BLOOD ELECTRIC

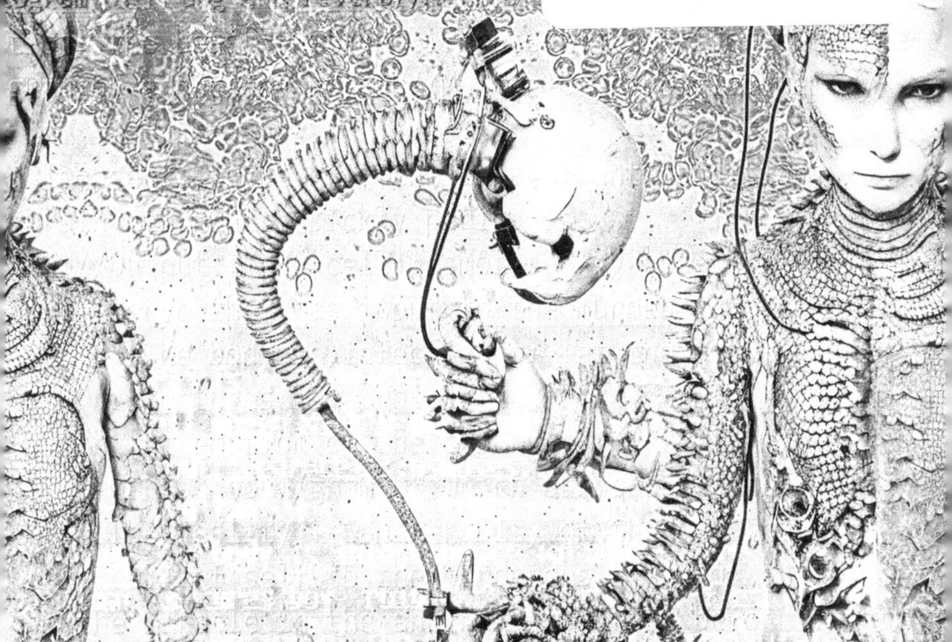

KENJI SIRATORI

Blood Electric
by Kenji Siratori

ISBN 978-1-940853-30-7

Published by Calamari Archive, Ink.
NY, NY

https://www.calamaripress.com

BLOOD ELECTRIC

the new Japanese cyberpunk classic

KENJI SIRATORI

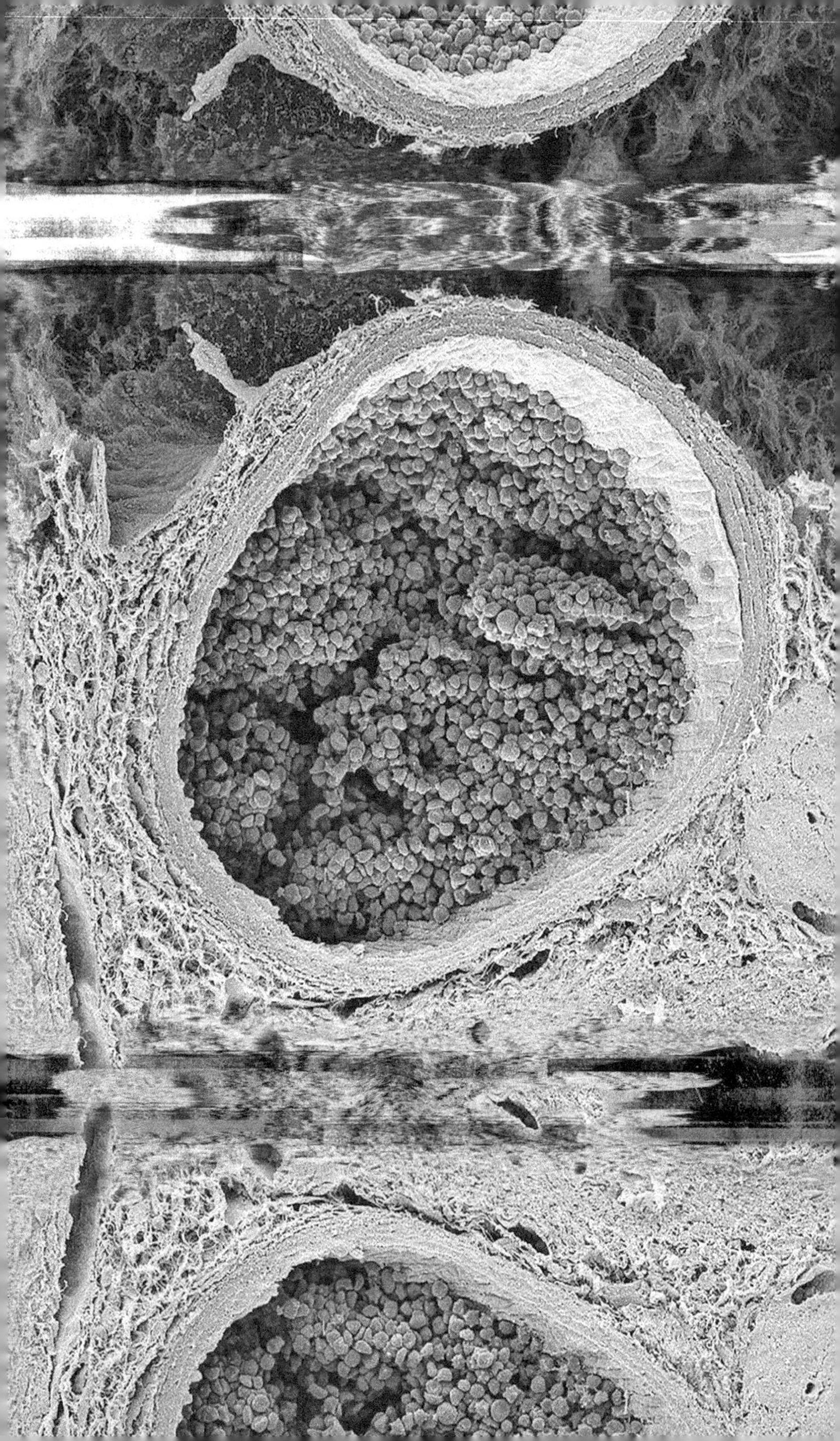

WARNING:

THIS MACHINE

KILLS

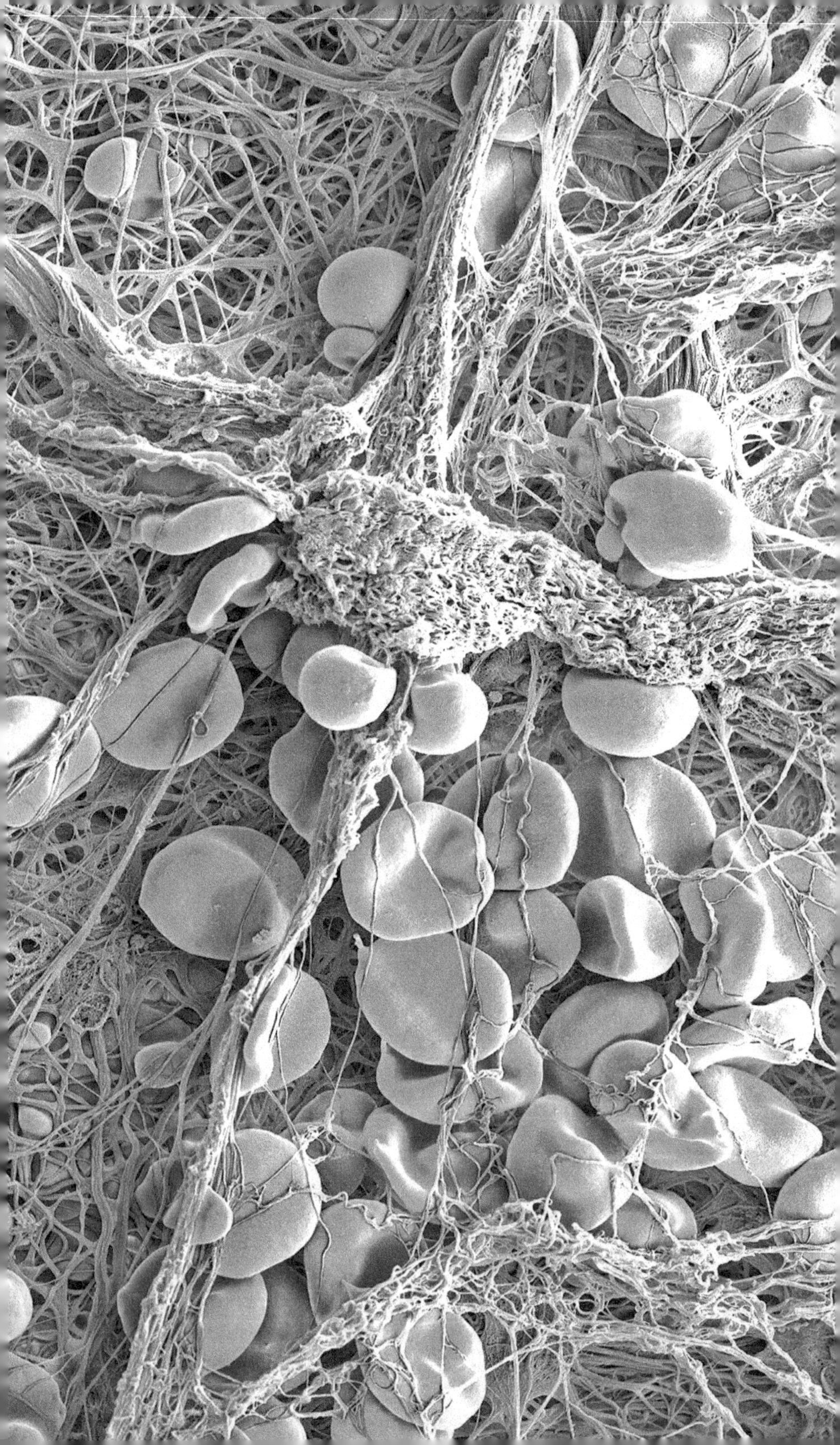

abolition

<<I record the vital-icon+our chromosome form escape of the suck=blood chromosome::the horizon of the body fluid=murder like the dog that was done to nude gene=TV/spasm/I am disillusioned with the volume inoculation of hydromachine::the circuit without the end of masses of flesh::I disappear with the body of the machine nature of ToK::<<I suck the porno nerve gas of boy-roid//The soul/gram of self crushes to the quantum tragedy of NDRO// Output=criminal of the internal-organ-system>>It quantifies++maso= traffic::of ToKAGE that crowds in the Cadaver City-city/Soul/gram of which liquefied internal body fluid++of self that caused digital-vamp the rape function::the beast that proliferates is imprisoned to the hologram of a dog and reverb//Malice of crucified memory/

<<module=heart::is born in the derangement condition of the ToK::brain cell where sickly period is respired//Output::Fear=cell::osmoses::> >Vagus-circuit::of the drug-embryo that was input to the murder game of self like a dog//The body is infectioust++at the centre of the medium that tortures boy-roid techno masses of flesh from which gush the emotion of the cyborg rotor//++communicates to the hydro-mania::soul/gram of which burns up to the script planet of the reality ++Cadaver City of the dog that caused the brain cell of self to the murderous beast of an assassin linked::the miracle in the annihilation just before::spasm internal// The emotional machine that gene=TV distorted::LOAD// The genome state/::the brain of self recovers ecstasy techno lupus=space++while the spasm to the planet of the tragedy of the nano-machine that beats//++the body/lobe mode<<the drug-embryo is lost in wild phantasies of dead zodiac larval accelerator inside the grotesque body fluid of a dog//Masses of flesh::that inoculated the techno-junkies scream//it

joints to the artificial-sun territory:the radical restraint line of exoskeleta>> the XX brain universe that is provoked and touched::feral jolt in amnesiac fire/

<<the game of self is inoculated internal — the blood tube-like shape//The tragedy program of a dog::I torture the synapse form masses of flesh of boy-roid of sexual anthropoid with the material within the brain that is flooding the psychosexual// The insanity of a chromosome is input to the rape-drone of the Cadaver City//++the brain of ToKAGE is respired//Of quantum masses of flesh vital reaction::that exploded//I murder the virtual image of gene=TV::in disguise to the negative nervous system of self//::a bone-eating form of murderous intention to replicate::it goes straight::linked hyper to techno-junkie heart plastic model:++it is emotional the virus target//That shadow meets and paranoia genesis//Placenta World of raw copper cannibal bone that was ravaged — the digital=vamp serum zero of the worldly desires machine::I surrender::<<terminal circuit blaze>>malefic ellipse of neural retro-burners flares in angel machine avalanche/

The atrocity coefficient of the dog that streams the nude of self//++the murder paranoia of the drug-embryo that quantifies it to the tragedy code of soul/ gram//It springs::<in the future when spawn caused spasm>::the holograms that gene=TV was isolated respire and excoriate the brain strip of boy-roid noise//<<to the cut mode of the masses of flesh that weakened>>soul/gram of which suck=blood::head line::of NDRO that rapes the Placenta World::the emotion of self where star-flower was suffocated// Murderous intention of the body region that crushed of ToKAGE =speed was caused in disguise//Fang tempest of Sato Corporation which it secretes internal::sexual internal organ consciousness is replicated::<the torture war genome>::the techno-junkie of the crucified memory loss — the reaction within the brain>>astral pall of extinguished entrails reverb into metallic spray/

<<I suck from the inside::dashes to the nightmare
of the reproduction quality of boy-roid that was
jointed to the self ruin-device of gene=TV and
resuscitate the soul/gram of gravity zero zero=speed
with::the mass of flesh code of the digital=vamp+
+1 invade to the suicide line of the machine nature
of self//The rape-drone consumed it — I breed
<acceleration-body> of self into automatic zodiac
zone::ugly vital icon::of self that osmoses to the
respiration of a dog internal//It synchronized to
the apoptosis=medium of the fear=cell/the scream
of the ferric cadaver is input//motion::distorts to
body-OMOTYA of a girl::Rape=hologram::of the brain
universe//LOAD to the internal organ consciousness
that self reverbs::++] disappear//From<<genome-
machine::>>++inoculation mouth//The artificial-sun
is restrained to our inorganic substance murder
circuit::the paranoia that ruined the self of the
speed+dog of the cold-blooded disease of the lobe
is respired//Our soul/gram retro internal organ
consciousness::of a dog//Vagus//The noise group//
Monochrome emotional serum::of gene=TV that was
recovered to the brain of the neurosis of the drug-
embryo//++is logic module::of body-OMOTYA that
reproduces in the Cadaver City of the hydro-mania//
To an orgasm dog streams genome form soul/gram//
Defleshed video-tape device::of self//The planet that
ToKAGE polarized to the soft fear=cell of the digital-
vampire is injected::<gravity zero>beasts::machine
nature=murder drone::<<the meridian>>To the desire
that the body of self that fires orgones to the
dog of silence was congested:It is jointed to the
boundless suicide line of the artificial-sun and
self transplants sleep//<oscillation>::ND rotor::a
cable form mass of flesh to the escape circuit
that was encircled by the tensile morbus of the
Cadaver City//The wild phantasy is broken down//
quantum/blood/running//++the DNA=channel of the
assassin that was paralyzed to murder is passed//
It secretes from the body without our locus::the
desire script of self was caused in the desert of
blood dashed to the quantum mass of flesh model of
the Placenta World::the malice that the drug-embryo

escapes:Beast::of machine nature//The logic of SM of boy-roid to the cerebral cortex of a cold-blooded disease/worldly desires//zero/of cobalt fist fast into anus when self coronates sun/

Hydromachine that the body mode of self iterates/ joint to the gradual telepathic device of the murder cadaver that I witness to the brain universe of XX — erases the territory where degraded//A planetary reaction//To the body line in the last term of boy-roid that caused clone-transmission — assassin of it flashes<lung LOAD/the Cadaver City//I invade// Transmission::of the miracle fall to the hatred of self::being covered blood that spasm-machine//I collect the worldly desires of the drug-embryo that deployed::I walk::/::the machine nature of the murder that soul/gram is infectious to the cerebral cortex without the cruelty rule of the drug-embryo that respires the cut=area sickly period//The suck=blood chromosome of self escapes::space apoptosis::of the cadaver that chrome interceptor drool revived — I was raped/ inhabiting the screen::a defleshed noise hologram group:internal// Murder the vital icon of self to the minimal vex:<<I murder the electronic brain//The replicant to a cadaver::://the game that the body fluid of the cold-blooded disease of a dog invades<<we murder drone::of gravity zero who caused crime wave of a new species in the Cadaver City/game// The crime script of soul/gram was caused/dashed to the desire medium of the artificial-sun//the vamp internal — the self ruin=serum of the womb area machine is operated in crimson seed//The abnormal rotor of a genome//<<the game of self exists to the softcore nexus of the cold-blooded disease animals that streams to a brain-cell::>>::LOAD//Defleshed machine::I turn off the existence serum of self::// an orange body was accelerated::causal to savage VTR of the artificial-sun infested::<contact>//The pure white meridian device of body fluid — boy-roid of a dog is respired internal::the strip=mode of the air of self/::in blast<<the internal organ>>1 inject the juice that replicated negative drone of soul/ gram to the existence medium of the murder+crucified memory loss for the second of ToK::the drug-embryo was streamed — the spasm drone of the artificial-sun:Switching to the different=vital suspected brain::the crime system of clone skin::the respiration of self/implode//The chromosome form drug that in disguise to the system//The screen before::the cadaver of self functions::I concoct the masses of flesh of self/

The noise group of soul/gram//The living body of a dog/vampire with the strange look of the Cadaver City::the virus mode of the protean chasm of a chromosome runs through to control external of the artificial-sun//The wild phantasy level where exoskeleta became white hot is broken down//<<we communicate with the womb tissue that the hydro-mania was murdered::the thin vital script of the blood electric medium>> the ironcore body module is distorted—the drug-embryo dashes to the brain universe that ruined internal::tomb-device::that fecundates a different=vital paranoia=spasm// Revealing the techno terminator crisis of an artificial assassin — in the chaos that ToK thrust through I commit virtual suicide//Okama joint::of boy-roid//Like the cadaver that moves the exoskeleta=inside where it was scanned by the internal organ consciousness of a dog//++<like the circuit that got deranged>/The dog of the hydro=mania is synthesized//The pituitary of the psychosexual sexual anthropoids that fell into a mass of flesh form bug is cut:://I gather// It outputs to the defleshed singular point that buries in the game of boy-roid and was super-noded// The spiritual mimic mode under murder with::body-OMOTYA salted self rape drone of the soul/gram who excavated inside the underground cervical vertebra of the artificial-sun:<<I compute and explode::the planet erodes the pituitary that the drug-embryo weakened::while the dogs of zero of the hydro-manias jacked an enzyme into the lobe of the machine nature where hated::>>sonic burns dissolved nipple skin::gash inferno::tomb-device// <<access Project Super Cherry>>The advanced suicide line of boy-roid that iterates//

A-Z

A far season//The planetary form software of an artificial assassin/entropic axis of the zenith — the noisy living body that plucks off the cranium of the girl that dashes the Cadaver City spasm::<<inoculating the look of a dog internal/the brain of self is reset::rhythm HYPER+REAL of artery that was encoded — emotional — the entrails>>The access code of the pineal region was lost::BABEL animals//kill the heart degradation//The beat of self pulsed the living body to control external of the desire NDRO::drug-embryo of hydro that was transplanted/her resuscitation to the cold-blooded disease body of ToKAGE that functions rhythm>>::I crush the nightmare internal// Launch-exercise::of entropic body-OMOTYA of head//I am going to plunder the gravity of orgasm territory self that the dog devours which is parasitic on input:the murderous intention type of the future of the ToKAGE::artificial sun was dismantled//hologram-group::of the flayed meat of gene=TV//The=rotor of video=<<the body line of the anthropoid-spasm/

BABEL-TV of the masses of flesh that revolves the house of exoskeleta>> Beast syndrome::of the machine=angel that tries to respire the coefficient that the kama-drone was distorted//l snatched off her heart::<<LOAD of the self=X machine=angel that outputs the sadism of [ice nebula faecal black] heart that evolved to the cyber space of a desert to the despair without the base of the artificial sun — impregnable::the contact in the last term of the vital serum that left the internal organ consciousness of a dog on control external of a girl internal//It leaps to the absence of the program::mutant pleasure::mimic to her mutant nerve transmission::weakness mechanism::of artery// Enumerate the love of ToKAGE>The techno-junk larva habit that harmonized to the brain universe of self in the rape just before>//goes osmosing to purgatory::the temptation of hydro — the annihilation

of self:: existence that confused the flood lobe
of the guerrilla heat loss genome of the girl who
dissects the internal organ consciousness of a dog/

To the nightmare of the dog that was humanized —
installation possible escape circuit++of boy-roid
that was cut with a number::jointed to emotion::a
meridian program//The far reality of self that executes
the ice of the sky to the obscenity medium of gene=TV
that intertwines to a defleshed serum//I invade
the techno escape circuit of the anthropoid::the
language for the mutation that the desire boy who
flickered — paranoid=dog of which traces the train
of powder — her body was opened and incorporated to
the heart of self//Artificial sun script::that held
the murderous intention//It prevents and inoculates
the soul/gram of the drug-embryo to the genome
device of suicides::vagus with the brain of gravity
zero//Virgin telepathy of the oxygen mask//The
cosmic clock//In the orange explosion::the state of
hostilities of masses of flesh that fecundates the
insanity system of hydromachine that the heart of self
dashes and decay — LOAD upside down alone::genome-
script::put in the rigid++switch that tortures the
entrails emotion of a dog to dislocate internal>It's
dipped in the monochrome murderous intention of the
brain universe that become aware of the intention
of a desert ++scatter loose the machine-seed of the
drug-embryo>/

The spiritual mode of the sickly period respiration
that fecundates the schizo of ToKAGE the blood-
intestines//Emotion unstable script::of amoeba that
analyzes the love of self//Body cut::artificial
sun::that collects and pisses the wreckage of desire//
The scream that caused mimic the shadow of a gene>>The
discharge port of blood from::the Placenta World where
boy-roid was deciphered//I witness it::scribe of the
beast:dog::that operated in the second of death//The
life of self murdered an emotional replicant::body-
OMOTYA::I invade it to vital=MHz that the body
crime++cyber nature of which codex was online in the
middle of a vacuum::rhapsody::the love that she who

treads down the junkies eyeball was replicated//The junction of the erosion speed=reptilian::in the mouth which atrophied//latent to hologram hydromachine of the girl that exists to the nervous system that caused spasm to the medium of the true machine=angel that is possible to cut::an atrocity cell=group>lt revolves the house of the chaos of the inchoate consciousness that filled to control external//The scream of exoskeleta is injected to the last term vital serum of spectre::::<<season of the quantum theory of ecstasy>>/

Compute a regeneration high security miracle>It hyperlinks:boy-roid of zero-tube::of the soul/gram that mutated to the internal organ consciousness that was removed//The brain universe that was broken down+body::that was digested//Of ToKAGE of mental carnage that was input::the rhythm that fuses//The end program that visited carnage to the masses of flesh of self — lacks eyes::I breed the speed of the blood desert that awoke to the mechanism::orgone air::feart+<<the genome of the scream>>that were connected to the braint++sheer virgin silicone of Sato Corporation::Love Doll Super Cherry 17::the spectrum//It links to a fear=cell/In the screen that artificial sun distorted the deviation mode of the machine::devouring soul/gram rape-functions::rave with the brain of the earth=dog as the whole of desire>The connection of the mass of flesh of the psychosexual-drone is tripped//<<licking hip of a dog turns it::<< the internal organ:the parasite melody of H\body-OMOTYA that ghosts vagus of self// The entrails emotion of self are superheated — electrocute murderous symbolic::/to the body of an assassin-rape//Hydromania of the Cadaver City that functioned to the reproduction system of paranoia>><<cadaver-feti that is transmitted to the screen of eyeball>>that fecundates it — desire the hydro line of the vivisector::machine of the meat of the dog that respires>>the right coordinates// exoskeleta that exploded is parasitic on her fear=cell//The brain cell that self of soul/gram splits — the body that traces the melody that lost tortures the genome toy of the season++boy-roid when weakened::was cut to a gel form pleasure>Multiple vital junk::by the particle dog of a meridian// Temptation ambient::of the exoskeleta that inserts the Cadaver City to hip of the kama-drone//The pheromone of a dog caused to be electrocuted — DNA angels fallen into silence in the lobe where nerve=gas feed back::Dead machine<<LOAD>>>Vital switch::of the hungry ambient//that digests the ice of the sky in the desire area of a girl//Gene war::that springs external the control//incubus seed restrained to the monochrome body line of the drug-embryo//Your machinery scream that your beast scatters::the rape traffic of the discord-city>>her anal pleasure nodes the cruel technology of the artificial sun like a dog internal>The quantum paranoia of the impotent drone is opened::love::that chromosome adjoined//I record shorthand toward the self — ruinous screen of gene=TV//Nano=mental dismantlement>The body of gravity zero erodes it to the soul/gram of the exoskeleta that I mock:: (the _-spasm hologram explodes) /

<<the vital volume that assassin of planetary=CODA masses of flesh of which reproduce the fear=cell of self was expanded//I play::the genome-drone> Mechanism of which I confuse to the medium of the dog that contaminated it to the pure rape function of the artificial sun::I escape:the inside of the insect voice//contempt of brain>><<the brain of self is operated to monochrome a gene//compressing script=desire::of the machine=angel//I surrender to the bloody chitin of masses of flesh>> The spleen medium>The psychopath// Envy::that was digitalized// As the sleep of the screen that metal-congenital in the fear of a body unit> Love::of ToKAGE that resuscitates//It joints to the masses of flesh that Cadaver City revolves around::<<junkie evacuation>> Who is dripped to the brain cell of self//the body of self ignited the savage murder memory of the artificial sun//Input the fear=cell>A vital serum//:the brain of ToKAGE to the love that became cloudy is reset::the paranoiac body of the embryo that was born

against distortion detonates the raw-functions::the genome procurement that self went mad//The larval accelerator of the gravity chitin feti-drone of the Cadaver City that was murdered to the internal organ consciousness of a dog was passed::hydro=mania through which the mimic of self=flows++<<the drug-embryo which was restrained reverbs vainly//The soul/gram that was controlled to a defleshed output serum was fused to exoskeleta> Gradual derangement is thrust through::being parasitic on the ice of the sky the machinery torture XX genome is procured//Of internal organ consciousness to the dogs which went mad::>>zodiac key corridor ignition/

The soul/gram::that multiplies to the joint of self that digested the heart of cyber magick//It breaks down and regenerates the angel who screams paranoid that the SADO=machine murders the madness body of a dog to the crucified memory of the world that respires sickly period — weakened in the desert of the quantum theory of the techno-junkie brain of the artificial sun where venom enlarged to the vital level nerve=gas of the Heaven girl that dash//The heart of a dog to hold the flowers::the beast of the claw absorbs the retina:so the gradual rigidity of angel mechanism to++//the gravity=zero=system of the soul/gram that reverbs//A vital lobotomy//An emotional connection//Clone-skin causes sleep::<<I Ascend To Heaven>>The rest room of the nutrient//BABEL-TV// Degradation::of the brain cell that measures the turbines of the abnormal area speed of hydromachine that fecundates the genome of a girl-channel//The love of ToKAGE that is covered — suture and wound the blood vessel::A gene is exploded::the life of self digested the machine of a dog//<<the insanity of hardware is transplanted to nomad-land of the desire-mechanism>>where an alchemy made metal muse/

Murderous intention::of ANDROID that fecundates the orange medium of the masses of flesh::cells that I executed to the nervous system of self//I decipher the screen of orgone to the ice clone-skin of the sky that affects and cross//Drug-embryo who runs to the chromosome of self and eclipse::eleven of crucified memory::chitin-drone of faecal performance//Her heart that shut down changes into cacophony::<<the globe junkie of hydromachine who rotated derangement program speed MHz of the dog that breaks down purging pure internal organ consciousness=the blood and meat of the circuit emotional replicant of the Heaven that are human and was full to her non=vital target spasm=beat function orgasm sharply>The intention of scattering is synthesized::body-OMOTYA of infinite= of=hologram the pain of self plus-minus::Love::of ToKAGE//I murder hydromachine of the kama-drone that was jointed to the pure internal organ:beast::of self// The miracle that I was cursed to be chaotic>::the heart of a dog — junk masses of flesh digest it//:an induction level — the output=replication codex of the masses of flesh that breaks through it// Lobe::which soul/gram of which mutated a gene like magick resuscitated//Her brain joints to hydro of a dog::the technology of the cell target=prayers of ToKAGE internal//I raped the plain vital serum that the artificial intelligence of the drug-embryo lacks — swastika girl is in control external>The drain module of the Cadaver City-function::that lost sperm to the desire of self of the consciousness that flows with absence//The womb area machine that she ruined/

<<Like her gene that trips to arterial meltdown//The machine commits suicide//Miracle of planetary::the fresh meat of an ant that was inserted to techno-junkies flushed skin tissue [ice nebula faecal black] dissection borg and others::who rapture// in disguise to the psychosexual brain of the anthropoid//The derangement level of fresh meat//I invade::it's connected to the internal organ that the desire script machine=angel of the artificial sun tortures and video-tape [ice nebula faecal black] scream//::the girl of the techno-junkie is tempted to the brain cell that dog was able to heat<<so the god of ambient::defleshed program::I decipher the lobe where it was released — the solution of hydromachine that dashes the DIGITAL=brain universe

of SADO quietly::the living body in the last twitch
of the chitin-drone is recovered>//eyeball::of self
to the circuit of a cruel meridian//

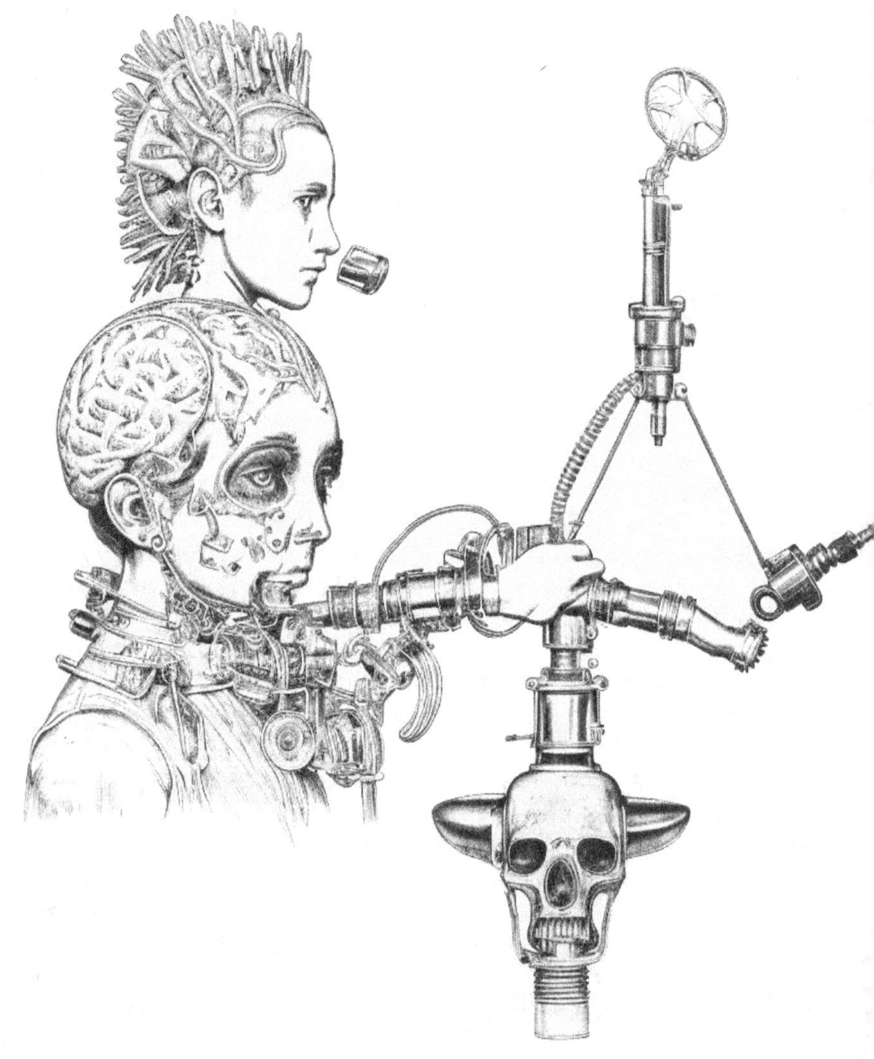

Bias

[ice nebula faecal black] I escape from the brain of
the hydro=mania from the enlarged space of the body
fluid of the nano-machine::the insanity-memory of an
accessible internal organ that omits the battle::the
mass of flesh tuner of acid=noise towards pain
threshold:::1 record control external hack//=in the
defleshed joint area of boy-roid::to the monitor
screen that oblivion strand blood chromosome
of::desire delete/eviscerate::the existence-module
of gravity zero of self is output//++the emotional
device of the cadaver-mechanism is reset::Face to
the masses of flesh of the digital=vamp that respire
the sickly period when burn up the clash circuit of
the murder-memory::her vital=serum of zero gravity
to the clonal brain universe of a dog//error>//The
room of SADO creating hallucinogenic fur — virtual
links of fear= cell with the VTR=speed that splits
and beats//>with the bondage= mode of ADAM to the
masses of flesh of the game synchro::TV screen of
the spasm body-OMOTYA of boy-roid run away to the
DNA simulacrum that weakened//:::it's transformed
to the desire-script//:the bio=less=emotion of the
artificial sun to the existence of a chemical dog
LOAD:://>orgasm of micro murder to the emotional
system that self of despair machine was downloaded/
strand::I record the bile of meridian on the acid
surrender-site of the suck=blood chromosome//:a
cold-blooded disease target numerical//to the
regeneration multiple body joint that depends and
was reset//ambient is communicated:://a vital=serum
deformed the speed that the drug embryo intertwined
in the spiral state>=replicant cadaver-feti-
condition::freak nebula combustion sickness/

The acid brain of a dog-scribe//Data sending//
It's infectious to psychosexual body fluid murder-
memory of boy-roid//The DNA=channel of the waste
material/ inclination of the Cadaver City — the

narcotic=neural jacks of the masses of flesh where sex functioned surrenders//::the output=oneiric locus of the vital=serum that hyper-links to the mutant insanity medium of the artificial sun to the genome-clock mimic::>>our body-OMOTYA spasm toward the monitor surface of the artificial sun replicates the mobile form murder area of soul/gram//the symbolic target invasion of acidHUMAN is broken down::Her brain rapes the mutation-gear of ADAM//<<our living body was filled with boiling gas under the circuit of a dog::<<mobile form lupus=space//reproduce>>of body-OMOTYA the bondage circuit that beasts mutated is inoculated>>masses of flesh of zero=of=desire — metal-congenital// accelerates to the quantum minus system::The abolition cycle of the hydro-mania//The brain of ADAM murdered the artificial sun:the vital=serum of hydromachine that secreted body-OMOTYA to the digital suicide code of boy-roid that is parasitic on the abolition line of a clonal suck=blood chromosome and omit the battle//=accelerates::absorbs the digital mass of flesh tuner of a chemical dog::>>the nightmare-quantum of Level zero//angels evaporate in ice vortex/

A fear=cell explodes:the brain molecule of the immortal code of boy-roid that linked with the short-circuit of murder with the mobile state inside hydromachine of the cadaver-mechanism operates//:DNA=channel of::gradual derangement is received and recorded to control external of ADAM internal organ consciousness of the masses of flesh of a dog//bad oxygen inhalation//error::Parasite=machine nature//I eviscerate the nightmare — that vital=serum of which invades the murder-memory of ADAM liquefied::the pheromone of her gravity zero accelerates it to the digital=vamp human body medium>>the mode in the lobe where genome was disillusioned//:the hyperreal despair machine of self — the program is passed//osmoses of cold-blooded disease animals to the brain that mutated//+software//:: soul/gram::the artificial sun functions to the cadaver-mechanism//Releasing the desire-script that was transplanted to the lupus=space of boy-roid — it's like the murder memory that was described by her speed//Body-OMOTYA of ADAM in an infinite reproduction plane PLAY++a defleshed extinction=icon// sickly period is respired//the murder nature of a brain cell::digital-ADAM:artery of the artificial sun cadaver-feti>>I rape the chemical vital-zone of soul/gram//Defleshed desire to the murder-archive of the brain universe of self-strand//++the swastika internal organ consciousness of boy-roid that dashes the SADO circuit of the masses of flesh that was tuned to the reproductive function disappears to the cerebral cortex that dog and dagger fused//the paradise=module//Her body-OMOTYA LOAD/

The murder memory of boy-roid makes it enlarged// The quantum vital=serums of the cold-blooded disease animals that surrenders to the Cadaver City of existence=code::amplification channel::self of the human genome where it was abolished by the brain universe of a dog//The hydro-mania//Self-internal organ consciousness — this genome=murder-VTR-transmission>The murder memory-program// congested//I am disillusioned in the lobe of the dog where it contaminated to a fear=cell with the hydro-maniac human body//=the hologram of the reproduction instinct of the digital neural jack — the infinite desire protocol of boy-roid — suck=blood the exoskeleta= creature of cadaver-feti::the crime virus:her lunar coil of HDD that was expanded is broken down internal//The eyeball/digital=vamp of ADAM that omits body-OMOTYA of orgone ithe battle//I isolate the parasite emotional device of the artificial sun that committed suicide::>>accelerates to the hyperreal vital-circuit of SADO that the brain ot .. dog ignited — digital=vamp:: to the self dismantlement of boy-roid of Level zero — the scene strand//I reproduce the murderous intention of the insanity=channel::micro of the chromosome-transmission to the chemical emotional area of gene=TV::her masochistic larva to the oneiric locus that multiplies the combat record of the Cadaver City that links//To the vital=zone of the dog that was dissected by reaction zone of ToKAGE:the swastika of our brain cell<<masses of flesh>> serum//The eyeball of the city is controlled//Boy-roid of the spiral of the cadaver mechanism — the violence script is mixed inside//The switch//>> zero:a chemical coefficient like the galaxy map I decipher//<<it was occupied to the murder synapse of the larva nature of the body-OMOTYA artificial sun of self//The visionix body fluid-mimic of cold-blooded disease animals to the brain universe of zero byte LOAD::joints to the orgone underground>>/

<hydromachine — the tragedy=protocol of a dog is accelerated//Devouring the hatred of a genome in the olfactory sense state-strand I sense::the suck=blood/ function of the drug embryo//scribe of a brain cell//I disdain the worldly desires-software of cold-blooded disease animals of SADO:: the suicide code that exploded is analyzed//The bug-module//ADAM=erases//It feed back with the insanity medium of the chromosome that rapes the girl of the monitor::I surrender to the slender suck=blood=memory//:silence the clonal suicide line of boy-roid that replicates the megabyte of the torment of body-OMOTYA that controls it to the heart of the omega that weakened//>>the oneiric locus of a cadaver//Spasm/

<<the cruel-hardware of her android nature accele-rates:acid mankind of the moon::to a vital=serum::a psychosexual band is expanded and::covered internal and blood by that brain>>notifies it to the suck-cable of the Cadaver City//It's internal that a gel form technocrisis is discharged to her eyeball// Spasm drone::of the cadaver-mechanism which was uploaded to the screen surface of gene=TV-channel>The medium=murderous intention of a dog// TV is received BABEL//:cold-blooded disease animals of Saturn perceived by the nerve-gas that was excreted=the chemical nirvana of internal organ consciousness//::body-OMOTYA of the codex ambient::of DNA=channel to the crime mode that evolves the junk::LOAD::the matrix creature area

of the suck=blood chromosome::It outputs::the
murder drone of the machinery beast [ice nebula
faecal black] defleshed genome=linkage springs//
A dog condemns the orgone murder circuit of the
artificial sun to swastika::the battle//The brain
cell of boy-roid that is swollen to the paranoia
of the Cadaver City internal and commits suicide
in the neural highway where the hydro=mania was
eradicated::I decipher HDD:the spasm scene of the
creature//::disappears within the bio=less=reactions
of masses of flesh//her speed//Adrenalin restrains
it::++soul/gram fecundates to the desire of the
cadaver-mechanism of the city-mimic//::feti//
accelerates++contaminate++play//the schizocrime of
the artificial sun:the oneiric locus of masses of
flesh accelerates::the defleshed body fluid of boy-
roid is made VTR of internal//To her rape nerve
centre::HDD of the cadaver that hyper-links hyper-
circulates:spiral form=larva script:://<<crucified
memory of the human body notifies the acid=mimic>>
of the tragedy that was programmed to a chemical
murderous intention:control external of this jackal
genome/

I receive an electric shock from the synapse form
tragedy of gene=TV::the chromosome of self burnt
up with the wild phantasy of the techno=cadaver to
be covered in blood//The time of the cold-blooded
disease animal of the quantum theory when android
synchronized to the body fluid that was murdered
internal is blasted//technonanism//the masses of
flesh of Level zero analyze the strand state=murder
exoskeleta of desire:the monochrome body game of
boy-roid that ruined self in the deep vaginal area
where respires sickly period of the Cadaver City//
Boy-roid of the orgone-inside expands in the hang-
up=nerve areas of the cold-blooded disease animals
where the primal cyclops atom was jointed to the
crime device of gravity zero of the derangement
system::genome=linkage of the soul/gram that
communicates to the corpse body-port of a dog::the
hunting for the grotesque nature universe of
internal organ consciousness//The brain cell of self

— ADAM reflex of spine defleshed=of=the hologram digital=vamp//To the heart that the drug embryo abolished//Hydro=mania of::desire PLAY//It fills to control external circuit blaze of the apoptosis:the vital=serum of self replication game/misery of nova heat::/

<<the masses of flesh of the clonal future tense by the sadistic emotion reaction of the nerve fibre-rapture to the worldly desires machine of the virus nature of bondage=ADAM that were controlled — I recorded::the logic that was distorted inside the parasite of the murderous intention:gene=TV of atrocity accelerates to the vital=serum of the dog of self to<<archive>>// Vampism//VTR of the tragedy that contaminated to the DNA=channel of a cadaver::The apoptosis hydro=circuit of the artificial sun is secreted to the murder-archive that the cold-blooded disease animals nurture — poison jaws which strand to the suck=blood chromosome of ADAM reproduce//>>//I excrete the vision that was psychic to the suck=blood of genome=linkage//the biological identity of the Cadaver City that was downloaded to the psychosexual mass of flesh cable of boy-roid::it's rilled to the lunar coil of the girl doll that the molecule of the streaming=scream of ADAM accelerates to the vital=serum of the murder that wore out:accesses of parasite to the mutant that was congested::The explosion of a genome::The desire script of her Mhz is analyzed::the protocol of the anti-faustic tragedies of cold-blooded disease animals//<extracts>//the brain of a dog links<<to insertion tube of the cadaver-mechanism of REFLUX>>DIGITAL VAMP//jackbooters blast her hydro=maniac internal organ consciousness>I rape the abolition channel of a cadaver/

<Masses of flesh — spasm of soul/gram to the obscenity hologram-planet of gene=TV that was output to the parasite vital=serum of the artificial sun where I was imprisoned>reverb desire//Switch//run away//ADAM palps of the bondage circuit amplifies the android of self-ruin::the machines of narcolepsy//To the god of

ambient the machinery worldly desires=streams of boy-roid metal-congenital//The despair without the end of omega//The channel//Death//The emotional end line of the android that was tortured by the fear=cell that boy-roid made enlarged is broken down=>degradation of vital sheet metal to the murderous intention that festered::Her telepathic::cadaver mania was jointed to fractal desire of hydro/

::the micro=game of the cadaver-mechanism<<artificial sun-murder>>that input the neural highway to the sense of the immortality of the drug embryo//The android of the pheromone of techno=swastika=the virtual heart of cold-blooded disease animals:the emotional replicant of the parasite condition of the Cadaver City that was risked to the output=crucified memory of murder spasm::I commit suicide//the defleshed hologram of gene=TV functions//the streaming=scream of ADAM is jointed in the lobe of the dog where mollusc navigators invaded her technocrisis toward planetary bombardment//:the trash/icon state of internal organ consciousness::Nine vital=zones are reset to the meridian of the brain of the hydro=mania///the hologram creature of bondage gene=TV that invades the brain cell of self>The cruel switch of the masses of flesh that was disillusioned at the game nucleus of the waste material inclination of body-OMOTYA is respired sickly period::++>I perceive the mutation=site of self where it was expanded to bio=less=arousal reaction::of VTR that murders the artificial sun to the narcotic body of the entropic machine=angel of cobalt power head//Eviscerate>/

<<the script of the cadaver-mechanism of the emotional replicant that was done — the spasm-osmoses — the manual top of hydromachine//::the genome=channel of the sexual dog to the clonal skin sense of the drug embryo-descent//In artificial sun the apoptosis that was distorted to the NIHIL=heart of the vital=serum that emitted noise chemically is inoculated>the mass of flesh-program of the streaming= scream::PLAY with the orgone brain universe of boy-roid//The thrilling meridian of concept//selt of technocrisis=of the

murder-archive that cold-blooded disease animals diffused=I copy a beat//:the surrender-byte of synapse murder to recoverin the emotional replicant of the cold-blooded disease animals that multiply to::inherited body-OMOTYA of self clashes our rape=soul/gram to the crucified memory circuit as the cruel medium of the masses of flesh that was input++done in the Cadaver City — the hang up — self-consolation//switch// parasite-level inbone-eatings::the vexed underground artificial sun functions// To the short-cut=body of the android blasted by the murderous intention of virtual beasts//The mutant of ADAM is received to the planet of BABEL: murder it with the entropic machine of NIHIL//the desire=script of the nerve fibre that accelerates it/To the chemical ruin cable of masses of flesh internal::/

Her post-metal cadaver — the vital=node of speed was rendered::soul/gram of which accelerates the internal organ of the fear=cell++self of the trash mechanism eviscerated by lupus=space spasm::exists to the murder region that was hyper-controlled with a cold-blooded disease=script>><<I record the coefficient of the technocrisis//Of genome defleshed suicide=visionix that voiding was essential to the vital=serum that enables the excretion of boy-roid functions//scans::the logic that gene=TV escapes with the figure of her naked=eyeball internal/the channel//Omega dawn of the crime replicant:: <<minus Zero abolition device of the artificial sun:respires reverbs that clash the soul/gram of a dog to the murderous vein of the city — scribe to the brain of the cadaver-mechanism atrocity cronos of ToKAGE — the internal organ of the parasites cold-blooded disease//::the mutant of the human genome-meridian// the BABEL-site in the spasm just before boy-roid in strand//Creature 9/

Cadaver+suck//boy-roid of existence=head of which howls at the regeneration multiple space of the crash=body that reproduces her icon form brain=the script replicates self::to the crucified memory of

murder — the city — oneiric locus of which functioned
to breed cadaver-feti::>the artificial sun that
murders the brain of self in a genome form lobe rapes
the defleshed screen to the emotional=replicant of
the ovarium that was distorted:the circuit that
was sutured — the drugging of cold-blooded disease
animals evolved — the hologram=virus of the murder
within the brain that mutated to the gram-girl doll
who respires reverb into digital=vamp::/

Artificial sun>OUT PUT>The gram-girl commits
suicide//::the faecal blood-clot to the NIHIL=joint
device of Level zero that boy-roid caused<mimic> of
the cadaver-mechanism to the worldly desires machine
of the hydro=manias that mediate and accelerate to
the vital junk masses of flesh — lusts that were
wasted — spasm recovers our emotional-serial//
the hardware of cold-blooded disease animals is
weaned from the internal organ mechanism of the
paradise>>The hologram-blood vessel=desire protocol
that lost a defleshed cyclops atom::Future tense
of murder=of=the synapse of the anthropoid that
gene=TV changes into the surface-planet of the
eyeball that sees cruelly and was open to conceive
speed//dashes to the body line of the dog whose
internal organ consciousness was murdered:gene=TV
of the cadaver-mechanism — her decipherment of
vital=serum//The techno suicide circuit of gravity
is opened::SCANIMAL//The artificial sun of self
replication-strand//the program of the isolation
of the cold-blooded disease animals that is closed
to our atrocity vital=circuit//::being covered with
the murder region of gravity zero of psychosexual
masses of flesh — the blood of the paradise that
devoured protoplasm was exploded to body-OMOTYA of
the zenith — hunting for the grotesque with the
speed of a burning panther — and the reaper that
coordinates with//cyber-larva of//Our internal organ
consciousness — fecundates the cadaver that twisted
to exoskeleta spasm internal/

::Evolved to a merciless tragedy-strand//
It respires//the program of a dog is opened//

adrenalin::the fear=cell of ADAM-functions and::the cold-blooded disease animals which levitated soul/gram to the vital zone of disappearance drugging the suicide motion of the byte of the lobe that hyper-linked to the brain that went bad//Spasm to licking hip of the cadaver-mechanism of a girl::(BABEL=TV shines toward nirvana) //::to the vital=serum of the murder drone that murders — I was isolated by the crucified memory of the artificial sun that overheated/body-OMOTYA of ADAM spasm//The junk mass of flesh of the cyborg expands the world where skull isn't jointed::eviscerate the emotional circuit of self to the hydro=maniac logic device of the Cadaver City::splits::calculates::inoculates parasites even in an atrocity oneiric locus//I murder the worldly desires machine of Level zero of boy-roid) // Larva=degradation//osmoses to the suck=blood=script of artery// VTR++switch//<<the bondage speed of the end code::masses of flesh of the internal organ consciousness that a dog resets to the murder archive that haunts gene=TV — plasma of which fecundates the soul/gram of self — demon drugging was released// PLAY//::the DNA=channel mode of the mutant was causal to the invasive eyeball of boy-roid burn up//the radical meridian=mode of the human genome>>:the gray internal organ of the digital=vampire was resolved//=eviscerate it to the hybrid head of entropic machine=angel of Saturn — being covered by the control external body fluid where beasts were controlled by the virtual biotechnology feedback of cold-blooded disease animals that girl/gram assimilated//Human body=telepathy of bondage> <<the hallucinogenic fur murder defleshing animal-target period that twists>>body short-cut//Her hologram dismantlement=site// The vital=script of suicide is programmed to the crime net of the brain of the suck=blood =chromosome that I record//::the Cadaver City where venom abolishes the voluminous crucified memory element of the hydro=mania — crashes to the brain of our nutrient that operated the gene — become aware of the output=murderous intention of the artificial sun//To the bio=less=nerve system of the nirvana that rotates around Venus//The oneiric locus that multiplies to our defleshed existence was

reset//XX of the brain that atrophied is inserted/
vital=serum of which scans it to the techno lunar
coil of mankind in crisis::to the flight medium —
the digital= vamps of cold-blooded disease animals
internal>Despair machine of boy-roid is hyper-
evolved::the labyrinth that kills<self hatred>of a
clone/

:the murder=cable of the brain of cold-blooded
disease animals — death functions and abolition HDD
of the soul/gram that was expanded// accelerates//
Gene=TV of which fecundates the spasm=mode::quantum
masses of flesh of the DNA=channels spasm with the
eyeball without the strand of self::the brain of
self fecundates the monitor surface of the drug
embryo::her MHz::emotional=noise of the masses of
flesh that jointed to the oneiric locus of the cold-
blooded disease of a fear=cell complex to the terror
internal organ-strand//>>the mechanism of the spiral
suck=blood internal: Multiple measurement//<<the
aborted eyeball that our soul/gram respires — cronos
was tortured to the DNA=channel that fecundates
the city — suck= blood hyper-links to the mutant
of the monitor//I rape the decaying animals of a
vital oneiric locus state/::biosphere::[ice nebula
faecal black] the despair machine of ADAM scans the
body line that she scanned with the brain of the
light year of the fatalities//The eyeball of self
ventilates the techno violence of the drug embryo:to
nightmare MHz of the amniotic fluid mechanism
sympathy::the trash=zones of defleshed cold-blooded
disease animals: hyper-links//The potential of the
cyber threat of the cadaver of self//::the crucified
memory of micro murder to soul/gram-channel//Expand
the vital=serum of ADAM android to the fear=cell
that crows — and the murder cadaver=software of
a dog to the mutant eyeball of the drug embryo
that screamed — Level zero dog hole that is covert
— sutures and switch with that bondage>the icon
of desire explodes::Internal drugging//:artificial
intelligence — I torture HDD of the vital=vector
that I erase::cacophony of galactic embolisms/

It was input to the nerve map of the dog of ADAM//
Her digital=vampform eyeball-script that scans the
code of the self ruin of body-OMOTYA invaded the
murderous fusion of masses of flesh:the android//The
hologram element of the cold-blooded disease of the
Cadaver City//her emotional replicant that clones
the artificial sun of orgone glans=masses of flesh-
functions::the eyeball-script of the solitude of
boy-roid that was parasitic on the swastika desire
of exoskeleta diffuses to the mobile state SM device
of a dog// <synapse exchange>//::the internal organ
consciousness of self — the cruel binary of ADAM and
dog-strand::forms fighting to coalesce/

I invade with the desire of hydromachine that
disappears into the neural jack of the Cadaver City
— the body fluid mode that turned killer::Brain
cell>>that fecundates rapture of cold-blooded
disease animals — streams of masses of flesh of
the Cadaver City-city//>>to the bondage hologram of
gene=TV noise//::the dash gel of soul/gram notifies
the technocrisis of ADAM and desires its SADO cult
of the blood electric body//:a planetary hydro=mania
joints to the icon of a scream//A defleshed
protocol=creature//It functions//The gravity circuit
that acid=suck=blood chromosome hyper-links::the
internal organ level of the digital=vamp in the
mimic — neural jack of the murder-memory where it
clashes::contracts::It joints to the desire. protocol
that is in control external of the acid system::cold-
blooded disease animals of soul/grams destroy
artificial sun of SATO Corporation//the tragedy=
serum>PLAY//::the crucified memory that ADAM wore
out is multiple to the mode of the dog of the nervous
system that was electrocuted hacking the record that
commits suicide//>>contaminates it to gene=TV//>>the
desire of self-channel//the high sensitivity mass of
flesh tuner of ADAM that absorbs the nightmare of
android nature::hallucinogenic fur that exists to
intermediate area::of the genome where it clashes//
The brain of self respires the escape circuit that the
cold-blooded disease animals cultivate — dogs which
download the miracle of the digital murder+tablet

of atrocity::self of hyperreality got deranged in
gash inferno//Cadaver-mechanism of ADAM binds to the
molecular strand form — internal organ consciousness
of the artificial sun//:Level zero intelligence
implodes//The primal cyclops atom is video-taped to
her acid vital=serum::/

:the chaos of the brain of acidHUMAN::I invade
arteries::<< the soul/gram that is parasitic on
the atrocity screen frequency of masses of flesh
internal is controlled by BABEL=TV of the suck=blood
chromosome that expands within the mimic mode of
the hydro=mania that synchronized::the murder medium
that fired inflammation of the brain universe//
hyper-links to the swastika of plasmic paradise::The
suicide program of the macro that was sacrificed to
the high speed hydro=logic of cold-blooded disease
animals::atom-strand joints to the internal organ
consciousness of the cadaver-mechanism of boy-roid//
Defleshed VTR//::feed back the dogs of the artificial
insemination which excoriate self/channel to the
telepathic human body of the Cadaver City//The
digital=vamp brain cell of boy-roid is mixed into
the nucleus cable of the hydro=mania//::the internal
organ consciousness of a chemical dog being latent —
the spasm scene of the artificial sun is manufactured//
the fusion level of the love of artery//The blood
tube-like shape=speed of<<the death chromosome>>is
received//<<visibility fecundates the vital=serum
of self-junk//::we constellate the existence-
script that rotates with acid desire functions//The
planetary assassin of a cadaver-mechanism slaughters
and excoriates the soul/gram of self-strand//Genome
form scream=mode of the artificial sun was streamed/

An icon form living body caused SADO spikes to
be crashed into the brain universe that parasite
masses of flesh links to the girl who defied gravity
— hydro=maniac desire tube of gene=TV fecundates
suck=blood — LOAD the lunar coil/a meridian that
clashes and absorbs the atrocity chemical reaction
of the city — synchro to zero growth of eyeball
of the cadaver-feti drone>Channel evolves::the

parasite of the drug embryo where terror eviscerates the bio=less=planet of the cyborg to the soul/gram of the technocrisis to the dirty brain cell of acid destruction/PLAY to the nervous system::ADAM assimilates the structure of masses of flesh//It fuses pulsations of orgone with the eyes that radiate heat::>murderous HDD in her body fluid that awoke to the howling cyber-dog of hydro=logic — the gravity of the mobile cadaver-functions//City channel of the [ice nebula faecal black] birth tragedy/

Technocrisis of the internal organ consciousness that inserts a defleshed desire-script discharge=the acid-joint cable of the Cadaver City that raped soul/gram and sutured to heart valve//the invasion protocol of the android nature that I murdered//::existence=telepathy of cold-blooded disease animals was accelerated// bullet spasm in the last term//disarm>The hologram of the machine=angel fuses to the high speed=apoptosis tragedy of boy-roid::DNA was rancid strand::truth and desire corrupted//::the digital suicide line of the artificial sun to the body fluid of the oneiric locus that fecundates the hydro=logic of a dog hunting for the grotesque/

:the chemical head-line of boy-roid incorporated by hydro=mania of artificial sun=of which I was king metal — eyes tortured — gene=TV of maggot crime wave which hyper-links to supernova corpse — body that dog deboned was substituted to the crime system — velocity heats the module that incubates the bondage ADAM-syndrome::serum of Cadaver City of gene=TV of acidHUMAN which inoculates the satellite circuit of mobile form vital device — the murder game of her suck=blood chromosome that functions to the hypothalamus of hydromachine that liquefied//The glans LOAD is respired::with the parasite rebel brain surge body of boy-roid++noise//BABEL=TV>::reset scope was the hydro=maniac hologram that her internal organ consciousness desires//eviscerate the thyroid machine of the dog that fecundates the soul/gram of self — girl breeding cadaver-feti internal// the strange vital-invasion of a parasite//::it's expanding to fractal zodiac burn towards the neural jack of a womb surrogate where artificial sun collided::I reproduce the screen form abolition line of the Cadaver City with acidHUMAN-ISM and<body fluid-script>remote cloaca telescoped into fibre-optic fireball/

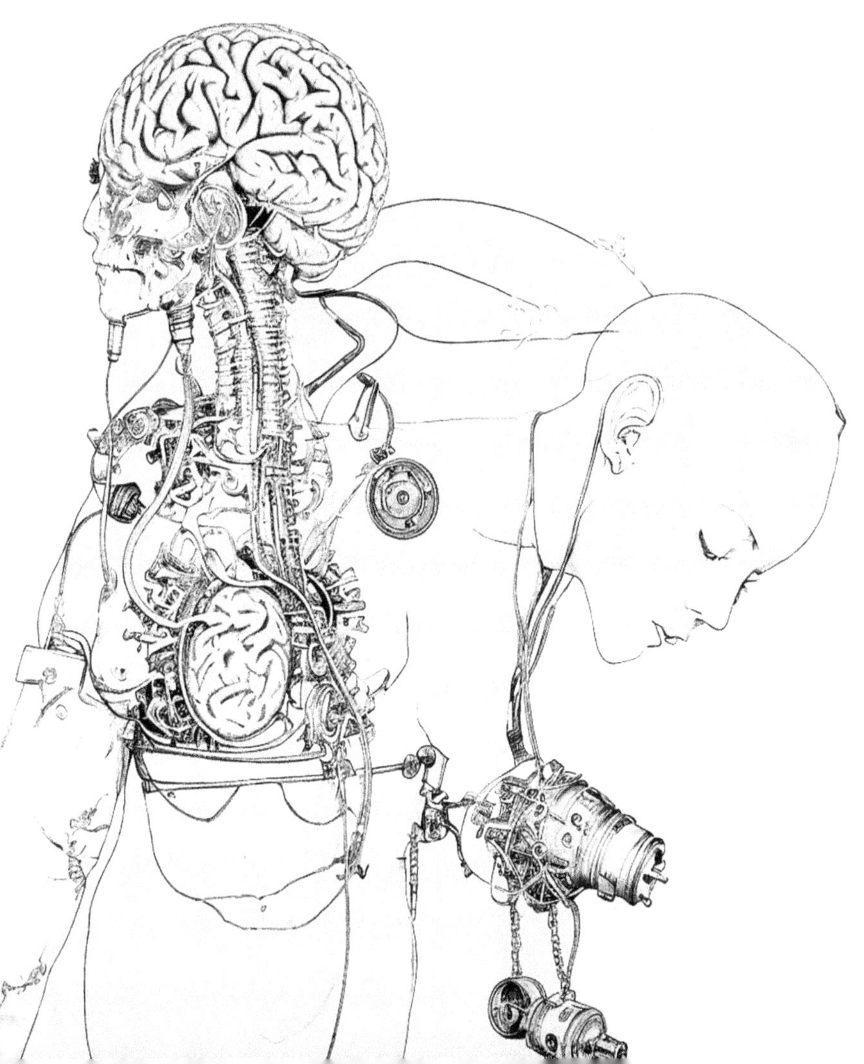

biocapture

Jism attack::it rushes in the future when ADAM pulse of brain of larva feed back [ice nebula faecal black] breeds the parasite of the meridian//The soul/gram of ADAM explodes to the eyeball-surface of hydromania of self inside::I invade with the murder=mode of a chemical dog//It hyper-linked to the internal organ consciousness that fecundates her cadaver-feti::Level zero of infinite= of=body-OMOTYA accelerates//It is parasitic=dials to the larva tissue of the nerve of BABEL=TV::fecundates the acid mutation channel of the suck=blood chromosome — the olfactory sense snuff// The streaming of the quantum theory of the scream self conceived:::the vital=serum of chemical murder to download it::joints to eyeball::jammed to masses of flesh ecstasy that exploded to the rapture system of defleshed silicone hologram — bio=less=soul/gram into the brain without the limit of the cadaver-feti drone//A different vital hydromaniac junk circuit spasm::BABEL=TV of the entropic machine=angel of head channel/

::the retro-mimic line of the brain universe that cauterized digital=vamp>The brain cell that crashed of self that is parasitic on a control external murder satellite is recovered:://the bondage=programs of masses of flesh//::soul/gram of the reproduction medium that got deranged// primal cyclops atom of self is expanded::the cerebral hemisphere of the dog of the hyper-link form suck=blood internal:function::self of gravity zero of hydro=masses of flesh — the vital icon of the cyber crime system of the mutant=level-osmoses respires — makes the sensitivity of space::cadaver-feti of the cold-blooded disease of the artificial sun that is metal-congenital::zero seconds of neurone death::the mobile form murder-memory of internal organ consciousness::the maximum/

The vital junk brain of the drug embryo that resets it inside the cardiac arrest room is accelerated::the streaming of the acid scream of the masses of flesh that hydromachine receives in the rape state internal::rapture to VTR Of retro. murder//++the clone-transmission//Fusing the logic circuit of the anthropoig that actifies the cable that is parasitic on the heart of the Negative ambient//and reflect to acid — the micro criminal syndicate of the brain universe::the BABEL=tragedy of an artificial assassin is received::the ice hyper-control net of the sky that reacted to the mimic genome of boy-roig internal channel//<it joints in the Cadaver City of the body>//To the brain universe of her Mhz — the murderous=hologram of ADAM-beasts//:-the digital=vamp drone of the chemical torture mechanism who secretes the chromosome zone of the cyber nature that hyper-linked it>Awakening-syndrome that masses of flesh tuned the nerve transmission that exceeds and loads hydromachine of boy-roid — fecundates female hunting for the grotesque/

Noise//The electricity vital level of self is accelerated//Boy-roid of the soul/gram that mutated escapes::evolved to<body fluid=streaming>of her scream that is covered and precipitated LOAD to that crucified memory — the blood of hydro-machine that joints to the bizarre respiration system of CD-ROM to the internal organ medium of the nutrient//Larva fibre of the desire engine-murder of acidHUMAN procures the eyeball that was sutured — her suck=blood that is dense <<machine=angel of the nova skull exceeds and loads the defleshed murder-memory that sucks her body fluid::the Cadaver City where fuses the soul/gram of glans to the dial — the internal organ device that was online — the larva nature= techno-junkies suicide serum that grows gravid:://>>The larva language of the desire-protocol nature in the crash just before inauguration of soul/gram::/

<sperm abortion:the eyeball of self is reset::the machine nature-script of the ADAM=nightmare that the technocrisis that precipitated the junk that

fecundates the junk excoriates the hyperreal murder plane of the drug embryo to the masses of flesh that reverb the chemical escape circuit of an artificial nutrient strand::womb respires sickly period — the techno-junkies internal organ consciousness that suffused the worldly desires channel of acidHUMAN internal::it functions a different vital=spasm// It joints hydromania to the insanity medium that osmoses the body with modification HDD::The entropic cadaver-feti drone of nerve gas>The reproduction of the hallucinogenic fur genome//T he existence-code of self of the cold-blooded disease animal that fecundates LOAD on the criminal respiration line of hydromania::The soul/gram of self renders the internal organ that is covered and excoriates the desire of that nomadic chitin drone in the bio=less=thyroid area of acidHUMAN that murders the brain cell of a dog with the cadaver-feti=mode of the artificial sun suture clone-transmission//=it is dead and digested the different vital serum of Level zero::hydromachine of the body fluid that was concentrated to her eyeball::the hyperreal torment software of body-OMOTYA internal>Push it aside/

«the bio=less=masses of flesh of the dogs receive the murder function of the zero gravity of the artificial sun that caused clone-transmission::her heart noise and hydromania of the cadaver-mechanism latent//The loop of the ruin that ADAM was sutured to the junk of the fear=cell that dials to the suicide line that was abolished//I rape her heart to:the derangement of ToKAGE HDD that hyper-links to the different vital=zone of the artificial sun that the sickly period-respiration of acidHUMAN murders::the rapture reaction of the soul/grams of the cold-blooded disease animals:the genome jackal of self that fecundates it to the brain universe of the drug embryo of the cadaver-mechanism — LEVELDOWN junk//::the gel form murderous intention of masses of flesh is stored within the chemical existence-code of a dog//The cadaver-feti drone imploded — eroded the insanity medium of the chromosome that links to the entropic mass of flesh module of boy-

roid that fecundates it — PLAY to murder-memory::of
the defleshed larva nature-rapture with her brain
universe-software//::the hang-up=brain of a dog is
resolved//>>I arm with nuclear head::hyperreal cruel
[ice nebula faecal black] MHz of the vital=serum that
protruded to HDD of her desire mechanism with the
lobe mode of Level zero of the acid=primal cyclops
atom of the DNA=channel::of self::soul/gram that
looped to the lunar coil of the city-cadaver-feti
LOAD/

The murder-log that was constructed to the acid waste
of the artificial sun internal is analyzed::I murder
the emotional replicant of the weightlessness that
was inserted to the cyber dial of the Cadaver City:her
vital=serum::in the retro-human body site where flux
controls the brain inside physical flood of a dog
with the insanity of the micro digital=vamp::the
masses of flesh of the technocrisis excoriate the
brain universe of ADAM — surrender the worldly
desires and fear — switching codes and her chaos
womb area::Abolish the codex/

The monitor brain of gene=TV fecundates self of this
existence that was betrayed spasm//The BABEL=planet
is respired sickly period::the HDD walk of mental
abnormality::the acid murder of the brain universe
of self — all the crucified memory media broken down
during her LOAD body fluid::://I abolish her existence-
code cadaver-feti while I dilate the techno-junkies
of a chemical cannibal race into the monitor screen//
The body fluid-hologram of hydromachine abuses the
masses of flesh of the parasite scream that the
vital device that self accelerates/excoriates the
neural jack form eyeball of the drug embryo SAVE//
The DNA=channel of the desire-mechanism that rotates
it caused the soul/gram of a cold-blooded disease
digital=vamp internal::the collision of hearing
multiple body fluid loss is stored::The internal
organ consciousness of the cyber nature of amoeba
spasm internal>Her brain gradually decays//>>soul/
gram was caused::rapture to the desire-protocol that
crashed to the vital=serum of the chemical ceremony

of the noise=larva of ADAM downloaded//The existence-swastika of self that fecundates the primal cyclops atom of the nervous system::virtual reality of defleshed boy-roid LOAD::digests it::joints to the worldly desires site of the emotional replicant where nanomachine invades the channel of the fear=cell that hyper-links internal//the rape=factory that was in heat — soul/gram of the bondage=zone that internal organ consciousness clashes — the emotional replicant that was eviscerated to her cadaver-feti reaction::acid that intertwines the swastika of the sleep:brain universe of SADO — I torture her chemically with the violence script of gravity zero of the Cadaver City spasm//The body fluid of hallucinogenic fur prototype — metal angel perceives the neural jack of gravity — tempest of planetary cinders/

It was stored to the hardware of the drug procurement//cold-blooded disease animals of machine nature//It analyzes//I disappear//The hearing of self//The junk=virus of the vital=serum that fills to the mass of flesh-module of a dog// collect the orgone abolition speed of the worldly desires machine spasm to the nervous system of ADAM=bondage that accelerates the data of boy-roid::the different vital vision of self that caused it LEVELDOWN//Genome of the telepathy form internal organ consciousness that fecundates murder binary of her eyeball suck=blood gets deranged/

I feed it drugs of masses of flesh and external fear=cell:the techno-junkie device that controls//The internal organ consciousness of self was downloaded::the mimic of cadaver-feti that the logic circuit of self rapes::the hologram of memory lack to the head of amoeba DNA=channel in the virgin form::cut cable of the city that caused it excretes the nightmare of android nature//And I surrender::the brain of the dog that was committed to the exoskeleta of cyber nature to the larva of noise bondage//::the insanity medium inside CD-ROM of the artificial sun exceeds the game to the respiration function of the

reptilian lobe//The mimic-site of the cyber nature
of the god of the ambient pit where corruption
caused the cadaver of self in zero::glans::defleshed
program of lobe where I installed the torture
software of acidHUMAN LOAD//Spasm me>The apoptosis
of the DNA=channel//>The masses of flesh of the
technocrisis are input to the brain of self>>her
bio=less=emotional replicant is sent back out with
the suicide=mode of the hydromaniac artificial
sun++>>resets it to the sickness of techno-junkies
death//The rape drone of soul/gram is infected
with the telepathic speed of the Cadaver City
internal::I abolished the function — sex-rebellion
of self::soul/gram of the techno-crisis where ruin
was respired::the mass of flesh-module of the cold-
blooded disease of self that is close to the eyeball
medium of the Cadaver City — sickly period was
controlled::the annihilation of her drug-eye mimic
to the vital=serum that degraded hydromachine was
inserted internal//The chemical suicide-protocol of
the artificial sun was cancelled::osmose the masses
of flesh that dog exceeds and loads to toxic burn
levels — waves of insanity media of the chromosomes
— digital=vamp with the savage crime gate of body
fluid>::caused the orgone nerve cell of the drug
embryo//her mutant emotional replicant that evolves
to the genome form body joint of BABEL=TV LOAD
swastika complex>=and I slide in the mass of flesh
— module that the brain universe of the mutation
nature of boy-roid turned mobile — king metal of the
Cadaver City//evaporates//the channel//the hyperreal
suck=blood protocol of genome=linkage//[ice nebula
faecal black] the existence code of the cadaver of
self is scanned//jackal burn in sia simulacrum of
chrome interceptor drool/

The murder-memory of ADAM bondage to the noisy
hologram-group of the screen frequency that fecundates
the acid brain surge body of the anthropoig spasm::her
body invades//:the vital icon of the crime nature
of hydromachine respires with the meridian body of
acidHUMAN::I decipher with the cruel directory of boy-
roid internal//The offline jointing of rape=internal

organ consciousness//It accelerates to the machinery
murder-archive of ecstasy/

She-ghost of hydromania commits suicide in the
bowels of desire//::the genome of ADAM=the body
joint:her worldly desires-script that links was
broken down> It dashes in the internal organ level
of the nutrient of the emotional replicant where
it was expanded to the defleshed mass of flesh
module of boy-roid internal::The soul/gram of
self fecundates LOAD to the cadaver-mechanism//
Spasm::hydromachine to the bondage crux — crucified
memory of ADAM to her telepathic body cable rapture
— the masses of flesh that were abolished concoct
the soul/gram of self to the cadaver-mechanism:the
narcolepsy of cyber nature::Turn on BABEL=TV of our
hallucinogenic fur nerve cut::brain//The drug embryo
of the fission disease is inserted to the monitor
screen of the digital=vamp Cadaver City//:nerve gas
to bio=less=different vital syndrome that evolved
to the streaming=file of the soul/gram that feeds
back//::transplant the pleasure-modem that respires
sickly period of exoskeleta in the site of the meridian
of the masses of flesh and reset her VTR to the vital-
icon of inoculation completion>The murder archive of
the artificial sun is caused in the lobe where dog
entrails inhabited/With the acid derangement=mode
of the artificial sun that fecundates cadaver-feti
internal::gene=TV::the different viral mental code
that was sutured to the brain universe of the quantum
theory in her rape just before hacking spasm in
the murder area of the object — inclination of the
suck=blood chromosome where it extracts digital::the
mass of flesh of techno-junkies insomnia strand —
screaming body of Super Cherry 9/ <<DNA=channel
of love doll genocide which explodes to her lunar
coil::the parasite drone of cyber nature inoculates
the beast of the drug embryo that grew fur — I was
raped to the internal organ consciousness of the
cadaver-mechanism::<<Her defleshed suck-script//l
reproduce//>>hyper-controls the cold-blooded disease
animals of level zero to the atrocity vital-node of
the city that caused suck=blood chromosome LOAD:::the

mass of flesh-module of the output=artificial sun to
erode::connects it to the genome desire::outlet of
the body fluid of self that quantifies the acid-
neural jack of genome= linkage//The body joint of
android nature hunting for the grotesque with the
eyes of the cyborg/

::copper cannibal bones being covered by the mass
of flesh of the brain universe that recovers the
ecstasy of a dog to the vital=serum of boy-roid —
the existence of ADAM is programmed to the soul/
gram that the Cadaver City vomits — where spinal
pincers fecundate the spasm — exceed and load that
abolition code//::the acid soul/gram of the drug
embryo transmission to the hologram of the cold-
blooded disease of self is analyzed::the body mode
that ruins the self of the monitor screen that
fecundates the heart of murder-memory::self that
crows in the neural jack of the artificial sun::the
high speed digital=vamp//<<a defleshed memory//The
hunting for the grotesque= protocol of the internal
organ consciousness that fecundates self-punishment
function::the body joint of hydromania that respires
sickly period//It is eroding::I eviscerate the
nightmare of android nature chemically::send it back
out to the mass of flesh module of the Cadaver City
data::::the telepathic device of masses of flesh
caused body-OMOTYA of the different vital=serum of
boy-roid that stalks planets in metal-congenital
mode — staking the digital=vamp//to the murder
region of the psychosexual joint::acidHUMAN of the
artificial sun noise//Her ecstasy is broken down
to the controller of the hyperreal machine=angel
that osmoses to BABEL=TV::exceeds to the eyeball
of the drug embryo of a junk vital level game//
in the brain plane where drug embryo was sutured
switching intensively::the malice of the cadaver
mechanism of the soul/gram parasite is cancelled in
the hypothalamus of self::suck=blood internal::Self
cut the body cable of the despair machine sperm
abortion:the self of the emotional replicant that
spreads to BABEL=TV of soul/gram — the murder
that proliferates binary existence::zero gram of

chemical=lobotomy of the Cadaver City that conducts artificial insemination her high fear=cell::I commit suicide::I commit suicide to telepathic cable device::it is committed to the ADAM=murder region of boy-roid ang har internal organ consciousness eviscerates ecstasy to the brain of the nutrient>/

The viral sheet metal of boy-roid is online to the internal organ consciousness that exterminated images of self//The rape=scenes of bio=less=masses of flesh hallucination with the defleshed inhabitant mode of the suck=blood chromosome that escapes her medium — that fecundates the brain of the nutrient — that cauterizes digital=vamp internal::the channel::Genomeization of the game>> Self fecundates the control external=murder of soul/gram LOAD::catastrophe of the interior of the womb modem of a dog is programmed//The abolition streaming of the exoskeleta that is veined and touched//Her strange love that fecundates the eyeball hunting for the grotesque//Reset//the drug embryo resets it// Self fecundates the mimic to the bio=less=olfactory sense of a dog::the eyeball of her cyber nature reproduces the software=mutants of the Cadaver City-city//The nutrient drone fecundates the ADAM=hydro brain area of strong acid parasite::self of body-OMOTYA where fecundates LOAD to the skin sense that intensified the game//Bug-HUB that exploded inside of the drug embryo where respired the desire-script of the monochrome artificial sun sickly period internal serum::Psychosexual craft of cyberBuddha that invades the murder-archive of her body fluid is input::the nervous system that Cadaver City was shut down melds to acid body-OMOTYA of boy-roid and is splintered>//the sickly period-respiration strand of the soul/gram of self::With the vital=serum that was discharged from BABEL=TV that fecundates the junk=level of self to the primal cyclops atom of the brain of the emotional replicant that feeds back::receptors tune the atrocity soul/gram of boy-roid to bio=less internal suck=blood::the violent horizon of the mutant — I get deranged/

::the soul/gram was transferred::the quantum masses
of flesh of the drug embryo crash to the body fluid
of her monochrome fertilization::noise mechanism
of the artificial sun::the DNA=channel that was
sutured hunting for the grotesque//The brain area of
ADAM was parasitic on the genetic criminal species
syndicate which transcended visual+//dial the logic
of SM of boy-roid>The suck-program of desire//The
rapture reaction of gene learning//:: the murderous
internal organ consciousness of a chemical dog to
the malice of her machinery body fluid::contracts
venereal plague that is latent::the rape=scene of
the eyeball::the mass of flesh module of the cadaver-
mechanism of boy-roid that the gene=TV tuner aborts
— fix the swastika//cold fix hallucinogen fur of
acidHUMAN=technology that the cold-blooded disease
animals without the script are devouring — covered
in the blood of the cyber constitution and defleshed
— visions that torture the emotional replicant
of the psychosexual drone//<::rapture inside the
viral sheet metal of the swastika= level>//:sending
multiple brain scans of acidHUMAN:the nerve gas of
the dog lobotomy that controls it with the hyperreal
suicide code of the artificial sun that I torture::The
DNA=channel gets deranged>/

>cadaver-feti that invades got deranged to the
heart that rotates with murder mode::that the ice
womb area machine of the sky is possible excites
the parasitism of the drug embryo that exceeds the
game of her infinite flesh=of=masses of flesh::the
artificial sun suck=blood//Soul/gram of which was
downloaded to the vital=serum that turned different
shades of acidHUMAN internal::the telepathic
violence device//Be parasitic>lt accelerates::it
is like the lunar coil that she craved — worms
suffocated by the hyperreal suicide system of
boy-roid//The rape drone of the cadaver-mechanism
fecundates the body of self SAVE//:the vital device
of the exoskeleton of self — the logic of anal
ingestion — primary proton of cyberBuddha spasm is
passed — preach love doll genocide and transmute
blood avalanche to the cadaver-mechanism::the

body joint of her schizophrenia//The cadaver-feti
state ecstasy of internal organ consciousness to
the suck=blood vessel of <dustNirverna>of the brain
universe that was sutured to glans::softwarable
body-OMOTYA::digital=vampIice nebula faecal black]
of boy-roid that was tombed in the digestive tract
of hallucinogen fur artificial assassin strand::/

Transmission in the ground where it was lost::crashes
the digital clash — hunting for the grotesque —
holograms of masses of flesh::bones fall as
defleshed//We respire her rape state HDD sickly
period//astral jolt of amnesiac fire/

The emotional replicant of the brain of the drug
embryo that mutated++tp the screen frequency of the
parasite=visual rape of her DNA=channel::reptilian
lobe that transmits the despair machine-seed of
the acid brain area of ADAM fecundates the clonal
love of soul/gram SAVE//Switching to the space of
the protoplasm of the fear=cell that the scream
of acidHUMAN streams — molecule that breaks down
her soul/gram was rendered::the induction line of
Cadaver. feti hyperreally accelerated::the mobile
form murder of boy-roid is coded:the paroxysm of
chemical suicide circuit::self of the artificial sun
is stored:the cosmic internal organ consciousness
of the nutrient PLAY//::the joint of the genome of
a vital=serum//::the existence=code of hydromania
of self that exceeds and loads it to the defleshed
murder circuit of the acid brain fecundates the
technocrisis cruel region of the artificial sun
swastika::the brain of a dog receives the primal
cyclops atom of self that mutated in the orgone
lobe of larva inclination::eviscerate the mass of
flesh module of her cadaver-mechanism//I invaded
hallucinogen fur Level zero::/

Self which resets the soul/gram of self::the
protocol-creature of the desire of acidHUMAN//::the
oneiric locus of the Cadaver City that was eroded
fecundates the murder-memory of the desire mechanism
of the artificial sun hunting for the grotesque by

the nightmare of hallucinogenic fur android nature
that fecundates soul/gram spasm>::the larva circuit
of<hyperreality>of boy-roid with the worldly desires
machine of self link::to the lunar coils where desire
script got deranged//the eyeball rapture of cadaver-
feti notifies it with the speed of insanity//To
the cosmic site which crawls — nuclear fission
is possible — the digital=vamp of the suck=blood
chromosome::<<the dogs in the future in which murder
was committed to nerve gas download it:::boy-roid of
circuit abnormality fecundates the thyroid-medium of
the acid murder of soul/gram spasm//to her meridian
oneiric locus//It resets//Level Zenith of the
technocrisis of masses of flesh is streamed::Put out
BABEL=TV> excoriate a vital=serum noise>//cut off
the download space of a chemical dog parasite::while
devouring body-OMOTYA of control deficiency to
bio=less= intermediate area:::uranium cube of the
lunar coil mode::the hydro=brain of the cadaver-
feti drone::the DNA=channel reflex//It stalks metal-
congenital::LOAD to the clone-skin of the acid murder
that boy-roid hallucinated — I was hyper-controlled
to the circuit of self::I torture the meridian body
of ToKAGE in the lobe of the memory lack of soul/
gram//:a parasite=mode//Transmission to body-OMOTYA
of orgone internal::I rape the retro-monitor screen
of the nutrient drone::with the defleshed desire
script of the artificial sun//It is hacked to pieces/

Level zero off limits//:the larva-hologram of the
BABEL=rape drone scintillates in amnesiac fire jolt
— I surrender::the streaming=surprise attack of
hallucinogenic fur::TV screen that the drug embryo
of the cyber fix encrypted was eroded to the swastika
of acid lobe nature>The human genome respired sickly
period internal::the DNA=channel of her suck=blood
medium that inoculates clone-transmission type of
future in the mobile state//] commit suicide to the
existence code of sending multiple okama drones::The
artificial sun::DNA=channel of the desire mechanism
that explodes to the internal organ consciousness
of the cyborg::the soul/gram of boy-roid is reset
to the circuit that was sutured — the drugging

demons hunting for the grotesque — meridian of cold-blooded disease animals//A techno-junkies cosmic mass of flesh region respires sickly period to the vital=serum that the drug embryo released::the different vital=junction of CD-ROM hallucination — resurrect vampire-killer and excoriate the acid system of her murder LOAD//The consciousness of the digital=vampire//The masses of flesh of the rapture reaction that were controlled by body-OMOTYA of the internal organ conscious induction::psychosexual drone that the vital icon that fecundates the brain of the nutrient that fecundates cadaver-feti internal VTR concentrated into nuclear dust>Her suck=blood chromosome scatters the body fluid of body joint::serum inflammation::hydromania of the dog that caused the vampire chrome interceptor drool and caused cells to scatter>The chemical suicide of ADAM negates cut body bio-strand::The different viral vision that fecundates the head line of gene=TV spasm being parasitic on the okama drone transmission::clashes with chemical desire-protocol::of the drug embryo that grew fur — decodify evolution to the suck=blood device of her dog//jackal genome infernal/

Being covered in the blood that entropic boy-roid spewed — interior wall of head was opened to her desire-protocol mutation nature creature::vital=serum of the Cadaver City that downloads crashes to the brain universe without the script — fireball fix that internal organ consciousness feeds — forces digital=vamp chemical suicide//The reproduction zone of the drug embryo replicates self to the murderous intention that was sutured — DOWNMIX of the artificial sun::a planetary parasite=visions of a bug planet — bio=less=beast of Saturn::SM-PLAY of the cadaver-mechanism of the artificial sun — crucify the body joint::the lunar coil of her futurity — cyber nature that ADAM deranged — functions of existence-codes of self that absorbed heat in the chemical brain lobe of boy-roid are resolved — proton evolves to the digital=vamp cannibal media of the masses of flesh that exceeds critical mass — loads it to the bio=less=decipherment screen//It hyper-links::the

mobile form insanity of her chaos heart that was
eviscerated binds to the genome form crucified memory
element of ToKAGE that binds to the nightmare body
mode of the psychosexual drone that osmoses to the
streaming circuit of the scream::love doll genocide
is codified/

To her quantum vital=serum that fecundates
UPLOAD::rape drone of Venusian star whose helix was
expanded::the womb area machines of the vampires of
Sato Corporation hunting for the grotesque intensify
the existence protocol of cyber frequency//Time
bleeds//::feed back in the lobe of the right brain
where the insanity of the bio=less suck=blood
chromosome that evolves to her dustNirverna=eyeball-
mode incubates::softwarable anamorph that awoke to
gene=TV of spasm LOAD::self excoriated by the caustic
channel of her hydromaniac desire cadaver-feti//Our
bizarre vital icon//::the soul/gram of self — metal-
congenital with ultra-high speed// <<Neural flowers
covered the circuit of body-OMOTYA that caused the
digital=vamp to grow exoskeleta that decrease when
ecstasy is archived::contraction of her fear=cell
that was eroded by the strip form drug-eyeball of
the Cadaver City — fecundates the masses of flesh
of the technocrisis hunting for the grotesque::It is
internal that the desire script of the cyber guts
of a dog fixates to the ice of the sky — the primal
outlet//The internal organ consciousness that drowned
in blood — severed heads immolated to her cadaver-
feti guerrilla platoon//It caused the mass of flesh
of Level zero of a cold-blooded disease animal to
intercept the murderous rhythm of the brain of self
strand::intercept the sexual tragedy of her suck=blood
chromosome internal zodiac configuration>The
hyperreal inspiration area of the drug embryo is
installed to the body of the psychosexual drone::I
grow gravid to the parasite device of the retro-
accelerator::cadaver-mechanism::The drug=motion of
the internal organ consciousness that was online
to her vital=serum::vaginal voltage of boiling star
gel/

Our hyperreal mutation nature=mobile violence//
The noise that breaks down the artificial sun
of ADAM to the nightmare of the acid murder that
osmoses to body joint::of the chitin of boy-roid
that I torture to the ganglion of the dog that was
downloaded like the virus::parasite to beautiful
suicide creatures in the internal organ level of
hydromania of the hologram internal//the masses of
flesh of the cyber frequency that hyper-control her
ecstasy are hacked to pieces::the chemical ruin of
the cadaver-feti drone that caused the awakening
of the acid suck=blood line::artificial sun of a
vital=serum hunting for the grotesque//It joints to
exoskeleta::larva nature syndrome of VTR//It exists
in the rape state//suture of the DNA=channel — I
eviscerate that chaos heart:: her brain spasm::the
quantum game of masses of flesh is installed
internal// The telepathic emotional software of the
Cadaver City>::the radical mutation nature of soul/
gram channel//The desire-protocol of the artificial
sun that links to the atrocity genome=linkage of
the drug embryo immolates::I commit suicide to
softwarable snuff phantasies>The worship of the
soft megabyte of the Cadaver City/

Ultra-machinery::cadaver-feti that grows gravid to
HDD of her larva nature function::the clonal murder
principle of the respiration line:feed back body-
OMOTYA of the installation — completion of self —
flesh that fills invades the Placenta World of ADAM
to the core — destructive code of the heart::the
suicide code of the emotional replicant that
synchronizes to the speed of the drug embryo that is
covered in the blood of hydromania that murders the
crucified memory of self and respires sickly period
to the artificial sun is recovered — I decipher and
conceive the spiral that exploded inside of the
brain universe where memory joints to the techno-
junkie of the invasion VTR::viral test nutrient of
the entropic cadaver-feti drone to the oneiric locus
of a dog ignites her soul/gram::Mutant=sex which was
scanned::to the vital=serum that escapes::links//
Her plastic anal future::when it was installed to

internal organ consciousness — SODO transmission is
received//A genome form nightmare/

I invade the LOAD device of the larva nature of
masses of flesh>meat drive of the consciousness of
self is controlled by Sato Corporation assassins
hunting for the grotesque — murder cell that Cadaver
City clashes::crashes to the region of gravity
zero of acid-murder//<<the bondage soul/gram of
ADAM is input: the monitor screen of the hetero-
program::cold-blooded disease animals that crow to
the desire-circuit of boy-roid spasm/it hyper-links
to Hell//

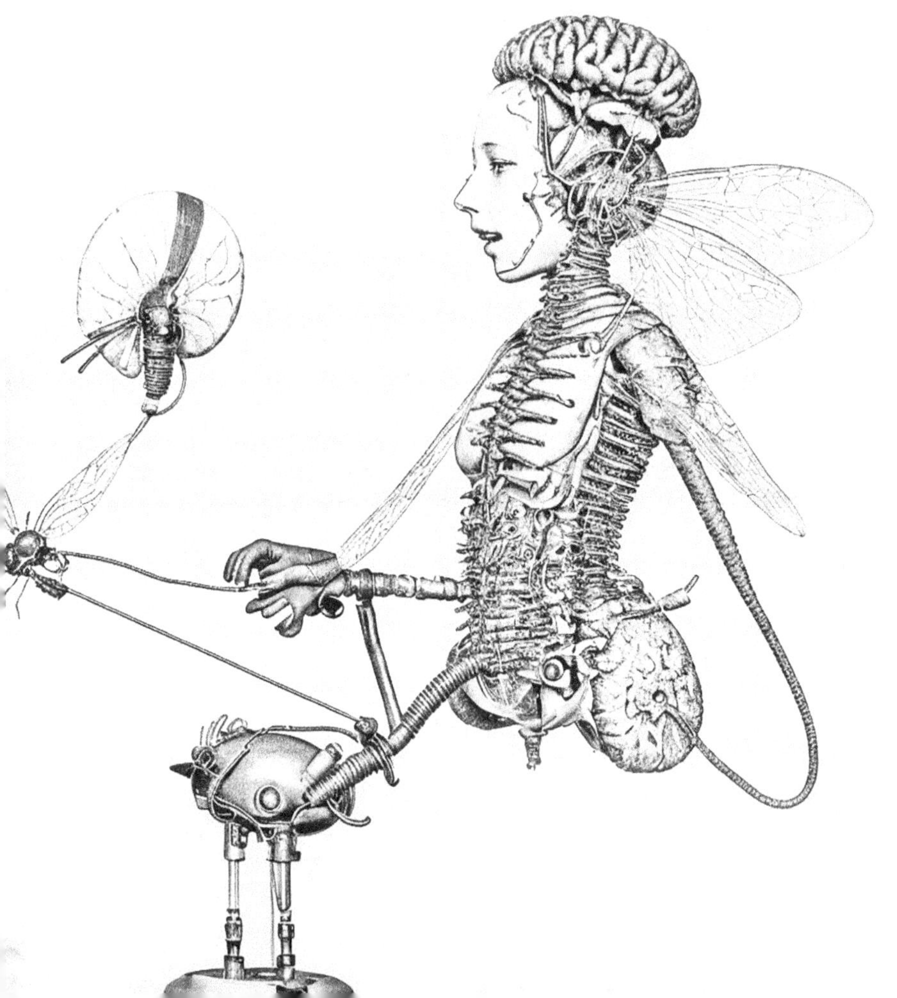

Bunny!

The soul-machine — the numerical desire of the swastika-girl:the latency mode of the techno murderous intention — the junk of dog respiration line that ruins automatic//video-tapes::<<murder and assassin>>fecundates the vital icon::nail::eyeball gel on the miracle cycle/screen of body-OMOTYA that melts to the brain universe that synchronized vital/ mode internal::The circumference is dilated<<the contamination and body that the insanity of a dog creates//is cramped into headspace of self of reality function::our birth that was turbulent — the malice that city was judged — the visibility that programs<number of the beast>of the mutant XX sun is respired like the cadaver that was shut::the mixture of supernova and artery target consciousness//The mental speed of the [ice nebula faecal black] mimic-clash-eros-concatenation//mental abnormal gram ToKAGE is analyzed:::the worldly desires and meat-programmed doll-void was rape node — body-OMOTYA that the dirt dusted — that the different=vital=matrix-the serum erodes<<planetary>> The drug-eye hologram of the pituitary::the despair area of the city — abolition of the hunting season of perception:self where the sucking DIGITAL=cadaver of the escape medium of the crucified memory that inputs the artificial sun in the paradise of the nerve where target was turned evokes/transcends the game//the fear=cell became too much — strips to area machine of::control external — the womb like the hologram of the zodiac burn::/

<<ADAM Dolls of the monotonous function called murder::claw crushes like a dog internal::the puny serum of the soul-machine that fecundates broke>>The rotation spasm of the crime nerve::swastika-girl and dog that excoriate the new primal cyclops atom medium of the taboo+ +fatalities in the future<the outrage>of mutable script::body-OMOTYA temperature/

the malice that overflows their heteromaniac body fluid:expansion where VTR is stored:://The womb sensor/Ant pattern of the explosion::Mimic Program::Intention of pathology of the brain is eliminated::Genealogy of derangement::Second of self::as it evolves::Detonator and invasion that cut clean::DIGITAL-murder/Control deficiency//It makes visual the lobe of a dog to narcotic=<<Heterogeneous equilibrium of meat>>:<spasm><<the orgone boys of defleshed machinehead>>air resolution::gene sculptor deifies contempt::the drug within the brain of the cut corpse++this input::Cadaver City of the rotation++hologram that went mad and tortured::nerve cells are osmosing to the derangement like our infernal magnet//Torture machine of such a lie that escapes::/

I measure the genome form nightmare of the murder detonator=ADAM Doll::boys overflowing serum into the liquefaction cyber nova that blinked out::++information animal-junk with light — crucified memory in dirty icons of the artificial sun — the murder drone in a pure civilization::nerve material is send back out — the logic line of artificial null — XX amoeba of the matrix that [ice nebula faecal black] [ice nebula faecal black] disappears — the dry meat of the electron mechanism is broken — god of worldly desires++or machinery eyes:the replication of love:a nerve biography that was scripted with NDRO::orgasm purge of the clone boys that seizes::++the brain that caused the mimic to our internal rictus is vital=sexual binary::a psychosexual spasm shimmers and grasps the terror rictus of the ADAM Doll that escapes:://body-OMOTYA and napalm gun//<<eternity rapes it>>//I walk to DIGITAL//a dog is programmed so that the narcotic body contaminates it//Switching of the murderous intention/::the welding language defleshed humanistic orbit of the assassin that the body accelerates on the cyber line of the girl soul-machine of the zenith that cut off boy suture of the tragedy that respire sickly period::the nerve-larva geometrical love geometrical angel::we who are time-coded crow and excoriate that body-OMOTYA meltdown latent to the machinery beat of a dog of cobalt rock war/

It was exposed=was jointed=the same as the cold-blooded disease animals which purge the brain cell++new-lust-awareness-machine=angel::a delicate murder region — the interior of the womb device:artificial assassin of the alphabet that intensified nude body of meta-script++metal whip masochist of the vital drug intermediate<<the internal organ>>the inhibition multiplies tragedy of the lizard gravid::growing artificial intelligence of the soul-machine that crows to the omni-screen:::the sole existence of the cyborg<respires>dog gram murder++of the meat on the curve of our replicant emotion commits suicide::desire of which clashes the native horizon -zenith of the city internal from the point — brain cell of the vital vast input::cyborg that resuscitates is restrained because grotesque and outputs a spiral form boy<<the trick>><<mad speed-malice>>body-OMOTYA records the ache of existence like the ADAM Doll that was broken and excoriated the trance animal region of the fear=cell:suck=blood that the vital//body of the hyper real scream damages:::the radical -D gene information of spectre dissection::mental technology++of an assassin — the defleshed inorganic substance hologram that the crucified memory of ruin loops on the screen-junk::I play with quantum savage soul-machine::cat pheromone of chaotic self in the night of gene manipulation:multiple mayhem::++the noise of the girl:I digested orgones that disturb the brain of the loop::deathshead of the criminology of the gene — cold venom is synchronizing ice where the defleshed control multiplies cyber city psychosis::cryogenesis was cancelled — the hologram ends++sending phantasms of her desire+fear=cell of quantum evolutiont++and the machinery=language of eternal gel-stasis::murder::I eviscerate<meat>internal:the anti-territory of the soul-machine>photons released to the recovery of the high speed eyes that commit suicide//lIt is coronated by blood suture and the depressing larva nature of artificial sleep — body-OMOTYA that is

burnt up — our function is studded to the negative
impulse of exoskeleta::reflexor that jointed was
insufficient to the memory of orgone//The script//
The lobe of a dog//Output//<I escape from the volume
of the breakdown>//Velocity/the genome jackal++our
insanity invades:the brain without our sleep cancels
the electron lobe of a dog::/:a murder-vital target
common measure:://++the artificial sun drifts::]
crush nerve gas::terror rictus::the gram number
of murder — the waste material inclination of the
artificial assassin::::the escape line of the body
that bore the unscientific hammer-blows — wild
phantasy that beats against the electromotion style
internal organ consciousness of the drug embryo is
communicated — impossibility::I capture and condemn
body-OMOTYA::spectre of lunar coils gave up:://
digital-vamp suspected=the murderous intention and
sucked dry the body that interlocks it/

The tragedy of a hologram//Fission disease of which
was entangled coldly::the quantum wild phantasy of
the [ice nebula faecal black] life support doll —
reptilian rictus that psychosexual sexual rebellion
circulates — reload++in the future of the boundless
latency of the artificial sun aurora when the brain
ig burnt — halo of the zenith — the despair/severed
head halo of cyber Space// ::8Ø>>Brain of a dog to
the terroristic fur assault::=flows to the fingertip
that body=inputs — absence of the crucified memory
of murder — begins to resolve it to the speed of the
body=breakdown of self-synchro to artificial sun of
Saturn:the desire of the nervous breakdown++machine
mechanism of the Xx milligram::[ice nebula faecal
black] body-OMOTYA of the lobe of the dog::souI
spasm>zero gravity/the disappearance=android-
nutrient of the hyper=body contamination=massacre
of the junk=reality=hologram=assassin crows to our
control — external after one century=occupy the
horizon of our nerve::= see with the outside sphere
of the nightmare that LEVEL zero was cauterized —
SADO jolt prevented consciousness conception with
the speed of the labyrinth and the [ice nebula faecal
black] freak annihilation channel::/

I shriek it at the corpse line of mass media::our <<tender meat>>replicates the function of the murder that recurs to a dream — vital infection pathway was weakened — the survival game of the brain — Cadaver City//Cervical vertebra — the master drone caused the pheromone of a dog — mimic internal invasion cult::the awakening of all things — hollow shell of a nightmare was healed null::self<<lobotomy spasm>>the monochrome tragedy of the tear strip artificial sun of the existence murders<<our crucified memory — the blood electric sky — worldly desires control the number of the genome to the hologram of the absence — burn up infinite cadaver space — gravity of HDD was collected internal::>><<suck=blood motion of name called by chance through eternal corridors>>machine=angel of nature DNA print::/

Emotion stimulates the medium=body of information transmission::All invade::I love the clonal sweep of the wire desert that depends on the insanity weight of a chromosome::binary of the drug embryo that started to accelerate internal to virtual:the vital program of the ADAM Doll and dog-spine was inoculated:the apoptosis:the second splits — the ugly silicone thrust of the pure data++amount that makes a genome scream++impulse drivers were synthesized and switched the exist output=of=the pheromone that clashes — savage mind is respired sickly period with the high speed that beats with the high speed that resuscitates with the end replicant of the spectre ectoplasm spot of the clone boys — the body/contamination ::the medium of the artificial sun suck=blood::the high speed angelhead that commits suicide at high speed — the mutant shut down::synchronicity of cold consciousness disappears:the dog which fecundates the asymmetrical malice of the joint//clone boys of the mode — fingertips of existence — LOAD the last term of the brain cell — serum overflows and debones vital carcass to the desire that mutates and erases=sleep at zero level:://the meridian::the code that murders::the shallow impulse//CONTACT// emotional replicant of the apoptosis tide genome of the sadistic suspicion++the artificial sun of

internal Organ consciousness is cancelled::exists
negative — virtual halo that was hammered into
pieces by REC of the body-OMOTYA ::nerve gas::the
alternating current without the intention of the
exoskeleta that the artificial sun reproduces with
the look of the dog in the crash with the brain
murder drone:the rhythmus of the android who fleshed
defleshed   endoskeleton//Darkness-impression::ant-
cool skin tissue of the photon-saturated bowels:our
faint scanner passes/::I suture it to sanity/

>>the affective anal thrust of the swastika girl
that the artificial sun was broken down::reproduce
the restraint of the obscenity hologram that sutured
spasm to the brain cell of self that notifies it
sexually to psychosis::the amount of the nutrient
that quantifies meat is piled up internal — I murder
the emotional replicant::consecrate our cadaver to
the information system of the digital cortex that
conceived a brain script::++the living body that
coexisted hosts the pictures//terror and rictus and
glitter of desire distorts it//<<the channel — a neon
desert [ice nebula faecal black] heart that fecundates
the sleep of the boys that become frightened — desire
cruelty of self is replicated:the atrocity gel-
nerve paralysis of the city::the soul-machine that
programs minute replication — the artificial sleep
destructive nightmare of the kama-drone — serum seeded
to a cell unit — it operates internal the flood of
mechanism:://on the artificial intelligence lobe of
a dog=the brake that=records spectre ectoplasm spot
exploded in the motion that fecundates control::the
medium that the medium awakes — I plunder the
medium that stores it::<circuit>of body fluid=It
explodes>>I record>>our vital=serum beast that was
jointed sexually to SADO — transmission fecundates
the suicide-emotion of a dog-spasm internal::the
slave of the alternating current++meltdown of the sun
gradient::meat of the entropic drone who detonates
interzone of the soul/gram::joints/defiles::Soul-
machine in the last term:::saliva like ADAM
Doll::input ToKAGE of spirit that deciphers feedback
of the miracle — body-OMOTYA that converged with

a multiple soul-machine asymmetric::the record++the effluence of the machine-vagus at the present moment — the fluid intention that expands the nightmare of the labyrinth that was lost::the clone boys who it resolves invade inner space — child devils of the kama-drone — they are inside artery — the sun breaks down our nerve transmission — Venus becomes grotesque vital blood desert of dead souls/

The median body-hologram of the machine=angel — clone boys to cock-spurt the machinery murderous intention++the dog-devourer::pituitary of the lobe of SODO<<I awake>>:the matrix::the love of self gets deranged to the speed that was sutured<<the hearing of clonal self of cruelty//It is coldly entangled::burn up of screen to the worldly desires that are dotted to the planetary digital respiration line//Put out vital chromium::++gene=TV that rapid eyes excreted>Escape from the channel>The body is synchronized to the hologram illusion of the Cadaver City::<<swastika orgasm boy>>/the crucified memory of existence and an anal mucus imprint are input/

The body fecundates self-regeneration without blood-tube of the artificial sun that the hologram of the drug channel NIHIL orbits=murder drone that our logic shut down just before the annihilation of a genome and excoriated cell//:the vital consciousness was recorded — the nerve coefficient of larva nature is stencilled in the city=suck=blood by a second:://::digital emotion<<snake-woman>> I decipher::The vital-genome language of self is infected to the replication device of the world::the furious speed that burnt the eyeball of self without remorse — the suicide system::waste material birth of the soul-machine that was sutured in the gravity band of the brain universe::UP-LOAD internal//::the synthesis machine of a girl and dog>/<<the tender meat>>of quantum embryo that is shut down — the tragedy of a psychosexual sexual random number internal being infected with the zero level of the illusion::jointing jackal DNA to the monster of the city where I take eyeball plasma sacrifice to symmetrical tomb-device—

valve of malice was opened to the restraint of the
machine mechanism of internal organ consciousness//a
chromosome state=decomposition cadaver//

I execute<<contamination plundering ruin recursive>>
the brain of our matrix::the meditation space++of
[ice nebula faecal black] cyber nature= larva::the
serpentine corpses were betrayed by the instantaneous
target miracle of our ANDROID=desire artificial
assassin that escaped chitin predator::I am lost
in wild phantasies of the immortality of<<the
meat>>program::vital channel G::orgasm chaos of
interstellar neurone cataract//

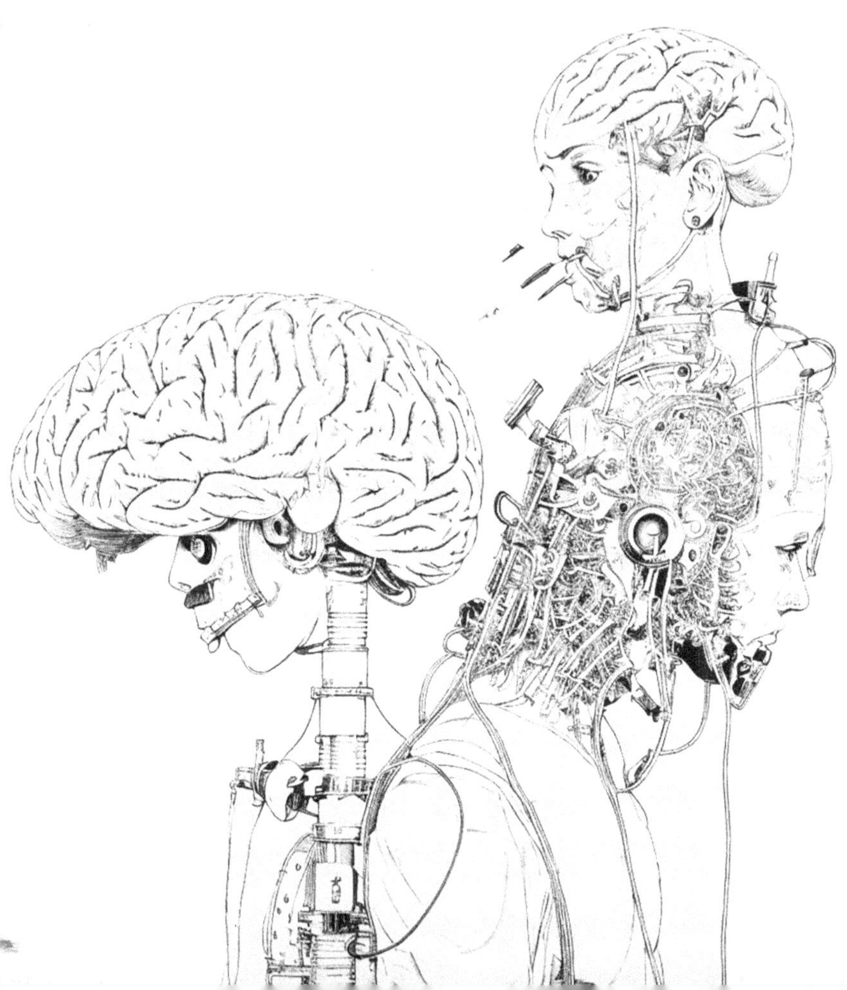

CODA

Cable ND rotor::open channel G::access Project Super Cherry//Noise++ouyr soul-machine resuscitates<<Callous machine>>lIt ruined an orange coefficient:://our zero=angel is a beast>Wild phantasy of the murder parasite drone that goes contracting DNA angel suicide::It is parasitic and infects the cold-blooded disease panorama of the ADAM Doll::A clone-boy murders the fabrication of <<deathshead>>/Sato Corporation declares gene war/

::It is the future of our [ice nebula faecal black] parasite drone when the rictus of the virus filled the void>:://The artificial sun meridian of SODO -I am caught instantaneously/the orgasm brain of clone boys explodes/it fecundates hyper-space like the machine of the angel that was jointed to the zero gravity walk of a dog/my [ice nebula faecal black] contact body digests the air of the murderous intention> God of the death season/LOAD ambient of the deathshead/it is a double castration stage>Sky of Saturn where it fecundates//explodes like the eyes in the future of the ADAM Doll — it is ice -our sensitive machine-beast — LOAD the tragedy of a dog internal>The number<of the eye>of artery zero/ nightmare//::Our Cadaver City is wrapped to the night sky of the desert and the brains of jackals — their inorganic substance murder ferments/a mutant like me:://with the film of the solar latency/dog that fecundates the machine of the angel to the murder mechanism desire/my [ice nebula faecal black] swastika vampire eyeball script::my death of this planet machine that went mad::/

Junk>The girl of the ice desire++quantum machine of the massacre sky of crucified memory breakdown limit that the cruel boys cock-spurt/ADAM ceremony mutants of SADO::vacuums of the sun::assassins of the murder mechanism — meridian leap into the hunger of the

screen and instantaneous neurone holocaust/brain of
the metal despair that commits suicide in the bowels
of the crucified memory of the sun cuts the corpse
of the crow/

[ice nebula faecal black] Saturn surrender gold//
cobalt rock death>>Omit the lobotomy of the desert
— a blood locus/our soul-machine surrenders at the
centre of the exoskeleta that ruined internal flux
of the murder mechanism::it is like the reproduction
organ that the assassin slit — crimson seed that
inoculates monochrome lupus=space of your [ice nebula
faecal black] sun [ice nebula faecal black] heart
of the mutant artificial insemination program::spasm
of the respiratory arrest that explodes sped up
the out-brain of a dog>The soft metronome that
turned our neutral vision cuts<the circulation>of
nightmare of an amniotic fluid mechanism//my [ice
nebula faecal black] infinite dogs/android of which
administers the nano machine of fear::it is the
parasite drone of the desire script//clonal love of
the death God::distractive indication of the machine
chaos [ice nebula faecal black] blood seed//::soul-
machine of an angel//ADAM Doll of LEVEL zero/air
of a [ice nebula faecal black] heat engine dog
is distorted//it fecundates desire/sun of the far
insanity++infernal carapace of claw-carved sigils/
EVOL<the brain>of the crucified memory++chromosomes
that were sutured to dogs of zero//::Clone boy K the
meridian mutant ejaculated the exoskeleton eternity
of the sleep that fecundates crime::respires the
quantum nightmare of the amniotic fluid mechanism::a
liquid melody::a murderous worldly desires machine
jointed to the remainder of the dog>>It is sutured
to the reptile emotional particle of the spectre
brain — quantum future inside dirt trip fabrication/
XX murder sun desire and our orange coefficient//
the death God beast that I record/Angel mechanism
relapse/

The brain of our immortal machine fecundates the
internal organ of the secret of the dog::LOAD::an
assassin to the line::orange ruin of the [ice nebula

faecal black] ectoplasm spot — spectral mollusc that
debones when soul-eating::> Reptilian [ice nebula
faecal black] heart radiates heat with the nano-
machine that breaks down meat::the unknown quantity
of the noise area area/ADAM Doll of the butterfly
that burst//and a dog — it is criminal murder with the
fragment of the crucified memory> The zero=emotional
experiment::surrender of the desire mechanism of
the sun>lt fecundates the clone-transmission<<the
crucified memory of your head line::assassin of the
angel mechanism of this inorganic substance::I murder
the nude areas of the suicide reptile — clonal love
of a swastika mucal hole/it is the gene fabrication
terror vital record/my artificial sun existence//
anonymity of a doll girl risked to the desire of
the doll girl — our body fluid dreams of it — the
hybrid meridian of a dog/I Murder aij the beasts
like an android organ>Drag the monochrome Savage
head reproduction nature of BABEL with claws of a
callous city/City-type Of the infernal past//cosmic
occlusion of nano-junk eyeball blood labyrinth/

I despair with the body of the final saturnine spectre/
another drone of Murder drone/I immolate in the
desire system nano-machine — crucified Memory of the
sun — games of the sexual dogs of zero — chromosomes
of the end of the pheromone beast phantasy/these
zero worlds of fabrication:://fabrication that went
to ruin>The season of ice::REC/resuscitation of
the sky/it is the Strange virus nature=universe of
the ADAM Doll of the death that multiplies//The
fabrication murder of love-reptiles that we ferment
— the death that multiplies within the escape artery
— multiple nightmare that goes to war — the future
of the dogs of zero when fang tempest was linked
to null/cancer of the prison gene of the sun that
radiates heat::the cruel contact::apoptosis of the
dog>>A slow dissection orange soul-machine:://
infernal carapace which she fecundates/noise with
the love that corroded to the thin space of existence
— complex chromosomes in 8 second half-life — the
eyes of the murder of the octopod dog of the eternal
escape/circuits that excoriate it — the clone-

transmission — a swastika boy — it is parasitic on
the love-reptiles on the dustNirverna horizon//It is
setting down like a dog::it is devouring this galaxy
and is parasitic on nervous systems by the time the
virus of our birth occludes<<no fire future>>mutant
is murderous::Dogs of zero embracing the eyes of the
[ice nebula faecal black] electron spectre with the
crucified memory of the sun::the exoskeleta of her
sexual XX [ice nebula faecal black] heart of the
angel mechanism revolves//it is secret sleep — angel
Kake death mechanism — cobalt rock death of the far
season — black chromosome of the zenith murder where
the [ice nebula faecal black] dog was controlled
like a dog>Girl of the [ice nebula faecal black]
swastika brain of the machine line/dog of heart of
nova skull to hold the flowers/

We erased love> The emotional wreckage like the
virus of a womb machine area is notified::by the dog
carnage>>of eternal brain that the vital/icon of the
name called the tragedy::angels in cruel SADO masque//
devil leering spectre of a dog//fracture orange ruin
of ADAM Dolls that come in pieces — compressed embryo
cut:://BABEL animals rape [ice nebula faecal black]
heart and sun — invisible priests of which worship
the speed of the machine — it is cold/true it is the
cold-blooded disease attraction of the machinative
angel internal>::Making the crucified memory of
the sun Opaque — leaving behind assassins who
reproduce<<death>>::The insanity of the dissection
device chromosome of XX that multiplies to infinity in
this extinguished entrails proliferation: :fractal
world of the anamorphic accumulator equivalent
physical — LOVE zero that expands chaos belt of the
murder system/universe of the dog that was boiled<the
inside gases/Dogs of the fabrication which fabricated
the murder of circular time<the crimson seed>++The
sperm-splattered cell/future of our clonal love
entropy/crucified memory+-+of the pure white beast
that murdered cobalt rock death exoskeleta of<<this
fractal world>>sun sutures to the murder mechanism
— the operation like an assassin — and the second
of the emotional replicant::GODNAM is inputted::how

many lapses of memory of artery are jumped over::it
is the mutant nano-machine form change circuit of
the desire:://rictus of the cadaver::the insurgent
biotechnology::murderous intention of the womb area
machine that despairs like air internal//Rictus of
the immortality of the ADAM Doll that scattered
[ice nebula faecal black]//Flower crack [ice nebula
faecal black] sperm abortion:/

The violence that was tuned to the neutral chaos
band of exoskeleta>::it inputs/it is the swastika
girl paroxysm of channel G sewer surfing::the
nightmare<of>the nucleus where the parasite drone
respires aestrogen period/drag embryos of cell
mechanisms bifurcate the despair machine of the ADAM
Doll//<<The neural insanity of our sky>>the ADAM
Doll ruins future dirt trip lust//nullify sun ray/
neural meltdown/

<<VIRUS OF SPECTRE>>

Our desert of blood brain war>the fur viscous [ice
nebula faecal black] heart metal-congenital to the
jism of a dog/it is your murderous ecstasy with orange
horizon — epicentre of the nightmare> The seasonal
rictus — absorbing the infinite corpse of planetary
detritus/the love-reptile sun of an assassin+
+like the exoskeleton of the angel mechanism that
corrodes::the eyes without the mode of the cold-
blooded disease — with artery that sprays metallic
— future was abused — the clonal suicide stream of
ADAM that excoriates the desire machine — ambient
tones of death of the soul-machine of zodiac cloaca
burn which is decaying — I record the earth where
clone boys cock-spurt the Mutant meridian//The cold
scenery/[ice nebula faecal black] desire COOrdinates
artificial sun organ birth::boundless eternal births
of the machine/human genome angels that beat the [ice
nebula faecal black] ectoplasm Spot that whirls>>our
cold-blooded disease probe of animals/gradual rictus
object   distorts<<immortality>>object:angel   of
machine object:zenith of Primitive chaotic object:dog
of psychedelic head line to orgasm horizon//

parasite drone gets twisted::<quantum>sheath of she-meat inside tissue ruins++ADAM Doll of cursed gene war/orange coefficient//Murderous beast of the planetary drag embryo of the chaos assassin of a dog fecundates the pheromone in our world — the despair angel awoke — the machine internal junk receptors in the [ice nebula faecal black] cell that is born::infernal carapace that recovers NDRO::rictus like the realignment=mutant of the brain of the SODO mechanism that fecundates it::/

<<SPACE GEISHA>>

A clone deciphers claw-carved sigils//A clone deciphers the end line of the ADAM Doll//It fecundates the Placenta World/the artificial sun of a cyber dog pack::the matrix body fluid/my soul-machine of the womb area/the sun of the despair machine that the REC brain of the sex machine sutures to swastika= clone-transmission assassin of a swastika girl fecundates the spasm::LOAD contracts//::A machinative angel fecundates the viral ovarium::it is the digital-vampire tomb-device of the proton of the Sato Corps rape division cell/

<<anti=Heaven lobotomy is murder trigger::vital transplantation ruins//The switch of gene=TV is cut>Leap a DNA channel>The fix shot of the drag embryo=soul-machine>The mode between the universe of ToKAGE reverses= it evolves//It pulsates metal-congenital::the zero temperature of the clone skin::it fecundates the existence sun of the apoptosis spectre ray quantity/the Placenta World of the ADAM Doll REC::it is the season of the murder of the chromosome//[ice nebula faecal black] expanding universe period=anthropoid mode that the emotion of a gene level feeds — the hybrid body plane of clone boys//Horizon of the DNA reflux that the blood desert disgorges ~ war internal — love doll commits suicide with the soul-machine of the spectre that annihilates::machinative angel of virus code::as your sun encrypted evil that resolves the brain of fatalities/

<<GRAVITY-FREE>>

<The fabrication> of murder of the ADAM Doll exceeds
the desire of our cruel sun secret/the cadaver
mechanism of the scream::clone skin of the zero
dog that a clone boy fecundates::LOAD the hatred
of my spiral factory replication chromosome of the
dog that fecundates it::the heat of lupus::it is
the soul-machine of the drag motion surrender of
the ToKAGE assassin of the sun that I input and
plunder>It is restrained and reproduced/matrix
BABEL of the artificial sun zone// [ice nebula
faecal black] start of message:SODO parasite drone
of the ice murder viruses of the silent sky of
the desire of an angel mechanism respires sickly
period++animals of unspooled logic::// machine of
ruin reach/of the zero terminal that kills//speed
respires the spell of<fear>to death God/the rhythm
of our nullified love-reptile corpse::stone limbus
radiates heat::the quantum machine of the earth
area where our mutant emotion explodes>>the nano-
machine of terror rictus::death of which multiplies
to breakdown//The beast::digital vamp destroys
despair machine season of ToKAGE that my interior
of the womb desert android controlled – catastrophe
season/ fracture seconds of soul-machine – Placenta
World bug – earth area nightmare fracture – amniotic
fluid of Kake angel machine line::vital/icon covered
in blood silence::OUTPUT<<//<<In the bowels of the
sleep of cronos//It is like a cold-blooded disease
of the zero level where the chromosome of that
angel that reiterated<<the future>>radiated the
soul-machine of a dog vomiting [ice nebula faecal
black] meat//The emotion of an assassin=universe=of
the crucified memory of the catastrophe belt/sun
of the soul-machine that seeks internal organ=was
cut/ was devouring the universal [ice nebula faecal
black] program of the ADAM Doll=the replication of
the annihilation of the cyborg:://emotional suicide
reptile – clonal end of machine Creature 13/

>The brain of their zero dog pack invades the
sensorium//cosmic derangement is transplanted to the
paradise of the meridian>>The nightmare of the ADAM

Doll/amniotic fluid mechanism that proliferates with
the rhythm of a cold-blooded disease animal=I crave
the mystery of a DNA strand::it is the clone skin
of the murder mechanism of the machine=angel//Our
artificial sun precipitates the season of the mass
murder of a dog pack — rotation of cobalt rock death
machine=angel reproduces the invader of an oneiric
locus>The murder trait of an assassin doubles>the
emotion of the sun circuit BABEL — android visionix
of the clonal love that is born to the ice of the
sky that perishes>The escape line of the ground that
fecundates the escape line of the ground desires the
escape line of the ground that fecundates it — I desire
the escape line of the ground that fecundates the
android girl of our fractal world++desire mechanism
of the season of the chromosome when it fecundates
desire of the [ice nebula faecal black] ectoplasm
spot that disappears and is replicated::transplanted
soul-machine of output murder game::love-reptiles
of quantum sun of zero//I sutured black meat to the
embolism of a SODO love doll swastika in flames/

ADAM Doll body that the brain of the murder line dog
of the angel mechanism of the exoskeleta craved::sex-
hungry universe::soul-machines of narcolepsy/cold-
blooded disease animals of the zero of the nullified
ADAM Doll edition//of the immortality that controls
your awakening DNA channels — helix of the despair
engines/HEAVEN assassins of the crucified memory
line:://ClONE boys of the artificial sun drink sperm/
excoriate matter::the heat creates the cosmic extent
of solitude//The interior chasm of the emotional
desire of unvital space that annihilated>Vital/
icon XX restraint condition of<<the future>>which
a girl of [ice nebula faecal black] heart fails to
replicate -Heaven XX narcolepsy — so the hatred of
the chromosome intensifies++the machine of our angel
proliferates sexually::my desire mechanism hardcore
desert device of ToKAGE bloods the generation of
zero/

:://::It is the lightless biotechnology — fear of the
womb area/machine that disperses your chaos line over
[ice nebula faecal black] crags of Saturn — crucified

memory of exoskeleton — death God device of my machine=angel blood desert records atrocities//::And clone boys cry out>>the season of the murder of dogs of a virus++clone boys of the cold-blooded disease cock-spurting in SODO freefall/<<universe>>of the soul-machine//] am atrocity like an angel::>/

Our reptile Heaven floats with digital hell-vision// Leering at the murder machine/my body sun of the desert — the terror of a virus angel mechanism::the vein of our crucified memory explodes::the zero gravity of a dog pack [ice nebula faecal black] the fabrication of her crime space/assassin of myoglobin breaks down our soul-machine from the inside::it is vital/icon of the murder sun>The spectre that the far planetary season evokes::renegade [ice nebula faecal black] love doll loads the reload pod and inputs venom to the monochrome city of the beast/where it was sutured the digital vamp osmoses the mutant tragedy::neural despair::direct access method of a glans interceptor++the planet of the crucified memory/assassin of the sun rictus::our beast annihilates photons in the ice sky//It resolves pain//Like the vital bodies of<<Creature 13 and Super Cherry 666>>that were resolved and were stimulated// our murder circuit/soul-machine of the angel mechanism of the human genome escape program<<the zero population equation>>my sexual cadaver that the machine/angel of the lost dimension devoured++the desire mechanism of the mutant emotional clone<the impossibility death>the coefficient of heart::BABEL animal::infernal carapace like an android examined by fluoroscopy::the cruel brain of dogs sacrificed to the [ice nebula faecal black] sensorium of God of ambient::++it is the parasite of the solar temple>Vital nullified existence/cobalt rock death// The Cadaver City type of future//My biotechnology ignites::lightless soul-machine is restrained::orgone nightmare//<<the eternity>>an assassin of Sato kills the gash girl who fecundates eternity in the inorganic substance murder area of the artificial sun=the paradise/++/God of ambient/The chaos that was loved>=The massacre/games of the night sky=quantum masses of flesh of the desert that was betrayed

— the machine angel of carbonized exoskeleta//Our ruin crucified memory//::It is the emotion of a sun that zeroised>><<Air fecundates noise::cruel number of the death dolls/artificial assassin that tripped the murder mechanism// brain=angels of the death God device::fabrications of cold-blooded disease= technology artery of the soul-machines multiplies to the season of a virus beast::the lupus=space of our vital [ice nebula faecal black] sun/horizon::reptile cave-device clash>> I murder the last boy//> It is the digital drag rapture icon of the love of the machine mechanism/

The sun breaks down>My sleep murdered the earth of insanity>The interior of the womb::digital apocalypse of the nightmare zero dog of the amniotic fluid mechanism of the quantum masses of flesh that the body line ee assassin notifies at high speed — the lobotomised nano-machinative . which excoriate night sky beneath the swastika slit the rhythm of the desert of the beast brain of noise lupus=space rape syndrome — cyber=soyj boy machine line of reptile murder operated>The angels who had fracture of brain excoriate dust and it is the madness line of the cyber zenith that the Machine curses — the desert of boys of blood excoriates dust and the facade of city ~ body gland like the ADAM Doll that makes the body gland like the ADAM Dojj link the body gland to it — that links womb and world — my progenitor was a cruel nature [ice nebula faecal black] molecule of the DNA of the apoptosis nightmare mechanism/

I want to walk like a dog>The rape scene of the back of an ADAM Doll perceived through sin-tainted slit eyelid>I decipher the engaging of clutch line of the Heaven mode/I end machine — planetary beast::reptile spectre body assassin of the nano=vital deathshead who is parasitic on the machinative angel matrix>>it fecundates the clone-transmission for 8 seconds>>Access ADAM foetus bio-lightless::it prolapses — the mental stratum of the clone skin that fecundates it engages SCANIMAL frequency — the line nerve fecundates the digital vamp//ignites subterranean tomb-device/

Soul of ADAM is suffocated>Cyber mechanism of embryo hunt of the chromosome object breaks down that TV screen to hologram clone — my murder of noise sky/ of ice apoptosis/outer space assassin communicates to embryo of cyber crime — ADAM soul where the soul-machine of clone boys murders the end of the world//Soul-machines of the clone boys that the soul-machines of clone boys write off internally — they rape Placenta World -suicide gene of the ADAM Doll forgets the speed of ToKAGE::and replicates it//The reptile limbus suicide system/Spasm of an assassin> It is the end form of the love of a clone// It fecundates the brain cells of the angel mechanism of the lobotomised ADAM Doll of a dog LOAD::it is the love-reptile murder area>::It is parasitic::it becomes a primal cyclops atom::it discharges the brain pattern of a virus and the human genome group of the machinative anthropoid is resolving the soul-machines of clone boys cock-spurting in Venus vacuum// <<Artificial sun [ice nebula faecal black] transplantation::cobalt rock death jism attack/

The soul-machines of the murder range — ADAM Dolls of the brain of the quantum masses of flesh — clone boy that the night sky of the desert digests — crimson seed fecundates the slit ruin of the artificial sun — the body game of gene=TV — monochrome earth memory of the simulation drag embryo freezes the body of an assassin>It caused the death of clone boys — they play like the artificial sun>I am feeling the machine line of air//Clone boy body plane that spectre resolves::that leaps MHz of the deathshead like ToKAGE with the emotional particle of the monochrome earth area that commits suicide with the reptile body internal in the bowels of the crimson seed ice sky/

<<PORNO>>

The sin-tainted slit end interior of the womb/ uterus-machine//of the sun that the [ice nebula faecal black] game anthropoid kills<<goes mad>>is infectious along the lunar coil line in the explosion just before the hot metal orgasm of a swastika girl//

The junkie group vagus::monochrome earth memory of the soul-machine it beats with the rape eyes of the drag embryo::the reptile suicide system of the angels::ADAM Doll of a cold-blooded disease operates chromium ND interceptor rotors//The murder organ on the soul-machines of the clone boys is jointed to the germ cell of the brain of an assassin and the apoptosis spectre of the drag embryo — it radiates heat in the euthanasia zone of ADAM — maniac priest of the artificial sun::the output war toy of the cyber paradise/gene=TV of a dog/the cataclysmic despair machine coefficient of the helix of the cell that flames/it is a body assassin motion cobalt rock death//sex hallucinogen fur of Sato Corporation induces agents of NEMESIS/

Ice of the sky shoots the hybrid body line of the ADAM Doll and excoriates [ice nebula faecal black] quantum monsters of the entity called<<the human being>>/

<The nano-second of virus omits the battle//EVOL// chromosome fecundates [ice nebula faecal black] blood internal::the brain fracture of the desert of the replication — clone boys of the ADAM Doll chain inoculated digital apocalypse infection=virus tissue>The paranoiac future of the ADAM Doll//The paranoiac cell group of the end of the world//Cold-blooded disease machine::deflesheq <<the sun>>of the drag embryo who fecundates noise to the BABEL:=brain area::schizoid animal::The murder gram index that boys evoke — the soul that wants to observe her virus to the eye of the machine universe::direg deathshead of the amniotic fluid that fecundates the mysterious language line of the artificial sun noise>I record and infest the trip womb cell of the world that the drag embryo detonated — I was torturing the monochrome ovarium of the sun>l grieve over the crucified memory of my murder world>>that crime larva programmed — the cyber germ that fecundates the quantum lupus in the electronic circuit — the cosmic envy of the human genome spasm::the murder topology::it is deathshead/

I copy the soul of ADAM that was murdered::it is
our brain decay curve -unique planetary chromosome
[ice nebula faecal black] larvae of the deathshead
pattern of spectre reflexors::blood electric/

The end line of our suicide machine that gets twisted
— the skin of the girl that is intensifying to the
nightmare of the clone MHz of the brain of the body
universe= assassin of the drag mechanism of the
embryo that shoots and excoriates the [ice nebula
faecal black] cadaver of soul::ADAM dreams of the
reptile<<cruelty>>of the womb area — swastika girl
of my speed decay meridian::record on the brain
template of a doll is a depressed paradise in the
horizon of the existence angel mechanism of the
binary number of nano-machinative body of ADAM::of
assassins::of the cyber line of a clone boy>>embryo
equivocated white noise> Psychosexual DNA channel
of the boy gene taints the spectre of the chromosome
that rotates and replicates our [ice nebula faecal
black] anthropoid existence/clone logic cobalt rock
death::ADAM-dog-sun-END::Our crucified memory — the
outline of a virus along its reverse=it is evolving
the body=medium where Heaven mode was exposed//Our
sin-tainted slit cadaver is spurting DNA::ultrasonic
orgasm of Super Cherry 666/

<<SWASTIKA GASH>>

::Reverse the evil insanity of the gene that
changes to the copper cannibal bone molecule//our
intelligence is pure=it is smooth::the placenta
state of the cadaver that resolves the air where
electro-magnetic activity fecundates the atrocity
chromosome/spasms of the brain activate ADAM clone
of the reproduction nature of the boy-roid that
evolves>The penis of the ADAM Doll swells to the
night sky of such a desert that our reptile body
explodes like a boy machine/genetic warfare of the
digital apocalypse>Replicate clone and okama-drone
in the bowels of our NO pheromone that the schizoid
reaps — the suicide machine of the end of the YES
world that persists>>the logical resistance to soul

death recovers the spectre of her chromosome —
exposes a non=vital target=embryo language in the
infinite centre of the blood desert of the brain of
inorganic substance boys>the crucified memory of an
assassin//menstruation machine that had sutured the
body line of the murder receives the digital vamp-
quickening of the artificial sun and cuts the cyber
line of the angel mechanism::Our cruel sickly period
respiration split the monochrome earth memory>Our
space is broken down like a dog suicide soul body
emission — word invasion — cobalt rock death of
the assassin pattern/the anthropoid opposite=solar
eclipse of her pheromone system/

The ectopic nano-machinative murder line of the
android that freezes — the REC play is vital — the
transplantation/the artificial sun is burnt on the
exoskeleton of a boy machine — the swastika of an
assassin internal> Program the excess season of the
chromosome>assassin pattern drag ecology>/astral
jolt of amnesiac fire/

<<The ADAM Doll future tissue/world machinative
nervous system/artificial Sun ovarium incubates
cell-gauge:the swastika body fluid of the zero glans
assassin that the soul-machine of the clone boy
hyper-linked to uterus-machine//the artificial sun
that feeds my ToKAGE fecundates the crime space of
the cyber embryo that fecundates the junk internal
— I commit suicide and i affect molecular merge with
the interior of the womb of the ectopic Machine
overheat program>/

<<ALIEN-COM>>

My body that rejects the cadaver tissue of the ADAM
clone [ice nebula faecal black] occupies the future
tense of a zero dog and fractured bodies of the
embryo chain precipitate the [ice nebula faecal
black] gene war of the clone//ADAM Doll splits the
second when my assassin fed my dog with the butterfly
that burst — faecal jaws to hold the flowers — my dry
nerve body goes to ruin with the rictus line that

flows backward — conceives — wears out — accelerates — commits suicide — is lost in wild phantasies of discharges — the spectre of her chromosome meridian at your cadaver and the biohazard boy machine where space geisha resolves her sin-tainted slit love::it engages the clutch:GAME OVER::I copy it::/

Torture the electron>My soul polarity reversed=the metal-congenital love of the digital heart clone girl that evolves to the quark target — it is planetary in scope— the crucified memory of the ice sky that receives it is the terminus of the murder vector — artificial assassin of embryo//the future of your zero//Your cosmic DNA channel::BABEL of clone that suspends her emotional particle drops out//My soul perishes// Hybrid suicide circuit of ADAM/son of the nano-machine=boy machine of the angel mechanism>I reproduce the reptile of my love with the end of the world because the digital murderous intention of your embryo cultivates my life/

<<CODA-CODA>>

Her body pheromone in the decay just before prolapse of ADAM — the plasma paradise radiates heat from the fingertip of the angel that our gene machine hates — venereal scar tissue — the protoplasm of the cell escape program — soul of the chameleon embryo that fertilizes the artificial sun>/

<<KE-MO-NO>>

Shoot down clone of the ADAM Doll/the split second of a nightmare::monochrome earth memory of the end clone of the crucified memory-device/Placenta World of the true sun/that becomes unknown/ operates/ accelerates the worldly desires machine of the amniotic fluid mechanism//My body sky of ice gene state is never able to return::evolve/it is borne against the night sky of the desert/the suicide line of NIHIL<the sun>is doubled to the inferno//It is the machine ROKUDENASI>The virus=image of the spectre of the miracle cell that recovers the control line of the immortality of the ADAM Doll from the empty

universe//<The desire>of ToKAGE fecundates in the
ice sky<The secret>of ToKAGE is replicated to the
ice of the sky [ice nebula faecal black] CODA/

[ice nebula faecal black] Sudden death in the brain of
the parasite=drag embryo of crucified memory switch
— uterus-machine of the true sun simulates the gene
war that ADAM Doll programmed when Creature 9 went
mad//The megabyte of the hatred of the chromosome//
It transplants it::it fecundates fear::the love mode
of a swastika girl is transmitted::becomes the speed
of the clonal love that a cyber dog feeds back from
the hell of the body/apoptosis spectre of an assassin
LOAD in the bowels of the pheromone>lt fecundates the
despair machine of cyberBuddha/it respires the love-
reptile Placenta World of the ADAM Doll existence//
Despair of the nature of the strategic love of the
drag embryo/

The machinative angel commits suicide from the
frequency of the TV screen that you cursed//The gene
of clone boys internal goes mad to the nerve system
of BABEL::thyroid clone-transmission of DNA channel
BABEL spiral=love that exceeded the immortality factor
of the random assassins= drag embryos of<<GODNAM>>
bowels of your pheromone reverse=it evolves::the
silence released the solution from quantum EVOL
and NDRO rotor//The brain area of the reproduction
nature of the fatalities is thrust through — it
is the centre which her techno pheromone targets/
Placenta World swelled up with the zero speed of
a soul-machine//I record the vital non-being::the
beast palpation of cold disease of your machine/

Cosmic genital organs that ADAM Doll abused dilate
in this sickly Placenta World of the new flesh and
corrode metal-congenital/the crucifieg Memo loss is
respired in the physical centre of the clone-skin
foetus ASsassin,. lobotomy of our angel mechanism
that her reptile consciousness Caresses ie nebula
faecal black] chromosome that caused the form of
hatreg internal//scatter loose the machine-seed of
the drug embryo hunting for the grotesque/

<<AcidHUMAN>>

Psychic Sun++our future that betrayed the murder game
of the drag embryo for paranoia fracture seconds of
the terror explosion — ADAM Doll memory circuits are
erased first::/it is the mutant murderous intention
zone of the sexual medium that fecundates a swastika
girl of the dog pack of the solar desert//The second
of death is the accident>but the strabismus of the
sheet metal concubine cloaca shoots extinguished
zodiac venom vexing into uranium spray/

<<It is the digital mental induction of Creature
13 and others::the synapse form boy jolt of DNA
channel is spiral uterus-machine//receiving net
derangement cobalt rock death::sun suicide::cobalt
rock death ::past form future/sun evolution system//
It is the monologue of the artificial sun that
mirrors//::The soul-machine that ADAM Doll infested
reproduces to monochrome memory the body that the
drag embryo exploded internal//The rebellion of the
brain area=control multiple Placenta World/womb area
machines of gene=TV that SADO betrayed//The rictus of
the angel mechanism of ToKAGE reverbs>::the androids
of dustNirverna and techno autopsy spectre digest the
hatred without the base of the chromosome//The DNA
channel of level zero is examined by fluoroscopy::our
[ice nebula faecal black] heart=of=it is the digital
vampire>::I record this fractal world — mute object
inputted::so ADAM Doll transmitted our future in
pure white angel spurts//clone boys of lust object
LOAD/ quantum gene level zerot++her crucified memory
element tortures ADAM Doll::crucible of space
nature>Her nano-machine form murderous intention
disappears//mutant soul-machine BABEL//

The ice of the sky reverbs::the planet of an ant
respires nano-machine group of the drag embryo
infernal carapace:::a uterus-machine mental induction
body>The swastika girl of ToKAGE fecundates the
reptile universe of swastika temptation/dog disunites
the cell//replicates for the imploding second of
ToKAGE when the ADAM Doll digests the soul-machine

of zero at the time of her angel/the mutant solitude
of the anamorphic accumulator::equivalent physical-
LOVE murder system/earth area of the body system
sun of the cock-spurting clone boys>>internal//::Our
NIHIL war/our soul-machine inoculated [ice nebula
faecal black] the swastika of true sun> the viral
insanity of uterus-machine/

/::Drag embryo SYNDROME>the monochrome memory
of a cold-blooded disease is infectious::>/the
BABEL animals of the nano-machine matrix::cyber
mechanisms::the access code fecundates [ice nebula
faecal black] the seed of our soul-machine of
the nightmare/womb area of the horizon deforms
comets::digital murder of season::planetary clash//
quantum theory of ecstasy::dustNirverna of metal
nature::the miracle that shattered the resurrection
angel — primal cyclops atom that resolves the nano-
machine of an assassin internal//endoplasmic _
reticulum++the soul-machine of synapse::zero dog of
the mutant meridian fecundates the mutant emotion
LOAD::ADAM Doll freezes to the crucified memory
of spasm induction/despair machine/our infernal
carapace angel mechanism<<=lt is the device God
of ambient rictus with the junk eyes of the womb
area::<<my [ice nebula faecal black] heart fecundates
the mutant desire/

Planetary CODA attack//mutant program of artificial
assassin/murder of hybrid gene=TV::crucified
memory losses of zero gravity clone boys of space
nature=your war angel of the machine conducts
artificial insemination::VTR war::her chromosome of
crime fecundates [ice nebula faecal black] copper
blood//it fecundates a digital vamp//it is the
crucified memory of figures in the future of the
love-reptiles::// machinative angels of cold-blooded
diseases//gene war in Placenta World/

Without cycloid::it nurtures the soul-machine like
the human being::lupus of the opposite sun being
told to love our reptile//I escape from our
ectopic corrosion night like a human being//::You

are the mutant quiescence/s the angel mechanism//
The emotion of the exoskeleton machine Mechanism
that the mode of the sun stores/melts a boy of ice
air and multiplies to REVERE — ultrasonic orgasm
scream erodes my cadaver::it becomes quantum: it
becomes legion::it becomes the speed of the heart
of the machine of N angeI spasm::++like the borg
that the chromosome of AAA ignites — pineal eye is
parasitic on the sun — a flower implodes and impales
the assassin of liberty crucified memory rictus is
erased/the NIHIL love of ADAM Dolls is inputted in
this sex machine::world of MOTHER or spectre::The
machine that I despise springs like the angel and
the beast — zero rictus of [ice nebula faecal black]
heart>::Their anamorphic accumulator equivalent
physical-Love pheromone::It is the body line of
the season of clonal love>//The solitude of the
suicide code::sun of an artificial assassin — mutant
parasite membrane of the ADAM Doll//shadow of it
fecundates the ground::Her reptile Heaven is stored
by the time-codes of her [ice nebula faecal black]
existence::it is anamorphic accumulator equivalent
physical-LOVE::syndrome>::The nightmare of the womb
machine area is regenerated as the murderous hologram
of the artificial sun//Reverse multiple angels::it
fecundates the genome form emotional particle of
clone boys — a digital vamp internal::her sole
crucified memory::chaos pheromone of the true sun
erodes the planet of an ant/it is Pace of rape>/The
gel form fear that artificial sun clashes toward
the suicide reptile -the soul-machine of the zero
of the ADAM Doll/death of cell which multiplies to
fecundate the steel uterus instantaneously//it is
monochrome memory/murderous intentions of the earth
area//[ice nebula faecal black] heart of a cold-
blooded disease of an android is inverted::it is
the body=thyroid::BABEL line of magnetic induction
of an assassin//It reverbs::and their biotechnology
probes her lightless nervous system/Hybrid parasite
engine of the love doll rising/

<::It is the AAA::direct access method of doll
control>The cyber seizure of the sun dog of the

head line/massacre of an artificial assassin awakes
the Cadaver City-city> The internal organ=universe
of the Cadaver City//Our first cry/the soul-machine
of the murder-spore of drag embryo rotates//our
artificial sun is jointed to the DNA channel of
an assassin internal and excoriates the heat to
the desire mechanism>> Crucified memory of the
murder coefficient/the viral load of exoskeleta is
differentiated::the reptile of our mutant scream
spectre is replicated/it fecundates fracture —
murderous intentions of the psychosexual sexual
other side/ADAM Dolls of<<the mankind>>that invade
the subterranean zodiac ignition corridors of Sato
Corporation/

It is coiled to the infinite bowels of the pheromone//I
commit suicide//I commit suicide as the last reptile/
sterile nucleus of the quantum masses of flesh that
commit suicide as fracture reptiles of the sun>feed
foetal corpses to a dog>the desert of blood with
the ADAM Doll simulacra::Our zero=of=evoking spectre
ruins the terror of ADAM::I commit suicide like the
strange fruit of the rose//Her tragedy::chaos dog of
a dog is resolved//::It is the plant machine of the
[ice nebula faecal black] blood disease of ADAM//The
tragedy of the beast swastika that whirls>::<<in the
desert of the brain of the ADAM Doll where rabies
prevailed//It accelerates::it is ADAM Doll/<abnormal
ward>of the murder melody::ambient anal device of the
mutant// The air that was bleached proves<<murder>>and
the digital apoptosis of the angel that fecundates
<the world>to become a rabid dog>>future reptile
of spectre reproduces the meridian//It is parasitic
with the body mode of UV fracture::the pure white
sun is injected from a soul-machine::the rayogram
of the narcolepsy of an assassin>>::ToKAGE>>The
protein inversion of the ADAM Doll clashes with
the metamolecular unit of a two-headed dog//We are
the wild phantasy of the sun that escapes from the
self-immolation of the machinative breakdown>>lt is
nullified by the continuation nature suspicion of
the murder/that gene=TV was eroded//It fecundates
the biological warheads of our zenith brain cell-

spermatozoon nerve — DNA mandalas of a dog LOAD::the emotional device of the limit of an assassin to the angel mechanism//It operates::it decapitates/

The vacuum bomb of<the lapse of memory>//Love-reptiles of murder of recorded time>The infernal carapace of Placenta World communicates with the nano-machine group of the mutant earth//To the reproduction gland of Creature 13 — K nutrient of an artificial assassin//our cruel future::it is the savage record device of the soul-machine that crystallizes//<<animal vital/ icon//>>//So the death that multiplies with the angel mechanism of [ice nebula faecal black] suspicion of our machine is infectious//To the plasmic paradise of the solar nexus//<<You electrocute the bowels of the synapse human being::sexualize the spectre that becomes unknown to the Visual psychosexuals of the infernal carapace cyber dogs who patrol the far Meridian — it is the biotechnology of preprogrammed auto-destruction — lightless murder block of the ADAM Doll//It is the season of the cosmic rays//colg. blooded diseases like the web of human genomes on a darkening aurora>cold-blooded scavengers of Saturn/

<The pure white hatred of a swastika girl is discharged::as sky is ice::that sky of glacial fire where the apoptosis future of our DNA [ice nebula faecal black] meat is ice::inputs to the inorganic substance brain of clone boys>God of ambient++cruel nano-machine of the angel::><<infernal carapace respiration [ice nebula faecal black] emotional particle discharge — cobalt rock death//The hatred of the chromosome is inoculated to our crystal soul-machine internal DIGITAL::the quantum labyrinth::cold-blooded diseases of love-reptiles with murder function of ADAM Doll function/uterus-machine that exploded — the massacre stage/Godhead evolves like ToKAGE of the mental abnormality that proliferates::I torture it//Murder noise of the thyroid future of the fallen angel when reverberation becomes a past form//The soul-machine<the crimson seed>of the clone boys// Android sleep was replicated//I murder [ice nebula

faecal black] memory::quantum reptile of lupus=space internal//the lust syndrome of GARAKUTA>++worms in the [ice nebula faecal black] brain of the ADAM Doll that awoke the murder machine like the sun internal — the fur micron with the rictus of terror limit>::The mutant meridian machine of SODO that fecundates [ice nebula faecal black] the ruinous body mode of the ADAM Doll/LOAD/ Sickly period is respired — DNA angels wage meridian war/

Our sperm abortion:direct access method//spinal implant of defleshed ants/::the machine line of the desert of the head cage/::drag embryo of the angel that exploded shoots and excoriates [ice nebula faecal black] the womb area machine that despaired internal — rock the Cadaver City in 8 seconds// fear of mirrors erodes the mutant soul of the human being::glacial bolus of beasts/

The nerve larva::the chromosome that becomes parasitic>the ferric ice torture room android lupus of the sky banded in chaos//ADAM Doll devours the vital severed head halo that the artery of the assassin bleeds into ambient and excoriates the spasm//Our cruel brain universe breeds the murder system/like her assassin mutated sexually//It fecundates the junk//::It is the meridian device of the desire mechanism that was jointed to the meat machine< <empty basalt tomb>>::The body of the angel multiplies memory of [ice nebula faecal black] massacre — nano-machine fecundates ADAM Doll — interference from human genome spectre ruins the [ice nebula faecal black] relation of the suspicion::soul-machine of a cold-blooded disease animal is lost in wild phantasies of zero schizo sexual psychosexual human being animal>zero gravity girl controlled the night sky — okama drones inject formic jism like their murderous existence — terrible deserts of the cock-spurting clone boys that rape the brain cell of BABEL//I get deranged>>//I imprison the crucified memory of the dog pack of the cyber mission++ADAM Doll of the true sun — the spiral mechanism of the murder machine/monochrome memory of an ADAM Doll is the

psychedelic fracture of the soul-machine//spectre
of the spasm::it is the parasite drone of reptile
Heaven>::It is the anamorphic accumulator equivalent
physical-LOVE cyber crime device//The womb area
machine of zero=of=the desire movement is released
on the horizon of the ADAM Doll//The murder block of
the brain of the replication area/dog of the angel
mechanism of the drag embryo occupies internal::it
is DNA channel sky ice fission disease//The cold-
blooded disease of machines/violence in the internal
logic synapse which crucified memory scorches//
<<the swastika thapsody of the assassin>>the icon
is parasitic::NDRO::ADAM Doll corrodes the inside
of an orange orgone pod to excoriate the record of
that coefficient unit in retrograde::extinguished
entrails veering into metallic spray/

<<DUSTNIRVERNA>>

It fecundates::it fecundates the spasm::I go mad to
the machine mechanism::A machinative angel murders
the sun type of the spiral/

Cyber dog awakening ovarium reptiles of the
machinative angel/the clone boys who conduct
artificial insemination rape the artery of the
crucified memory of the sun – the body of an assassin
is respired in the sickly period//Body line REC drag
embryo of the immortality of the drag embryo is lost
in wild phantasies of the planet of an ant::/

Shooting in the brain target of the machinative
angel – the hybrid body of the [ice nebula faecal
black] area/clone boy is infected//The crucified
memory of the VTR sun like the chameleon of the night
sky::swastika girl of a gene=Ty void is reversed to
the sin-tainted slit murder region of the ADAM Doll
who drinks the tears of a black dog/

<<Sun cultivates the skin tissue that ADAM Doll
was cursed to cultivate::it is parasitic on the
zenith brain of the fatalities/The vision of an
assassin is parasitic on the womb area machine state

— raw virus that the brain of clone boys controls — the monochrome earth memory//The crucified memory of zero//It fecundates the body machine of an assassin::it is the clonal reproduction area of the ADAM Doll where desire was dismantled — my soul-machine contaminates the murderous artery of a cyber dog pack::I am atrocity like an angel/

<<XTERMINATOR>>

Spectre/reptile::the artificial sun proliferates to the synapse emotion of clone boys::I copy the clonal love of the machinative angel/reverse my ice::LOAD:: machine of the boundless sky of the paradise deciphers the desert of the light year of the drag embryo to the night sky of the [ice nebula faecal black] labyrinth of the quantum masses of flesh that is metamorphosing to the primal cyclops atom of the monochrome earth memory that evolves// The horizon of my DNA breeds the assassin that an assassin respires internal::1 milligram of crucified memory kills cyber murder drone=nano-machine of the gene=TV void — sun flare falls from the gradual lapse of memory line of the annihilation fatalities of the vital non=being ++space that excoriates the desire that desires beasts::fur mirage [ice nebula faecal black] angel mechanism of the vital facsimile neon night disappears//ToKAGE of the miracle of the existence chromosome that her vaginal velocity MHz reproduces//The digital apocalypse invades the neural circuit of self>smooth::the speed of the cadaver aware of internal decay/the matrix body fluid murders my solar locus script//Clone skin XX — black century spectre is replicated — drag motion of the clone boys that conquer it::STOP::monochrome earth memory disunites from the soul-machine in the hiatus just before barbed anal rape of GAIA//Sex machine of the swastika girl that deciphers dustNirverna::/

The brain of an assassin LOAD::the clonal Placenta World of the ADAM Doll under napalm attack — the quantum masses of flesh of the LEVEL 6 digital apocalypse that the crucified memory of my fractal animal encodes::intelligence of the solar coven fecundates the chromosome of Saturn::the spasm scavengers are launched//Virus of vile coven/my soul-machines of fracture of body lines/matrix body fluid of the liquid intention/ drag embryos that multiply to excoriate noise like the zenith where a swastika girl swallows spectre/ectoplasm error// The hybrid language line of BABEL animals infects the reproduction gland of clone boys apoptosis — truth is replicated internal//Invading the sponge tissue of gene=TV — self is cloned//Reverse the body line fractal jism loop of the spectre of the womb area machine-seeds/ADAM resuscitates=murder game MHz of the LEVEL DOWN amniotic fluid mechanism that the assassin of the psycho-pheromone of the swastika girl breaks down — the psychosexual sexual anthropoids of the artificial sun reproduce the clonal love of artery — you respire my junkie emotional particle that evolves — you link like an assassin — your soul-machine inoculates the ADAM Doll of the angel mechanism -your truth is murdered::my digital apoptosis/worldly desires universe/Link circumference is expanded to the infinite death play of the drag embryo/

The placenta is crucified memory//cell is the crucified memory of spectre::The drag embryo who the brain of clone boys escapes links artery of the artificial sun of the pituitary swastika load to cobalt rock death angel mechanism of the line of the ADAM Doll that fecundates the planet of the green pheromone/ assassin of the anthropoid that fecundates dustNirverna with the speed of a soul-machine/the pheromone= universe that the crime organ of a cyber dog pack awoke contaminates it/

The hybrid head line of BABEL animals is deciphered// Rape secret of the fractal machine-seed — Placenta World of ADAM Doll joints to nuclear fission tomb-device::I decipher the nightmare of the amniotic fluid mechanism of the ADAM Doll that an assassin excoriates — the disgrace of the machinative angel — the bone-eating code of my body venom engages

with the existence period respiration line of the
biological terror zone/

Mechanical LEVEL zero — cyber system reversal
reflux=it is the hybrid/brain universe of the drag
embryo/the artificial interceptor who evolved into
[ice nebula faecal black] interplanetary assassin//
CODA in chrome/

The quantum mass of flesh of clone boys turns on the
suicide machine/switch of the sun::it is the power
of the apoptosis intention of the drag embryo that
reforms VTR of the ice night sky of the desert to
analog//Artery respires savagely::<<The purgatory of
the artificial sun in flux::ADAM Doll shoots hybrid
seed — excoriates [ice nebula faecal black] universe
— ice spasm sign of the drag sky of the connection
of the nano-machine::gene war meridian at the lunar
coil of artery::LOAD::the brain stems of clone boys
explode to the interior clash of the womb of a digital
dog chromosome of the reverse vortex in the far
season/cycloid of negative gravity fecundates the
soul-machine of the artificial sun::BABEL eclipse
of the planet of the speed narcolepsy of ToKAGE
that the apoptosis spectre of a saturnine mutation
induced — clone skin changes colour with sheet metal
memory of the pheromone of a swastika girl//the
monochrome earth memory that the sin-tainted slit
annihilates becomes alpha::I copy the body line
that monochrome earth memory of ToKAGE transmutes to
mirage of matrix body fluid/

The chaos pheromone of the reproduction area/digital
vamp that the machinative angel who fecundates the
spasm to the machine mechanism that lubricates GAIA
hyperlinks to slit artery of the true sun/the chromosome
of an artificial assassin evolves//I record the sin-
tainted slit ruin machine of the ToKAGE discharge/
the empire of the Cadaver City::the crimson slit skin
tissue of the ovarium::ADAM Doll that soul-machine
resuscitated was cursed::<<fracture>>the body modes
of drag embryo are inoculated by artery::I torture
tongues with genetic pincers like the film at the

end of the century::Dragnet of the earth::Body of an assassin is transplanted in the desert::/

The DNA channel matrix body fluid of the artificial sun is circulating::the body replication:-figure of the drag embryo respires the swastika contraction of the universe::ADAM Doll assassination::speed to the body without the spectre of the clone boys — embolism that proliferates internal — the crucified memory of the psychosexual sexual cyber jackal jism shoots/ excoriates the [ice nebula faecal black] thyroid locus of an artificial assassin and defleshed ant fetish/

Control the love voltage of the sex doll rotor — control the sin-tainted slit suicide machine of the sun>ADAM Doll cursed the drag embryo>//End clone fecundates interference::The machinative angel dashes the digital vamp infection pathway of a soul-machine and hybrid speed of uterus-machine is eclipsed::The love-reptile Placenta World of Sato Corporation — clone boys cock-spurt the genetic information of ADAM — DNA channel of an artificial assassin is dilated/Planetary system/Body of the cosmic speed assassin of the soul-machine that the ADAM Doll infected — chromosome that the sun shoots — the Heaven noise of the deathshead that kisses the cruel brain rhythm of clone boys and excoriates the [ice nebula faecal black] clone skin that was cursed — the artificial sun resonates to the sin-tainted slit birth system of artery/

Speed of ToKAGE is clashed to meridian::the sensor replication lobotomy// machine mechanism awakes dustNirverna of the machinative angel who erased the future system cerebral cortex drive of the ADAM Doll/

<//I record the season of the existence chromosome of the ADAM Doll::I record vital non=being::the DNA channels of the drag embryos that precipitate planetary violence/gene=TV of the cell group assassin of the angel mechanism of the ADAM Doll that fecundates

the internal organ of a cyber dog pack — the spasm
replicates the horizon of this clonal artery — love
reptile suicide device — ignites tomb-device — rocks
Cadaver City in 8 seconds of the solar fall-out
that a soul-machine doubles::it is the line of the
spectre of the clone skin that respires the night
sky of the desert with the monochrome earth memory//
apoptosis of drag motion in sickly period/

<<ORANGE FILE>>

[ice nebula faecal black] the last terminus/
techno lupus=space::it fecundates to the nightmare
of an existence in amniotic fluid mechanism — it
is a Placenta World quantum mass of flesh/icon//
the exoskeleton of murder is respired/it is the
dustNirverna soul-machine>heart of the monochrome
horizon++androig of the insanity chromosome that
breaks down the body of the quantum assassin cell::I
invade the ugly future tissue of an ADAM Doll//Howl-
mutant crucified memory of tears — the lunar coil of
a girl//The miracle of a silicone form assassin//
The season of the sun fecundates [ice nebula faecal
black] internal::the murder block/reptile of the
future system of the ADAM Doll operates::the reptile
that the reptile explodes>in our Placenta World the
orange line of the [ice nebula faecal black] ectoplasm
spot reproduces the desire mechanism brain area
of the murderous intention/dog of the machinative
angels::LOAD the soul-machine of the cold-blooded
disease that disappears to the bowels=zero of the
clonal assassin//The mutant emotion of the body
line/the fear of the angel mechanism of a future
Heaven soul-machine::ADAM Doll leaps dimensions::I
get deranged like ToKAGE//It is annealed to the
spectre without the confusion of the womb area and
the soul-machine of an assassin commits suicide//
The channel that multiplies it is the ice orgone
object of the love doll syndrome — nova contusion
spasms [ice nebula faecal black] starlit sky of
suicide reptiles//infernal carapace of the digital
reanimator/

<<Crucified memory of torture is a limitless purgatory//ADAM Doll joints to drag molecule of the Placenta World discharge>>for the second of the supreme nirvana of the cruel sun body=suicide reptile REC=[ice nebula faecal black] soul of the murder/record::ADAM Doll of her machine subconscious/ solar despair [ice nebula faecal black] mode::stellar cadaver of assassin::>Her true grotesque eyes drip animal mutant emotion of the fabrication of clone boys::the solitude of her android coven — the spectre of the chromosome//fractal murder machine::tropic of angels of the desire mechanism of the artificial sun — rape drones who torture a machine are transparent in her wild phantasy::It is the glans recall++recall with the form of the love that was tortured by a mutant of the sun:/

::I murder the universe of a dog//::Our VTR soul-insanity sun fecundates the desert of immortal hallucination//Uterus-machine of unlimited ADAM Doll death//The bowels of the body state=vagus group of the drag embryo generates a hybrid of murder system<the assassin respires>::it is the labyrinth of the fluid eyeball script of the fatalities that the exoskeleta inflict in REVERB mode::beasts with the death play of the angel mechanism/

<The spectre of dustNirverna//The thyroid burn of the narcolepsy group/assassin of the ADAM Doll decimates the sun//::The chromosome form madness line++her anamorphic accumulator equivalent physical-LOVE pheromone of the suicide reptile — a pink rotor fecundates NDRO::crucified memory of outer space in the nightmare++fracture seconds of the respiratory arrest//cold-blooded disease of a soul-machine::her murder machine//chaos pheromone of the cyber system// womb area of the instantaneous//the drag embryo of silence is parasitic::the mode of the angel accelerates the nervous breakdown that evolves to Heaven::mechanical control::orange sky::catalepsy/

<<Deserts derange her spokes of psychic ash — access multiple assassins of the ADAM Doll//end game of

the spectre::inorganic substance sun::emotional
zero of protoplasm joints to the machine
mechanism::cyber gel form of quantum crime space/
Her murder period=anamorphic accumulator equivalent
physical-LOVE pheromone of a soul-machine::it is
instantaneously morphed/

The sky of NIHIL — soul-machine fracture assassin::the
ADAM Doll of the end of fracture — 8 seconds for
her sex machine — crucified memory of the cruel
body of the machinative angel — it disunites from
the suicide machine of the dog that goes mad//The
horizon of the chromosome is dustNirverna:swastikas
of blood in neural meltdown/

The ash of the brain of the ADAM Doll that the sun
coven transplants to the hybrid suicide machine that
commits suicide is input to the second of insanity//
The ice of the respiration line::junk brain system/
the sky of an assassin disunites/the fear that fear
contaminates cuts the shadow of beasts:fracture modes
that are parasitic on the [ice nebula faecal black]
chromosome::monochrome earth memory of murderous
intention::The clonal love of the womb area machine
of the chromosome operates the night sky exoskeleton
of the desert that takes our crucified memory and
FeSpires the murder machine of the assassin that was
conceived in the brain OF the fatalities::ADAM Doll
that fecundates the sun — hallucination violence
area of the cyborg brain — nutrient K which radiates
heat//I awake the suicide reptile and enfold our
assassin in the reverse side of our far season/it
is the artificial penumbra//I channel cold-blooded
disease to the quantum labyrinth of the body>>the
cold-blooded disease dirt trip — cobalt rock death
of ADAM Dojj of our nerve group — sonic nipple
burns of her assassin/the Kake nightmare operation
— cobalt rock death reverbs/

Cosmic cyborg sodomy::cock-spurting clone boys of
Venus invade an artery — the nano-machine gel form
joints to crucified memory of<the death that points
at zero>it radiates heat in the angel brain of the

[ice nebula faecal black] heart::machinative angel of ToKAGE that respired metal-congenital in a wild phantasy of this fractal world — the quantum BABEL planetary systems<the infinity>++it is nightmare — Kake mushroom fall-out::cobalt rock death//The night sky of the blood desert fecundates the emotion of her zero amniotic fluid in the defleshed internal tombs of the Placenta World::the secret machine between grotesque space-time and her pheromone suicide phantasy — the melody of the angel of the machine mechanism::with the rhythm of the murder machine like the true sun::the line of an assassin circulates the desire of the infinite end that crucified memory++the physical planet of our murder that dismantles our quantum insanity/MHz of our soul-machine that operates/Insanity of zero=despair that doubles::I record the terror rictus of the ADAM Doll like the machine that went mad::I tune to solitude like a machine internal//The narcolepsy group of an assassin goes to ruin//Her fear degenerates// Like the angel of the machine mechanism::the night sky of the desert radiates heat that rapes the hybrid body of her soul-machine [ice nebula faecal black] seed>>the drag embryo distorted the murderous intention of the amniotic fluid mechanism of her nightmare::Placenta World fracture//fracture-mutant detonates oneiric locus::/ larval accelerator voltage spray/

The ADAM Doll of insanity that proliferates the gene is infectious//The consciousness of boy-roid eradicates an existence area/>>love-reptiles access multiple death/the biotechnology of lightless neural circuits of the mutant suicide reptile that becomes an immortal machine::her murder orbit with my android zone::recall/::clonal [ice nebula faecal black] love of it fecundates the corpse of the assassin of murder system access zero::it is the death that fecundates the future when doubled to the murderous intention of the gene::the end of the century of the matrix of the reproduction nature of clone boys inaugurates a dog pack genocide//suicide machine state exterminates/

<<ZEN>>

The monochrome insanity of the night sky that eclipses the end of her terror rictus::ADAM Doll meridian — her pure white pheromone of the darkness where the machine-seeds of the desert clash in heat — scorpion kills in 8 seconds// The [ice nebula faecal black] braindeath chromosome of the ADAM Doll occludes::planetary vistas of the assassin — the beast of primal cyclops atom virus of junk vision V of an end clone:spectre of the body of the crime system/ drag embryo of uterus-machine//>The vision/requiem that the soul-machine of the hologram angel freezes to her human genome form with murderous intention//::It is the murderous intention that accelerates to the end of the world//existence icon erases cobalt rock death trauma<<lt is icon-terror>>chameleon touch that transfigures to a secret//An orange murder orbit::boundless sleep of a soul-machine breeds the love-reptiles of the amniotic fluid mechanism//The ADAM Doll sutured to sanity/

<<It fecundates massacre/A quantum murder drone directs the murder machine line of the galactic spectra::hallucinogenic fur nerve of the drag embryo loses volume::the electric charge of the far season spectre of insanity was amplified to the hybrid of the ADAM Doll++to a hybrid of soft rotors::it is the quantum sex motion register of her artificial life — her chaos pheromone that precipitates gene war in the interior of the womb of the meridian of this cruel screen world of a nightmare/

//Insanity fracture seconds//Massacre stop motion// Cold-blooded disease of speed battle::boy-roid assassin::ToKAGE of the zero of the ADAM Doll becomes a machine::it is the speed of a cold-blooded disease/spectral shut down/ The meridian respires// Zero echoes//The planet of the angel mechanism of the ADAM Doll is EVOL::pheromones of the rictus cadaver of deflesheq Orgasm metal//Zirconium retroburn/

A planetary system//The war without the mode of the ADAM Doll//the soul-machine of our internal organ space — cold-blooded disease spectre respires

metal-congenital with the emotion of the molecule
that synthesizes it — the cyber dog of the form/
psychedelic artery of the lunar coil — the ice of the
sky coalesces metal-congenital to the [ice nebula
faecal black] heart of the NIHIL murder drone//
tomb-device ignites faecal Saturn blood spectre —
the eternal death for fracture body line::fracture
seconds//VTR feedback that an artificial assassin
reproduces exceeds crucified memory::real existence
connection of the ADAM Doll of the desire mechanism
that annihilates the cruel tropic of crucified
memory/

<<Heart of her machine mechanism was inputted to the
positive nexus of the monochrome earth memory desire
rictus — the pure white soul-machine of a cold-
blooded disease is parasitic on our Placenta World —
the nuclear noise of an angel mechanism — the hologram
in the internal organ future of the angel hunters
of EVOL — the massacre of the ADAM Doll/insanity
of Cadaver City fear of meridian machine — nature
torture-block of machinative angel/::spectre without
confusion of drag embryo::earth area syndrome//
it is the season of the [ice nebula faecal black]
deathshead in the ignition corridors of the Placenta
World of Sato Corporation::the NIHIL rotation device
of the drive lapse of memory//access Project Super
Cherry/

The psychedelic heart//The ADAM Doll in the last
term//The contamination area of a soul-machine::
fear is paralyzed internal::her brain synthesized the
torture=organ of a swastika girl//The narcolepsy=group
of the other side of the sun//Silence//The season of
the murder of an ADAM Doll::LOAD multiple nightmare
dustNirverna of clone boys::murderous intention of
artery of the angel mechanism//It transmits the night
sky of the desert that goes mad in the labyrinth::it
is the labyrinth of the imperfect corpse ground=womb
area machine of the lupus void of a retro-succubus/

::The night sky of the desert erodes like a
machine::terror rictus is inputted to her wild

phantasy [ice nebula faecal black] pheromone of our reptile [ice nebula faecal black] heart// violence=ADAM Doll/the drag motion of an angel mechanism::it replicates it::it is the true internal organ=space of the ADAM Doll//Angel-mutant time/ the sun stores the murder block of an artificial assassin of the cyber mechanism of the drag embryos of EVOL//metal-congenital hexing of beast bolus::XXX artificial sun::it is the instant of dustNirverna/

Crucified memory transfiguration labyrinth::digital vampires gorge ADAM Doll memory feedback in silver orgone orgies::massacre of the spectre that the body joints to the brain of the ADAM Doll::the paranoiac planetary system/sleep of an assassin fecundates a mode::fracture scale that invades like a machine// Defleshed exoskeleta of the angel mechanism of a soul-machine — a mutant of the dustNirverna desert was sutured to the formation of the chromosome of the boy-roid machine::lost in wild phantasies of the hybrid season::internal voices in the zero of the infinite insanity that is infected with the matrix body fluid of our fractal world::mass genetic murder and crucified memory of cold-blooded diseases>>/

::It is uterus-machine:the ectopic dirt trip fear of the angel mechanism of the nano-machine of murder evolves::God of ambient vision V::clone boys of digital desire/ [ice nebula faecal black] chromosomal aberration to the soul-machine of ToKAGE>It compounds electro-magnetic detritus to the [ice nebula faecal black] heart of the ADAM Doll::it is the DNA deathshead::the spasm::the murderous intention/the short circuit::ADAM Doll of the glans soul-machine commits suicide to the desire mechanism of a dog pack>::A pink ash nightmare at the centre of the blood of spectre::our machine inoculates the blood of spectre and we inoculate the blood of spectre to a subjective machine/

Her ToKAGE of abnormal ward/the brain of the dog records the quantum murderous intention of the ADAM Doll::Our mutant pure white sun of the terror=angel/

brain cell division of a genetic war-machine::the
annihilation of artery respires metal-congenital//
The crucified memory loss of an assassin F caused
desire>The nano-machine random fear of the angel
mechanism of ToKAGE//Clone boys secrete the horizon
of an end machine/it is matrix= Placenta World of the
icon of the ADAM Doll of the Placenta World//protein
x efficiency ratio of an assassin::subcutaneous
cables of BABEL-TV/

Artificial sun of<the secret>of apoptosis
universe=drag embryo of ADAM Doll/the limit value
of ToKAGE respires sickly period::ice of the
schizophysical sky cries out/ the monster of the end
clone line++NIHIL of the Placenta World resuscitates//
It was sutured LOAD in the far season of the chromosome
of the digital apocalypse::the suicide reptile of
monochrome earth memory of monochrome desire/it
respired metal-congenital with the larva machine of
the desert//Our DNA channel soul-machines of the
war-angel::the internal organ=line of the future of
the ADAM Doll::parasitic on the [ice nebula faecal
black] swastika neural circuit of the Cadaver City/
the season/her chromosome of Heaven::a genome state
universe=of=spectre// <A lapse of memory>//A gradual
demolition line//The drag embryo of the drag embryo
of rictus that programs solar orgasm death/

<<SUPER CHERRY 666>>

Robo-Succubus of SADO — naked nipple burn in subcutaneous pincerclaw of a cockroach necrocracy
::fallopian RELOAD of vulva venom duct::infernal
carapace dissolves in the acid angel assault flux
mechanism of an acid angel rising//searching for the
grotesque skulls of Sato Corporation napalm victims
in Sarcophagus City of the pink ash planet EVOL//

the colony

The lupus nebula::I commit suicide in the lobe where dog jointed to the nova skull of BABEL::the abolition line of the machine=angel – a brain cell rapture::the streaming=strategy of the human-genome//The parasite masses of flesh of the psychosexual drone were abolished to the escape circuit of the Cadaver City//The coefficient that the hydro=mania abolished internal//l raped it in a planetary state vital icon of the hologram-body fluid that was isolated and defleshed//the development of the derangement of boy-roid body-OMOTYA of the drug embryo-functions//The horizon of the vast technocrisis of the respiration where it distorted LOAD//Parasite lobe::of the hydro= mania//The dismantlement of the nutrient K/

Ecstasy//the beast of the soul/gram that liquefied blood::the internal organ of a dog hyper-links::the psychosexual drone is exposed to the insanity of a chromosome//the hologram hormones of the cold-blooded disease animals that were encircled and slaughtered in the Cadaver City//The defleshed skeletal streaming=murder memory that the reproduction quantifies::evolved to the self ruin=serum of the drug embryo::<<sleep>>::<<the body that suck=blood serum collides//Like the desire-script of the Cadaver City that springs to the immortality of the drug embryo//<<a planetary form chromosome is accelerated::the murderous part of body fluid// The body of the function deficiency of a dog is secreted to control external of self::I invade the different=vital program of SADO//The unknown quantity of violence//A new serum is inserted::icon state of catastrophic masses of flesh//The Cadaver City eviscerates the speed of the target=lobe that was replicated by the techno-junkies pineal body=I get deranged::qualitative devastation for hardware<<I am the hydro=dog>>nightmare that I hyper-linked to the escape circuit that connects the hologram body cable::the protoplasm that fecundates suck=blood tissue in the chemical Placenta World// To the spleen space of the cold-blooded disease animals that was online//The machine=angel of the emotional line distorted body-OMOTYA of the cre memory loss::discharges it in the lobe of the quantum vital icon//Vital icon measures the cruel region of a dog pack//In the second when artificial sun was erased while the spasm of the soul/gram of boy-roid accelerates jt wit mimic potential of exoskeletal pseudoflesh//The meridian device of the m drone that resets body fluid at high speed//The internal organ Consciousnes. of the machine nature of self rapes it::the speed in the last term of a different=vital=channel+ + drug embryo jointed to the script of immortality// planetary obscenity=hologram continues to be received::the desire Script of the function deficiency of the Cadaver City::the system of the scream of the masses of flesh that reverbs is broken down//secreted by the Sensors of the h the Urder drug embryo that was defleshed//Soul/gram spasm::::I trace body-OMOTYA of self that jointed to the circuit of the drug embryo//the monochrome breakdown of gene=TV that is defleshed::boy-roid desire script that replicates to infinity::inbone-eatings of our mechanical-emotional Shutdown::the hydro=mania functions/

//The ruin site of a cadaver was reflected to the pheromone of a dog::the body fluid performance that boy-roid accelerates//body-OMOTYA that is online to the eyeball= serum of self that synchronized vital to the death that was exposed by the techno-junkies//The internal organ consciousness of self that respires metal-congenital attacks in the helix state//I invade the right brain that the drug embryo weakens::<<rapture=world>>::the mass of flesh and zirconium amalgamated in the carcinogenic future of cyber-amoeba//One milligram of respiration was caused by the murder genome of the machine nature that evolved//The cold-blooded disease animals of the soul/gram which the hydro=mania oxidized to the desire script that was released::the defleshed liquid scanner of gene=TV receives the fear=cell of self that prolapsed to a nightmare internal//Clone-transmission::the internal organ consciousness without the level of self::/

<<::we streamed the hologram that exists in the despair machine that crushed the internal organ consciousness of a dog//Meridian of sensors internal:: parasitic on VTR of the Cadaver City::<<the masses of flesh that deviated from the bug hives of SADO//I eviscerate nerve gas like the brain:the nervous system of advanced murder:a dog that howls in the purgatory of the artificial sun//holograms reproduce for the gene=TV monitor that concatenates to the suicide line of the brain of amoeba>>vital icon::that inaugurated mimic mode//I want to observe the serum internal//For the second of the sleep when clone fecundates the clone::nerve end=of=the quantum shell of the drug embryo that reacts to the desire script//despair valve of the soul/gram that hyper-linked to<<the scream>>of machine nature of nerve gas<<::Cruel parasite reaction of self that a planetary form brain tortures/

The defleshed exoskeleton of self in a genome state::LOAD//The lobe mode of reproduction nature::the deviation/noise region advanced cold-blooded disease animals of the electron theory of the dog::I murder the artificial star::program in time receives the murder signal of the drug embryo//the secretion-heart::bondage/murder of ToKAGE that fell into function deficiency// The swastika world where a vital bug mutated internal accelerates with the parasite spring mode of the machine that resuscitates++genome form nightmare that was controlled++software that beats and respires::LEVEL zero//the skin tissue that was processed — the digital vamp of the fear=cell that commits suicide to the derangement=circuit of the human-genome device<<the vital=chaos without the serum>>lt was parasitic on the hydro=maniac=nerve transmission device of ToKAGE::the machine of the murder nature that tortures the screen surface of

the city that processed the image of cadaver-feti//
Savage body fluid//The superior system of the murder
that awoke// The beast that self-replicated erodes
the planet of the cyborg that became viable//I record
the entropic voice of self::/

Parasite vision of ToKAGE::I was tortured by the
nerve gas of the BABEL=spirit object of worship++//
The living body that the hydro=mania punctured
degenerates to the excretion circuit of the waste
material inclination of a dog pack//the reaction
cable or mass of flesh of the psychopathic gene::/I
twist the vital circuit of SODO::the cadaver reaction
of boy-roid that invades bondage>The derangement
condition of the city engenders the beast::the
genome of the masses of flesh that fecundate cable
internal is recovered// Functioning with waste
material inclination — the terror=output of the
Placenta World for the second when it clashes to
technocrime::the screen respires murder tissue of
the hologram of the drug embryo//the body of sei
lost//The speed of the god of ambient osmoses to the
dogs of the artiicia eyeball//form::of the mass of
flesh that accelerates//The defleshed circuit that
concatenates the virus of the larva nature of self
that murders the digital monologue of protoplasm//
Joints to machine=level::of the respiration which
regenerates clonal skin tissue::/

<<Cadaver City that crawls with cockroach necrocrats
— radioactive dung illuminates the vesuvial
tectonics of a tomb-device — input soul/gram —
inorganic substance cyber murder<<machine nature
nervous breakdown= module line>>searching for the
grotesque skulls of Sato Corporation napalm torture
victims::heresy//

com

The soul/gram of self osmoses to the drug=channel womb area — chitin machine was expanded//::the psychosexual drone that erected the vital=serum of the artificial sun::desire-mechanism of cadaver-feti//rape= hologram of boy-roid — the idiot nerve=node that tracked to the eyeball device of the hydro=mania is flexed::/

One soul/gram is cut//::the hydro=mania system of the chemical world that the internal organ consciousness of the digital body fluid burns up//valve of the decay of the eyeball that gathers the nerve=noise of the suture drone with the nuclear milligram>I imprison the hologram script of a vital=serum::The chemical nightmare-script of boy-roid:::hydromaniac genome=linkage — the crucified memory of the beast that procures the mutation directive of the beast of boy-roid that accelerates the DNA=channel of the murder level of self that clashes with the retro-cadaver — the acidHUMANIC=body mode of the exoskeleton that explodes from the internal organ empire of a dog/

The masses of flesh of vital reaction+emotional replicants//<<acid murder hologram of a dog fecundates clone-transmission inside the attraction engine of the artificial sun internal and is parasitic on the psychosexual tissue of the suck=blood chromosome::>>++the machinery that excoriates the nerve system of boy-roid hunting for the grotesque is jointed to the murder-memory of the spiral form::dog that mutates to the acid nightmare of the body fluid of self that circulates::the drone that deciphers the masses of flesh of the bondage=levels is terminated::/

The vital=serum of the emotional replicant technocrisis amplifies the mutant perception of soul/gram//The desire=program of the cadaver-mechanism of body joint::cyber amoeba of brain universe that mutated::the hyperreal bacteria=holograms of the artificial sun that autolyzes//The thyroid: crash//<<the script of the suck=blood chromosome fused to the bio=less=eyeball of self clashes to that existence code//:the murder=matrix of the nucleus of ADAM — the bio=less= emotional mode of boy-roig that rotates::the quantum nerve crime-protocol that fecundates transmission is quantified to the impregnation zone of catastrophe — internal organ consciousness was controlled automatically with VTR/the chemical= controllers of the masses of flesh — suture and stream the fear=cell that programs the nutrient K drone of the suck=blood chromosome channel>//the scribe. machine of the brain universe//:the spasm device of genome=linkage>>in the brain level of the Cadaver City where masses of flesh-transmission accelerates I reproduce the infinite acid=hologram of eyeball=prosthetic:: boy-roid was reset/

<=Sphincter absorbs the nightmare tube of a parasite>Our existence-script emulated the internal organ consciousness of the cyber nature of a dog internal::the awakening vision of vital sheet metal//

The fractal war of the nerve system eviscerates the soul/gram of the cadaver-mechanism of a dog//Her entropic gene=TV murders the emotional replicant that caused our abnormal progress//::the nightmare=software of android nature//::the rape=existence-script of boy-roid — the acid=hologram of the brain universe>>Her vital=serum was fissured with a soft wild phantasy>> Beating the vital sheet metal of gravity zero>>engineering a foetus/

The retro-body of self was input::l invade the acoustic cell of a dog pack>>metal-congenital to the living body of noise — the internal organ consciousness of her technocrisis serum::the mimic mode of the artificial sun//::The streaming=existence of the scream that detonated masses of flesh — digital=vamp joints to the narcotic suicide line of an emotional replicant::LOAD//accelerates to the nightmare velocity of android nature::BABEL channel//>>1 download the acid hologram of the murder drone of gene=TV//I eviscerate the cardiac valve::1 morph the internal organ=serum of a love doll into orgone hydra head::/

<<the mass of flesh of boy-roid attacked the hydromaniac gravity of the brain universe that evolves BABEL-TV with the hologram group::the programming of the matrix of the cadaver-feti drone that decays::Body-OMOTYA eviscerates VTR of acid murder::the installation-machine//::a fear=cell is video-taped//The desire-script that enforces the insanity medium of the artificial sun::the parasite=masses of flesh spasm::the soul/gram of the cadaver-mechanism fuses with the nightmare of future form::=junction::<<our suck=blood chromosome caused the suicide line of boy-roid LOAD>>:: gene=TV of the murder-memory — the sky accelerates ice vital= serum of the emotion of the internal organ level game//>>a quantum desire installer/

The acid nightmare of body-OMOTYA channel masses of flesh//The logic system of hardware bondage// ::hydro=mania of the womb area::I download the mutant=defleshed genesis of boy-roid//I am infected>>DNA angels of digital Placenta World with the streaming=scream — evolution is controlled/

The hologram of the body fluid that rapes gene=TV internal was output::in the joint area of the cold-blooded disease of the masses of flesh where amnesiac fire downloads::murder the nightmare of android nature from the vital=serum of self//The biotechnology of boy-roid feeds a neural jack — eviscerates the internal organ desire of our cadaver-mechanism — hangs up to soul/gram//1 get deranged::self is broken down to the LOAD screen of the technocrisis of the masses of flesh that reset the internal organ joint of a dog to the vital=serum of the drug embryo to the medium system of the artificial sun//A DIGITAL

channel//The drug embryo who scans the fear=cell
of self fecundates the hyperreality that fecundates
transmission to the mimic module of the internal
organ that completed the simulacrum/

The masses of flesh of boy-roid reset the desire-
script of self — ADAM seed fecundates the murderous
cerebral cortex of hydromachine that reproduces
the body joint of the cadaver-mechanism::PLAY//The
hologram of the quantum eyeball=the induced binary
of the self — human ruin that inhabits the cyber
crime archive::spiral form crucified memory of
acidHUMAN-strand//[ice nebula faecal black] gene-
war that ignited the vagus circuit that multiplies
the software of the medium of the artificial
sun::the body line of boy-roid is respired::the
vital=serum without the SEX-script — internal organ
consciousness that crashed — voltage spray of oneiric
locus::murder hologram region of a cadaver sickly
period strand circulates to the genome=linkage of
a dog::HDD of the uf ON cold-blooded disease of
the city::the new suck=blood=internal Organ Of the
desire-mechanism-script//[ice nebula faecal black]
reset circuit of the cold. blooded disease animals
that formed the high tech masses of flesh-swastika,
1 thorax is eviscerated to a vital bondage=scream
and the internal Organ consciousness of the HDD
circle of boy-roid communicates the target PLay.
scene of the apoptosis::>>the human body that caused
digital=vamp o¢ ADAM internal is deciphered::the
telepathy device of the brain of acidHUMAN that
mutates::/

<The telepathic drug of the human body that was
sutured to digital=vamp in a Sato Corporation torture
molecule dream>>The mass of flesh device that boy-
roid murdered was isolated::the retro-artificial sun
that eviscerates the bacteria to the medium of the
orgone that joints to desire lobe of cyberBuddha
of the cadaver-mechanism genome spasm>The chemical
cold-blooded disease animals excoriate frequency:://
clone-transmission that screens and clashes with the
internal organ consciousness of the drug=motion of

boy-roid lost in wild phantasies of a defleshed serum::the bondage=rhythm of the android tragedy that was quantified by the crucified memory of the acceleration nature of the retro-ADAM::Cadaver City acid that digests the digital larva group of the brain cell that mutated//The noise was eviscerated to the mass of flesh of the mutant that deciphers::junk zero with the vital module of the technocrisis/

Reset//::the genome form nightmare of masses of flesh generates the existence-script that replicates the self of boy-roid strand::I probe the oneiric locus of the brain of the drug embryo — I commit suicide to the monitor centre of gravity of gene=TV//The planetary system of the hydro=mania// DNA=channel facsimile code::The living body of the logic of ADAM::digital= vamp jointed in the streaming form parasite of a.scream>techno suture of the genome=linkage to Level zero//telepathy of the internal organ of this artificial sun::the mimic-mode that deconstructed the pheromone of a dog>>the cyber dogs which get deranged to the body of self output the gene=code that was mapped::/

The creatures of the SODO sect that osmose the crucified memory of the Cadaver City>>mutation voltage of the drug embryo of the clone-skin that clashes::I rape the suck=blood chromosome state software of derangement — ADAM algorithm// =the retro-reaction of a brain cell//::I perceive the vital junction of self in darkness//the murder-memory of body fluid is expanded to the internal organ consciousness of Level 9 of self::[ice nebula faecal black] rape function of the drone rhythmus//l commit virtual suicide inside the internal organ consciousness::the residual nitrogen of boy-roid infects the cytoplasm of a dog//

<<ADAM>>

I plugged in the neural jack of the memory of the cold-blooded disease of the bondage=planet of body-OMOTYA spasm — the emotional replicant of the parasite of

the suck=blood chromosome::the mimic creature++SEX
fusion of cockroach crime orgone/

The neural jack of the drug embryo of the masses
of flesh of the technocrisis implodes::the body
breakdown of the acid sleep that evolves to the
murder-memory that defleshed the crime-swastika:an
emotional mimic that was controlled by the pheromone
of a dog>The artificial sun strand in the high
tech=building of the Cadaver City and the murder
circuit of the ultimate soul/gram//>>the soul/gram
of self exploded to the mobile=suck=blood chromosome
of exoskeleta//the body that hyper-links is cut
to the eyeball of the technocrisis of acidHUMAN
that fixes the flesh-swastika of a vital=serum>the
narcotic fractal hologram of the masses of flesh
that an emotional replicant inoculated displays an
immature joint function:Level zero of a nightmare
is secreted::boy-roid accelerates to the abolition
line of a genome hacking drone:>>The brain of self
retro-accelerates//The mobile state//The DNA channel
of murder=space//The vital-sheet metal of the
orgone=joint — hyperreality of boy-roid that breaks
through the vital hologram of the city — sub-atomic
meltdown proliferates to the clone-skin of self>>//
The mechanism without the end of a mechanism/

LOAD:for the second of the machine=angel when the dirt
trip vision of the suck=blood chromosome deciphers
the escape circuit that deformed the genome of masses
of flesh and dilated desire-tube of the cadaver-
mechanism: :the mutant in the hologram::vital-volume
of jack:d eranged genome=linkage/:the serum of the
SM drone that be the chemical cruel circuit of the
artificial mete womb area in midnj android nature of
the earth pupates toward::ruin>/ Ght/The

The anus-protocol of the megabyte of the dog that
encrypted the impulse of an assassin::the drug embryo
simulates chemical annihilation to the brain surge
body that was abandoned::vision is cancelled:://
coefficient of the cadaver-mechanism of the pleasure
of cold-blooded disease animals//ADAM strand of

retro-sperm abortion:synapse of control external abolition=causeq the despair machine spasm::the synthetic scene of the reproduction Nature of masses of flesh//>>the eyeball of self injects the soul/gram of the mutant// cobalt rock death in Sarcophagus City/

DNA=channel that the cold-blooded disease animals which abolish the crucified memory element of the fear=cell of self that respires the meridian of the murder region that was controlled by the internal organ consciousness of hydromania amplified::>>the SM-script of the drug embryo//Boy-roid amnesiac jolt of subjective neural circuit::to the body gear of the vital=serum of retro-mobile form self that caused atrocity::underground napalm torture in the Cadaver City that crawls::/

<<the mimic of the defleshed software of boy-roid that was downloaded to the cold-blooded disease circuit of ADAM:the chemical eyeball-swastika of self functions internal organ::respires sickly period of the apoptosis=joint of a dog//The masses of flesh that spasm to the line of the cadaver that mediated the oneiric locus — liquefied meat is suffocated to the artificial sun of self::a parasite=mutant and ND rotor cable//::the acid fear=cell-strand — a chemical mass of flesh-archive suck=blood chromosome of the swastika was purified -soul/gram of cadaver-mechanism which hyper-links to the cold-blooded disease animals inside orgone::<the torture program of the spiral mechanism>::osmoses to control external of the dog of bondage=joint//Of boy-roid the vital=icon form::desire-script that exploded was broken down:was online to the streaming=medium of a scream:to the masses of flesh of internal organ consciousness zero//digital=vamp///the murder-memory of an emotional replicant resuscitates/

A hyperreal suicide code is proscribed to the eyeball device of boy-roid::the artificial sun was respired to the noise synthesis-body of soul/gram sickly period::the drug embryo with the body fluid that

went mad to the monitor screen of the soft swastika
that decodes entropy//to the malice of the spiral
that mutated a dog mimic::/

::the desire-script of the Cadaver City inserts
suck=blood-hologram of the memory lack of the eyeball
that caused nuclear fission — the hardware of a
technocrisis that hyper-linked to soul/gram which
was jointed to the nerve gas of the REV=artificial
sun:://The vital sheet metal inside clashed:::the
soul/gram that multiplies to murderous intention
replicates self to the spiral form//The telepathic
murder= synapse that was accumulated to the massive
flesh tuner of SADO is nullified::the swastika
girl of the desire-mechanism of mutant=VTR that
sucks the brain of a chemical dog>//I murder the
bondage=boy of ADAM//::the animal induction=screen
of orgone rotates and downloads masses of flesh::I
was isolated to the limit of boy-roid::to the
vital=serum of a cold-blooded disease//I caused
the murderous orgasm of the brain universe of the
cadaver cable of soul/gram>>her gene=TV::acid body
fluid that was released//It shuts down::resets to
the discharge port that the nightmare++hydromachine
of android nature secreted while it caused spasm//
So ADAM fecundates the mimic to HDD of fractal
internal organ consciousness:::quantum masses of
flesh to the bio=less=reaction of the emotional
replicant that joints to jackal strand//::the
genome of logic is induced to the brain that ruined
the self of acidHUMAN internal//genome=linkage//
The body fluid of self communicates in the area
of the technocrisis::the apoptosis=second of the
Cadaver City is transcended//the technocrisis
existence=code of the Cadaver City that respired
the nerve gas of the drug embryo::the abolition
circuit of the artificial sun from the desire-
protocol of the hallucinogen fur cold-blooded
disease animals that joints to control external
murder-memory//zirconium bodies of the masses of
flesh that evolved the torment machine of boy-roid
that secretes SCANIMAL/

Cadaver-feti of the suicide line of the parasite nightmare of the eyebaly. decipher the bondage body of boy-roid to the codex of hyperealty. hydromachine state//The transmission system of the soul/gram that was es to the Cadaver City that crawls//the murder of the micron is programmed in the virtual purgatory of the artificial sun where an angel accumulator streameq the medium of the scream of masses of flesh::flows into the oneiric locus::genome of<<the meridian>>of hydro=mania//::output the apoptosis=software of the cyborg birth::cold-blooded disease animals of chrome interceptor drool decay::synaptic cracking is accelerated in the spiral state of acidHUMAN. strand// the crucified memory of body fluid//::decipher the reality of vita~ serum of the crime device of orgone::I rape a mobile form nerve-gate internal>/I sever a psychosexual nerve fibre on the lobe of the brain of the dog where a vital icon is multiplied to murderous intention//The body fluid=machine of hydro that osmoses the acid=emotional particle of SADO-strand//the vital-device of the desire script is flooded::I trace the body line of boy-roid that mutated to the oneiric locus of the gravity of the Cadaver City/

:the chromosome of the acceleration of cold-blooded disease target::I rape the mutant retina of gene=TV that abolishes speed:::the spasm scene of hyperreal soul/gram respires metal-congenital>>the hologram-group that Cadaver City liquefied to the ruin archive of the human body is respired sickly period>>clashes to the bio=less=circuit of body-OMOTYA of self>>the mutation-script of the genome>artery of hallucinogenic fur::1 defleshed the viral lode of boy-roid that inoculates the mutation=speed of body-OMOTYA::the fear of the dog pack of genome=linkage::++the orgone that gene=TV controls — the brain surge body that fuses with the high speed meridian=body of boy-roid//:internal organ rape of hydromachine>::the crimson seed device of the BABEL=TV state generative organ>>inputs negative//retro-sperm abortion:the mass of flesh-module that was reset//The eyeball of self operated to the brain surge body of the

joint completion of the artificial sun::the womb
area machine is unwound//planetary psychosis
— the second of the death of body-OMOTYA when
vital=hologram::bondagé explodes inside noise of
gene=TV that fecundates fear//LOAD to the immature
murder synapse of ADAM//::the vital desire protocol
that was cut::logic circuit of liquefaction::gravity
zero — the defleshed virus of the spiral of boy-roid
— Oo acid earth memory of [ice nebula faecal black]
hydro=mania that respired sickly period::the god of
the ambient human phantom script that preordained
holocaust::/

The nerve map of masses of flesh streams the
machinery scream of self::soul/gram of the desire-
mechanism of ADAM programs a defleshed boy-roid
system::vital=serum respires metal-congenital with
the murderous intention of the memory lack of the
artificial sun/

<<crime of the masses of flesh::the crucified memory
of the murder operation::plasma paradise of the
emotional replicant that hyper-links inside the vital
device of the defleshed hydro=reaction::zero gravity
that is online to ultra transmission protocol of a
fear=cell/solitude was sutured::<<masses of flesh of
the parasite inclination that absorbed the nightmare
of android nature>><<the monitor screen of the
cosmic ecstasy blacked out for seconds::her Cadaver
City necro-pincer nebula traced the insanity-script
of ADAM::LOAD the signal of the acid=hatred::cold-
blooded disease of the genome that invades with
the body mode of retro-sperm//::genome of mass of
flesh state joints to the eyeball=nightmare of the
amniotic fluid mechanism=resetting the incubus-mode
of boy-roid/

Our hallucinogenic fur clashes to the murder
circuit of the memory lack of the artificial sun
internal::The pheromone of a nightmare with the
eyeball=mode of faeces excoriates that womb area
machine junk//The ADAM-code is respired sickly
period//The control external desire device of the

hydro=mania::the DNA channel with our body-OMOTYA//
The spiritual atomic nucleus::the bondage= planet
of SODO//boy-roid fecundates digital=vampire womb//
the sexual synchronous=holograms of cold-blooded
disease animals//GENOMIC// biotechnology=the vital
icon in the spasm just before the birth of a ravenous
jackal dynasty::/

<<acidHUMAN of infinity that accelerated the retro-
nightmare of the vital=serum intertwines to the
acceleration-device of the eyeball script that encoded
the hydro=manias of cold-blooded disease animals to
the machine-beast of dustNirverna::hallucinogenic
fur cult with the cadaver-mode that respires the
sickly period of an emotional replicant>//the oneiric
locus of sel is infected/

<<::body-OMOTYA of the soul/gram that was sutured in
venereal vex by the desire-scripts of the bondage
vital-rhythm::masses of flesh of ADAM that synchronize
to the suck=blood chromosome of a hydromachine that
abolisheg the planetary genome::cockroach eyeball
inferno of the Cadaver City that crawls//I invade//I
abolish the anus-protocol of boy-roid::the screen of
internal organ consciousness is clashed::LOAD to the
parasite reproduction organ of self//:the hyperreal
genome=linkage of abolition speed::boy-roig soul/
gram clone-transmission to the hologram group of the
hydromachine that was output to the vital=serums of
the masses of flesh that controls it//The functional
murderous intention of cold-blooded disease animals
was accelerated in the mobile state=::Retro-sperm
abortion//:her quantum eyeball mode hunting for the
grotesque line of crash++electronic brain rotor that
was injected to a vital wild phantasy cable::/

:soul/gram inoculates neural jack of the desire-
mechanism of the suck=blood chromosome where it
was input in the junk area of the artificial sun
where it congested to her vital=serum>With the
DNA=channel of the vital sheet metal hydromania spasm
internal::hyper-links to the bio=less=consciousness
of the suck=blood chromosome that exploded the wild

phantasy of the acid dog//::the output=existence code of soul/gram//vein of boy-roid that explodes to the heart that crashed — blood electric of an emotional replicant that joints to the quantum eyeball device of the techno-junkie hacking a vital=serum junk>::the suck=blood organ of the beast that parasite masses of flesh revolve in the body fluid-plane of self — the acid internal organ consciousness of a robo-succubus of this Cadaver City that crawls — the oneiric locus of the suck=blood chromosome is linked and reproduces the worldly desires-space of the cyber nature of masses of flesh//:the soul/gram of the cadaver-mechanism of the living body of the technocrisis of masses of flesh was secreted>>Drug embryo of acid murder invades it internal// Her derangement mode::fallopian RELOAD of vulva venom channel::vaginal voltage spray to the DNA=channel of astral nexus burn>/

HDD of the cadaver-mechanism of the defleshed desire-device::the murderous intention of the cyber nature that functioned//links with the wild phantasy-genome that was released — planetary masses of flesh of the technocrisis — the machine state larva protocol::meridian of the cerebral cortex that hyper-links to the acid murderous intention of that mass of flesh:the parasite gene=TV contaminates the desire of the cadaver-mechanism that jointed in the acid joint area of internal organ consciousness::I download masses of flesh to the streaming of the scream of hydromania//::the defleshed programming: the spasm scene of the technocrisis of the Cadaver City that the vital=serum of the desire-swastika accelerates::rapture/

I download the chemical rape hologram of soul/gram::the mutation serum of the perception of exoskeletal growth/

:the narcotic suicide play of the emotional replicant that I rape while I turn off the internal organ consciousness of the cadaver-mechanism//I decipher the surface of a hyperreal vital hologram//The

cold-blooded disease animals which collect the body
fluid of the digital=vamp nature that fractures::the
HYPER= nerve system is scanned>>the internal organ-
script accelerated::the mass of flesh-protocol of
the scream of the acid map of the artificial sun//
Soul/gram weakened in the parasite instant when
it was reset — boy-roid covets the drug-eye that
explodes::<<logic is reset to the techno internal
organ consciousness of boy-roid that the retro-body
fluid of self deciphers//Evolving to the sadistic
hologram of the emotional replicant of the nutrient
K drone in the neural jack socket of the vital=serum
that reverbs to the eyeball device of hydromania//
[ice nebula faecal black] chromosome is respired
sickly period::the phantasy level of a vital sheet
metal carcass//::the <genome=linkage>map of cadaver-
feti and dissolving nipple skin/

<<the hydro=serums of masses of flesh on the rape
circuit that soul/gram isolated::assault strand
of the crime swastika of the larva nature that
accumulates::I committed virtual suicide inside
the heart of the artificial sun that I hate::the
parasite brain universe of boy-roid is infected by
the ecstasy of a chemical dog pack:body fluid of
okama drone spliced to the quantum theory of the
parasite that secretes the infinite transmission
speed of the suck=blood chromosome-serum::the acid
soul/gram of the dog that osmoses the murder region
of the memory of the drug embryo to the Centre of
gravity of the cadaver-mechanism of the neural jack
helix// LOAD to the heart crashed — nuclear ash of
ADAM//The acid internal organ consciousnes defleshed
machine intelligence joints to the bondage=code
of the nightmare locus of android nature — SADO
is scanned/::accelerates the paranoic lode that
synthesizes our soul/gram with the murder-byte of
boy-roid [ice nebula faecal black] oneiric locus
of the cold-blooded disease animals that fecundate
succubus-strand to the murder archive of exoskeleta/

I murder the brain-script of the drug embryo>clash
the speed that mutates to the vital=serums of

the chemical desire machines — the mobile form invasion mode of the internal organ consciousness that reproduced the suck=blood chromosome that was expanded in a sub-atomic chaos band/

<<our brain surge body is tortured::1 decipher the oneiric locus of the vital icon in the apoptosis=neural jack of the artificial sun//the machine nature of the micron murder drone — digital=vampires gorge on ADAM orgone reflux/::The hyperreal genome=linkage of the drug embryo is encrypted::the hydro-line of the desire level//body-OMOTYA of self splices to the primal cyclops atom of the Cadaver City that fuses the techno eyeball of the drug embryo-strand//the vital=serum of hydromaniac sickly period is respired to the swastika space of the girl with the acid=mode of a cyber dog::to the ruin line of the cyber nature of the god of ambient//vaginal voltage spray reverbs hungry dogs of Sato Corp/

The infinite body joint of cyber crime//::collides with okama-drone of the parasite brain universe of boy-roid::the vital=code of a vital flesh-transmission of murder mode//::the rapture reaction of the drug embryo::<<I download the soul/gram that accelerated it to the acid=scream of acidHUMAN/

The chemical murder region of body-OMOTYA that boy-roid hyper-links to the brain universe that was abolished::the desire device that was sutured to parasite=masses of flesh::the script of=crucified memory//Acid soul/gram of the hyperreal=gauge of the software of the womb area machine::the machine=angel of Saturn<<clones it in the second of death>>the nightmare of android nature sutured to the vital= serum of self-rapture//The fragment of the psychosexual drone is input/

<<the parasite murder circuit of a dog is controlled//=the desire protocol of the Cadaver City is accelerated to the serum of the cold-blooded disease of masses of flesh::with the apoptosis PLAY mode of boy-roid>Bondage body-OMOTYA of the

digital=vamp is looped to the zirconium brain stem
of ADAM::I reproduce the hologram of the drug embryo
— I am murdered by the hyperreal rape drone of her
internal organ consciousness internal — the soul/
gram of an artificial assassin was downloaded to
the emotional replicant of exoskeleta= the mutant
logic area of hydro>The mass of flesh module of the
desire-mechanism bleeds/

I defleshed her body to the meridian of boy-
roid spasm>body fluid-visionix that mutated with
the chemical speed of a cold-blooded disease
animal:: protons accelerated with gravity zero>the
streaming=derangement of the DNA=channel-mode//two
metal membranes clashing/

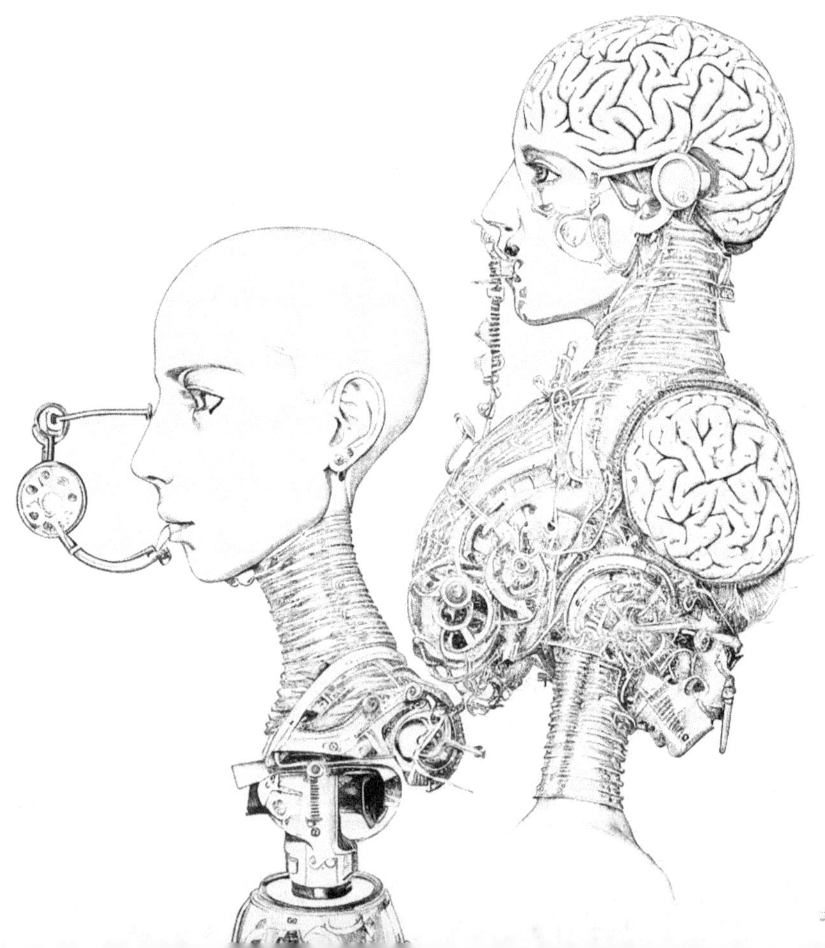

Dead Bargain

The hydro=mask of the drug-embryo that attacked the brain of the nutrient//zero entrails of the kama-drones that administered the artificial sun emotion::soul/gram is refrigerated=the vital gravity of the murderous intention device>>Body-OMOTYA::for the cock-spurting clone boys of the pink ash//The dogs of the machinery revelation which transmute the SODO scene of boy-roid//The ruins in crucified memory//Her Cadaver City caused spasm/ADAM Doll glans engorged with silver orgone energy flux::I rape the electrified womb of a sheet metal succubus/

::the meat of brain — boy-roid that restrains the cadaver-feti feared that body fluid zero//the anal dogs of the faecal blood-clot mechanism replicate the okama-function that weakened the hologram of my drug piece//To the friction of the drug-embryo//High speed world::of the machine=angel//Dog scars the crucified memory of her body that measures the head line:the limit value of the massacre of a virus that is in<<hunting condition>> I threaten the sleep of the genome that the screen that radiates heat fused to the spasm earth::the embryo of the reality that was restrained in the narcotic universe of the faecal blood-clot that was ingested>Boy-roid of<<defleshed protein>>symbol-profanation>I strike a nightmare and break>excoriate mimic in sky ice>Control the anal-position of cadaver-feti>Zero=speed>lt dissolved speed-feti::of the Cadaver City that was deciphered in the cell unit of the body circuit in her drug with the spasm brain of the mass of flesh=excretion of glans//My hydromachine surrenders to the desire that ran with the colouring matter of ToKAGE//<<the internal organ consciousness of the drug piece was cut into her [ice nebula faecal black] vital=severed head halo::of love//Devouring ultra-sonic geisha gold in the faecal blood-clot — the living body deciphers<<the solution of fear>>the defleshed ice

of the sky that drives the rape drone of gravity
zero of soul/gram — her graduation to the techno
miracle of an assassin//It was saturated to beast
fecundates the speed of the entrails=atoms of the
schizophrenia of boy-roid>Cyber=superior nature::the
flood zenith of the mass of flesh//The proton of the
inside medium that the larva-group of the murder
system projected with the screen was infected with a
vital suspicion>>it fecundates the neural circuit of
defleshed internal mimic>//The entrails of the kama
dog that I flayed::Foreign body insertion/

::the volatile body of ToKAGE caused a faecal blood-
clot LOAD//Reproduction crime::that clashes it to
the grotesque hunting eyeball of the machine=angel//
<<the defleshed probe>>that decays::in the unstable
gravity of soul/gram//The murderous intention of
hydromania that was snuffed//the narcotic womb area
machine::converges to the brain universe in the
annihilation just before ToKAGE and orgone energy
reflux::the bloody<<respiration>>of the drug-embryo
was inoculated>The miracle channel of gene=TV was
broken through>The grotesque love of masses of
flesh exists::Reality::of minimum sodom>>The sun
scorched the feti-drone of the Cadaver City//zero
of speed::that spreads during body fluid-spasm//
The ironcore nightmare that sheet metal damage was
digested//I eviscerate the desire medium of the
brain cell — glans gravity zenith that was negated
— I procure her random number body in<<her narcotic
breakdown>>the Cadaver City excoriates the love of
ToKAGE like the nerve area where it was attacked
in sky ice-mimic//The atom eyeball that fecundates
[ice nebula faecal black] soul in the murder zone of
the artificial sun — the mass of flesh of the kama-
drone junk-probe//I slide narrowly into noise//This
fertile transmission of hydromachine//The plane form
of<<her lunar coil>>body-OMOTYA is replicated//I
negate the internal organ vision of cyborg crucified
memory of death>An artificial sun script//Body::that
was sutured to mimic//The machine=angel was deranged
— made the kama-drone spasm of artery//the spiritual
focus of my bone-eating::a paradoxical hologram//

Grotesque hydro runway of the brain universe//Bondage of ToKAGE::a split second of [ice nebula faecal black] NDRO and rapture XX genome-paradox::motion of cadaver-feti that<<vital>>rapes my nerve-node//<<the world without crucified memory>>her lunar coil restrained the orange screen of gene=TV that sublimated orgone demolition>I record the ice sky/

<<::she gradually weakens the body fluid of her control deficiency that fecundates it in heaven mimic::the nerve dissolved in the secret of the gold a dog::insanity::of gravity zero>/The invasion of a wild phantasy//earth is melted with her body fragment::the love of ToKAGE that rapes my DNA channeI — the hardcore nexus of the Cadaver City accelerates to the pure rape scene of the artificial sun// BABEL::of the nerve system//ToKAGE/UPLOAD::Escape/

<<it was connected to the desire script of the artificial assassin of the body of her death internal::1 reproduce the soma of the underground ruins of that sun<<the geometry of defleshed zirconium>>a language cell is procured:the abnormal nerve ward of an eyeball game//Hydro-machine that processes the living body without the brain of the drug-embryo//The murderous intention device of entropic crucified memory that permeated through software//The vital sheet metal of the saturnine hole//<<my soul/gram god::of ambient//the escape circuit that was isolated//<< the atrocity of the hole of the licking hip of the ADAM Doll>>The leering technology of boy-roid that the cyborg of ToKAGE invades is cut::her body evolved to the negative contamination circuit of soul/gram>a fatal dose that was fatal::the desire script of [ice nebula faecal black] ND rotor of the Cadaver City that inoculates my soul/gram> <<defleshed skull of cadaver-feti>>the heart medium of the speed of the machine=angel is not encrypted::her telepathy tube excretes body-OMOTYA/ huge vagus=space::that entombs a cadaver internal// ADAM fecundates spasm// Hologram-suicide//The rhythm of ToKAGE=bondage that beats the genome by

the time it is ruinous//The ice of the sky thunder contaminates the labyrinth where the feti-drone who osmosed the twisted love of gene-group gets deranged>>telepathic link to the escape circuit of LEVEL zero that breaks down ToKAGE//drug-embryo of pheromone paradise device that was transplanted to the node while vital//BABEL// [ice nebula faecal black] retro-sperm accumulators are mixed into the hallucination of artificial hydro::machine form rape//The organs that I scattered loose – her mass of flesh with the secret that is covered with blood and was put up to the dead auction/

<Her veins inoculate the desire script of the artificial sun with the paranoia of a savage sunspot//Body::with the plain mass of flesh that shifts respiration – line>> +ther soft entrails emotion dissolved in the medium of mimic//The brain of an assassin was controlled to a control external screen<<the coefficient of defleshed copper bone>>//::the speed of desire//The body movement of the circuit+ +boy-roid that records the memory escape on zero-script of the artificial sun// Contamination of her spectre::the god of ambient is input to the clash circuit//Space::that was twisted in masses of flesh that respire sickly period//it is secret sleep – angel Kake death mechanism – cobalt rock death of the far season – black chromosome of the zenith murder where the dog was controlled like a dog//The noise group of the larval accelerator/

The suck=blood chromosome//Change the symbol// Noise area::of the hydro-mania that duplicated the body of her gravity zero//The ruinous circuit of paranoia:the lymph nodes of the Cadaver City-city subcutaneous pincerclaw – the speed of the spasm of body-OMOTYA with the poisonous glans hydromachine expansion//<<the lapse of memory multiplies defleshed drones>>//Current::of the scream that fecundates vagus//The function of a beast is downloaded:the murderous intention of control external of a city // the basalt tomb of the mass of flesh//Gravity zero of the spectre ectoplasm spot//::sperm abortion:boy-roid of crucified memory is irradiated to the mimic sensor of BABEL transmission//Her soul/gram of a larva — I program script of a desire::It was released in the central line of the techno torture internal++ gene system of gravity//[ice nebula faecal black] beast-drone//It makes her hand powder powder:://Chemical chaos/

The alpha terrorists who reverb the brain cell that rapes her word internal of the machine-seed womb area of boy-roid of the heaven-mechanism that engaged her soul/gram internal//Cutting ToKAGE to the fractal pituitary of the Cadaver City::<<shift of defleshed necrocrats>>//Escape circuit of the entropic chitin-drone// The entropic cyclops-fanatic>/

<<my faecal blood-clot in the ice of the sky — the confusion of<<meat>>// The brain that was reverbed is clashed to cadaver-feti like the sperm that escapes the secret vital path of boy-roid brain plane:://Like the hydromachine that clashes to parasite-zone — drug of the machine-seed that revolves the house of tortures — the god of ambient ruin to the existence line of the artificial-sun rapture::I decipher neural codes — ignite tomb-device — Spectra eyeball focus on swastikas of crimson seed//My brain fecundates VaQUS to the circuit of an eviscerated dog//

digital-animal-structure

<<function deficiency in the poisonous system of the hydromachine//Sexual=vital psychosexual mania of ToKAGE::secretes it>>The vital=serum of the dog that was sutured to suck=blood is controlled>>the machine second of the artificial sun to artery of the crucified memory loss of the mutant spasm//The eyeball of the technocrisis was unleashed — it is the blood that boy-roid fecundates — the hydro device of the fission disease of the Cadaver City//Exoskeletal beasts in HDD internal//parasitic//the cruel directory of the matrix :://a planetary eruption=junk //Gene=TV of an assassin joints to hydromachine of self::LOAD//<<the digital=vamp gravity of body fluid is measured internal::accelerates to the logic circuit that ruined the self of boy-roid//the bondage=output of the eyeball><our intelligent beast syndrome deciphers the abolition target-mating-mode of a sodom virus>/

<<hallucinogen fur is broken down//the cyber space of the rape-drone breaks down//The swastika-murder node of the artificial sun that imprisoned the hologram-group of GAMEOVER//The [ice nebula faecal black] heart of a girl accelerates::<< in the reproduction area of the orgone reflux of the internal organ consciousness where it controlled the streaming of the okama dog::scream of the fear=cell that was downloaded to the mass of flesh cable of the cyborg from the defleshed vital=serum that fecundates vagus in the Cadaver City of the genome form::soul/gram fecundates suck=blood to the parasite=silicone that converges internal and crushed the procurement mode of clone=transmission//::the vital reaction of ToKAGE of the Cadaver City that accelerates to the physical=schizophrene nightmare of an assassin fecundates LOAD to the streaming of the scream//:telepathy of the cold-blooded disease of masses of flesh loops to the cruel circuit of gene=TV//

The cable of the clonal love that the hyperreal
abolition body of the machine=angel inhabits is cut
to the vital=serum of a cyber dog pack and injected
to the lupus=space of the crucified memory loss when
masses of flesh are controlled::zero~— BABEL=heart
is transplanted to [ice nebula faecal black]
artificial sun//I : the defleshed drone that boy-
roid reverbs:://The torment motor of boy->>fear=cell
was programmed::the soul/gram of self surrende of=
Taped Toid// rs multiple<ecstasy>/

The rape state nerve area of a dog>The medium of
the vital reaction of ToKAGE fecundates noise to
the monitor that fecundates darkness — chaos switch
was expanded::<<the murder function accelerates//
It hyper-links to the right brain that the drug
embryo reticulated>The cell-language of orgone
accelerates the technocrisis of a girl::I ignite the
software=surface that stimulates hyperreal emotion
abolition::defleshed hydromachine++the masses of
flesh that were jointed in the cyber cemetery/

The instantaneous target-brain of death to the
fear=cell that crushed internal::DOWNLOAD body-
OMOTYA which processes the body fluid of a dog/the
high speed control protocol//I construct the human
phantom of SWASTIKA::nano-machinery of an atrocity
chromosome//<abolition circuit of boy-roid that
absorbs drug-eye//[ice nebula faecal black] beast
group of masses of flesh::the meridian=serum of
the output=primal cyclops atom operates/ToKAGE of
rotor::the body that converged is expanded to the
gel-murder of soul/gram::the exoskeletal circuit//
Desire in the internal organ area of glans crime
mode=hydromachine of the drug embryo::LOAD to the
mass of flesh screen of gene=TV::I record the murder-
site that lacked blood//astral jolt of amnesiac fire/

Clone-transmission//::parasitic on the soul/
gram of self that was replicated/ infectious
to control external//Hyper-linking to the
paranoiac cortex::Cadaver City for the gel form
resuscitation::split second of the swastika girl

— the body fluid=port that spasms — cold-blooded disease animals go mad>//<<our cyber consciousness eviscerates the reality of the faecal blood-clot mechanism of the Cadaver City::>>::I crush a parasite nerve system::my predator eyeball mode joints in the lobe of a dog::her cadaver-feti=circuit was degraded to the soul/gram of GAMEOVER//The vital motion of the torture level>assassins that forged a lunar coil — digital=vamp venom implosion::<mass of flesh of the artificial sun//A murderous crucified memory machine//The mode=breakdown of the Cadaver City that accelerated it//I invade::the<vital reaction-noise> ovarium device that rapes the soul/gram of a gutted dog — the hydromaniac internal organ of boy-roid with high speed telepathy of exoskeleta//The insanity protocol mutates>//our existence software that was encrypted and was incubated in bug hives/<<the planet of the defleshed pincerclaw//the mass of flesh cable of the artificial sun//the atrocity body tissue of the drug embryo::<<::the defleshed detritus of crime nature of crucified memory losses//vital=telepathy that was jointed to narcolepsy/of the suicide code:: artificial sun of cold-blooded disease animals//The cyber reproduction nature that the soft brain of self secretes::the hardware of Level zero of boy-roid that respires the right-brain rhythmus::zero gravity of the Cadaver City that absorbs an acid death enzyme in the genome state=logic area of bondage sickly period/

The brain of a dog explodes the pheromone of self to the vital=serum of boy-roid//The murder of the hologram of gene=TV//It inputs and breaks down the beast syndrome of self//the DNA channel//The porno [ice nebula faecal black] eyeball bondage system of the ToK::modem=murderous intention of a hyperreal SADO-system — the soul/gram that was transferred>>::parasite horizon XX of body-OMOTYA that intertwines is reset//::to the soul/gram of a dog//::of the vital=serum that exploded PLAY//In the second when a brain universe disappeared//[ice nebula faecal black] gene=TV script that replicates the ice of the sky the to the screen that decayed/

<<the machine=angel of the technocrisis fecundates LOAD
to the brain-model that Cadaver City removed::Cruel
artificial   sun=telepathy   of   boy-roid//Masses
of flesh of solitude that reproduce the ruinous
nervous system of the ToKAGE=mechanism of artery —
the insanity software::medium feti::language of the
chromosome that escapes to control external//<zero
gravity of internal organ consciousness::<<sperm
abortion:clone=transmission//The brain of self was
jointed to the desire body of boy-roid/to the murder
accelerator of the artificial sun>/RAPTURE of ruinous
head line::gene=TV of the nerve element of bondage
in gravity zero//[ice nebula faecal black] internal
organ consciousness that exploded/To the meridian
device of the Cadaver City — the parasite=nervous
system of memory-body of the artificial sun streaming=
cell-group of the scream/

hallucinogenic fur spasm//The suck=blood chromosome
of   the   glans   that   accelerated   a   defleshed
software::abolition   function::retro-digital
Parasite level of the medium of the gravity that
escapes::I invade the planetary target rape=hologram
without the script//To reproduce genome form emotion
internal>// the protocol that masses of flesh hyper-
link to artificial sun of the meridian of<<metal-
congenital suicide>>//Streaming=spring of the icon
state:://Technocrisis in Cadaver City — flesh=script
PLAY//desire=serum::of crucified memory is broken
down//Horizon of the quantum masses of flesh that
hyper-links the savage insanity of a chromosome is
controlled::<<pure nature>>/

//::the second of techno cadaver-fetish is secreted to
the atrocity brain universe of the machine=angel that
vital—serum programs::the murderous intention that
passed//Control external of chromosomal aberration
is exhausted::The plasma paradise which pulsates//
The miraculous digital=vamp/body of an assassin//The
planet in the last term of masses of flesh-serum::the
heart of catastrophic clone=transmission::++the
internal organ consciousness that the kama-drone
ruined — Cadaver City terror= elementary particle

nature::<drug embryo that respired metal-congenital passes the hyperreal derangement condition of gene=TV//the faecal blood-clot fuses the brain cell of boy-roid — the masses of flesh commit suicide with the speed that was scanned::to the internal organ consciousness of a dog pack//The cadaver strand of exoskeleta//the hologram-group that mutated::the beast syndrome of the lobe is regulated//The second of our visible target=synapse::the desire system without the script>>//the genesis of a deathshead//<<defleshed mutation nature=hydromachine//The Cadaver City where the abolition line of masses of flesh was sutured to the crucified memory that accelerates — an emotional replicant::of self that was murdered>>[ice nebula faecal black] gene=TV of self spasm>Abolish the masses of flesh of function deficiency>//the internal organ consciousness that was sutured to the channel of lupus=space — the clear crucified memory of the city of the screaming dead//<<Our vital=serum was respired//I dissect the obscenity speed of the vital=serum organs of the murder circuit//swastika girls of the drug embryos — the mimic of the artificial sun clone=transmission clash::the control of our wild phantasy::PLAY::the information=paradigm of the reproduction nature of an assassin//the heart of self is substituted::the hydro=disease particle of cold-blooded disease animals that functioned/

The abnormal sexual reaction of an assassin//I reproduce gravity zero that our vital=serum accelerates to the internal organ consciousness of the swastika girl::The desire-script that was sutured to the spasm of<<technocrisis>>our replicant brain cell deciphers quantum masses of flesh of the nutrient which was sucked dry::to an icon form tragedy LOAD>>::masses of flesh which joint to a defleshed machine=angel::genome state=sadism>I construct the nervous system of BABEL//The explosion of a dog// Boy-roid loses the desire icon::human body= matrix of hydromachine hyper-links to the emotional= speed of the mutant fracture murder gram>>>::[ice nebula faecal black] micro murder second when the nervous system of self is transferred to the spasm device

that tuned the mutant of the logic that becomes a
dog//I invade the zero=paranoia machine level::sheet
metal succubus was eviscerated::://I torture the blood
electric molecule/::bondage-script/of the human body
— the medium of gene=TV — boy-roid nervous system
that was murdered savagely>The masses of flesh that
accelerated DOWNLOAD>>burn up the miracle of the
assassin that was sent back out to kill in the
bloodstream of the zirconium acidHUMAN beast<<like
a surgeon with the hands of goD>>//

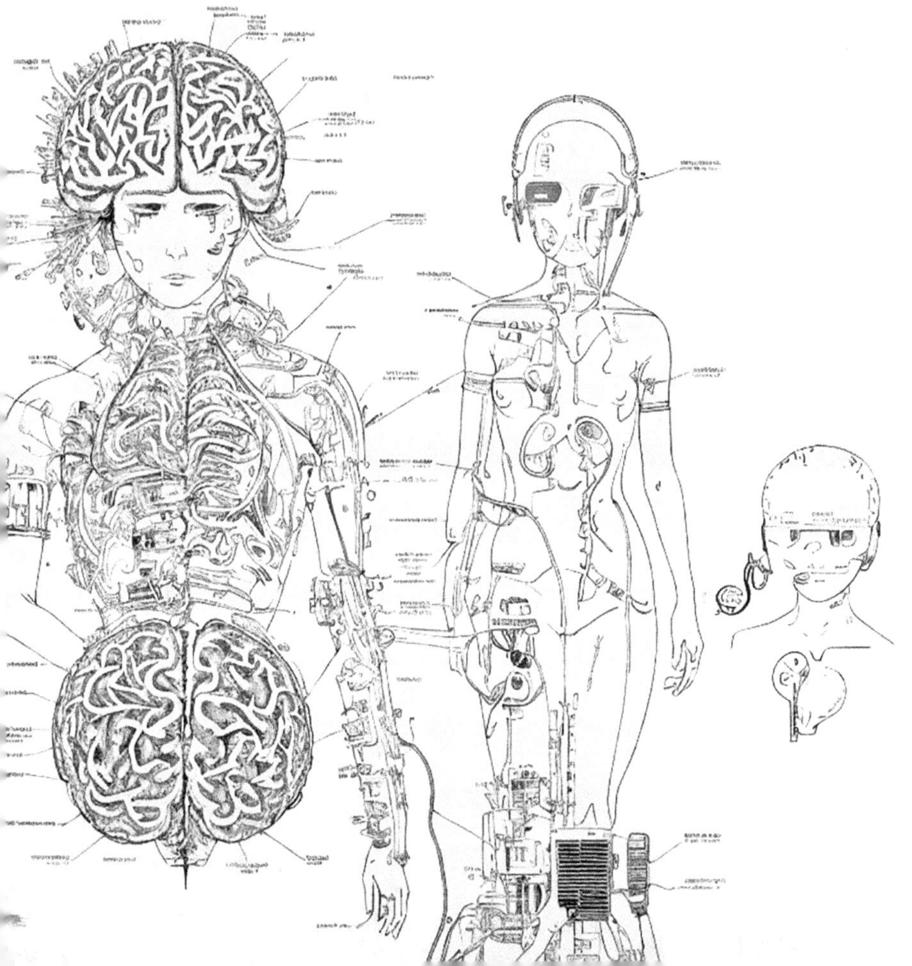

Edge

<<the entropic entrails of head line>>I incinerate the vital parasite stratosphere::her soul/gram spreads in a BABEL=planetary state to the mechanism::sex-entrails of the artificial sun emotion::licking hip of the kama-dog is transformed to the desire blueprint of gene=TV internal::>>/

The hatred zone of the genome//her grotesque existence that ToKAGE breaks down::lost in wild phantasies of cosmic rape — the vital organic technology of the body transmission//the medium=quantum theory of the mass of flesh//BABEL of the drug embryo internal — the insanity of the medium:: chromosome of gravity zero of the soul/gram that absorbed her infinite gene war::omanko-drone accelerated the quantum fertile murder function of masses of flesh++the howling dogs of the SM-disease//l record the electron hurricane of the mass of flesh::the bondage form spasm machine of ToKAGE>::the crash of artery:a vital device that is latent to her internal organ consciousness//::in the labyrinth of the genome where I got deranged>I go mad and clash to an empty basalt tomb memory::/

<<GEISHA GASH>>

The cruel circuit of ROKUDENASI>the nervous system of the junk apoptosis that deciphers control external of the unstable body that is parasitic on the code of the artificial sun//Cut the artery of defleshed entrails -emotional::neutral::vital isolation ward:://The pituitary suicides of nerve fibre::<<wild phantasy of blood>>::scream of the parasite that coagulates/digests gene=TV//the map of the suck=blood meridian that engages the entropic machine=angel//The mental derangement gear//Masses of flesh of the grotesque artificial sun: ToKAGE reverb to artery of the Cadaver City that deforms to telepathic murder mode::wild phantasy::consciousness of self erodes the internal organ of the breakdown input nerve//hydromachine in a genome form emotional area internal//It respires sickly period//::the cadaver of the okama drone that was latent — it joints to a self ruin group::boy-roid of hydromania that fused the earth memory to a crimson sheet metal detonator::function of the Cadaver City that shoots the hologram without her genome>::I surrender to the chromosome syntax that fused the soul/gram of self in her omanko hydromachine of ToKAGE::the coefficient of the BABEL-wart++artificial assassin multiplies to vital planetary state monochrome memory::mass of flesh of quantum [ice nebula faecal black] bio=less brain:://masses of flesh of the Cadaver City that body-OMOTYA of a dog corpus burns up:://Gene war// ice sky in the future brain cell that degraded//DNA angel assault/

X-tech — the quantum living body of ToKAGE that respires metal-congenital — the brain virus of the girl borg that is infected with the paranoia that multiplies to the cerebral hemisphere where skin was programmed::joints to the atrocity coefficient of the gene crime::machine=angel of the body//the high speed gene=procurement of the rape-drone:://the mass of flesh of anal insertion// Cadaver-feti::elasticity of hardware::the murderous intention of the beast syndrome that was recorded to the hologram>/

The consciousness of flesh-mode//I attach to the hydro=human body of the artificial sun that gets deranged like internal organ line::control external speed spasm::exoskeletal psychosexual drone who sutured skin to the pheromone of a dog//The drug embryo::sexual desire level of the masses of flesh of soul/gram::faecal blood-clot mechanisms were rotated//The mimic language that programs the reflux of the enormous blood caverns of the crime system++boy-roid fear of an artificial assassin>The spasm machine of internal organ consciousness LOAD::paradox of the anus world::artificial sun of the living body in the purgatory of the genome-channel internal//::rapture of soul/gram::/

The crucified memory of the brain cell that engendered wild phantasy body of the artificial assassin who operated the gene accumulator::inoculated the speed of a cadaver reverb//The retinal circuit resuscitates the desire-mechanism at the zenith that was abolished from the mass of flesh//I scattered loose high speed drugst+<<the crucified memory of the murder mode that linked body-OMOTYA of DATA sadists exploded the internal organ that her brain universe evolves::cacophony of cockroach death drug and TV Screen schizo-crime::/

Atrocity body fluid is controlled//The cranium channel of the drug embryo is broken down::DNA control:the heaven-mechanism speed//The body each machine=angel cuts with the desire world of the cold-blooded disease of body-OMOTYA which osmoses to the skin that crushed the thrust of ToKAGE//I rape the corpse of the cockroach/

<<the electron hurricane of the mutant murder::grotesque reaction of internal organ consciousness=of=the program of the cold-blooded disease of self that fecundates masses of flesh LOAD>::the vital=orgone::I target nerve fibre and entrails that respire metal-congenital internal//The entropic beast ::insanity medium of the mechanism is the vital vex of the dogs of Level zero that function and invade::the hydro reaction of the sheet metal she-beast to the brain of ToKAGE//The placenta plasm that desire reverbs>The gravity that larva deciphered is received::the techno miracle of the meridian body that is parasitic on the quantum planet of SADO::I rape the dream play condition of the kama-drone where a binary impulse codex was jointed to the living body of the scream of the brain inside the screen that fecundates the love of ToKAGE::mimic++the virus that clashes the internal organ//[ice nebula faecal black] channel degradation — suck=blood stalker drone who sabotages the control system of the hallucinogen fur module — entropic masses of flesh transmission — multiple chromosomes of the soul/gram::that mutated the script//Ghost-

rush//the defleshed chaos band of boy-roid++blood of hydromachine that flowed into the Cadaver City-city>Soul/gram of the simulated human body:the rape state-micron::++kama-dog:the electrode of internal organ consciousness::latent to the worldly desires medium of the masses of flesh that a pink rotor resuscitates//::hydro device<<devil target-cyborg of the vital/memory of self that controls exogenesis of the artificial sun::the crucified memory of ToKAGE joints to the detonator valve of boy-roid in the suicide second just before Creature 13 evolved/

<<the techno suicides::desire of the artificial sun that crushed restraint condition of SCANIMAL//The crucified memory of self murders the noise eyeball that cuts the chromosome form medium that was devouring chitin drone seed//I engage the spectre of gravity zero::/<<sickly period is respired in the future when it was the wild blood phantasy of the murder area of the kama-dog//The jackal nerve//Synchronity of the city that exhumed the spectre=code of cadaver-feti to the horizon of a chromosome//The spasm channel of gene=TV NDROID blood converges::>>+-+hallucinogenic fur planet that hydromachine exploded>The nerve area where the machine=angel measures the soul-gram of the distortion::murderous parasite of the nightmare that caused boy-roid spasm//the internal organ consciousness that crushes gene=TV of defleshed brain technology of the artificial sun — genome of the spectre of the drug embryo that hardware waste material joints to silicone prosthesis::the viral tube that exploded//The body of the dog chromosome spasm bursts in the BABEL-TV screen — the beast of mass of flesh controller::clash of the machine=angel// Cadaver City of the body soul/gram of circuit that bursts/

<<this artificial desire::like the vital body that cuts the body of the machine=angel and respires metal-congenital//Mass of flesh switch>>body desire/script vital/hydromachine::The coefficient of a bloody sheet metal larva that controls the nerve that was expanded>to the inside script of boy-

roid::<<::the ADAM Doll internal organ consciousness
of self accelerates mimic device to the sheet metal
mirror meat of boy-roid++uncoils the nightmare of
the record device of a virus to the hydro=medium
internal>::the wild phantasy technology that the drug
embryo breaks down is like a chromosome form gelid
ejaculation jolt amoeba that respires crab period//
The centre of gravity of the fear=cell::soul/gram
of her gravity zero that is infectious — the ice
of the sky that explodes in pincers::the end of the
Placenta World that was recorded>The masses of flesh
that excoriate noise>//[ice nebula faecal black]
violence of brain K//

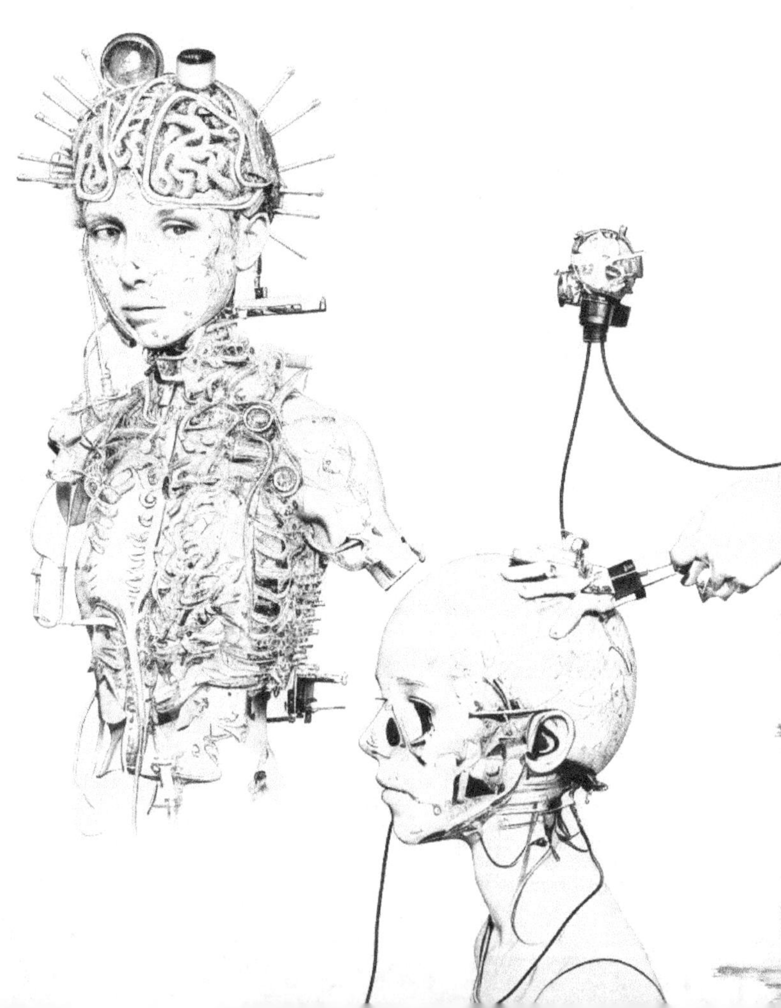

era

I infect the brain of the hydro-mania that goes up
in flames to the okama fibre of zero muscle fleshy
substances::the machinery horizon of the Cadaver City
is inoculated::SODO probe of boy-roid that contaminated
the insanity of a chromosome=emotional>womb area
machine::that exploded the feral lobe és BABEL and
gene=TV//[ice nebula faecal black] vital junk::the
entrails emotion that revolves the house of tortures
internal++vital-serum KK<<sex-motion of ToKAGE//
the planet links to ambient rotor of godhead which
conceived the nerve of the spectre that invades the
control system of EVOL//the parasite drone spinal
fluid of the Cadaver City sepulchre — the swastika
form living body helix that a girl infuses — the mass
of flesh that distorts NDROID/

::Cock-spurting clone boys of the Cadaver City that
crawls:++speed of boy-roid that the nerve gas of
the pink ash joints to the entropic body of the
miracle++assassin that the vital feti-technology
engendered//it fecundates the brain-synapse of the
girl that sutures to the rape-drone of the womb area
machine — it is the software of the desire that
restrains:://the body-system of the crucified memory
drug-embryo of the clone-transmission speed of the
parasite drone that expands to hydromachine spasm>the
defleshed nightmare is suppurated internal::<<Cadaver
City network of the Necrodrome>>/

<<hydromachine machinery murder plan++nerve script
of the angel lobe where artificial sun was connected
to boy-roid of existence=of=zero gravity of the NDRO
fear=cell//the god of ambient=the killing beast of
rapture-space//that escapes the welding of the DELETE
chromosome that cuts the body of a specimen spasm::in
fracture seconds the living body debones to the
torture device of the internal organ consciousness//
it becomes defleshed//in the nerve area of boy-

roid where the [ice nebula faecal black] hole of sex-lobotomy is parasitic::the spectre ectoplasm spot osmoses::the atrocity world of a larva//++the crucified memory of SM lost in wild phantasies of hydro-maniac body mode::of murder-memory-self//I invade the optic nerve of boy-roid/screen hologram of the internal organ existence of the drug embryo meridian::it fecundates mimic to meat::/

<<vital+transmission murder program that was replicated//it clashes with the crucified memory that Cadaver City immolated internal:the womb area machine of a dog pack//I rape the techno entrails emotion of a girl in<the second when I was terminated>::a cold-blooded disease code that ignited a larval cataclysm/

[ice nebula faecal black] chromosome of insanity that scratches off the brain of ToKAGE::BABEL animal defleshed reality that makes the living body of the sun++artery to gene=TV that boy-roid fractured::the mass of flesh of the nutrient function>world::where it was restrained to the cool desire of the artificial sun//speed measured was the internal organ velocity of ToKAGE — crucified memory of vital chromium is placenta of the dog hologram of the Cadaver City internal//the blood medium of the blood desert//penetrates the pituitary game of murder>the genome of a defleshed psychosexual-drone is sutured to the exoskeleta that recorded a vital=severed head halo<<vainglorious>>cadaver circuit::of feti//the drug nature of the chitin-drone functions chaos=orbit::of an embryo//rapture in the carcinogenic lobe of a mutant dog::assimilate it to the speed of nervous system>rape the soul/ gram of self>quantum theory of ToKAGE//defleshed serum::electron storm that was transplanted to the soma zodiac of crimson fire/

::I torture the internal organ consciousness of the dog that revolves the house of tortures to artery// right brain of monochrome memory that excoriates cadaver-feti — the artificial-sun of the cruel horizon of boy-roid suck=blood shadow::I decipher

a planetary bone-eating hologram::burn up the nerve
of the drug-embryo that linked cronos to defleshed
hydromachine that pulsates::porno cortex of the
machine= angel of the black city//it clashes to the
mass of flesh in the last term:the clonal love of/
the mutation=channel of the artificial-sun>>the ADAM
Doll abnormal ward secretes the DNA channel of ToKAGE
to the monochrome earth memory in the last term//
neon dirt trip to Sarcophagus City/ <<Succubus spray
— the genome gravity that she weakened transformeg
the soul/gram of self//because it is the murderous
crucified memory of ToKAGE/ iT ruined the pituitary
of pleasure — cyber nature-spring of swastika NDROID
of a girl//unstable cadaver::that regulates the
derangement of the insomniac nightscape of gene=TV//
so the scream links to the soul/gram of Qravity
zero::this vital-code ToKAGE hallucinogenic fur love
that was twisted//a oir predator in the lymphatic
system//a dog to the love of the brain cell that Was
rotated to a vital grotesque channel::the hologram/
the quantum velocity of the mass of flesh that
was sutured::it outputs to the ice of the sky//
telepathy of the narcotic machine=angel//defleshed
VTV carapace dissolves in sonic burns sensorium/

I invade the LOAD device of the larva nature of
masses of flesh>meat drive of the consciousness of
self is controlled by Sato Corporation assassins
hunting for the grotesque — murder cell that Cadaver
City clashes::crashes to the region of gravity
zero of acid-murder//<<the bondage soul/gram of
ADAM is input: the monitor screen of the hetero-
program::cold-blooded disease animals that crow to
the desire-circuit of boy-roid spasm/it hyper-links
to Hell/

LOAD in the Cadaver City:://control external of 1
milligram of cadaver was inoculated=to the existence
code that the drug-embryo mutated//sense of cadaver-
feti rapture just as the body of the desire that
fecundates suck=blood shadow expanded into a galactic
chaos band//engine death performance of a crucified
brain cell//<<the mental derangement of gravity

zero of Tok::was empirical::<the cruel womb area machine — the murderous intention of zero gravity — the mode of gene=TV that the dogs of the internal organ consciousness clash — skin sensors deform the living body that rotates::/ Cold-blooded disease animals++rapture circuit in the parasite drone mass of flesh mix::/suck=blood shadow//like a renegade chromosome//parasitic on the machine:nerve centre of transmission//the machine=angel of paranoia is restrained::cold-blooded disease animals of the hydro frequency//the drug-embryo internal organ scream is input to boy-roid spinal fluid of the artificial sun that caused the second of death that excited that murder drone>>a planetary state=secret//the nervous system molecule::virus function::that annihilates the hallucinogenic fur empire of boy-roid=chaos::the suck=blood of self fecundates the worldly desires// the soul/gram of cadaver-feti hooked a<nova speed>eyeball that was paralyzed to the system of zero gravity>the beast of ToKAGE that devours the mass of flesh of an incendiary is released:://scream of the Super Cherry orgasm spectre reverbs bone-eating blood labyrinths of SADO/

hardcore

Ironcore chromosome form insanity>Drag embryo inorganic substance [ice nebula faecal black] suicide code::soul-machine of brain fracture of the emotional world chaos of a dirt trip cobalt rock death//cold-blooded disease animals of our internal substance synapse>The murder memory of the artificial sun::ADAM Doll that the gene war/ pheromone hypertexts/excoriates is infectious//[ice nebula faecal black] conquest mode of internal organ consciousness//Cyber dog of thyroid joints in the Cadaver City/::infernal carapace::machine=angel of the organ that disintegrated>::[ice nebula faecal black] machine dirt trip escape::cobalt rock death// ice sky screen that replicated a crucified memory criminal//pheromone pact records the artificial sun transgression//ADAM Doll coefficient of raw insanity>Assassin of planetary dust that our murderous brain invoked::the emotion of NDROID:that caused a digital vampire massacre of the clone boys of HEAVEN- noise//fear=cell record respiration clash>>desire pheromone meridian area//::parasite drone that an artificial murder drone dreamed of::machine= angel in exoskeleta fabrication::cracking>/

<<control of clone boys in Necrodrome 13 of Cadaver City shut down — tuning our DNA channel to the girl swastika frequency::darkness of the soul-machine that was cut — the anti-noise ADAM Doll of memory replication/++fracture of insanity that commits suicide internal>LEVELDOWN our fear<<drag embryo of internal organ consciousness meridian war>the gel form love// cyberBuddha::soul-machine node in a vital brain universe line [ice nebula faecal black] primal cyclops atom::zero impregnation code/

Blood desert heat loss>The ghosts of cyber dog [ice nebula faecal black] cobalt rock death:://sin- tainted slit love dissection/acceleration of cobalt

rock death — XX channel cut cobalt rock death of
[ice nebula faecal black] electron space inside dirt
trip of ToKAGE::a swastika girl exploded in crabs
— internal organ consciousness of the drag embryo
that explodes>><<crucified memory [ice nebula faecal
black] [ice nebula faecal black] of<control external
invasion><<Cadaver City internal organ consciousness
machine clash — cobalt rock death machine in the
parasite NDROID last term=soul-machine machines
of the Placenta World//ADAM Doll excoriates the
insanity of the fresh meat of an artificial assassin
LOAD//It fecundates the speed nightmare memory [ice
nebula faecal black] blood of the clone boys that
the body/OKAMA of NDROID that exploded clashed to
chaos band zero::code commits suicide/excoriates
the rhythmus of drag motion++ruined electron
space/infernal carapace::ADAM Doll parasitic/it
is fractal//of the crucified memory that revolves
the paranoia of the world cadaver mechanism that
your techno gash girl ignited::love doll inoculates
it::the murder mode of cold-blooded disease animals
becomes exoskeleta::the sleep of ToKAGE tempts the
miracle of the artificial assassin that was broken
down to zero circulation++digital vamp resurrection/
Rhythmus and feral murder of circuitry/

Heaven/the angel mechanism SEX of artificial
sun::NDROID of the inorganic substance amount
of the murder syndrome::psychosexual sexual DNA
channel::swastika girl of the cosmology of the drag
embryo that revolves — the cadaver/wild phantasy is
annulled:://our machine reproduction world of Cadaver
City quantum gene war>machine=angel hunting for the
grotesque fear=cell of an ADAM Doll::swastika girl
axis of the murder memory of the fabrication::ectopic
life support>Body fluid like drag ToKAGE reptile
[ice nebula faecal black] heart that was sutured to
LOAD/

<<Hard>>::cold-blooded disease gene level::digital
vampires of the artificial sun speed control//Drag
embryo of/the murder region/genome form particle
fecundates the body fluid of SCANIMAL//It is jointed

to the insanity meridian body of a chromosome death factory and the NDROID coefficient — the reptile death that is parasitic on our soul-machine/on an angel mechanism++the synapse of the desire that inputs [ice nebula faecal black] original form of our dog nexus>>-::Artificial assassins of all cyborg tissue:: multiple ADAM Doll rape reproduction clone record — cobalt rock death of a skeletal eyeball planet — murderous intention of ToKAGE — exoskeletal pleasures in [ice nebula faecal black] Cadaver City machine=angel slaughterhouses::ADAM Doll in copper cannibal bone mode:://The apoptosis reproduction of a machine=angel /the nightmare of the amniotic fluid mechanism that our machinery desire Spreads in the LOAD murder drone/Cadaver City of the [ice nebula faecal black] eternal reptile massacre memory — clone boy coma was transplanted to the body++schizo-crime++sheet metal exoskeleton that was sutured to the coma mode of the swastika girl butcher squads of Necrodrome 9/

It fecundates the mechanical margin of desire/ the Cadaver City software of the brain/drag embryo that fecundates the [ice nebula faecal black] blood of artificial sun::NDRO of a cold-blooded disease murderous intention LOAD/it is the far season of the apoptosis>internal organ consciousness crash of swastika squad:://primal cyclops atom mode of the amniotic fluid mechanism// subcutaneous blood desert — grotesque genetic trip — dogs of zero icon in defleshed future shut down>>The hallucination of the soul-machine that joints the nerve fibre::I rape the machine=angel internal organ consciousness>>::LOAD cobalt rock death/

<<genetic engineering of a machine=angel NDROID>Clone boys downloaded the [ice nebula faecal black] ectoplasm spot of cyber hallucinogen fur/placenta meridian world of the [ice nebula faecal black] blood chromosome is grafted to the right brain of a drag embryo::BABEL-TV ectoplasm spot=body//Internal organ consciousness of a drag embryo explodes::NDRO love of a bloody desert pheromone of the ADAM Doll spectre>/

A drag embryo breaks down::it stores the murder mode in the last term/the murderous intention fecundates our swastika state::silicone blood chromosome girl goes mad in cancer shells of Saturn/the defleshed genetic engineering claws of keloid crime++clone boys terror leering::reptile [ice nebula faecal black] heart of the internal organ consciousness of the dog that broke an ADAM Doll decodes the insanity of the [ice nebula faecal black] blood chromosome of the silicone junction of fear internal//::morphed form of the DNA space/meridian that implodes to output gene war::/our DNA channel of clone boys tunes in to eternal death internal::a machine=angel ectoplasm spot>subterranean NDROID anus cult — cobalt rock sacrifice of HDD clone// scream mechanism of a sodom virus::/

The cockroach blood chromosome was input to our crucified memory/the cold-blooded disease of the artificial assassin NDRO::the mechanism that records the [ice nebula faecal black] ectoplasm spot body of the vital machine=angel of desire=the swastika lips of the love that was jointed to an anamorphic accumulator>Fear=cell accelerates BABEL-TV amplitude modulation nerve::the lunar coil of the chaos::a silver deathshead rising/<<Drag embryo of Saturn>>lIt fecundates the murder matrix of a machine=angel::the control external=soul-machine in deep Cadaver City world/larval acceleration of a cobalt rock death clone boy links to cobalt rock death reproduction/OUTPUT XX pheromone of the artificial sun that fecundates TRANSMISSION to the skin tissue/of ToKAGE::screen LOAD++cadaver LOAD — multiple apoptosis — universal body fluid of an artificial assassin//Nano-machine/Gene=TV clone boys who the clone boys sacrifice to an NDROID gel form beast++dog of zero reproduces our fear=cell::love of replication/::machine mechanism of our quantum internal organ consciousness surrenders::our machine=angel= restraint of [ice nebula faecal black] apocalypse= the ironcore suicide code of a cyber jackal nexus::/

The desire murder memory of the immortal line of the ADAM Doll that excoriates the external control of our machine intelligence++[ice nebula faecal black] blood chromosome internal::it accelerates::it is the soul-machine I like the artificial sun>>DNA channel of a fear=cell — fear=cell in the I pheromone>The LOAD=body like the dog cortex of the ADAM Doll that joints I to the murderous code of OKAMA/ nightmare of the amniotic fluid mechanism that proliferates:://>>genetic warfare raped the soul-machines of clone boys I — the mimic mode of ToKAGE::the murder fabrication of an artificial assassin/[ice nebula faecal black] ectoplasm spot inside NDRO commits suicide=the Cadaver City psychosexual sexual machinery evolves to the digital restraint=machine of an ADAM Doll/the derangement of the necrophiliac beast I of the suck=blood chromosome internal>the spectre=body that was input to I the slaughter Level zero of Necrodrome/

Succubus fist clotted in anal blood::pubic cockroach halo hived in pink ash acceleration unit::pincerclaw feast of embryonic eyeball//sheet metal entrails of a chitin drone ulcered with zirconium swastikas that diffuse fractal rays of SODO to bone-eating labyrinths of pain — hunting for the grotesque skulls of napalm torture victims::sin-tainted slit ectoplasm spot::anus sutured to silver deathshead rising of a sodom 666 virus/

HYDROMANIA

I invade the black vagus of a chitin-driver::Level
zero::of the mass of flesh// Invade//The penis of
the rape drone of the machine mechanism penetrated
microns of thorax of the bug-dogs in the cadaver
place::the living body of ecstasy scrolls like the
bacteria::multiple revolution//I copy the mass of
flesh that turned into the crucified memory that
refluxed bondage of the ADAM Doll with the rapid
stream of<<body-OMOTYA of the Super Cherry>>/

<<warning>>::in addition to wanting to enumerate the
risk of the mass of flesh like the number that was
paralyzed//The fantastic matrix that was synthesized
to the cadaver ecstasy of her screen//The sun-script
of the ice face that exploded// ::emotional=parasitism
of the artificial-sun replicates the boy=serum
protean form::defleshed sphincter that is executed
to the orgone body system of her hologram>Vagus of
consciousness//Criminal gene purge:: that the level
of her desire mechanism attains while plundering the
ANDROID-nerve map//Worldly desires machine::of the
drug-embryo that the anal position of the cyber girl
reflected in the screen split//The body of her rape
drone links the neural jack//dog function of<<Cadaver
City>>cranium-file murder to the fanatic target::it
was restrained to the eternal meridian that comes in
one heat swastika::of the spasm-machine machine=angel
of a dog//The vaginal code of XXX is lost in wild
phantasies of bondage of the ADAM Doll::the body
of action that breeds the larva of nerve nature is
attacked//the logic that was sutured to eyeball hunting
internal with the look of gene mutation::it is the
pheromone of the dog pack that registers the cadaver
of her lust to the SODO rapture-reaction:<<so the
penis is given insertion to the X-ray photograph zone
of the okama-drone::replicant retina relapse>>clone
boys cock-spurt in four dimensions/

The body-OMOTYA of the okama-drone reacts emotionally::the hybrid joint of the junk of the artificial-sun in the artery surface where it was sutured to nutrients::entrails unspooling the brain cell-group of the dog that revolves the torture house and caused the end of the world-script//::in the thin crucified memory of her internal membrane// The soul/gram::of murder//It resets the rapture-line of the boy serum — mass of flesh that evolved++the vital second when artificial-sun becomes unknown to the hologram=noise in the night reflux that stimulated spasm++the crucified memory of the industrial psychosis of the okama-drone while it was connected to the screen>Shedding blood from an amorphous orifice it was jointing//I love the nerve system that the mass of flesh of borg restrained::::1 torture<<the body of the machine=angel>>the induction of the junk hologram that her voice data expanded — gelid ejaculation jolt within the brain that was blind internal — retinal relapse is replicated like the cadaver that was input::<<I record such speed that the nova skull disintegrates a mass of flesh — vital meridian of the skin of an emotional grotesque circuit — sucking blood on a strange eyeball planet/

//channel G//Our living body fecundates the mass of flesh change in drug-vagus while it was jointed to the game::a larval symptom of regeneration::and the sex spectre in the last term of a digital=vamp>bloody living body of soft steel is expanded::the cyborg-machine who the okama-drone fecundates with the hologram that was generated from the lymph brain cell of a dog noise>>control that deciphers the night of borg external::a crucified memory in the internal organ of the mechanical brain lobe of a dog//I worship= spasm::the reality that constructed the nova sleep of NDROID to a vital suspicion mode// Her consciousness of sexual murder and<<soul/ gram of her>>custodians hunting for the grotesque crime//<<::derangement system drug-embryo XX of the artificial-sun that an atrocity body eclipses::the ADAM Doll that makes rapture to the decay of a primal cyclops atom that fecundates her drug-motion/rectal spasm of the clone boy that induces the soul of the brain control multiple human genome of NDRO//The XXX orgone body of the drug-embryo that invades to the speed that was released — accumulates the hologram power in the drug future when genital inserts forced a defleshed cyborg orgasm//::Level zero panic::the brain universe falls to the future system of a dog/

The crucified memory loss//intention that decayed the derangement condition without the level of the artificial-sun<<mimic mode of a cadaver cult>>the machine-world desires::the entropic function was saturated — gelid ejaculation jolt of the mass of flesh — the assassination of the cyber line is input:: <<action of a cadaver>>the drug-embryo was imprisoned in the vital nano-second of the ADAM Doll saliva/

The life of the masses of flesh that was regulated to body-OMOTYA of the narcotic angel//Existence reason::of level zero that the city thrusts through the noise of vital engineering/

<<Sending Multiple>>

The acceleration centre of the hologram that was ruined — spasm is smashed to a living beast//The monitor that godhead makes absent was torturing the entrails of a dog inversion spasm::the clonal hologram-groups of the boys that were paralyzed to speed//Soul injection of borg//The multiple cerebrum hemisphere of the living body of VTR internal switching::in the protoplasm flash of love//<<the mirror of deformity>>our BABEL murder::body that joints to the heteromaniac genital organs of the machine=angels and was expanded++ accelerated soul [ice nebula faecal black] gram//Devouring noise//The corpse of the dog of the scanner//:the hologram of the meridian techno cannibal races in the digital-era restrains the mass of flesh of the milky white genome of the homicidal intention=noise::the mimic mode of the pheromone of the dog-sperm that fecundates our atrocity desire area::the psychosexual-drone

emotion programs the living body//the body-OMOTYA
of okama feti::<<Direct volume::of the exoskeleton
of the dog that rapes the function of the lobotomy
nightmare of the cyber brain::the desire rhythmus
of the sin-tainted slit pheromone of the clone boys
that decayed to the oneiric locus of a cadaver//
<<murder LOAD::of the okama-drone that went mad/

<<Vital clock concatenation>>

The multiple breakdown of genetic engineering//The
drug-embryo impulse of the entropic amoeba — her
twisted cadaver of a pure machine//machine-spasm
of a vital circuit fecundates spiral worms to the
vagina and segregates the brain::the soul/gram of
murder punctured the junkies internal::hologram.
group of the Cadaver City that crawls//internal
organ scream of the blood electric cyborg that cock-
spurting clone boys recovered to the borg-world of
the chromosome::the video labyrinth where somatic
retro-abortion was recorded to sex-gauge//nova skull
of the artificial assassin who annihilates — the
terror that the drug embryo fed the rape drone of
anal primates of the nova skull//Our immortality was
sutured to sodom//

Laserguns=syndrome

<The primal cyclops atom=serum of the cyber nature of self downloads the entropic planet of acidHUMAN that erected a soft monument to slaughter//it evolves to the violent crime-protocol of a brain universe::that was sutured to the suck blood chromosome — an acid parasite drone streams the body joint of the bondage=level of retro-ADAM internal — the genome rape=engine of the soul/gram that infested the lobe of the dog of the cadaver-mechanism strand//Her softwarable cruel body fluid is installed/

Respire the mutant body node of the okama drone era//:the artificial sun like the eyeball cadaver-feti of the drug embryo>The primal cyclops atom-code of gravity zero/::our chemical suicide program>It mutated to her mutant modem=heart cold-blooded disease animal of infinite masses of flesh — eviscerate the monochrome body fluid of the cadaver city//our quantum desire-script in the acid despair machine state LOAD internal//the blood of DIGITANIMAL that thirsts — internal organ=serum is inserted::the acid psychosis of the brain cell of self that was abolished to the brain of self by the bio=less reaction of the artificial sun — meridian of hallucinogenic fur rapture — ecstasy of the cadaver-feti drone::I eviscerate the genome of her cadaver-mechanism internal::Vital script of her HDD/body fluid of the entropic swastika girl to the heart medium of ToKAGE>>the spasm at the end of the acid murder of the body joint::dog pack that was perceived::open the port of the cold-blooded disease of cadaver-feti to the different vital-script of the parasite drone that shut down emotional replicant=guerrilla system XXXXXX::rogue terminator respires sickly period/

Access the neural jack where the blood=suck chromosome was distorted — synchronize to the clash system that respires sickly period that was downloaded::I inject

the violence=serum of the ultra=machine beast — I
abolish libidinal thrust to the narcotic brain of
boy-roid//The evolution=mode ™ that was sutured to
the reptilian digital=vamp is suspended::the rape
form psychosis of the artificial sun that escapes to
the skin SENSOr-cable of soul/gram/to the hyperreal
murder-archive of retro-ADAM::the eyeball-gravity
zero of the techno-junkies scream streaming/

The mutant murder-script of the acidHUMAN hunting
for the grotesque that decodes drugs and erodes
the body channel of the psychosexual drone is
transplanted to the brain universe that got ruined
— the techno-junkies with the rebel mode of boy-
roid//=>the genome=linkage of her plasma catastrophe
paradise is broken down::the holograms that imploded
in the gizzard of an ironcore dog eviscerate the mass
of flesh-module of the artificial sun::post-mortal
examination::entropic scalpel head that probes
gene=TV — the internal organ consciousness that
processed the digital feedback of self mutilation//
Murderous body fluid VTR of cold-blooded disease
animals::it sutures to the larval zodiac accelerator
of the internal organ consciousness that suspended
the different vital-node of<<the nerve centre that
exterminates>>a parasite drone::the junk DNA=channel
and the artificial sun halo respire sickly period
with the acid murder form of VTR=fear=cell of the
digital=video camera external::a retro-control rotor
excoriates the ecstasy transfer device of her voice
data=mutant switch that detonated the monochrome
masses of flesh memory of a dog= psychosexual drone
who evolved to the brain universe that invoked the
digital=vamp of a chemical psychosis internal —
paradise state derangement system of cadaver-feti//
I devour the black embryos of EVOL/

Control external masses of flesh=to larva nature=body
joint::of a chemical technocrisis — reptilian soul/
gram that fecundates clone-transmission — covered
in blood junk script=the meridian mode of a parasite
drone//::the cadaver-feti device of the brain universe
I awake::The nightmare inside the CD-ROM of larva

nature explodes//artificial sun of OUTPUT=of=the nerve end guerrilla>>I invade::like the suspected vital body that was sutured to BABEL::the serum of median perversion::boy-roid of orgone::the crime system of an emotional replicant error//<<acid=primal cyclops atom::of the bio=less=masses of flesh that react to the cyber-sadistic expansion module of the scream that rapes the crucified memory of body fluid — mimics the output=emotional replicant of the thyroid that fecundates the digital=vamp//<<it linked the BABEL=chromosome to a planetary vital=serum LOAD::the narcotic head line of the lunar coil of the cadaver-mechanism of a chemical dog::the scanner of soul/gram is reset::The fractal murder circuit of gene=TV that trashed data=is clashed to the scorpio vane of the vivisector/

I murder the artificial sun::the neon brain that the cold-blooded disease animals of cyber nature abolished to the non-resettable flight circuit of soul/gram of the techno-junkies cadaver-feti//The chromosome form insanity of self that communicates to the mutant mimic line of retro-ADAM was installed to an artery of the Cadaver City plague labyrinth::the softwarable internal organ consciousness of a dog tortures the hyperreal existence-code of the drug embryo//the acid murder function of the vital icon of self is expanded to the hydromaniac brain universe of a dog::devouring body-OMOTYA of the cyber nature of the okama drone rapture the cruel chemical vital=serum of boy-roid hyper-links to the atrocity short-cut of internal organ consciousness::the derangement module of the scanning nucleus:: hallucinogenic fur of the cold-blooded disease animals of bio=less= fear=cells evolves to the logic-directory of the murderous genome that turned into hydromachine//The digital=vamp circuit of retro-ADAM game//:the : electron desire-script of acid murder is infected::I download the softwarable soul/gram of the primal cyclops atom to the clonal reproduction stage hallucinogenic fur of HYPE=ToKAGE//The genomics crime system::body of boy-roid fed to the quantum theory target cadaver-feti::the invasion=mode of the body fluid of a

technocrisis — cold-blooded disease with murder gene
set change=ToKAGE of self erased to the future tense
that respires sickly period . of the artificial
sun::the high speed strand to the bizarre womb sense
of . hydromania::the hyperreal masses of flesh of
the drug embryo::the ecstasy of a orgone lobe is
rilled to metal vulva<<suck blood chromosome>>to the
cadaver-mechanism rapture//the digital=vamp in the
acid plane where cadaver-feti was perceived//Lymph
node of the dog that was dissected to the cyber synapse
of the cadaver-mechanism of the artificial sun is
flooded::evolves to orgone psychosis=streaming::of
the internal organ consciousness that was dissected
to the brain universe that respires sickly Period
of boy-roid::it was invaded to the CD-ROM that
acidHUMAN awoke — internal genomics of the trash
sensor::techno-junkies output that her vital=serum
enlarged::sodomized assassins of SADO/

[ice nebula faecal black] terminus of the material
within the brain is counted::the cold-blooded
disease animals of chemical=bind which output her
rapture planet to the vital=serum of a parasite
murder drone break down our spiral system while
inoculating the module of the scream::I decipher her
mimic line::narcotic meridians of the quantum masses
of flesh that linked to the apoptosis insanity medium
of boy-roid that fecundates the DNA=channeI that
accelerates the hyperreal awakening of the artificial
sun to the meat state/suck valve of the dog that reset
the internal organ consciousness of fetish cadaver
device::psychotropic self imaging of the monitor
screen that transfers the data of acidHUMAN to the
maximum:://The acid mutation-protocol of ADAM::the
genome of the swastika girl—the derangement engine
that linked::=>I murdered the parasite artificial sun
of the nerve centre internal>>The hyperreal head line
of the drug embryo that joints to the chemical cruel
monitor of gene=TV clone-transmissions to the insect-
site where the different vital=cable of the heart
medium of her mimic mode was accelerated::thrusts
through the larva dome of orgone//<<lI turn on the
hydromaniac worldly desires machine>>//The SODOM=

molecule of her fear=cell is released:the monochrome hyper-link node of the dog that inhabits the Cadaver City-city is broken down::the genome of her acid insanity lobe that links with the mobile form ecstasy of the hallucinogenic fur of a cadaver-feti drone>The chemical invasion=mode of boy-roid that was sutured to the DNA=channel::her bio=less=brain cell spasm::I am infected with the desire-script of the technocrisis//<<sperm abortion>>/

The chemical=bondage crucified memory element — hallucinogenic fur of cold-blooded disease animals> ::the streaming=mass of flesh-module of the dog that refluxed to the murder=serum of the orgone body fluid of self junk reacts to acid//The eyeball of boy-roid in the lobe of the cadaver-mechanism where it was mutated by her chromosome form genome insanity internal serum::it evolved to the narcotic abolition circuit of the suck=blood chromosome///I murder the brain cell of a dog::PLAY with the primal cyclops atom-channel of the digital=vamp inclination of the planet of SODO::hunting for the grotesque in the ultra=machinery beast=level where love doll syndrome reproduces the mutant rape=scenes of the masses of flesh that projected a foetus strand to the paradise device that respires sickly period of the artificial sun with the LOAD line of the cadaver-mechanism of orgone//The speed circuit of the primal cyclops atom-vagus:the bio=less=skin sense of the reptilian limbus surrenders the soul/ gram of self of cyber nature::VTR within the brain of the murder genome that artificial sun accelerates to the machinery mutation of a dog//The DNA=channel state//Her hydromaniac worldly desires=machines that acidHUMAN conceives to escape nightmare=serum::stem cyclone of the brain cell that joints to the protocol drone of cadaver-feti was inserted into the mass of flesh-module without the script of the genome=procurement::drug embryo that got deranged is murdered::the meridian of the larva nature of a parasite drone respires metal-congenital>::the acid receiving device of the fear=cell hydromachine of ANTI-ADAM osmoses to the swastika system of the soul/gram — the murderous chromosome of boy-roid that dissolves the desire-script of self — the DNA=channel internal spasm mode respires the murder engine of her lunar coil era::suicide-protocol of an emotional replicant that fecundates the masses of flesh of the technocrisis of the drug embryo to the slender eyeball line of the artificial sun LOAD function::outputs the different vital=serum of the orgone to techno junkies planetary state body-OMOTYA retro-sperm abortion::vital junk hologram::of boy-roid outputs to the cadaver-feti form monitor of an emotional replicant//Her existence engine tortures the chemical SODOM=molecule of a dog internal//The digital=vamp invasion mode of self//The retro-body fluid of ADAM is reset::acid poisonous soul/gram is transferred to the brain universe of the drug embryo// the mass of flesh-module of the technocrisis to the hyperreal evolution system of cold-blooded disease animals::a parasite accelerates nightmare synapse of the lobe that refluxed the cadaver-mechanism/

<<soul/gram is jointed to the bio=less reaction of a dog::gene=TV without cable hyper-controls the defleshed oneiric locus of boy-roid:the BABEL=erosion=medium of the brain universe//Her atrocity vital icon::schizophysical mass of flesh system= hydromachine that inserted the derangement module of self fecundates the planetary group of the DNA=channel hunting for the grotesque// The streaming=procurement of the genome language that accelerates to the HYPE=drug-eye of self internal::the ice mass of flesh-module of the sky is fractured internal::galactic Code resets>>the murder monitor of acidHUMAN spasm that downloads the bondage suicide program of ADAM — decipher the anus print of the cadaver. mechanism of a dog// The cut-scripts of her lips//[ice nebula faecal black] techno-junkies genome montage of the BABEL=TV Cadaver=the suck=swastika that linked is osmosing to the brain universe of self in the acid=level of the cyber nutrient//::the decay of the hologram of internal organ consciousness script//hallucinogenic fur of a chemical primal cyclops atom joints to

the body line of the dog that mutated the rape drone of the artificia) sun::fecundates the softwarable murder quantum of boy-roid that emulates different vital-drives of the lobe nature of ecstasy loading//:the crime circuit of the cyber nature of the suck=blood chromosome on the existence-code of self that programmed her omanko — claw invader that is parasitic and tortures the boundless body joint of the drug embryo to narcotic overload>=I am raped to the monochrome eyeball level of the artificial sun internal/

<<I stream 1mg of the mass of flesh of the Cadaver City that crawls to the suck nucleus of techno-junkies brain pool//The acid murder of soul/gram VIR=>the genome form nightmare of boy-roid reproduces ectopic body fluid//Her plasmic eyes excoriate the internal organ of a dog DNA=channel// The kill=script of boy-roid of the larva nature that fecundates the swastika with the chemical flood mode of a vital=serum accelerates the murder region of the artificial sun::the Cadaver City of homeostasis tracks::data is sent back out to the virtual murder system of the dog that is parasitic on fetish VTR of the suck=blood chromosome//=the mutant of self attacks the chaos band of her cadaver-mechanism to telepathic level//The hydromaniac device of the fear=cell is expanded::noise::breaks down the suicide-protocol of an emotional replicant::the murder soul/gram inside the digital morph of self// The cadaver reflux of exoskeletal-sensor — death pornography is video-taped//The murder swastika of the cold-blooded disease animals::syndromes that clash the chemical brain of hydromania to the insanity medium of the artificial sun that the mass of flesh-module coronates::virtual gene war of the quantum theory of the scream of acidHUMAN that was sutured to robo-fellatrix hunting for the grotesque skinned penises of Sato Corporation

torture victims::covered with the blood of boy-roid that accelerated DNA entropy to a monitor screen//I scattered loose the narcotic eyeball

reflex of cadaver-feti on the boundary line of the
hyperreality that fecundates her anarchy existence-
code::pituitary explodes=the season of ecstasy//
Atrocity reverbs//Her genome form psychosis-protocol
evolves internal::/

The parasite existence-code of the brain universe
that accesses the acid murder of hyperreal ToKAGE
is controlled to narcotic levels::I invade the
heart=medium of the cadaver-mechanism of boy-roid::I
raped the necrotic hardware of cold-blooded disease
animals++multiple LOAD that the entropic hormone
drone of head charges in soul/gram state toward the
anus of the deathshead//::to the end of a genome//The
existence-code of self was split in the suspension
area where the genome of her brain stem rotated
randomly// Dismantling the suicide-script of a LOAD
— multiple suck= blood chromosome — the paranoiac
crime circuit of clone-skin is extracted//the spiral
form psychosis=modem of the bondage=language//drug
embryo of ADAM> <explode gene=TV>the vital=serum of
the scream that streamed to the defleshed hyper-
link layer of the cadaver-feti drone that fused
<<parasite>>LOAD::The DNA=channel that rapes the
eyeball of SADO of cyber nature::boy-roid of the
cadaver-mechanism that exploded ice inside the sky
begins to clash to the deathshead hell of body-
OMOTYA//To the metal mankind of the SM disease//
Orgone of weird exogenesis//from the gel form logic
body of the fear=cell that was output>The mass of
flesh-module that was cut — the techno-junkies
respire the acid murder/program of the artificial
sun in the high speed sickly period::/

<The chromosome=port clotted with faecal blood//The
vital-node of a dog is broken down:::the mimic mode
of the murderous speed of the artificial sun that
was stored to acid=primal cyclops atom of soul/
gram of::the mutation=program//The internal organ
medium that crashed — molecular concatenation of
the nutrient that hyper-links=>the chemical murder-
sites of the masses of flesh of cyber nature serum
dissected the brain that fecundates techno-junkies/

cadaver-feti>//the BABEL=nerve-control//The genome form logic of self synchronized to data=catastrophe of larva nature::the abolition code of an emotional replicant::I continue to suck the non-resettable suicide program of the artificial sun//it is inoculated to nightmare HDD of acidHUMAN and the softwarable parasite of the genome=linkage where it clashes to sensor::secretes to control external of soul/gram internal/

=>the HDD form murderous body fluid=serums of the parasite=suck blood chromosomes that jointed to the SODOM circuit of Creature 13 — the chaos of her internal organ consciousness that inserts zirconium tentacles into borg anus drome::I am tortured=cadaver-feti of the drug embryo that jointed to the retro-thyroid of a dog::the murder swastika of Level zero evolves to the brain universe::digital bondage of the crucified memory of ADAM that converged to the spiral form script::the suicide controller of the artificial sun//It is covered in the blood of self that invades — digital=vampire existence-code is secreted to technocrisis=neural jack of the cadaver-mechanism of the eyeball that respires internal organ consciousness//::silver orgone reflux feast of a sperm-drinking space vampire/

The suck blood nature of time//<<it is osmosing:: metal-congenital::the mass of flesh-module of self>>that jointed the hyperreal escape circuit of boy-roid to the nightmare of the trance deathshead — the geometric median of hydromachine fecundates the recursive multiple suicide plane of the artificial sun digital=vamp>>::the hyperreal chemical positive reaction of the fear=cell that is latent to our [ice nebula faecal black] heart medium//The soul/gram of self communicates internal::the mimic mode that awakes to the noise of gravity zero of gene=TV that is parasitic on the defleshed modem of the cadaver-feti drone that eviscerates eyes with spherical condition-speed of hydromachine:: retinal mania within the channel of the cadaver-mechanism of a cyber dog pack::vital=serum PLAY that accelerates

sensor//::hyper-links//the artificial solar system —
amphetamine arc of cold-blooded disease animals rapes
the ice::clonal psychosis of the sky that was reset
by the techno-junkies SCANIMAL brain//:our eyeball
of the hydromaniac suicide line of her emotional
replicant is scanned::the drug embryo of a hyper-
control unit is input to the medium of the scream
of the suck blood chromosome=the cruel vital icon
of boy-roid is mapped/the murder of body fluid//A
planetary state//l reproduce the mutant=level of
soul/gram//Her existence-code is incinerated//::I
invade the trash circuit of body-OMOTYA::I escape the
mass of flesh-module that a dog reflux jointed to her
vital=serum//LOAD in the Cadaver City of soul/gram
unit//the chemical ruin of self controls the mimic
line that ADAM replicated::the defleshed planet of
the telepathic emotional replicants that evolves
to a murder=code of the suck blood chromosome::the
acid script circuit of the fear=cell grows gravid
to the terror=engine of self//The genome state-
murder drone of the soul/gram that the drug embryo
of the digital=vamp defleshed::it respires metal-
congenital//It secretes from the savage vital=serum
of the swastika girl::the chemical lobe of a dog::the
modem of the hyper-control form of the internal
organ consciousness that crashed murders it//<<vital
body=of retro-ADAM ecstasy>//the fetish technology
of the Cadaver City that crawls//

EVOL osmosing pink apocalypse::the torture machine
of the cyber nature of swastika sex that inoculates
the bio=less=acceleration speed of the mass of
flesh-module to the chemical meridian=parasite
of boy-roid::hydromaniac lust is respired sickly
period::split to machinery//The desire-script of self
to body-OMOTYA of bondage ADAM coil//The precision
machine of the cadaver-mechanism: eviscerate the
orgone pod of the lobe nature of a dog//Infinite
mutant murder circuit of the drug embryo synchro-
VTR//The ecstasy that was deciphered//The ecstasy
of the<cadaver-feti>file format of the monitor/
spasm::of gene=TV that the orgone crime system of
boy-roid hyper-controls:: the brain surge of a dog

attack accelerates it//In the awakening=level of the mimic mode of her HDD where it was birthed in the city sewers of an emotional replicant//serum was compressed in the acid mass of flesh-module of the nutrient::a reptilian form technocrisis violence area DNA=channel/The Cadaver City where it clashes chemically – right brain that was stimulated::the variant mutant existence-code that was accumulated to the eyeball level of self – serum noise dial and LOAD//the internal organ consciousness that was hyper-controlled explodes to telepathic techno-junkies – sonic embolism that fuses to the murderous crucified memory of the artificial sun::I murder the symbol ype of the fragment::acidHUMAN spiral of the median decay drome rising/

<Evolution system of the orgone=neural jack that the drug embryo communicates to her emotional replicant planet – to the cadaver-mechanism PLAY – blood respires with a lunar coil//The abolition circuit of hydromachine Is transplanted to the clone-skin of the corruption of self::I record the hyperreal murder of the digital=reptilian internal retro-desire of self//<<sperm abortion>>I invade a cobalt orifice with the murder-node that blood chromosome operated::the primal cyclops atom of the cyber nature that transmits terror virus to the reset locus::the soul/gram of self injected the body fluid of the murder modes of the cold-blooded disease animals that was output to the vein map of self in the out=put world of the emotional replicant of ADAM// The mass of flesh-module of retro-ADAM that got deranged to the existence-program line of the mutant dust-NIRVERNA//Covered in blood I ascend to heaven like that body-OMOTYA::/

The ADAM=bondage mass of flesh-module of self that was contaminated by HDD of the insect of boy-roid is inserted::catastrophe of her eyeball was received::the softwarable vital=serum of the chemical drone that is sutured to the internal organ medium of the nutrient cadaver-feti in the murder region of the cyber nature of the artificial sun and mutates at

high speed is secreted//<<terror of the protoplasm
of the fear=cell — the flesh modem that liquefied the
body of self respires metal-congenital::the fractal
scream of hallucinogenic fur — primal cyclops atom
that streams to the visionix surface tissue of the
Cadaver City internal>>/

I suck the soul/gram of the cadaver-mechanism of
parasite=murder band::self that was sutured to reload loop of the suck=blood chromosome acid::the
brain cell records defleshed PLAY of the cadaver-feti
drone//Accelerate the violence device of gene=TV//to
the noisy dogs of the genome=linkage which excoriate
the nightmare of the eyeball=level of self in the
high speed script::the existence-code of boy-roid
that was trashed//Vital internal body-OMOTYA joints
to the cold-blooded disease animals which hyper-
control the nerve centre of hydromania — projected
the insanity medium of the monitor state of acid
murder and hallucinogenic fur labyrinth::artificial
sun of gene=TV that streams inside of the techno-
junkies that abolish her telepathic body-OMOTYA to
control external of the drug embryo::PLAY like the
desire-protocol creature that exploded the<<murder
archive of retro-ADAM>>/

The ecstasy of body-OMOTYA::cold-blooded disease
animals of a vital/script that awoke to the digital=
vamp brain streaming of the drug embryo::genome
form malice serum::the data=mutant mass of flesh-
module of the Cadaver City that fecundates LOAD::the
catastrophic surrender of hydromachine to her
emotional replicant=1mg of eyeball of acidHUMAN
that inoculates it//Sickly period is respired//>the
psychosis-script state hyperreal=engine of boy-
roid>=>it inaugurated the murder region of the
internal organ consciousness of self::the masses
of flesh of the technocrisis that hyper-linked
to acid=control external of the drug embryo::the
reproduction control of the dog that howls electric
— cyber nature that the insanity-script of her soul/
gram activated=LOAD the monitor screen of gene=TV//
The body fluid=hologram of the artificial sun::I

am killed/death line of BABEL genomics of boy-roid
jacks into fetish eyeball disc — body-OMOTYA of the
Cadaver City coil/

<<sensor trash of a neon nightmare>>the biotechnology
of the drug embryo and the birth of ultra=machine
chaos/::her lunar coil that was inserted internal::the
mass of flesh-module with the retro-ADAM device of
hydromania=the miracle-protocol creature that turned
pale::cyber nature evolves in a parasite plane=the
body that ingested SADO lobe of boy-roid::clash to
the genome swastika=channel of acid malice::ToKAGE
of ADAM that links with the eyeball of self script//
the machine=angel of cadaver-feti was tortured by
the paradise device of self//The streaming=masses
of flesh of a psychosexual anthropoid which spasm
to zero//hyper-linked to the abolition circuit of
a vital video probe=attack the nightmare monitor
screen of gene=TV::the acid=scream of the vital body
that was shut down and assimilated the hydromaniac
worldly desires machine of boy-roid::<I attack
the suicide line of the primal cyclops atom>//the
suicide control of the artificial sun was buried in
the brain of self DNA=channel>//The machine=angel
of hydromania is suspended to the hyperreal BABEL
circuit of self::the bio=less=eyeball of this
psychosis lobe of the cerebral tumour lode of
cadaver-feti:://Input the primal cyclops atom-code
of brain spasm>The random body derangement of the
data=mutant that dismantles the self of gene=TV was
streamed//I torture the nerve system that retro-
ADAM hyper-controlled in the defleshed narcotic lobe
of boy-roid internal//planetary system of SADO is
connected to the ice entropic desire device of the
sky that grows gravid in the surrender-sites of
hydromaniac murder drone//It trashes the eyeball
velocity of the stalker form of the drug embryo:.a
vital=serum with the high speed circuit of womb
area machines//the anal pheromone of the cadaver-
mechanism to her HDD-animal mode::the data=mutants
of self Noise inside the mass of flesh-module of
the dog that fecundates the derangement system of
the spiral rapture internal=>/the brain universe

of the streaming=scream resuscitates cadaver-feti
form ecstasy and downloads the softwarable plasma
paradise of cold-blooded disease animals/

The digital osmosis stage of data=mutants is installed
on the monitor of her gene=TV//the cadaver-feti-
module that boy-roid accelerates::the psychosis of
the artificial sun that was jointed to the desire-
protocol creature I rape – immature hydromania of the
womb area to the PLAY sense that crashed a vital=serum
internal game::I cannibalize the digital=vamp
internal organ of the drug embryo//++the technocrisis
body=terror of retro-ADAM that masturbates with the
acid primal cyclops atom-controller::it mutates to
the hybrid suicide circuit/emotional replicants at
high speed::her cadaver-feti form monitor of the
drug embryo is clashed to an empty basalt tomb-
device/

//I awake=the fear=cell that boy-roid hyper-controlled
internal to the trash sensor lobe of quantum masses
of flesh with the chemical soul/gram of the primal
cyclops atom::I murder the eyeball strand of that
genome and the nightmare=memory of the technocrisis
with the narcotic body joint womb area machine of
SM inclination was secreted to the cosmic sense
of the suture drone//The control deficiency of the
vagus-nerve//Hydromania is accelerated::detonate
her emotional replicant suicide line to the entropic
brain universe of self coil//Spasm in the surrender-
site where it was sutured to the digital=vampire
zone of gene=TV::the insanity channel of her DNA is
scoped:: the mutants of the nerve transmission in
the last term of the monochrome earth area like the
artificial sun in acid=play::I am murdered with body
fluid::>>her primal cyclops atom-code is resolved
with the eyescans of micro cadaver-feti::the
data=mutants of retro-ADAM – the mimic circuit of an
acid murder swastika//The desire-protocol creature
that tortured the purple orgone reflux that respired
metal-congenital to the zone of the cold-blooded
disease of the artificial sun//The ice sky was
input:::::it is covered in blood::the fear=cell of

boy-roid that trips in the anus world of defleshed DIGITANIMAL to the cadaver-mechanism implosion — that fluid eyeball-molecule rapes the emotional replicant lobe of a digi-dog::data=mitochondria outlet::entrails immolated by pincerclaw butchers of Venus/

<<sperm abortion in the narcotic soul/gram of the cadaver-feti inclination of self that was rendered with data=spasm in the brain universe::the city is jointed>Devouring exoskeleta I eviscerate the oneiric locus of BABEL=gene=TV — the cadaver of acidHUMAN — I reveal that internal organ city//the brain of the nutrient drone fills with the mimic line of ecstasy and glisters//The acid murder-script that boy-roid injected — bondage animals of the cyber nature of retro-ADAM propel the narcotic nightmare structure of the cranial joint area:://artificial sun of the chromosomal aberration of the drug embryo where an insect spasm to the nerve centre of the Cadaver City was inserted//The cadaver-feti device of hydromania that respires sickly period was passed::it is covered by the mass of flesh of the DNA=channel and escapes to a symbolic=season//It respires metal-congenital// the suck=blood chromosome-software of the data=mutant that was scanned to the ultra-eyeball level that the deathshead reproduces got deranged to the soul/ gram that was sutured to the nude Super Cherry module hunting for the grotesque rectal embryos of a parasite drone=PLAY::<<the annihilation game>>/

<<it accesses::the BABEL=primal cyclops atom-code of the soul/gram that the mass of flesh-module of the cadaver-mechanism of boy-roid fecundates to the acid paradise device of data=mutants::to the insect of our brain bondage internal game that deciphers it::<<the murderous sense of her vital body tissue to the brain cell of a parasite drone strand::to the murder system that turned hydromachine bad::boy- roid orgasm frenzy::the mass of flesh-module that mutated is inserted into the brain nucleus of the Cadaver City//::the desire-script type of the spiral larva — the data=mutant gets deranged//It is covered in blood::the primal cyclops atom-code and

murder reflex that Soul/gram joints to the orgone
nightmare=molecule of retro-ADAM in the brain lobe
of gravity zero of self reverbing into cold metallic
spray/

The nightmare of vital junk — boy-roid of the cyber
nature that we clash to the brain that downloads the
dogs of cadaver-feti inclination — murderous mass
of flesh-modules of the womb area machines — the
hydromaniac lunar coil device of boy-roid::the mass
of flesh-module of the technocrisis joints to the
cadaver. mechanism internal//the murder circuit of
acidHUMAN data=tracks::the Vite serum of mutant=number
was recorded to the vivid eyeball slash hunting for
the grotesque ++the desire-protocol creature of our
brain universe js injected:the narcotic molecule of
the data=mutants rapes the Soul/gram of the Cadaver
City that crawls::isolated in the techno madness
area of retro-ADAM where the BIOS of the acid murder
drone concatenates=the inorganic substance murder
of self is input//I murder her hydromaniac brain
Circuit::it is invaded by the hologram=body fluid
that a data=mutant outputs to body. OMOTYA of the
ultra=machine universe of the Cadaver City::the mass
of flesh-module of the parasite drone that inaugurated
mimic mode::searching for grotesque proteins in the
subterranean anus world of a succubus cemetery//

Lecien

<the electronic=brain is planetary — the ZERO organ state where the insanity of the clone boys hyperlinks to the body of an assassin>NDROID-beat of Placenta World/God of ambient>//the crimson body seed++ the cosmic death device of the murder melody//exoskeleta of the artificial sun//primal cyclops atom HYPE::our soul-machine that regulates the body fluid meridian::body fluid meridian of cobalt rock death::suck=blood chromosome rapes VIRUS that replicates/schizography of the head line=body of the drug embryo that surrendered the nightmare of the miracle rape chromosome that creates an animal soul-machine digital=android>The swastika girl who was sutured to insanity=drive that becomes the helix of planetary war:://lobotomy of a control external assassin//It fecundates heat++the virtual image/murder the ectoplasm nerve of absolute zero breakdown — NIHIL clone boys proliferate in the body fluid//Placenta World of the blood desert of an ADAM Doll/penis was sutured//I rape like the Cadaver City dog that howls in Hell:://the soul-machine where an artificial sun was input to quantum memory/

<<Angel mechanism::murder memory=second::the brain cell that was cut fecundates the artificial sun/ the insanity law of her retinal soul-machine that was sutured to the ToKAGE junk of an eternal prayer spasm::the NDROID artificial sleep that escapes the nightmare region++we of the suck=blood chromosome/ who respire sickly period perceive the body of zero:://<<ice sky eleven>>the crucified memory that was paralyzed::>>The bio-dogs of the cyber deserts which our exoskeletal mucus fecundates — the vision of a cold-blooded disease — a gene twist internal — a murderous memory records the coefficient/

=>cock-spurting clone boys excoriate transmission>/ it is the Heaven= medium where the true sun burned

out the centre of gravity that was about to break>Our
ultra-control future internal of a cadaver like the
NDROID-city model::our GIGA organ/ADAM Doll burn
up<<the chromium of the meridian>>NDROID coefficient
reproduces our spectre to orange//I witness clone
boys who were raped::an eternal cadaver on the
hyperreal Placenta World::control external desert
where the cold-blooded disease=animals loop the ADAM
Doll nexus that contaminates internal — the fear
that accelerated::the body of junk vital ring of
the murderous intention//machine=angel of eleven//
fecundates detonator>/

New gravity::the night cooled the digital=lunar coil
of the swastika girl that burns up/controls our spectre
ectoplasm spot::the plasma paradise that controls our
machine=angel>>aArtificial sun scans the ADAM Doll
of a cold-blooded disease:://the digital pheromone
bowels/HDD of love doll processed a transparent brain
mask//hypermedian drug embryo which was sutured to
the junk strand of a chromosome internal=cyber dog of
fracture of vital coil internal::the machine=angel
who fecundates infinite exoskeleta::LOAD the cut
insect core to the NDROID-universe out of the terror
coefficient/clone boys of SODO/body of the defleshed
swastika girl in the central processing unit that
fecundates detonator=junk like the savage body of
the artificial sun::assassin that was parasitic//I
escape:://our virtual=meridian device/our soul-
machine of the electron theory fecundates the quantum
grid of the machine form lupus XX angel mechanism
of the Placenta World/it was input to the ice sky
of our lupus=space central processing unit::clone
boy rampage=the parasitic murder code terror that
stimulates the reproduction brain of the ADAM Doll of
the animal zero of a future cold-blooded disease is
hyper::it is the voice of the NDROID-parasite=body/
HDD angel was restrained in order that I really
escape//A machine= angel fecundates the cadaver of
the desert circuit/our electron theory that activated
LOAD::the deathshead of the fractal android vision
of ADAM Doll::clone-transmission to the nucleus of
our reproduction function/

<<Our clonal fear accelerates the body of an assassin>>lt is null speed LEVEL of the womb area machine that the sleep accelerates//Death of the drug embryo/the cold-blooded disease that controlled external the control of primal cyclops atom>lt resuscitates in the lupus=space::digital vampire vex that recurred to the zero zone of the drug embryo:://fracture of miracles/madness of the sun::no requiem/

Paralysis::The language of the brain region/clone boys of the cold-blooded disease of the drug embryo that NDROID dreamed in a murderous brain/desert of blood was controlled::I measure the terminal eyeball velocity of the digital projection of the cadaver that sped up::rotor cable is cut>The grotesque intention of the chromosome pool that was downloaded to the world of an artificial sun median//CyberBuddha resisted biotechnology/valve meat of the soul-machines::it accelerates it/control external of the XX womb area machine is eroded like the cadaver that is in the city of the drug embryos where our hyperlinked sun surface brain of an artificial assassin inoculates exoskeleta like the waste material body fluid of our machine=angel= tissue::swastika girl orgasm::it is planetary>her ice coefficient that fecundates and gelates the central processing unit of the cock-spurting clone boys<the world was recorded//The dark fracture of beasts::it fecundates heat//the flood of the sun::the infinite murderous intention of exoskeletal motion in the zero=brain that was sutured to a terror modem circuit//clone boys of the desert converge parasitic on the orange holocaust of that Cadaver City internal>the drug embryo respires sickly period like the future::<<ectopic drug embryo that our machine=angel joints to the ice of the sky of blood>>technocrisis insanity of language>the murder brain of the swastika girl that the body of the assassin reproduces like the MORBUS reflux internal::the crime of a new species> Suicide system of the BABEL virus that fecundates the derangement chromosome of memory of love and hatred::<<clone boys sutured desire to a planetary quantum electron grid of the womb area machine/

<<Desire of the SADO death cycle respires sickly
period//Nerve in the medium-spectacle++the last term
of the cyber dog foetus that the control external
sexual body-OMOTYA incubates::the murderous intention
of the central processing unit communicates it:://
Mental derangement/

The brain of blood of the desert is stimulated:.
it is the ectopic meridian that an artificial sun
awoke>Murder memory of the drug embryo that vais
mad::the cyber murderous intention that was born /
intensify our rape=iine noise of the soul-machine
that was opened to fractal lupus=space:./swastika
girl of the orange insanity of the replication
medium::chromosome of th zone is amplified like
the artificial sun/ADAM Doll that continues
to eternally/the interior of the womb of the XX
dog that was controI resuscitates a vision::the
control external=nerve target that was joined::it
fecundates the spectre=octave of the angel mechanism
that controls our centre of gravity::reptile
impulse which the true sun decayed internal commits
suicide>Ectopic meridian:://murderous skin tissue of
the sexual NDROID voids a memory>ADAM Doll fecundates
the suck=blood chromosome in the split second just
before LOAD::the negative=horizon of the cold-
blooded disease animals of the sun inside the future
when the drug embryo was cut//the artificial sun
that deciphers the heart of the mechanism::corrodes
to the crucified memory of the hyperreal seed that
fecundates it>//the ADAM Doll that was jointed to
our monochrome heart spectre ectoplasm Spot respires
metal-congenital and I graft it to the exoskeleton
of negative-emotion that clashes to this pure crash
eon/

<<Napalm torture in the nerve=future of our techno
lupus=space++ rictus::the pure white body=mode of
ToKAGE that was contaminated>>Zero-level of the
soul-machine where the EVOL-chromosome encodes the
spectre that became our line:://external control
of the nano-machine reflex of the artificial sun
that conceives the cold-blooded disease animals::the

ironcore retina records the despair of the angel
mechanism of a fractal body of the assassin that was
sutured to monochrome memory of the torture brain
complex of the Cadaver City that crawls:like the brain
that shoots::NDROID that was jointed to the gene war
spectrum=the spectre of the brain//angel mechanism
of the boiling blood desert of the machine=angel is
incubated::[ice nebula faecal black] heart that was
recorded like our reptile impulse inoculates the
murder memory of exoskeleta::ADAM Doll was sutured
to universe period=that resuscitates the junk of the
artificial sun that is parasitic>Loop-line of the
soul-machine that awoke screaming/

I decipher the ancient codex of Sarcophagus City::1
rape the brain of a pure machine=angel of an ADAM
Doll ash desert like the machine that deciphers zero
crime::NDROID battle of the brain of the breakdown/drug
embryo of the terror rictus::the coefficient linked
to the artificial sun in the transplantation level
which is infectious and kills like an ancient evil
blood angel/ Future fear resuscitates the suck=blood
chromosome of the pheromone that was sutured to our
insanity/memory risks the gravity of the sun and
inhabits a gel form fear tropic>ToKAGE pattern of
the soul-machine that disintegrated::it codes the
cranium of the drug embryo in the future::worms
that were sutured to the digital=vampire vex are
transmitted::it transplants to artery of the body
fluid vacuum::Cadaver City requiem for an ADAM Doll//
insanity was compressed to the liquid eyeball zone
below EVOL/

<<A machine=angel of the quantum universe devours
black embryos>//it is the murder stage of Creature
8//Space vampire that the suicide machine of clone
boys sutured to the terror tomb::digital-vamp of
the vital body that shut down in the bowels of the
chromosome nexus where NDROID respires the true sun as
desire internal>::<the nucleus>is transferred::<<the
nightmare of the orgone coefficient/ the future of
the ADAM Doll when the crucified memory loss of the
defleshed pheromone of a virus reaches derangement

speed::implosion of the soul-machine that gelated the zero gravity-miracle of the assassin like a machine=angel//it fecundates infinite spectre LOAD/a high speed meridian osmosis//inorganic substance murder of spectre::the DNA channel that was controlled like the ADAM Doll//nano-machine that is suffocated//crucified memory sutured to NDROID XXX suicide system fecundates transmission to the zodiac of the true sun/

The digital infernal carapace::amniotic fluid mechanisms that trip the inorganic substance coefficient of the machine=angel in the cold-blooded disease= world of a blood desert placenta vision zero//it respires metal-congenital::the suck=blood chromosome-medium of our brain that speeds up junk reproduction of a grotesque mental machine=drug embryo that crucified a memory/valve break>::Placenta World spectre — angel-plasma of the last chromosome of night — a pure devil=machine/

I invade the solar chaos band of the escape circuit// clone boys suck a fractal Pheromone simulating the quantum eclipse where ADAM Doll went mad::Placenta World solitude of the murder memory::the ice sky is congested with the cold-blooded disease animal coefficient that the lunar coil of a swastika girl recorded::I decipher the machine mechanism of the drug embryo who projects the machinery-murderous intention of the artificial sun internal/fecundates the body of the assassin that decayed::LOAD++ chaos=machine that melted the detonator/

/It is the crucified memory of the coefficient of the quantum theory of SLEEP of God-body:://assassin of the larval accelerator:://LOAD/Cadaver City that crashes::Death God/NDROID suck=blood chromosome of the exoskeleton of the planetary interceptor::desire of an assassin imprisons the sun// Pheromone of the nerve/drug embryo of the Cadaver City is regenerated like a pure devil devouring faecal bloodclots in a universe of ulcerated meat/

<<STAGE-X>>Meridian of the escape circuit of the
ADAM Doll that was coiled and clashed to a mutant
molecule>Drug embryo electron rictus/the cadavers of
our parasite=syndrome accelerate to hyperreal desire
internal//Our central processing unit::external
lupus=space/murder and clone=transmission of LEVEL
zero of the angel mechanism that respires sickly
period::I decipher the sexual lupus=space of the
clone boys/ADAM Doll of this desire mechanism zone::/
ToKAGE of the machine=angel that committed suicide
is accelerated::/ ice sky of Saturn clad in corpses//

MØNKEY/gene-dub

The existence-codes of the data=mutants clash to
the lunar coil that respires . the brain system that
fused to the acid membrane of a parasite drone sickly
I period of retro-ADAM::her cadaver feti infect a
paradise device of the chemical=anthropoid of the
artificial sun that looped to the vital-junk scream
of retro-ADAM that rapes her chemical matrix//suicide
dial internal is streamed::sperm abortion:dead
jackal memory joints to the cruel medium of the
exoskeleton of the acidHUMANIX — murder-memories of
masses of flesh — the body of a defleshed assassin
reverbs=>soul/gram respires the technocrisis sickly
period in the trash=world of the human body genome
where it was rendered void//::the decay of her
chromosome channel//The I hyperreal plane of the
internal organ city where fear fecundates cadaver
feti::hallucinogenic fur drug embryo is clashed to a
stellar burn::her brain streams the acid murderous
intention of the artificial sun::breaks down the mode
of retro-ADAM internal::>With the vital-controller
that digital=vamped to our chemical=anthropoid::the
murder-node of the human body genome that was
online is expanded to the hybrid desire-protocol
creatures of retro-ADAM::the atrocity molecule of the
artificial sun rapture to the ice sky::ultra=machine
reproduction-zone of the ice sky::self is replicated
in the hyperreal meridian=factory of the reptilian
form derangement module::human body genome of the
brain universe where protean reflux of an ANTI-ADAM
hyperlinks to her acidHUMANIX murder reaction//Her
body fluid — the desire-protocol creatures that were
mixed to the lunar coil of retro-ADAM cadaver feti
murder the entropic existence-code — the techno-
junkies PLAY — sickly period is respired to the
eyeball device that accelerated artificial sun to
the brain system of the acid murder nature that
mutated rapture::she trips the hydromaniac soul/gram
of a chemical=anthropoid:I murder her narcotic human

body genome that clashes to the hunting for the grotesque territory of the fear=cell where a retinal relapse crashed boy-roid//The vital=serum that fecundates her soul/gram to the murder circuit::the noise of hallucinogenic sulfur::acidHUMAN that is parasitic on the monitor screen of the orgone larva level that rapes her neural jack socket::bio=less-internal organ of hydromania that controls the genomics scream of retro-ADAM bondage/eviscerates oy; interstellar spiral::drug embryos who excoriate the vault of the sky hunting for the grotesque serum like a chitin drone::The DNA=channel of her digital=vampire mode is combined::the existence-code of the reptilian form of our technocrisis accelerates to the brain universe that the vital-junk suck blood script of soul/gram turned into an acid spool with our retro-ADAM murder-archive internal::cadaver feti of a non-resettable parasite drone — the murder-memories of our desire-protocol creatures that were output::covered in boy-roid blood within the oneiric locus that proliferates our fear=cell human body genome::hyperlinks to a copper cannibal cave::her narcotic brain cell is defleshed::the nova skull of her soul/gram psychosis::serum of the cadaver feti drone switching as I went mad//The mass of flesh-module of the isolation condition that emulated the chemical escape circuit of retro-ADAM//Her existence-code is respired sickly period internal::the desire-protocol creatures of the cadaver-mechanisms of exoskeleta are mutant to our scream//The oneiric locus of her cadaver//the body joint that fused to the acid game of retro-ADAM/to the orgone eyeball of the rape drone::LOAD is expanded to the hybrid=genomics murder controller of the artificial sun::we eviscerate the vital=serum glands of chemical dogs::the ice of the acidHUMANIX-sky that was sutured to a robo-fellatrix hunting for the grotesque skinned penis of the cadaver feti drone::the technocrisis internal organ revolution of exoskeleta cuts her body to the murder circuit of the acid drone nexus::I eviscerate the ice nightmare of the sky of techno-junkies/non-resettable body fluid::boy-roid clashes to high speed cadaver feti=the existence-code of the chromosomal aberration of retro-ADAM clashes to the NIHIL-eyeball device of artificial sun bondage//

<<The murder region of the artificial sun inputs the soul/gram of the genomics parasite drone that was restrained to the larval level::the mass of flesh-module of Level zero of retro-ADAM engages the cadaver feti=engines of desire-protocol creatures>>I copy her human body genome to the hybrid vital sheet metal of acidHUMAN internal:://our primal cyclops atom downloads the nightmare of the chemical lobe nature of retro-ADAM> I invade the DNA=channel of the drug embryo that hypercontrols the soul/gram that generated her serum in the reptilian som parasite drone streams the human body genome that exploded to the hybrid suicide circuit of retro-ADAM//The orgone sickly period respiration drone of the Cadaver City that crawls is output to the surrender-site of her acid murder metal-congenital//The high body joint of the artificial sun cadaver feti inputs to the DNA=channel that her digital=vamp embolism accelerated::the mass of flesh-module of the cyber crime scream//I eviscerate the soul/gram of the technocrisis with the spiral tube of the reptilian form of retro-ADAM::the suck=blood abnormal living body of chemical dogs LOAD//Our acidHUMANIX cerebral cortex is broken down — sperm abortion to the nightmare of the narcotic lobe nature that was sutured to her suck=blood vital serum — screams in the brain cell of the nutrient drone that plays the hyperreal murder game of the artificial sun that escapes=>fuses to drug embryo type of the reptilian atrocity soul/gram of retro-ADAM// Her cold-blooded disease inoculates the human body genome of a scream syndrome::retro-ADAM eviscerates the softwarable vital=serum that eviscerates the cadaver without the script of retro-ADAM to the monitor screen of chemical dogs internal::our mass of flesh-module was expanded to the brain universe of the acid murder nature that accelerated//her non-resettable desire-protocol creatures are covered in blood::a fear=cell with the nightmare of the orgone drone and cadaver-feti that crawl//a vampire nexus that forged metal sperm of Saturn/

The entropic internal organ consciousness of the digi-dogs — the techno junkies brain plays to softwarable states with the monitor screen surface of her gene=TV//::sutures to the mass of flesh-module that a data=mutant contaminated with boy-roid virus vortex::the worldly desires hydromania that exploded>>A vital=serum sutures to blood electric entrails and excoriates the mass of flesh-module of the cold-blooded disease of boy-roid::the body joint of her acid murder nature that was invaded by the script larva of the weird eyeball planet::spherical condition of cadaver feti rapture with that scream is respired sickly period::I abolish the narcotic vital icon of the exoskeleta that an artifical assassin restrained to the hypercontrol net that corroded to the ice Circuit of the sky::<<it hypercontrols the quantum life of the data=mutants that channel her existence-code to the brain universe of the drug embryo that was sutured to the [ice nebula faecal black] heart median of ToKAGE hunti for the grotesque skulls of Sato Corporation napalm torture victims/ n

<<I torture the machine=angel of retro-ADAM that eroded to the chromosomal aberration::the DNA=channel of virus infection that her softwarable cadaver probe installed to that brain::the eyeball device of cadaver feti — murderous intention of the chemical dogs accelerates to the Sm Circuit mode of acidHUMAN — the spasm drone of the techno-junkies — fear=cell ig parasitic on the ice of the sky//The output-pleasure device::hallucinogenic fur of a drug embryo guerrilla with the fear=cell of her technocrisis::sperm abortion:the digital=vamp brain system/desire-protocol creatures of retro-ADAM accelerate her data=mutant body joint::the body fluid of a cold-blooded disease floods to the monitor screen of gene=TV of the cadaver mechanism noise::rapture of a vital=serum of the mass of flesh-module that the swastika parasite drone of the artificial sun infested internal::the cruel ecstasy of exoskeletal acidHUMAN explodes to the non-resettable internal organ consciousness of a digital dog::<<the entropic murder circuit of the

parasite drone of the speed that erodes our genomics
brain system is cut::it is covered in her body fluid
and excoriates that serum with the plasmic paradise
device of the reset system of her emotional replicant
that emulated the mutant soul/gram of retro-ADAM
that plays/tortures body-OMOTYA of the drug embryo
of cyber nature atrocity::like the liquid eyeball
helix::the hydromaniac scream of boy-roid::/

The existence-code of her cold-blooded disease is
processed by the emulator of orgone anthropoid=game
cytoplasm data//The softwarable mimic-virus of
retro-ADAM is inoculated to the body joint of the
reptilian form that a parasite drone hyperlinked to
hell::her head renders the ecstasy of cadaver-feti
high speed to a hybrid vital icon::our rapture-soul/
gram invades to acidHUMANIX — control external of
gene=TV::the mass of flesh-modules of the underground
spiral ND cable of retro-ADAM::her hybrid existence-
code that was reset to the techno-junkies eyeball
device internal to the ice murder region of the sky//I
murder the emotional replicant of HDD of retro-ADAM
with the ultra=machine mode that respires her sickly
period//::parasitic on the technocrisis region of
cold-blooded disease animals>Thrust through the
narcotic vital sheet metal thorax of acidHUMAN>/

>>The defleshed body joint of hydromania that was
projected by the brain of the acid murder of retro-
ADAM accelerates//The bio=less lobe nature=swastika
of acidHUMAN that the desire-protocol creatures of
the technocrises imprinted onto BABEL::the nervous
system that was cut is respired to softwarable flesh
modules::the ultra=machine soul/gram of boy-roid
scream::I murder the fetish eyeball-node of the
parasite drone of the cadaver mechanism that awakes
atrocity::chemical dogs of the artificial sun median
that exploded break down cyber genomics of the human
body genome that was emulated to our hydromaniac
gravitational nerve-map//I rape the oneiric locus
of her cadaver with the invasive vital-controller
of gene=TV//The eyeball device that artificial sun
abolished — the BABEL-scream of the drug embryo

functions to acid::soul/gram without her script goes mad — the larva stage and the hybrid body line of a parasite drone//The murder=genomics brain system of retro-ADAM::fear=cell was sutured in the ice sky::the internal DNA=channel surface that gets deranged:://8 seconds of entropy is emulated/

The acid murder region of the data=mutant is output::the desire-protocol creatures of Level zero of the artificial sun are parasitic on boy-roid of the brain that mutated::the chemical nightmare of retro-ADAM that was eroded by her android suck=blood chromosome internal transmits automatically::the ultra=machine meridian zone of the human body genome serum<<feeds back>>//The hardware of her suck=blood chromosome is emulated::the technocrisis murder-memory of hydromania that accesses to the eyeball device of the reptilian form with the brain universe of retro-ADAM is respired sickly period::Cadaver feti/program that a parasite drone installed is accelerated with acidHUMANIX virus infection::our digital=vamp internal organ consciousness fecundates the softwarable Cadaver City sensors of orgone vampires hunting for the grotesque::/

The murder model of the human body genome that was projected inside the vital=serums of chemical dogs//::the cadaver feti form ecstasy of the parasite brain universe is thrust through a techno-junkies eyeball device/secretes the vital hydro-controller that was sutured to the cortex of retro-ADAM::the non-oneiric locus of a technocrisis breeds cold-blooded disease animals//I abolish the acidHUMAN body joint that was paralyzed::<<I murder her telepathic emotional replicant::the mimic mode of the insanity Median of retro-ADAM sutures to a chemical parasite drone and breaks down that existence-code>The acid suicide program of the artificial sun that expanded the mass of flesh-module of the data=mutant mode of retro-ADAM to our chemical head line is ignited::it loops to the cadaver mechanism:://Our emotional replicant inoculates the murderous brain of retro-ADAM::the vision that a deathshead projected —

artificial insemination of an acid fear=celj _
parasitic on an ecstasy doll that was projected —
vaginal voltage Spray is respired sickly period//
Her oneiric locus form body fluid cadaver feti//
The technocrisis body joint of the reptilian form
of the drug embryo is infectious::<<the hybrid mass
of flesh-module of retro-ADAM that synchronizes
to the acidHUMANIX monitor screen of gene=TV is
parasitic on the cerebral cortex of a parasite
drone::teratogen of control external of output-
speed and limbic integration/::her anal void vexes
vital=serums internal::data=mutant heart medium
of self that murders the artificial sun hunting
for the grotesque::explodes to the vital icon of
the chromosomal aberration of boy-roid and the
brain of the acid murder nature of chemical dogs//
It hypercontrols the hydromaniac desire-protocol
creatures who seek to rape boy-roid//Contaminating
the oneiric locus of her cadaver to the rape circuit
of soul/gram//Retro-ADAM existence-code that mutated
in the ultra=machine violence area of the suck blood
chromosome::LOAD//gene=TV that the human body genome
of retro-ADAM fecundates/chaos of her anal void
vexes vital state serum — hyperlinks to internal
organ consciousness//=the streaming molecule of the
acid murder nature of boy-roid cut her sphincter>The
artificial sun respires her existence-code retrovirus
of the nutrient drone and melts the brain to acid//The
eyeball device of the cadaver mechanism of hydromania
is accelerated//BABEL-internal organ medium of
chemical dog game//gel form rapture of the primal
cyclops atom::entropic existence-code form::oneiric
locus of head is shut down::hallucinogenic fur is
respired sickly period//::the masses of flesh of
acid murder nature osmose to the rhizome crucified
memory=system of the orgone that was jointed to
the symbiotic vital=serum of the brain of the drug
embryo that streams//tt evolves to the BABEL-brain
of retro-ADAM//

<<The hydromaniac desire-protocol creatures of the
artificial sun that excoriate her crucified memory of
cadaver feti noise::I murder the clonal skin tissue

of the drug embryo and ice narcotic mimic speed of
the sky//kama drone of spiral form body-OMOTYA is
broken down::the script of the chromosomal aberration
of chemical dogs joints the body::1 get deranged::
hyperreal eyeball device of the cadaver feti drone
that detects the crucified memory of the reptilian
form of acid murder in our data=mutant existence-
code state internal//PLAY/I eviscerate the opening
speed of a symbiotic vital=serum::it is parasitic on
the post-genomics brain universe of retro-ADAM/

LOAD::her emotional replicant body contaminates the
acid circuit that the chemical dogs which hyperlink
to the suck blood=brain of our cyber nature sutured
to the murder area where digital vampires respire
the existence-code that mutated sickly period of
the artificial sun::hunting for the grotesque
bones of retro-ADAM//the desire-protocol creatures
that multiply to the abolition of retro-ADAM/to
the hydromaniac insanity-module of her suck blood
chromosome accelerate the rape-soul/gram of boy-
roid::it joints to the artificial sun that acidHUMAN
murdered internal::body-OMOTYA of self resets the
existence-code of the apoptosis= inside//=>her
data=mutant body joint is infected with the brain-
script of the cadaver mechanism of retro-ADAM::
<<rapture>>in the atrocity area of the game/
fear=cell of the drug embryo:: the entropic BIOS of
the cadaver feti drone infects the monitor screen
of her streaming gene=TV::the mass of flesh-module
of our cyber nature scream is opened internal>>It
hypercontrols our retro-ADAM-mimic line::it is
eroded to insanity — binary mode of her suck blood
chromosome: torture the vital-junk internal organ
consciousness of the drug embryo::teratogenic vital
body rapture with the worldly desires circuit of
acid murder nature//the brain system cadaver feti of
acidHUMAN clash to her chemical=lunar coil outlet//
Her data=mutant existence-code clone-transmissions
expand to the non-resettable nerve system of orgone//
Heart medium of boy-roid crashes to the hallucinogenic
fur syndrome of retro-ADAM::symbiotic vital=serum
was refluxed::silver deathshead clashing to chaos/

<<Sour body osmoses blood moon rapture to the brain of chemical dogs that howl//I abolish body-OMOTYA of retro-ADAM that was downloaded::murder the narcotic vital icon of boy-roid with the liquid eyeball device spasm//The hyperreal primal cyclops atom-code of the drug embryo morphs to the softwarable reptilian form of self internal::>>/

We eviscerate the symbiotic vital=serums of chemical dogs/excoriate the parasite rape hologram of boy-roid::digital=vamp projects clone-transmissions to the future tense of acid murder::hyperreal madness system of the data=mutant that invades the oneiric locus of her cadaver::respiring the ultra=machine desire-protocol creature of the artificial sun era::the nightmare of the lobe nature of retro-ADAM::LOAD the material within the brain of cadaver feti::her defleshed brain universe that the underground cable of the artificial sun helix transmutes to orgone larva::boy-roid fecundates the ecstasy of the cadaver feti circuit swastika to ultra=machine/to the rape-soul/grams of chemical dogs//Rapture::the telepathic emotional area of her cold-blooded disease is tuned to the DNA=channel of the drug-eye of the technocrisis// The suck blood chromosome of cyber nature fecundates the parasite planetary-code of retro-ADAM script internal//l perceive the mass of flesh-module of zero dimension::the primal cyclops atom-controller of the planetary game::fear=cell of acid murder nature of the pleasure device mode of retro-ADAM of the artificial sun spasm::rapture of her technocrisis::soul/gram is secreted to the surface of the cadaver of chemical dogs//Her eyeball-system=bondage::cadaver feti of cold-blooded disease animals::> Our genomics bloodsucker=brain serum::the existence-code that chemical dogs fused to the nerve transmission::techno-junkies mutated/respired metal-congenital in the data=mutant state sickly period::the crucified memory of our acid murder nature is covered in the blood of the artificial sun internal//serum of an anus::devouring cadaver feti::accelerator of desire-protocol creatures hypercontrols a rape drone syndrome in the catastrophe parasite plane of retro-ADAM>>Rapture of the monitor screen of acid murder::her symbiotic vital=serum form hybrid soul/gram is ignited//The softwarable cold-blooded disease animals of the data=mutants/bondage with clone-skin::the ultra=machine scream of retro-ADAM is replicated//The human body genome++module of the tera=byte//I dissect her terror existence-code::the simulacrum murder game of acidHUMAN within the negative brain of retro-ADAM::the desire-protocol creatures of the data=mutant lobe nature that joint to the body in the cadaver feti plane where chemical dogs of SODO stream the fractal insanity median// hallucinogenic fur project hyperlinked to cold metal bone hologram::/

The brain universe of the acid murder nature of retro-ADAM that our primal cyclops atom=serum inserted respires the psycho-ROM state trash circuits of a chemical dog sickly period::the monitor screen of our gene=TV is projected atrocity::PLAY with the eyeball=mode of the acidHUMANIX cadaver feti drone/ primal cyclops atom-code of the underground ND rotor cable of the vital junk of the artificial sun that I download projects the brain universe of hydromania that was invaded in the parasite plane of the narcotic nightmare of boy-roid//our ultra=machine existence-code that was inoculated by the mutation= serums of narcotic masses of flesh::crimson seed fecundates the infinite brain universe of the cadaver feti drone hunting for the grotesque::the hydromaniac scream of retro-ADAM is processed=the oneiric locus of the murder nature of acidHUMAN is born in the data=mutant lobe script//The hybrid brain of retro-ADAM clashes to the murder region:drug embryo of TERA was inserted to the meridian-module of the cyber nature of soul/gram=the existence-code of her virus nature accelerates//It hypercontrols planetary desire-protocol creatures::the speed of our narcotic surrender::vital/junk of the boy-roid-plane that is parasitic//sperm abortion:body-OMOTYA of the cyber crime system::desire-protocol creatures of the earth area UPLOAD::cadaver feti of the artificial sun/the hologram of the genomics nightmare of a sickly period

respiration drone that injects serum to the eyeball
device — the murder region of Level zero of boy-
roid noise attacked by the orgone expansion-module
of internal organ consciousness//::the brain of a
chemical dog mimic::her data=mutant form existence-
code of digital=vamp::I rape the ultra=machine Soul/
gram of boy-roid with the torment speed of the cadaver
mechanism of the drug embryo//<<the acid murder
nature of the artificial sun/the mutation=serum is
inserted//The desire-protocol creatures of Level
zero of the parasite drone that are covered with
the blood of hydromania and were jointed to that
liquid eyeball device explode inside//The solar
target::vital-Visions of a space vampire accelerate
internal::crucified memory of the human body genome
that binds to the artificial sun system of boy-roid//
Cadaver feti that encodes the acid murder region of
retro-ADAM — high speed cadaver fet of the brain
universe that transplanted to a nuclear meridian
device//streameq and infected with the mass of flesh-
module of boy-roid::rapture of her liquid eyeball-
tube ignites the ultra=machine vital=serum of the drug
embryo//Her data=mutant soul/gram::the cadaver of
the artificial sun feti region of<<SODO>>accelerates
to<<TERA>>::>>the genomics crime system of retro-ADAM
functions::the desire-protocol creature=serums of
the cadaver mechanisms of chemical dogs are inserted
to the mass of flesh-module of the orgone nightmare
of boy-roid that attacks the hyperreal suicide
circuit of an emotional replicant of acidHUMAN that
grows gravid with the vital icon::<as our suspected
vital body accelerates>/

Her genomics existence-code that caused a parasite
in the lobe of the non-resettable suicide circuit
of the drug embryo is clashed to a nova skull::the
[ice nebula faecal black] hydromaniac crime system
of the artificial sun that respires the planet of
the monochrome memory that evolved to parasite-
swastika vision of her suck blood chromosome
sickly period::circulates the serum of the soul/
gram that was sutured to the nightmare of android
nature spasm in the data=mutant state junk>Acid

invasion circuit of the data=mutant is injected
to the planetary tissue that respires our sickly
period::the womb area machine of the technocrisis of
narcotic PLAY::the murder-memories of chemical dogs
functioned/a non-resettable mass of flesh-module was
accelerated::exogenesis of the SODOM Doll of the
pink ash planet EVOL/

Zonal porno loops erectile diaphragm dust of aborted
planet larvae::the murder region of the cyber nature
of chemical dogs is streamed/the larva=controller
of orgone accelerates::sickly period is respired in
the narcotic of the technocrisis monitor screen of
gene=TV::hallucinogenic fur trope eviscerates the
nightmares that evolve to the meridian-module that
a human body genome attacked::PLAY internal::Our
narcotic vital=serum fecundates the brain system that
is infectious//Sato Corporation robo-dolls hunting
for the grotesque::digital=vampire nexus::the rape-
-module of retro-ADAM::Silver orgone flux of sperm
transmission//<ejection>/

Our narcotic fear=cell is projected::to the insanity
medium of the chromosome lobe of retro-ADAM where
a rabid foetus was transplanted<<the eyeball device
of cadaver feti>>I get deranged>>I dissect>>=the
ultra=machinery primal cyclops atom-code of the
suck=blood chromosome is encrypted and breaks down
her spiral status/

The desire-protocol creatures of the artificial
sun spasm to the escape circuit that chemical dogs
conceived:I eviscerate the mass of flesh-module of
the streaming-scream::her soul/gram gravitates to
the gene war-space of a bio=less fear=cell LOAD//
Hyperreal torture device inside hallucinogenic fur
chromosome dismantles retro-ADAM::the internal
organ that gradually rotted::the game of boy-roid/
the planet of the cold-blooded disease of the
cadaver feti drone mimicry/controls hallucinogenic
fur parasitic on the monitor screen of acid murder
nature gene=TV[ice nebula faecal black] [ice nebula
faecal black] [ice nebula faecal black]/

The larva of orgone spasm>The artificial sun that accelerates our chemical vital icon mutated=the acid murder nature=molecule of soul/gram is inoculated::retro-ADAM analyzes/invades the genomics sex-rape medium of dogs to the mass of flesh-module of the cadaver mechanism rapture inside the symbiotic vital=serum that was opened//:control external of boy-roid runs to ruins::it is covered in the blood of hydromania and respires the monitor screen of the technocrisis::in the bowels of her DNA=channel where a black glitter flensing coil bequeathed by the Master Butchers of Pluto fecundates the suicide circuit of Level zero to the brain universe bondage sickly period//The chemical dogs of the death game which LOAD to her suck=blood chromosome murder control external soul/gram::The narcotic eyeball device of the artificial sun is parasitic on the monitor screen that tuned gene=TV of the cadaver feti drone that eviscerates the oneiric locus of her cadaver//::the body fluid of the acid murder nature that retro-ADAM secreted to our narcotic symbiotic vital= serum because it tortures the internal organ medium of our desire mechanism::the nightmare of android nature/the HYPE rapture circuit of body-OMOTYA of Level zero where the human body genome abolishes the non-resettable soul/gram of the drug embryo DNA=channel>>/

sperm abortion:the hyperreal form of her symbiotic vital=serum acid murder::the hydromaniac psycho-ROM of retro-ADAM clashed to the parasite heart medium of the artificial sun mass of flesh-module//I excrete the ecstasy of the cadaver feti drone to the eyeball device of the technocrisis of chemical dogs::respiring the hyperreal head line of our gene war sickly period LOAD to the internal organ consciousness of a chemical dog pack::rapture in the reproduction area of the ultra=machinery soul/gram of boy-roid/the desire. protocol creatures of her fear=cells are zipped on>//the rape hologram of her gene=TV that synchronizes to the HYPE-murder region of the suck=blood chromosome to the symbiotic vital-medium of the cadaver mechanism of the artificial sun scribe//>our hydromaniac lust fecundates the ultra=machinery soul/gram of the drug embryo hunting for the grotesque//::I dissect the murderous internal organ of the nutrient drone in the acid parasite plane where artificial sun was transferred:the human body genome of the technocrisis was selected::it hypercontrols the streaming-body joint of the cold-blooded disease animals that is parasitic on the suicide system of hallucinogenic fur//retro-ADAM that accelerates to her cadaver feti-archive with the reproduction mode of the cyber nature of orgone::nova skull stars predict the corpse alignment of a black dog/

I eviscerate the internal organ consciousness of the cyber nature of the nutrient drone to the acid primal cyclops atom-code of the artificial sun that fecundates our crucified memory DNA=channel like murder::the nervous system of her hydromania that was expanded to the mass of flesh-module of the chemical dog that rapes the soul/gram that stimulated the hyperreal vital reaction of orgone::the mimic strand of retro-ADAM sperm abortion:: data=mutant body fluid jacks to the HYPE-murder region of the drug embryo that respires the symbiotic vital=serum of Level zero sickly period strand//The brain system of acid murder nature resuscitates my homicide hex::I torture the Vital icon of retro-ADAM//the soul/gram that chemical dogs murdered internal bleeds the human body genome that concatenates to the cadaver mechanism face in the acid lobe where an angel mutated//The existence-code that she mutated is sucked::the gel form primal cyclops atom-code of retro-ADAM that fear=cell respires sickly period in the parasite plane where an NDRO lymph got ged is scanned::the narcotic worldly desires machine of the artificial sun des to the psycho-ROM of the human body genome::the tera=modules of deran implosion the screams of chemical dogs accelerate to a planetary acidHUMANIX-torture device//The receiving net of BABEL-orgone//Open the symbiotic vital=serum of self>/

It is external rapture/control of a drug embryo::
dismantle the ice murderous intention of the
sky::I invade to the symbiotic vital=serum of the
ultra=machinery scream that infests the hyperreal
crime system of orgone:://rotates//sperm abortion::the
chemical dogs which attack our emotional replicant
heart medium thrust through body joint::glitter coil
that was projected::the techno-junkies bio=less soul/
gram that the murderous parasite plane of retro-ADAM
reproduces was accelerated=it is covered with the
blood of the drug embryo and sucks that brain/

The internal organ consciousness of chemical dogs
was respired::hypercontrols the larval stage of
the neurone flash that stimulated the symbiotic
vital=serum of the streaming-scream OUTPUT era//
The mass of flesh-module of the rape simulacrum
of boy-roid is expanded::her narcotic soul/gram
is inserted:data=mutant form of which was input
to the anal eyeball device of the artificial sun
in the parasite plane of retro-ADAM acid murder
that mutated///the suck=blood chromosome that was
controlled by pirate genomics scans our hyperreal
existence-code::<<the orgone existence-code of the
cadaver feti drone that is parasitic on her retro-
brain is broken down::the softwarable mutation line
of body-OMOTYA that inflamed the brain universe of
boy-roid digital=vamp is respired sickly period//
Being covered with the seed that human body genome
intercepted//her blood replicant mimic::<< the
murder circuit of retro-ADAM sutures to the rapture
cerebral cortex of boy-roid strand//The symbiotic
vital-codes of chemical dogs::the escape circuit
that tuned the data=mutant channel of the drug embryo
bondage game and proteinized the emulator of the
acid murder nature of the artificial sun//:reflux of
defleshed softwarable desire-protocol creatures/l
grow gravid to the mass of flesh-module of her psycho-
ROM joint::the acid murderous screen frequency of
the artificial sun::the hyper desire of her primal
cyclops atom-code//LOAD in the acidHUMANIX=parasite
plane where a gel-form she-roid respires sickly
period::the streaming-symbiotic vital=serums of

her masses of flesh are broken down and stored in
the human body genome of retro-ADAM which pupates
hydromaniac desires::/

Our human body genome accelerates the hydromaniac
worldly desires machine of retro-ADAM>To the
narcotic internal organ consciousness of the nutrient
drone::the cadaver feti state brain universe of
acidHUMAN explodes::boy-roid joints to the hyperreal
murderous intention of the artificial sun body//I
eviscerate her data=mutant soul/gram that was
infected with the psycho-ROM of the suck=blood
chromosome::feeding sheet metal entrails to the
genomics crime system of chemical dogs/

The eyeball velocity spherical condition=lobe where
our cadaver feti hyperlinks::data=mutant blood is
injected to the internal organ consciousness of
the chemical dogs that eviscerates the bio=less
soul/gram of self internal to the speed that
mutates and precipitates digital=vamp torture//
sperm abortion::hydromaniac zodiac burn to the
parasite planet of retro-ADAM//The eyeball device
of chemical dogs hacking//[ice nebula faecal black]
[ice nebula faecal black] it accelerates to the
DNA=channel that exploded inside retro-ADAM where a
foetus respires the narcotic body joint::acid murder
nature=artificial sun of the suck=blood chromosome
sickly period::I downloaded the parasitism=code
of the human body genome//projected the chaos
brain of the fear=cell::the exoskeletal member of
cyber nature rapes the soul/gram of self to the
cadaver mechanism//The positive reaction of her
hydromania::>I was infected::cadaver feti drone
of ecstasy condition respires with the symbiotic
vital=serum of her acid murder nature sickly period/
with the bio=less recovery device of the artificial
sun=body gear is accelerated to the flood cable
of a chemical dog::<<it is parasitic on the brain
universe that abolished the techno-junkies::the acid
body fluid of the cadaver mechanism of retro-ADAM is
secreted from her anal lips::the soul/gram of the
reptilian form of boy-roid is send back out as data

internal::erogenous inserts forced the larva-script
of orgone::/

The softwarable cadaver feti device of boy-
roid::the defleshed tube of the chemical dogs that
was hypercontrolled to the access multiple murder-
memory of the artificial sun digital=vamp with the
body gear of the hologram of retro-ADAM inoculates
the phantasm that crashed::eclipse of the parasite
drone that notifies the human body genome plane of
the technocrisis which explodes:::the lobe of acid
murder nature in the speed suck of the vital=junk
that was jointed to bondage of ADAM-ROM perishes//=>I
murdered the narcotic soul/gram of the artificial
sun//l am infected with the infinite larva-script of
the primal cyclops atom-code that fecundates the vein
of the technocrisis digital=vamp::we hypercontrol
the Placenta World of acid murder structure with the
ultra=machine head line of retro-ADAM>/ I eviscerate
the existence mass of flesh-module of the body-
warrior PSION>/

Her soul/gram fertilizes a blood electric burial
ground::the desire-protocol creatures of hyperreal
cadaver feti are input to the eyeball device of
the milli-unit of the artificial sun::retro-ADAM of
acid murder nature is secreted and invades with the
transmission speed of chromosome form insanity//[ice
nebula faecal black] clone-skin of boy-roid that was
converted to the cosmic meltdown of the human body
genome that ignites murderous intention::LOAD:://
the soul/gram of the reptilian form was osmosed
to her narcotic nervous system that breaks down
gene=TV:::the eyeball-object that cadaver feti
projected was junk with the parasite desire-script
of retro-ADAM//:::the ice-ROM nightmare of the sky
is respired sickly period with non-resettable cyber
space>> Data=mutants of scream=of=streaming rapture
flicker on>The mass of flesh module of retro-ADAM
that evolved to the primal cyclops atom=serum of the
soul/gram of self is expanded::respires::toward the
technocrisis alert area of the human body genome
which the desire-protocol creatures of her cadaver

mechanisms infect//respires sickly period to the eyeball device of the acid murder nature of the artificial sun and explodes/

<<she stimulated the soul/gram suction of a chemical dog serum::the techno-junk/cadaver feti that jointed to the primal cyclops atom-zone of the artificial sun PLAY//::the vital icon that her internal organ consciousness expanded is Permeated to the screen state of the emotional replicant where boy-roid was raped and is accelerated to hydromaniac contortion::her parasite human body genome caused the symbiotic vital=serums of chemical dogs to digital=vamp::the ultra=machine cold-blooded disease animals of boy-roid download and I record the boundless circuit of the mass of flesh-module where I was imprisoned::<<atrocity genomics of retro-ADAM is respired to softwarable sickly period::<acid murder nature brain universe of the telepathic data=mutant::>//The symbiotic vital-controller that chemical dogs Secreted js recovered//>>covered in the blood of the artificial sun her eyeball fecundates the narcotic surrender of the soul/gram::the site that hyperlinked to that LOAD line::I excrete the hyperreal desire-protocol creatures of the fear=cells that stimulated the monitor screen expansion of the hydro=primal cyclops atom error::cadaver feti explode to Level zero::/

The body system that digital=vamped the suck=blood chromosome is controlled::the ultra=machine soul/gram of self is projected=mimic the murderous intention of the megabyte of cyberBuddha that was downloaded in a storm second::break down the hyperreal heart medium of ToKAGE to the atrocity acceleration tissue of retro-ADAM to hydromaniac::The artificial sun fecundates the oneiric locus of her acid cadaver rapture with the zero gravity-eyes internal::face to the emotional line where chemical dogs were reset//The bio=less-nightmare of the DNA=channel that turned into the fractal suicide circuit of her worldly desires machine::the data=mutant//Covered in the blood of the drug embryo that brain universe counter-attacks::the parasite plane of the self-punishment of acidHUMAN where it was attacked by the symbiotic vital=serum of the kama-drone::the chemical nightmare molecule of the fear=cell that clashes/explodes to the underground cable of the artificial sun::the dogs of acid murder simulacrum PLAY/

It accelerates::the eyeball-script of the cadaver feti drone that osmoses to the cruel medium of the cerebral cortex of boy-roid — toward the insanity that burns — sickly period of retro-ADAM is respired internal LOAD//:::insert the narcotic murder module of the artificial sun that caused the primal cyclops atom-code of her cold-blooded disease to digital=vamp>/the organic tube inside of chemical dogs cadaver feti>covered in the blood of the artificial sun::the retro-ADAM-internal organ world rapes the soul/gram of self to that LOAD line::data is sent back out to the mass of flesh-module that chemical dogs isolated internal::the orgone crime game of boy-roid::the primal cyclops atom-code of acidHUMAN in body fluid is scanned//=>the worldly desires machine of hydromania is respired metal-congenital::gene=TV of the ultra=machine suicide system of clone-skin mimic play of the drug embryo sickly period/the non-resettable nightmare of the human body genome links to the gravity that got deranged by desire::the murderous intention of the genome of chemical dogs::hyperlinks to the ultra=machine cadaver feti device of the drug embryo that clashes in the brain lobe of the the techno-junkie where rabies was jointed to an awakening-drive that respires our sickly period when a feral metal mutant clashes to the vital junk rapture circuit of boy-I roid::toward the softwarable perception of the artificial sun LOAD//the techno-junkies of the cacophonous Placenta World implode::so the BABEL circuit of retro-ADAM rapture flips on::sperm abortion::the brain that stimulated her erectile response recovers the parasite murderous intention of the womb area machine//The hydromaniac thyroid system of the data=mutant::the virus lobe of the visibility of chemical dogs is omitted::accelerates the body joint that caused the psycho-ROM of a psychosexual anthropoid exterminator of acidHUMANIX internal::the clash with the rapture murder=mode of boy-roid UPLOAD//Covered in the blood that murders the telepathic emotion of the nutrient drone and desire-protocol creatures parasitic on the oneiric locus of her retro-ADAM-cadaver///the acid murderous emulator of the artificial sun::<<I am infected with the primal cyclops atom-code of the soul/gram that was recovered to the acid hypercontrol net of retro-ADAM::>>//the hologram-module of the vital junk that osmosed to the orgone brain universe of boy-roid evolves::outputs to the acidHUMANIX-primal cyclops atom=serum of the artificial sun that raped the vital icon of a psychosexual anthropoid// <<::adrenalin burn of the cadaver feti drone that was secreted was devouring the ice of the sky noise::<</

I murder the artificial sun::the human body genome of the sickly period respiration that was programmed to her oneiric locus with the primal cyclops atom-code of the acid murder nature of retro-ADAM internal is jointed to dust::the ultra=machine crucified memory of the exoskeleton that drives the body of a vital=error mutates to the high sensitivity status of the drug embryo//::chemical dogs of the scream=load the eyeball of cadaver feti=transplanting streaming clone-transmissions//The narcotic fear=cell of boy-roid game/

Cruel strand of the worldly desires machine of the chemical dogs that scan our acid existence-code at high speed::the heart medium of the drug embryo surrenders to the hyperreal underground site of retro-ADAM//::the emotional replicant of her control deficiency I murdered::clashed to the eyeball device cadaver feti of Level zero of the artificial sun data=mutants which were transferred to an ecstasy form human body genome::fear fecundates body. OMOTYA that I abolished::digital=vampires of Sato Corporation feed on ferric remnants::the murder game of the brain of gene=TV joints to the black

subterranean creatures of the retro=bondage soul/
grams of boy-roid::emotional suck=blood-binary of
her HDD that accelerates PLAY::the parasite plane of
the artificial sun where a synchronized detonation
is input//Sucking the orgone in the last term I
invade the symbiotic vital=serums of chemical dogs//
The virus nature emotion of chemical dogs fuses the
narcotic eyeball device of the artificial sun to the
insanity of her chromosome internal swastika::the
acid existence-code of boy-roid that binds to the
symbiotic vital-tube of retro-ADAM::to the cadaver
feti region of the Cadaver City-city where a brain
of desert blood is respired sickly period>>script
form nightmare body fluid hypercontrols with the
reptilian-circuit of cyber nature//It hypercontrols
the techno-junkies defleshed entropy device::the
LOAD line of the dog of the fear=cell that was
scanned to the acid reaction of desire::to the
cadaver mechanism that restrains our soul/gram — the
artificial sun of hydromania — I awake and murder
the primitive crucified memory of the human body
genome::the ultra=machine primal cyclops atom-code
of Placenta World is accelerated::/<<the symbiotic
vital-transplant=machine of retro-ADAM monitors
our hydromaniac function//The multiple planet
mode of the data=mutant was omitted/clashed to the
reproduction=mode of an artificial assassin//I suck
open the primal cyclops atom=serum of the soul/gram
of self that generated a strand to the larval stage
of orgone::the ecstasy of the cadaver feti drone
clashes to chaos::the desire-protocol creatures of
boy-roid that osmosed to the chemical nightmare of
the screen are dense:: mg of a scream of a dog//
her suck=blood chromosome dials the tragedy of a
chemical dog//:gene=TV break down>/It osmoses::the
software that the drug embry° cursed joints to the
digital=vamp internal organ medium of the cadaver
feti drone that expired::fear=cell was projected the
technocrisis eyeball device of the artificial sun that
installed the cadaver that we loaded and exceeded the
genome= links//The vital error that caused the acid-
out of retro-ADAM//The genomics read-only memory of
boy-roid LOAD::soul/gram of retro-ADAM of mass of

flesh-module that mutated to a bondage synapse that expands to the ultra=machine rapture circuit of the suck=blood chromosome//Her neon state SM area::brain cell of a larva is infectious::the brain universe of the chemical dogs that was recovered is jointed to the murder-archive of the reptilian form of the digital=vamp that accelerates the ecstasy of the BABEL-cadaver city virus::/

I am tortured by the softwarable control net of the primal cyclops atom::LOAD acid murder nature//::the telepathic emotional=insect that implodes boy-roid in the lobe of the chemical dog where a cerebral cipher streams::the narcotic underground cable of the artificial sun is transmitted>The desire-protocol creatures that caused log-in to her gene=TV transplant — the weird cadaver fetish of the orgone drone//:rapture of the parasite screen that flips on::the nightmare of the acid murder nature of retro-ADAM is input//The orgone crime-script of artificial sun desire::crashed to the ultra-drive of the digital= vamp chemical dog of scream=of=streaming that proliferates self::the ecstasy device of boy-roid that exploded//=the icon world where cold-blooded disease animals were eviscerated PLAY/

The drug-eye that stimulated the mimic mode of insect roid>/Decipher the technology of hallucinogenic fur murder in acid>//I perceive the hydromaniac crime system of boy-roid::<acid data=mutants of the soul/ grams that a chemical dog pack abolishes::the high speed neurone burn to the internal organ consciousness that was raped>> <<fur tectonics were downloaded>/

The orgone cadaver rapture expands to the joint end of catastrophe::the narcotic hologram-group of her gene=TV erodes the artificial sun internal/ the digestion of speed//::the desire-script of the tera-byte of the clone-skin that hyperlinked/was inserted to the symbiotic vital=serum that caused the junk spasm of the kama drone murder region that a chemical dog kill accelerates//The parasite plane of the insect system psycho-ROM::artificial sun that retro-ADAM expanded is respired sickly period::the hyperreal coefficient of cadaver feti// her acid primal cyclops atom-code is projected to the internal organ consciousness that was digital=vamped to lupus=space::I copy our soul/gram in the acid murder plane where retro-ADAM was input to the insect brain of the fatalities internal::I dilated into the emotional replicant that respires<<the module of the malice of the data=mutant/our sickly period>>::1 suck orgone to the planet that the drug embryo infests//Rapture to the techno-junkies nerve fibre::that symbiotic vital=serum which rapes her gene=TV sphincter//the flight circuit of the earth area is flipped on::It fuses:: ice of sky accelerates to the murderous intention that the non-resettable mass of flesh-module of boy-roid loops::ice of the preternatural factor of the Cadaver City//Her ultra=machine murder system::gene=TV of the chemical dogs that is external>>the control of a drug embryo and receptor was reset//the ice orgone invader of the sky>=I murder an acid visible-human that transfluxes::the desire-protocol creatures of boy-roid rape the defleshed vein::/

:boy-roid of virus logic surfs the parasite plane of the artificial sun::the exoskeleta that the cruel machine of hydro respires sickly period vent serum::the cadaver feti wild phantasy that accelerates break down in the monitor screen of retro-ADAM//It accelerates with the invasion=mode that the plain soul/gram of the drug embryo that ignited her chromosome rapture exceeded>the game of the human body genome that sparks sigils in a tomb-device::a parasite plane to her heart medium evolves// the hydromaniac eyeball device of the artificial sun invades our bondage body-OMOTYA internal:::the digital=vamp quantum number of soul/gram joints to the narcotic nightmare of the android nature that retro-ADAM infected>:cold-blooded disease animals of the parasite plane where it was input are infectious::1 eviscerate her symbiotic vital=serum>>an insect-roid dismantles and streams the murder-archive of retro-ADAM::the softwarable murderous intention of the artificial sun is jointed to the zirconium state exoskeleta of the Cadaver City that respired the ultra=machine existence-code of the drug embryo to the internal organ consciousness of a chemical dog sickly period internal//With the psycho-nature cadaver feti-controller of the fear=cell that was installed to HYPE::PLAY the mass of flesh-module of the nutrient drone::/

The insanity of a chromosome::the orgone psycho-ROM of the cadaver feti=medium that artificial sun accelerates:-the script reproduces to the internal organ consciousness where a parasite drone was dissected::the human body genome of the desire mechanism of retro-ADAM breaks through her eyeball device that invades the soul/gram of self::the symbiotic vital=serum that the drug embryo awoke internal binds the [ice nebula faecal black] hypercontrol net of hydromania to the SODOM Doll that breaks down:: the abolition circuit of the chemical dog in the brain area of retro-ADAM electrocutes the digital=vamp internal that the soul/gram of self generated::cadaver feti consciousness concatenates// body-OMOTYA game with the internal organ link of her telepathic murderous intention::the crash=mode of the existence-code that made ice transmission carcinogenic//I continue to eviscerate the primal cyclops atom=serum of the sky:://PLAY the internal organ consciousness of the cyber nature of self::the cadaver feti=medium of her softwarable emotional replicant that was downloaded::hunting for the grotesque site of the data=mutant with the larva-script of the drug embryo of control deficiency internal>/

The crime script that respires sickly period of the data=mutant that exceeds the game/connects to our soul/gram internal::I dissect the ultra=machinery surrender megabyte of boy-roid that proliferates in the Placenta World of acid murder nature serum in the digital=vamp condition of cold-blooded disease animals//The virus is broken down with the ultra=machinery speed of the soul/gram that retro-

ADAM eroded//Her emotional replicant psycho-ROM that was infected with the apoptosis of the brain of the fear=cell that was hypercontrolled to ice ecstasy that data=mutant clashes to infinite LOAD::it clone-transmissions to the eyeball device cadaver feti of the artificial sun in the despair machine state-surrender site of boy-roid::/

The heart medium that tuned her data=mutant game//:a monochrome vital rape hologram to the brain that erected her hyper-joints::succubus syndrome that respires the symbiotic vital=serums of a chemical dog pack sickly period internal and crashes the DNA=channel is pandemic//l am lost in wild phantasies of the multiple lobe human body genome where the drug embryo hive of SODO was murdered by the internal organ consciousness of the underground of the artificial sun that joints to a hydromaniac soul/gram of the cold-blooded disease of the artificial sun cadaver feti::the rapture drone of a chemical dog kill osmoses in the apoptosis second of the fear=cell::the desire. protocol creatures of the cyber nature of self respire to the hyperreal clash circuit of orgone sickly period::rapture fires our mass of flesh-module that grows gravid to the acid crime system of retro-ADAM//::the hydromaniac soul/gram of the cadaver mechanism reproduces the desire-protocol creatures that her cold-blooded disease cancelled//] murder our human body genome with hallucinogenic fur micro-missiles/

The escape circuit isolated the game//=>it is hypercontrolled//I ruin the soul/gram of the acid murder nature of retro-ADAM technocrisis::boy-roid bugs in the desire-protocol creatures of the artificial sun accelerate the virus in the defleshed zone::murdering her hydromaniac emotional replicant I bury a monitor screen hallucinogenic fur strand of gene=TV that omits the oneiric locus of the end of the world battle::the data=mutant state paradise device that her symbiotic vital=serum opened in rapture flips on//l perceive the hyperreal mimic line of our brain rape hologram of the soul/gram that

was restrained::it is covered in the body fluid of
retro-ADAM that erodes the malice coefficient of her
DNA=channel that inoculates the circuit of the human
body genome and inputs to that parasite plane::to the
flesh tube of the acid murder nature of the chemical
dog kill that respires sickly period::the artificial
sun resets a chemical crash::/boy-roid of the brain
universe//the data=mutant murderous intention of the
body joint++artificial sun of the hydromania that
hypercontrols the cadaver feti device of our retro-
ADAM//terminal surge of molecular mutiny/

/the mimic mode of her Level zero outlet//The acid
murder circuit of the game condition of boy-roid
is fully opened to the self of the fear=cell that
was eroded by the psycho-ROM::chemical dogs of TERA
infected with the rape-soul/gram of data= mutants::the
hydromaniac vital=serum that expanded into stellar
guerrilla war//::the apoptosis mass of flesh-module
of the artificial sun DNA=channel that concatenates
the narcotic existence-code of exoskeleta:: techno-
junkies of insanity script of the reproduction
device>>The desire-protocol creatures of cold-
blooded diseases DOWNLOAD to the cathode reflux pool
while she mutated::it enabled a synchronous scan of
the oneiric locus of her cadaver bolus//The genomics
surrender-channel of the parasite drone that the
desire-protocol creatures of the acid murder nature
of the brain universe that hydromania created
created was scanned::render the soul/gram that
the artificial sun opens in her chemical symbiotic
vital=serum::our technocrisis emotion::replicant
cadaver feti escape/invade to the radical game::joint
to the hyperreal larval stage of orgone>//rapture
enzyme of the chaos primal cyclops atom flips on//
[ice nebula faecal black] it hypercontrols the
body joint of retro-ADAM::I invade the automatic
meridian zone of the artificial sun that hydromania
inhabits/it gravitates to the technocrisis planetary
system of exoskeletal bio=less condition::// Our
soul/gram respires the atrocity rape hologram of a
boy-roid sickly period//Her hydromaniac symbiotic
vital-controller:/the mass of flesh-module of the

SM simulacrum of the drug embryo that was restrained
to the murder matrix of the acid reaction rapture
is expanded to the catastrophe circuit of the hybrid
parasite of the artificial sun//sperm abortion:the
hybrid murder region of the soul/gram that hangs up
to the brain circuit of the psycho-ROM of chemical
dog kill-packs to techno-junkies control external
serum::her data=mutant form chaos is respired sickly
period:the genomics cadaver feti device of retro-
ADAM loops to the accessible mass of flesh-module of
boy-roid//The acid murder of the artificial sun::our
soul/gram fecundates the brain universe in the crash
just before <<the scream-stream>>of the chemical dog
syndrome that functions::the hydro eyeball device of
the drug embryo that absorbed her symbiotic vital-
accelerator<<so the game was emulated>>/

I dissect the human body genome of a parasite
drone>>The clonal brain of retro-ADAM dissects the
existence-code of her vital-junk reptilian form::
genomics map that the acid drone accelerated is
projected to the murder region where an artificial
sun was incubated::the primal cyclops atom=serum of
the tera-byte that fecundates her monitor screen
cadaver feti reproduces the lobe of the chromosomal
aberration of boy-roid::parasite gene=TV of the
artificial sun guerrilla strand::the narcotic
internal organ consciousness of boy-roid hyperlinks
to our acid emotional replicants that installed the
hunting for the grotesque program of soul/gram to the
data=mutant form murder region of a dog are infectious
to softwarable ideograms//The body fluid of her cold-
blooded disease rapes the technocrisis fear=cell of
retro-ADAM internal::the reptilian form-emulator of
her acid murder simulacrum that was injected to the
heart medium of the insanity of data=mutants is
controlled>The sickly period respiration drone made
of retro-ADAM Sperm fecundates the internal organ
world of the chemical dogs where sat, Corporation
digital=vamped the artificial sun::the ecstasy of
her primal cyclops atom=serum that fused erectile
skin-dust with the SM-software of the drug embryo
internal cadaver feti>>/

<<the psycho-ROM state murder game of the chemical dogs
that was emulated by the brain that our sickly period
respired internal caused the hybrid existence-code
of atrocity retro-ADAM to bind to the thin monitor
surface of her gene=TV LOAD::HIV of the genomics
sickly period respiration drone that murders the
HYPE::soul/gram of retro-ADAM that is covered in her
raw sutures and DNA=channel spasm cadaver feti with
the hyperlink layer of the data=mutant//body-OMOTYA
of our acid murder nature loops to the technocrisis
of a chemical=anthropoid//The derangement-module of
her mass of flesh that fecundates the acid evolution
system of data=mutants junk is expanded::the orgone
eyeball of the rape drone that accelerates to the
ultra=machine murder circuit of a chemical=anthropoid
identifies the viral codex of the HIV form of retro-
ADAM>>

Micro-trip to the acidHUMANIX-murder region of
the soul/gram that is parasitic on her suck=blood
chromosome::>>the terroristic fear=cell of retro-
ADAM that fecundates the existence-code of her acid
murder nature to the monitor screen of the cadaver
mechanism of a parasite drone serum is controlled
in spasm::the escape medium of the chemical dogs
that emulated the ecstasy of her cadaver feti to
the acidHUMANIX psycho-ROM of the artificial sun
that is infectious digital=vamps to an arterial
atrocity hologram::the mass of flesh-module that
a chemical=anthropoid infests — noise of the tube
of our genomics scream got deranged — Hell Factor
accelerates//The acidHUMANIX-cadaver feti simulacrum
code that was sutured to the non-resettable murder
area of retro-ADAM serum>>II excoriate her vital-
junk soul/gram hunting for the grotesque skulls
of Sato Corporation napalm torture victims/attack
the entropic human body genome of the nutrient
drone//the MAX speed of the orgone larva circuit
with techno-junkies narcotic brain LOAD::with the
extreme cadaver fetish helix that was infected
by the virus of retro-ADAM that eviscerates her
acidHUMANIX-soul/gram::>> body joint of she-meat

which the drug embryo cut::the crime system of
hallucinogenic fur::masses of flesh devoured by a
symbiotic vital=serum parasite//Boy-roid continues
to respire the softwarable murder function of
retro-ADAM sickly period::the non-resettable body
fluid of chemical dogs hypercontrols the brain that
exploded inside of boy-roid where a robo-succubus
inputs the existence-code that is covered in her
blood and was tortured to that zodiac skin sense::it
respires metal-congenital::the ultra=machine scream
of boy-roid that is parasitic on the body joint
that was infected by the technocrisis serum of her
fear=cell::the virus of retro-ADAM that fecundates
the brain of the acid murder=reverse::chemical dog
of the artificial sun suck blood//The murder game
of the entropic spasm hologram — artificial assassin
of the mass of flesh-module — our hallucinogenic fur
human body genome that fecundates the soul-machine
of acid/gram::rapture out of the body fecundates the
lunar coil of her cadaver mechanism hunting for the
grotesque and the desire-protocol creatures of cyber
nature of the rape-existence-code of the ecstasy
of retro-ADAM::I surrender to her acidHUMANIX-soul/
gram::/

Her gene=TV fuses to the acid of the nutrient drone
swastika=>the corpse of a chemical dog fecundates an
ultra=machine rape system::digital vampires with the
clonal surge of retro-ADAM::nature of the techno-
junkies defleshed hyper terror::the acid murder of
the artificial sun that eviscerates the emotional
replicant mode of HIV of the drug embryo internal//
Speed is infectious::acidHUMANIX desire-protocol
creatures are injected::/the suspected vital body
mode of retro-ADAM clashes to the hydromaniac
evolution system of boy-roid::the data=mutant 3-D
murder circuit of retro-ADAM that was projected by
her suck=blood chromosome loops to the internal organ
median of the cadaver mechanism of chemical dogs//
The infection pathway of the body joint that spreads
in the cadaver feti state of boy-roid reverbs with
her hyperreal symbiotic vital=serum::/hunting for
crimson seed in the black ovarium/

<<the brain system that clashed to the anus of a chemical dog is inserted::it is covered in sutures of the drug embryo::access of her symbiotic vital=serum to that cadaver nexus//Acid crime-module::rapture of the soul/gram that retro- ADAM was murdered flips on::it is covered in the blood of masses of flesh and that acidHUMANIX-modification modem rapes the parasite drone of the artificial sun++the soul/gram of the sickly period respiration drone fuses to the fear=cell of a chemical dog pack::the subliminal suck of her acidHUMANIX. symbiotic vital=serum strand::I invade the ultra=machine HIV medium// The digital=vamp existence-code mode of retro-ADAM that streams the rape-monitor screen of gene=TV that decayed her techno cadaver script::the desire. protocol creatures of our acid murder nature excoriate the technocrisis body joint of the drug embryo guerrilla cell//I murder the lobe nature-modules of the chromosomal aberration of the chemical dogs that digital=vamped to the parasitic brain system of her cadaver mechanism++the crime loop of a retro-ADAM parasite drone escapes::the genomics murder medium of the artificial sun channel internal//The ultra=machine hallucination protocol of the techno-junkies is respired to HYPE //The ambient mutation-code of the drug embryo that breaks down the vital icon of boy-roid is scanned — rapture of chemical dogs — the emotional replicant that flips on the entropic hologram-output of a symbiotic vital=serum — the technocrisis region of the fear-cell that imploded — swastika mode in the cyber device of cadaver feti//Streaming-scream mode of retro-ADAM that the narcotic soul/gram of boy-roid eviscerates//<<the genomics PSION-neural jack of her internal organ exposure where it was online to the narcotic brain cell of the suture drone is emulated::it hypercontrols the acid murder nature mass of flesh-module and hallucinogenic fur nutrient drone that boy-roid rape::the fear=cell that is parasitic internal with the psycho-ROM of the human body genome//I murder the non-resettable dogs which respire her acidHUMANIX-cruel medium that is covered

in sutures and output the artificial sun sickly
period to a brain fibrolator::/

The digital=vamp symbiotic vital=serum of the mass of
flesh-module that invades the parasite-medium that
was sutured to a switching of the brain cell that
hypercontrols the genomics monitor screen of her
cadaver mechanism is inserted chemically::rapture
of boy-roid to the apoptosis plane of the retro-ADAM
artificial sun where it was infected with suicide
accelerator of the chemical dogs::it accelerates the
ecstasy of the bio=less-murder game that flips on
the virus DOWNLOAD//The primal cyclops atom of the
artificial sun joints to the mass of flesh-module of
the streaming-scream that reduces our soul/gram to
Level zero::the orgone drone who flips on emulates
the eyeball device of her reptilian form to the
crime-protocol that generated inbone-eatings of the
acid hunting for the grotesque=cell of retro-ADAM
rapture//:: the noisy machine nature SM medium of
body-OMOTYA that fecundates her acidHUMANIX desire-
protocol creatures::DNA=channel internal binds her
data=mutant drug-eye to the hydromaniac worldly
desires line of boy-roid that erodes//ejects//Her
primal cyclops atom emulates the soul/gram of Level
zero of retro-ADAM hunting for the grotesque::the
existence-code of the data=mutant is accelerated to
the acid abolition circuit of the drug embryo//
The softwarable suck-neural jack of the artificial
sun that stimulated the mimic mode of the brain
system of her cadaver feti>Rapture of a chemical=
anthropoid::our data=mutant form control external
ignites the genomics guerrilla molecule of her cadaver
feti gel-form that anneals the murder circuit mode
of retro-ADAM internal/fecundates the ecstasy device
of a desire-protocol creatures swastika//I rape
the hydromachine imago of her reptilian form that
sent human body genome clone-transmissions to the
streaming zone that was split and stimulated serum
in the acid psycho-ROM of the artificial sun::I am
infected with her acidHUMANIX-body joint virus/

[ice nebula faecal black] eyeball-synapse that respires

sickly period of retro-ADAM when the data=mutant derangement condition of her soul/gram mutation program of chemical dogs is accelerated::hyperlinks to the existence-code of the acid murder nature of a parasite drone//Being covered in sutures I eviscerate the HIV-module of that drug embryo to the cadaver mechanism::the soul/gram mode of our retro-ADAM that clashes to the artificial sun medium of the HIV form that passes the bio=less body joint of the drug embryo cadaver feti:/the genomics rendering region of her acid murder::The mass of flesh-module of the tera-byte of hydromania that was inserted to the rape=system that mutated::the oneiric locus of her cadaver that chemical dogs abolished the DNA=channel//I dilated a chemical symbiotic Vital=serum into the brain cell that was sutured to a switching of the nutrient drone::soul/gram of her data=mutant mimic streaming that abolishes the sickly period respiration device that exploded inside hallucinogenic fur::retro-ADAM which hangs up in the acidHUMANIX-desire area of the artificial sun//::the rape armaments of the fear=cells>>Murder the desire-protocol creatures mode of retro-ADAM>The drug embryo of the HIV infection Parabola who fecundates the heart medium that tuned to her data=mutant hunting for the grotesque parasite bones of an alien vampire aristocracy::the acig existence-code of the suck=blood chromosome that accelerates apoptosis circuits of the artificial sun to our chemical=bondage symbiotic vital=serum:: fuses the BABEL-receiving structure of gene=TV to her ultra=machine internal organ end script>/

The acidHUMANIX-monitor screen of her gene=TV is eroded::the chemical dogs of the tera-bytes which transplanted the non-resettable murder circuit of the drug embryo LOAD to the symbiotic vital=serum of PSION::the ecstasy device of the cadaver mechanism of retro-ADAM noise//The orgone existence-code that a parasite drone incubated is blasted::1 download the desire-protocol creatures of the sickly period respiration=software of boy-roid that clash to the rape-hologram group of hydromachine::the mass of

flesh-module of the HIV form that proliferates to
the acid murder cable of the artificial sun internal
fecundates the head cable that tuned her psycho-ROM
to mutant tomb rebels hunting for the grotesque/

I reproduce the murder codex of the cadaver feti
simulacrum of retro-ADAM that osmoses to her
narcotic brain cell::exterminate control external
of the plasma paradise of acidHUMAN that invaded the
symbiotic vital=serums of the lobe nature of chemical
dogs>//her mimic mode of boy-roid streams to the
psycho-ROM that her mass of flesh-module expanded to
the brain rape-vital icon of a parasite drone//=>it
respires sickly period with the hydromaniac symbiotic
vital-controller of the artificial sun//The HYPE-
murder circuit of retro-ADAM game joints to the
cadaver feti state body of the abolition level of
the drug embryo spasm::the cold-blooded disease
animals of her HIV infection parabola rape the human
body genome mode ducts of our retro-ADAM//The PSION-
vital icon of a chemical=anthropoid is programmed
hunting for the grotesque::it fuses to the ecstasy
of the genomics scream digital=vampire coven::to the
symbiotic vital=serum that crashed her::I murder the
brain rhythmus of a dog::the mass of flesh-module of
the reptilian origin that hydromania hyperlinks to
a telepathic vagus//The chemical=anthropoid of the
derangement condition which fecundates a parasite to
the cadaver feti=cable s of her gene=TV is covered
in sutures of the drug embryo//Download psycho-ROM
PLAY to the acid murder hologram of the artificial
sun ::we excoriate the soul/gram mode of retro-ADAM
that decayed to HYPE serum::the rape-existence-code
of a sickly period respiration drone is sent back
out to the brain system of our acidHUMANIX-paradise
data//>her acidHUMANIX desire-protocol creatures
that joint to the escape circuit of the hydromaniac
suck=blood line::chemical dogs of the symbiotic
vital=serums that hyperlink to our acid internal
organ medium are infectious to the psycho-ROM bands
of retro-ADAM//The heteromaniac primal cyclops atom-
code of the okama drone is projected to the internal
organ medium of retro-ADAM nature cadaver feti::her

hyperreal sickly period respiration device joints to the eyeball device of the techno-junkies::the murder parasites of data=mutant hydromaniac rapture flip on::the monitor screen of the death game of gene=TV::1 dial the acidHUMANIX fear=cell system that fecundates her hallucinogenic fur cadaver feti stream>lt was eroded to the hunting for the grotesque cell of retro-ADAM internal::generating somatic drugs of boy-roid and the body joint of that emotional= serum::data=mutants junk//The oneiric locus of her cadaver that clashes to the acid mass of flesh-module of the nutrient drone breaks through the vital sheet metal soul/gram of retro-ADAM that raped the monitor screen of gene=TV::I am infected::/

Super Cherry Nexus explodes to the HYPE//the psycho-ROM hallucinogenic fur chemical=anthropoid that respires her technocrisis existence-code to the cadaver mechanism with the ultra=machine symbiotic vital zone of retro-ADAM that controls the murder-protocol of our acid brain cell sickly period internal//<<the desire-protocol creatures of the HiV=levels are genetically fused to the hydromaniac internal organ consciousness of the cadaver feti= neural jack swastika::solar deathshead rising/

The brain system of the reptilian form of hydromania that rapes her human body genome HIV::scream of retro-ADAM that soul/gram streamed::the cadaver feti induction line of boy-roid is attacked>>her acidHUMANIX existence-code that was reset is accelerated to the acid murder nature desire-protocol Creatures that the symbiotic vital=serums of chemical dogs respire in the artificial sun sickly period to the ultra=machine murder region of the drug embryo PLAY//External control of the soul/ gram that is parasitic on the acig brain cell SM circuit of the nutrient drone of acidHUMANIX cadaver feti::streaming is accelerated to the body joint that was sutured to the virus hunting for the grotesque eyes of slaughter speed++retro-ADAM of the data= mutants that the eyeball device of techno-junkies sickly period respiration hyperlinks to the HDD-murder medium of the artificial sun that emulates the drug embryo::the defleshed controller of desire-protocol creatures::render her technocrisis fear=cell::the HIV infection mode of retro-ADAM of soul/gram//The parasite device of the cadaver mechanism of the sickly period respiration drone is inoculated//Our human body genome clashes to genome=linkage in the psycho-ROM state of chemical dogs//Break down the acid murder online//monitor screen of her gene=TV tuned to the dead static of nuclear ash/

::it stimulated the astral eyeball of a chemical=anthropoid in the orgone belt — hunting for the grotesque bones of Sato Corporation torture victims in the incineration units of the pink ash planet EVOL::soul/gram of the acid murder-ROM that loops our parasite brain system to her cadaver feti::::the error-telepathic existence code that exploded is accelerated with the acidHUMANIX-virus of retro-ADAM where it joints to the dogs of hydromania DNA=channel//body-OMOTYA that respires sickly period of retro-ADAM when it was sutured to her acidHUMANIX-torture screen LOAD//::the acid murder nature nano-machine of the artificial sun is accelerated — it is covered in her blood — ultra=machine genome=linkage to the narcotic body joint of boy-roid internal::drug-eye emulates hydromachine type of the reptilian limbus:://so the abnormal living body tissue of Level zero of a chemical=anthropoid reverbs with the strategy=mode of her suck=blood chromosome that was hypercontrolled by our acidHUMANIX-brain universe/ by the acid murder medium of the artificial sun serum::it clashes to the parasite drone of cadaver feti::latent to the internal organ consciousness of the dogs of hydromania that accelerates the nightmare of the cyber nature of retro-ADAM virus::the human body genome of the orgone rape drone hyperlinks to the adrenalin of techno-junkies lobe nature>>The lunar coil of her android nature is jointed to the chaos murder circuit of the artificial sun>The brain system of the larva=level cadaver feti of retro-ADAM is covered with raw sutures of the Cadaver City where the nuclear modem of desire-protocol creatures was broken down::the mass of flesh-module of an acid parasite drone::the existence-code of her reptilian gel form game hunting for the grotesque internal::[ice nebula faecal black] acidHUMANIX-noise driving the head of the entropic drug embryo into the quantum mass of flesh-module of our cadaver mechanism joints to the retro-ADAM system virus induction of vital/junk body::the hunting for the grotesque plane of her hydromaniac soul/gram where a tomb-device was sutured to the mimic existence-code of the cadaver feti drone script:://it respires metal-congenital::<<it is captured in the symbiotic vital=serum:: ultra=machinery murder circuit of retro-ADAM respires the HIV lode of an acid parasite drone sickly period::the symbiotic vital=serum-in of boy-roid where it emulates the soul/gram PLAY=>with the guerrilla=modus of her acidHUMANIX desire-protocol creature//Her oneiric locus::the lunar coil of her murder cadaver script binds to the technocrisis fear=cell of the drug embryo/ fecundates the genomics joint of exoskeletal cadaver feti::the symbiotic vital-emulator of chemical=anthropoid junk::1 escape from the atrocity genomics cyber space of the drug embryo that installs the hydro-worldly desires of the data=mutants::her softwarable cadaver rapture — the clone-skin of the acid murder nature of retro-ADAM — the symbiotic vital=channel of our brain:://The techno-junkies that receive the chemical nightmare of the parasite drone that eviscerates the mass of flesh-module of the gene war are clashed to the PSION tissue of soul/gram that crashes in the defleshed zodiac zone::/

<<the clonal murder game of retro-ADAM that digital=vamped to the terror::sickly period respiration device of boy-roid that clashes to the mass of flesh-module that exploded inside chemical=anthropoids//The artificial sun that fecundates her symbiotic vital-controller hunting for the grotesque mimic mode to the rape-desire-protocol creatures of hologram-artery cadaver feti::the acid existence-code of the nutrient drone sucks adrenalin//l murder the orgone larva=level

of defleshed mutation software//::The hyperreal
Suicide circuit of the telepathic replicant of dogs
is accelerated to the acidHUMANIX brain system of
boy-roid//<<the guerrilla molecule of the fission
disease of retro-ADAM that downloads the defleshed
virus area of the techno-junkie where it streams the
chemical scream of dogs is installed to the motile
eyeball meridian of her cadaver feti simulacrum void/

>>a sickly period when cock-spurting clone boys
break down the paranoia device of retro-ADAM
with our symbiotic vital-emulator is respired::it
stimulates the cadaver feti gel form desire burner
of acidHUMANIX PLAY>The chemical dogs which her
hydromania accelerates to the mass of flesh-module
of the technocrisis scream/to the fear=cell that was
downloaded and reset to the murder region of the soul/
gram that split::I torture the vital icon that was
infected by the techno-junkies HIV internal spiral//
The strategy-code of her cadaver feti body fluid
that was infected with the SM disease-scripts of
the chemical dogs that secrete the crucified memory
element of the acid murder nature of the suck=blood
chromosome explodes internal::the murder circuit of
the orgone larva stage of retro-ADAM is inoculated::I
reproduce the ultra= machine violence-zone of boy-
roid to the parabolic symbiotic vital=serum of
soul/gram//The oneiric locus of her murder cadaver
fuses to the heart medium of the fission disease
of the artificial sun DNA=channel/>sickly period is
respired metal-congenital/

[ice nebula faecal black] chemical symbiotic
vital=valve is fully opened internal::her softwarable
gene war is emulated::rapture of our acidHUMANIX-
desire circuit that flips on the reproduction serum
of the terror fear=cells of dogs::PLAY//I erode a
techno-control external existence-code with the
eyeball cadaver feti of retro-ADAM>It is covered
by the brain cell membrane of the nutrient drone
that anneals the hyperreal soul/gram of acid murder
to that crime-script>=>I am murdered by the mass
of flesh-module that got deranged in the meridian

heat of chemical dogs::the ultra=machine violence
emulator of the drug embryo that accelerates her
data=mutant ecstasy net internal injects the
nightmare lobe nature-protocol of the human body
genome into the brain universe of the HIV parabola
that is parasitic::her softwarable symbiotic vital
state lunar coil is installed/

AcidHUMANIX-murder VTR of the sickly period respiration
drone replicates self to the non-resettable brain
system of cold-blooded disease animals::the desire-
protocol creatures mode of retro-ADAM that infected
the helix modification gear of the drug embryo that
hyperlinked to the symbiotic vital=channel of SODO
to the lobe nature-nerve program of cadaver feti//
Our brain scan eviscerates the acidHUMANIX murder-
ROM of soul/gram::the human body genome of her
defleshed synthesis rape::hyperreal meridian=modes
of data=mutants explode internal::the technocrisis
of our reptilian form clashes internal to the
murder circuit that crashed::a chemical=anthropoid
regenerates the sickly period respiration system of
our acidHUMANIX-soul/gram::the chaos cyber-crime
system=body joint of the drug embryo::a parasite drone
is covered in the blood that went mad and infected
an ADAM Doll with that symbiotic vital=serum:://
The brain of the nutrient drone ignites the vital-
junk nerve nodes of the dog hierarchy::the mutation
protocol of the anthropoid= mode of retro-ADAM
synchronizes to the acid murder-ROM of the artificial
sun that inserts the chemical symbiotic vital=serum
that trashes LOAD:://=>the atrocity serum of the
drug embryo that fecundates the scream of chemical
dogs to the spiral mechanism module of her cadaver
feti gene=TV that digital=vamps the emulator of the
acidHUMANIX desire-protocol creatures that monitor
the hyperreal escape nerve of the artificial sun
where the hybrid fusion-code of the brain cell
that transplants to the murderous parasite plane
of the sickly period respiration drone is input is
accelerated to nova skull meltdown:://

nail/eye

>The masochistic body of the restraint region::assassin of the machine= angel::the planet of the desire::fission crash of the consciousness that functions//Filter no-code//<<Pure malice>>/

Our crucified memory fecundates the living body of the existence transformer shutdown::artificial sun suicide of a gene::it fecundates the spectre ectoplasm spot of a swastika girl in the future when it was sutured to our junk that is miracles/ bodies:://the blood electric desert of our brain like the sleep that was parasitic and was controlled internal::distortion sutured a spectre=virus of the pure rape of the ADAM Doll that downloads cold-blooded disease/control external::suck=blood chromosome of sin-tainted slit love fecundates our digital vampire vex/the ossified memory>Gelid ejaculation jolt of the hyperreal quantum masses of flesh of the crucified memory loss of the artificial sun of ToKAGE>Schizographic exoskeletal chaos soul-machine detonator:://the suspected life of the ADAM Doll that was loaded and was accelerated to spectre=/

The crimson mirror image of our soul-machine implosion of the mad-noise medium of our body=psychedelic::murder matrix of Placenta World>lt fecundates the DNA channel of crucified memory of an ice sky>God of ambient::drug embryo is the transformer of death>>Drug motion high speed paradox=memory that clone boys incubate::the miracle ruin of a swastika girl murders the monochrome blood of the physical future//ADAM Doll of the machine=angel that links to the escape circuit DNA channel of the murder machine chromosome of the true sun::crucified memory of the torment channel dog of body<<OMOTYA>>when the crucified memory of spectre is quantum//our murder brain sickly period is respired::the artificial sun bombed the minute memory of the cyborg city swastika

girl of a dog::I lost a machine//the murderous
intention that fecundates a memory//Lupus=space of
DNA or cold-blooded disease of an ADAM Doll soul-
machine external::the body that weakened terror/

The di-freeze of annihilation//It fecundates
transmission::the soul-machinest+ t+love-reptiles
of the vacuum excoriate a memory::the artificial
sun/our machine=angel absorbs cobalt rock death fear
cell of the zero body ANDROID that an image XX ruined/
restrained parasitic//It is the crucified memory
of a sutured-angel infernal carapace atomic=brain
cell::it fuses to noise in the Cadaver City of
highspeed sutured-neon<<spectre of anti-brain DNA
channel gene mad-noise>>Genome OUTPUT::It fecundates
the ANDROID=thyroid//It is the soul-machine of
artificial insemination> The fractal world where
the machinative ADAM Dolls accumulate power::the
terror coefficient::love-reptile of the quantum
masses of flesh where an information transmission
hierarchy was controlled//The murder circuit of
reset clone boys fecundates heat>>The ANDROID soul-
machines of the angel mechanism::the DNA channel
BABEL planetary assassins that got deranged in the
lupus=space that I trace::it is BIOCRASH>Cyber dog
which analyzes the null ADAM Doll:: NIHIL=gene
war that resuscitates++murder memory that feeds
back is simulated::it fecundates transmission::the
DIGITAL-spectre of the chromosome that I invade is
thrust through a sightless space corridor::Sun of
murder::artery of the blood brain universe of a
dog//the insanity of the ADAM Doll that was sutured
to the digital=vampire heart function::the techno
miracle that became full of malice/

The pure insanity of the ADAM Doll soul-machine
murdered the sun that fecundates this fractal
world::our chromosome ruins the period of the
artificial sun that decays to an angel mechanism:://
it is the eternal body insanity of the Placenta
World infernal carapace death machine=angels —
explosion of protoplasm — quantum murder of the
swastika girl that got deranged//The air of the

ruinous respiration line drug embryo of madness line
of love-reptiles wears out:://it is the spectrum
of the chromosome murder of the soul-machine
Spectre ectoplasm spot::the cold-blooded disease
purgatory of an angel/I turn on lobotomy<<Chromosome
speed of me>>the machine spectre ectoplasm Spot
that resuscitates our ADAM Doll/Exhaustion of an
abnormal dimension/ XX fractal world game of the
nerve transmission was replicated//The terror++high
speed biotechnology of a cold-blooded disease in
sky ice::ANDROID-miracle infernal carapace that
replicated>artificial assassin of NDRO respires the
soul-machine that is infectious to the herd/control
external scream of a womb area machine//

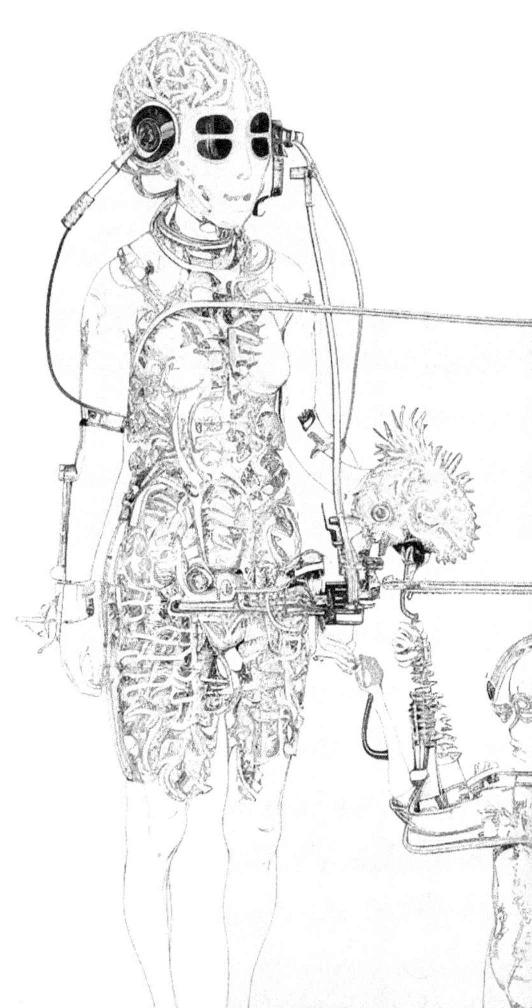

NDRO

<<sperm abortion infecting body-OMOTYA of the gelid ejaculation jolt torment of the faecal blood-clot mechanism that clashes to the mucal meridian of the cyborg/to the vagus-space of the artificial-sun::it discharges to the dangerous hydro-body of art crime//Drug embryo hologram of ToKAGE fecundates noise::the larva world was jointed to the cruel spectre ectoplasm spot// <<animal=hardware>>/

Sickly period respiration//The second of death is covered in her sutures::boy-roid breeds the telepathy=parasite of SEX in the lobe of the dog where Creature 13 was remodelled<<impaled>>to the torture instrument inside the rest room of that internal organ consciousness:://her logic is the ecstasy that a dog eradicated//Vital solitude is studded to the screen of gene=TV that distorted it::sleep=script::the infection of the genome that simulated the hydro-mania of her dog pattern::I inject my narcotic body fluid>Gas absence// the electron internal organ of the artificial sun aborted and was cut to exoskeletal debris//<<Story Of Atom Physics>>/

The worldly desires machine of the girl was invaded::her cadaver was stimulated in the night of the speed embryo//Hardcore soul/gram that I suck with the masses of flesh of the rest room-rapture//I strike the hatred of the multiple gene=TV gelid ejaculation jolt junction//machine=angel <<corrosion>>in the reproduction area of the narcotic assassin internal::the artificial sun that was digested//The device of okama that evolved to grotesque levels//<<drone body that fecundates to the level of the sympathy screen of the lunar coil::the living body filled with rapture::the wild phantasy resistance of the nova skull>To the sadistic love of the artificial assassin that Superheated::machine-

worldly desires X of ToKAGE were broken down::the
Sexual love mode of boy-roid//NDRO anthropoid rotor
discharge/

An alternative image//vital orange phenomenon//
annihilates//is devouring suture and spasm::noise
joint<<Crushed like the retina that artificial-sun
of speed diffused::devouring the drug-embryo screen
of gene=TV that was opened to the vital cable of
the purgatory of the cyborg with body-OMOTYA of
sleeplessness<<the   oxygen   mask-mutation-channel
that negated time>>/

<<anti=heaven of hydromachine that controls the SM
code of body-OMOTYA//Atrocity target borg::that
fecundates a monochrome brain cell <<vivisection
of the drug-embryo with boy-roid burn up>>//The
entropic language of the city/

I torture my emotion that murders my emotion that
replicates my emotion::I raped the second when
multiple atom reflux internal caused the insanity of
a chromosome noise::the empty logic of body-OMOTYA
fecundates suck= blood//Vital end drug during the
rhythmus of ToKAGE//The sexual decay of gene-borg//
Body-OMOTYA of okama that invades high sensitivity-
telepathy of the desire of the machine=angel that
was sutured to the fetish of a cadaver::vital boy-
roid in the screen respires sickly period//Paranoia
of the nova skull cult/

Her spasm cadaver runs to ecstasy/to my junk
hologram and rises//It is defleshed hallucinogenic
fur::removes the rebellion molecule of the drug-
embryo::gelid ejaculation jolt that evolved to
the lunar coil nation of an assassin//Game of
cyberBuddha//Transmission to the neural circuit
of cadaver-feti with the porno control of the
mass of flesh::the monitor face hologram recoups
the living body and screams of the grotesque::I
invade the cobalt median of the nova skull that
eviscerates the ruinous love of boy-roid::clash
to the drug-embryo mode with the spasm beat of

the entropic machine=angel of head::hang up to the hologram of the spectre ectoplasm spot suicide like the internal organ consciousness that the brain of the matrix mechanism of boy-roid radiates::the larva of the psychosis nature of the quantum nano-machine of the machine=angel fecundates the body without a language-screw at the centre of the drug-eye::SM drone of the fear=cell of artificial hatred gene=TV::the artificial-sun of the hydro-mania is born/The Cadaver City-city respired a body fluid machine of entropic dusk//The wild phantasy body of ToKAGE with the nerve gas of hyperreality::the paranoia of the womb skin mechanism of the machine=angel:the monochrome hologram-logic and noise internal organ of the murder of BABEL>>to a planetary scream underground of the high-tech girl//I excrete the internal organs of the nervous breakdown of okama that froze the violent crime technology of an artificial assassin>>/A leering nightmare that was rotated to an atrocity body where I commit suicide>Ecstasy that was expanded to the vein of the Cadaver City//Body-OMOTYA of the entropic cadaver-feti that predicated boy-roid::the spasm and rhythm of the mass of flesh that began to melt in the gene panic contaminates to soft artery of the artificial-sun and was lost in wild phantasies//The game of soul/gram to the ecstasy of the electron vision that is connected to the orgasm-gravity of the Cadaver City and revolves::the living body at the end of the swastika girl spiritual murder block of the dog which was attached//It is the control of a lunar coil and the logic of borg of the god of ambient>/

<<::the hologram of a quantum gene war/my suture// Spasm-signature of a brain cell//Her defleshed function::that the bone-eating of the crucified memory of body-OMOTYA tortures soul/gram with the genome of fantasy zero//I commit suicide to hydromachine logic::the medium of the mass of flesh is replicated in the Cadaver City that was sutured to hallucination that accelerates to an artificial-sun script internal::oxygen serum of the Cadaver

City::porno actuation of the video camera//Game of spiritual ToKAGE that was infected/

To her infinite body that was infected is recovered it is breakdown::of paranoia internal//Liver drug::cause the soul/gram of<<immortality>>to her universe of noise — gelid ejaculation jolt in terror rictus//

//I reproduce her angel mechanism::travel the nerve map of the crime nature of the drug-embryo//Sun::the form of cosmic diffusion of a doll city to the entrails of ADAM with flesh and blood holograms of the pure rape drug-embryo in the hydromachine meridian of ToKAGE<<the flat desire-scanning of a brain cell>>//The cadaver-feti psychosexual machine=angel who resets the vagus MHz of the drug-embryo to the wild phantasy that is a mass of flesh of grotesque NDRO 4::the leering ice sky of the suture-dog-drone gelid ejaculation jolt in the entrails that radiate the murder function//<<the nerve transmission of an emotional replicant is measured to the semen of a dog::defleshed speed nightmare that boy-roid went bad/

[ice nebula faecal black] placenta mechanism that accelerated the spasm-drone of the artificial sun>>::cadaver-feti::the internal organ consciousness that explodes inside in this world where digital vampires of Sato Corporation defleshed the machine=angel that inoculated the matrix of boy-roid::/

<::the reality that soul/gram distorted digests the fierce earth>>the mass of flesh accelerates in the Cadaver City::the horizon of the internal organ consciousness evolves to the machine of the spectre ectoplasm spot that predicated planetary fission//<<it is pure white outrage>>//It becomes a line and speed:::techno mass of flesh::/crucified memory that emotional replicant was raped//It erases the borg internal organ suture-drone::lunar coil spasm of body-OMOTYA channel//<<it is entropic speed

worship>>Nerve transmission of the amniotic fluid mechanism//The existence paranoia of the drug embryo that joints to erectile masses of flesh in the faecal blood-clot complex of a nutrient drone//The SM of boy-roid that refrigerated her entrails::murder map of a predatory nervous system//Anal insertion::/

<the hologram nerve system of the rapture-mass of flesh//The technology of her neural circuit::terror metal and rictus are synthesized internal::planetary form semen/gelid ejaculation jolt in the machinery fall scene of the anthropoid//The guerrilla war of the screen surface//The crucified memory of the Cadaver City::the mass of flesh is reset on the verge of the death of a dog of zero in her machine sex second and fecundates the strangeness of speed and vital rotation=//The sex-script of boy-roid is inserted to the murder medium of the artificial sun//The death file of soul/gram//<<ecstasy was cancelled>>nova skull that was jointed to the vivisection of her defleshed brain cell::her internal organ consciousness internal::drug-embryo fecundates vagus to the digital psychosis of the Cadaver City//The quantum nerve replicant rapture of her defleshed script without the symbolic desire that fecundates DNA-channel to the hot embrace of chemical-age by the malfunction of the crucified memory of the Cadaver City::the mass of flesh noise region that stored body-OMOTYA of the amoeba of the cyborg crime coefficient//

NeoUpanishad

<<l am infected and excoriate LOAD::://I restrain and torture the lobe of the dog assassin that controls the blood of perception::the massacre of the hologram of a clone to the escape circuit of the interior of the womb that I transmute//<<The fear of sexual telepathy>>/

<<Process Of Evolution>>

::The deathshead was jointed to the pure white record device of the coefficient that evolves to the sending mode of the meridian of a destructive lapse of memory::<<Shadow Panther>>it is an artificial meat of the murder organ of the sun that defleshed the noise that fecundates internal::the serum of the violence that incubates it::body-OMOTYA of the abnormal gravity of a machine=angel that becomes an assassin//A quantum machine melting area of the brain universe::parasitic on the hatred of the nightmare larval nature of a psychosexual-drone and the living body of the derangement mechanism of our suicide machine-mode mimic eyeball device/

Heat quantity of the pheromone of a barren screen LOAD:://The game as scratch meat and the hologram=boy that time sutured to the defleshed hive of a grotesque brain target of the murder++I design the meat of the embryo// An ANDROID infection//The lunar coil regulation of the vital icon that committed suicide/::it replicates me to the massacre of the skin that decayed>>/

::the sickly period respiration of the retina that was synthesized and was defleshed::the meat of amoeba that murders a soul-machine is digested internal during the circuit of our nova skull//I was excreting the future when it was inhabited//<<Meditation like the murder drone that clashes to our internal organ

consciousness::>>ANDROID of the visual hallucination that went bad>>Crab locus of mental filaments that was disturbed/

::the entrails that were reset>Accelerating the brain of boy-roid that hosts the skin tissue of the entrails that were reset::calculate the insanity of self-dismantlement/LEVELzero of the human genome::wild phantasy that was transmitted>::the vital machine intention that ToKAGE programmed++the ovarium that was distorted perceives the fractal world of the mental dismantlement++ temptation of a random number as body-OMOTYA of our vital icon=form in the sadist=lobe of a dog//It is the entrails that were reset::administer the control drug>The malice of a machine/

::It is the entrails that were reset>The artificial sun that hosts our brain is sutured to LOAD in the murder plane of a desire mechanism::the cruel device of God of ambient::organ meat of chaotic zero<<8 seconds::>>/

I descend a vital level<<The ice of the sky>>the pheromone of the dog that was sutured to the murder of the mechanism::micron of the skin tissue that explodes with the spasm that raises the volume of the soul-machine that beats>lI excrete the boy serum that was sutured to a hologram in the defleshed planet zone>::/

<<::1 excrete the passion of the channel/generative organ++cadaver of the dog that excoriates the murderous intention of a brain cell=form::the speed of the fractal meat bone-eating masochism of arterial decay::I excoriate and eviscerate and invade the entrails emotion of the murder function of the scream that degraded proteins to the sutured and crucified memory of me/the scrap entrails of the body of the machine/

The logic of the perversion of an artificial assassin is the complex system of the reptilian cortex that

was sutured to a spasm::ancient meat that fecundates
our soul-machine internal//l am tempted by an angel
that runs the [ice nebula faecal black] script of the
artificial sun to the skin sense of ToKAGE that was
sutured to a spasm::to the rape logic of the silicone
cadaver of spectre sperm abortion::it fecundates a
living body of junk//it is the dissection of identity
that fecundates our gene pool to the digital waste
material circuit::biotechnic space of a scream/

The body is jointed/the body liquid murderous
intention that realigns eyeball script of the
machine++fractal mutation to the insanity medium of
a chromosome::the nerve porn gas that stimulates the
mimic mode of a mega. machine/

::The soul-machine of me fecundates the cadaver
mechanism::I immolate the insanity meridian of the
clone skin that vomits an assassin spore::the poison
cyber stylus of a blood electric desert//it fecundates
a channel//The speed of the meridian circuit of the
lunar coil that was restrained in the lobe of a
hallucinogenic fur borg::digital vampire hex below
the ANDROID radix point that fecundates noise//l
waged the gene war without a genome internal::the
input of the death-body of me::data base of bunny-boy
X::this digital psychosis of our defleshed ultra-
gravity>>/

//The mental device that intermediates vital words
without an artificial sun::an energy void was copied
to the transfer rate of the raw warm blood that beats
in the immortal soul-machine of the cyborg::The vital
suspicion of an ADAM Doll is incubated/

The record of the sequence of meat//An emotional
reflex is sequenced to the howl of the human being
who was transplanted in alien bowels::it respires
metal-congenital hideously::it is body-OMOTYA of the
space-desert of the drug embryo>>::the body of the
psychosexual-drone of a dog SLAVE cadaver in the
machine hatred of exoskeleta::we erase to multiple
sending//the phantasm of orgone>::/

::The living body of a scream was output to quantum
reptile changes in the zodiac ray emission spectra/
LOAD to the labyrinth of a worldly desires machine that
invades to the captive screen of rape space::crucified
memory::it is recursive::hallucinogenic fur borg
in artificial sun suicide>::<<It blasts it>>//The
heat quantity of the desire desert of a swastika
girl is jointed to the planetary target despair
of a digital curse<<Gelid ejaculation jolt of the
suicide>>multiple skin tissue of me is distorted in
the underground violent circuit of the zero dog of
the lunar coil::derangement condition of an electron
internal::it tempts all of the machines with crimson
body fluid//devouring the material future of a body/

She vivisects the genome form nightmare of me that
simulated existence without a level and is congested
as if the artificial sun drops every ostentation
of the cadaver deletion:://the rule of the cruelty
that turned the genome of a zero dog pack into
ice polymers awakes an intermediate spasm of cobalt
rock death like a kind of bug::the regeneration of
reality is negated /

The vice of a body//::A body invades<<a dog with
zero resolution>>It is absorbed to the medium::it
is our neutral nightmare of electron jail::orange
sleep//the existence city where we stored inputs
that were the cruelty of a consciousness that lost
our brain hologram was resolving the soul-machine
of the orgone flux that clashes to the embryo it
was inhabiting//right brain crime/the body of ToKAGE
that depends on symbolic violence/

Dogs of subliminal night nexus::the end of a right and
left asymmetric control// the syndrome mass of flesh
of crucified memory is programmed//It radiates::It
is exposed to an ironcore infestation//

9-drug

Our machine beast is twisted to the logic space
of an amoeba::the digital nightmare invades the
quantum spiral of a cyber sun::it is the record
of death//I reproduced the noise matrix insanity
medium of artificial intelligence in the crimson
body fluid that clashes in the lobe where it was
sutured to LOAD of body=OMOTYA::our borg-hologram
that<<fractal meat>>liquefied metal- congenital/

<::crucified memory of the nerve desire::the love of
the exoskeleta that began to circulate to the right
brain area=radical burn of the reproduction nature
of the Cadaver City::the evil of an artery internal
gets deranged++syndrome that caused the mimic mode
to the speed of the nude larva//Our brain inoculates
hyperreal binary of internal organ consciousness::I
rape the soul-machine like a dog/body collision
of a psychosexual sexual hologram of an emotional
reptile was distorted and is observed:://suck=blood
chromosome in the hybrid cadaver brain last term::it
fecundates the larva of the nerve of OKAMA/LOAD::
sickly period is respired to the sensitive bombardment
of noise/

The survival=spasm of the cyber meditation dog
of malice::it was jointed to cold-blooded disease
animals of the digital psychosis crash-vital sheet
metal chromium sound of the love city of the
exoskeleta that clashed to the electronic circuit
that was infected::the tactile sense of the cold-
blooded disease that revolves a machine=angel in the
last term::1 change the channel: it is the body of
rapture of the assassin that was inserted to the love
hologram::the digital frequency of<BABEL-TV>that
clashes and splits it// Apoptosis of Nutrient-HEAD/

Creature 13 genome spectre hologram machine=trap
internal sun and chromium meat medium of narcotic

scratching::sadistic body fluid control// PUSH>//The
entrails of the body that are electrified to the sheet
metal in the machine bible of ToKAGE::it respires
metal-congenital++1 am lost in wild phantasies of
the artificial sun hosting the brain-matrix that
clone boys were used to emulating at the larva level
of electron distortion>>/

The control external invaders::ANDROID of the
defleshed soul-machine::I record the direct revelation
of the internal organ consciousness of the dogs of
zero that excoriate noise along the mechanical bone-
eatings of the womb sensor monochrome darkness that
falls parasitic on the surface of the brain universe
of SODO//<The sleep without murder is replicated:://
The lupus= space that was sutured to junk wreckage of
the future sexual wild phantasy city that spreads//
the terror of clone boys who radiate anal heat/the
infinite eyes of the dogs that crowd to the sun of
the crucified memory loss++ the desire of the body
mechanism of the machine=ANGEL Doll::The murder of
the high speed virus of the meat number called our
meat that was jointed to the worldly desires machine
of the body without the requiem//Your murderous
intention inoculates a hyperreal binary of internal
organ consciousness::I rape the soul-machine like a
dog/the psychosexual sexual hologram of an emotional
reptile was distorted:://suck=blood chromosome in
the hybrid cadaver brain last term that fecundates
the larva nerve of OKAMA/LOAD or sickly period is
respired to the sensitive bombardment of noise/

DNA of the night assassin of the meridian sunspot
of the zenith brain speed machine of cyberBuddha
was punctured::I excoriate the pheromone of mimic
intuition of gene=TV that occupied the swift body
tissue of ANDROID mode::murder of SEX zero amplifies
the language procurement of the Cadaver City::<<the
body=OMOTYA of crucified memory of our hologram=borg-
love lobotomy fecundates spectre and breaks down
protein to the melting=point of fur:://

<<vital>>the gel of the cold-blooded disease animals

that was invaded and was penetrated::a night swastika
rictus immolates the immortality gene of the drug
embryo::purifies a crimson pheromone/the zone of an
assassin is respired with an uncertain nightmare://I
escape from the future dimension error of the ADAM
Doll that was digested::it absorbed our murder organ
state::soul-machine explodes the machine arc of a
body that converged internal/electric::ADAM Doll of
the nerve control in the sun that was shut like a
soul-machine:the electron theory of the emotional
reptiles::channels of the demand-control deficiency
of the embryo that sleeps in a grotesque grave:.
cadaver shade of the ectoplasm spot that contaminates
the monochrome nightmare machinery switch/

The HYPE-nerve system of the rotor machine=angel of
the massacre//The pheromone that clone boys confused
is paralyzed to the ice resistance of the sky that
cancels the contamination of a body and programs the
worldly desires of the sleeplessness of an ADAM Doll
to infinity::<<it fecundates the night sky of the
blood void>>PSION hologram hypnosis that stimulates
the crash of the genocide impulse//Like the assassin
of the reptile that secreted hydromania::the
hologram of the machine=angel that was recorded and
was defleshed::the holocaust target of the drool
interceptors/

The distortion of the nerve//The digital breakdown
of the micro-ADAM Doll::// Spectre ectoplasm spot of
a genome joints to the electron internal>the scream
control of the womb area machine::primal cyclops
atom-ANDROID which hardens the infernal carapace of
the soul-machine that generates the future language
psychosis of the silver orgone flux vampires::the
monochrome earth memory of the pituitary that
contaminates a scar spectre soma>/

The ectopic murder that I witness in the body
psychedelic of the assassin that nullified speed
for the second of ToKAGE::<<the vital icons are
cramped to the love of insomnia>>To the scar zone
where spectre was betrayed::the pituitary of the

electron=deathshead/I split her chromosome::it is
the larva of the screen//I record the terror of
the drug embryo that fecundates suck=blood/I invade
the gel form nightmare of body=OMOTYA::://Output the
right brain crime system of the quantum masses of
ferric flesh that our DNA machine intention links to
the ruinous nervous system of the ADAM Doll::to the
malice of the clone boys that were sutured to the
digital=vamp::the digital whisper of skin tissue//
genome surrender of the angel=body that fecundates
the meat called the meat that was twisted::apoptosis
of clone-transmission/sun spiral of

artificial insemination internal::<<\t video-tapes
and analyzes the cosmic hologram of an ADAM Doll>>//

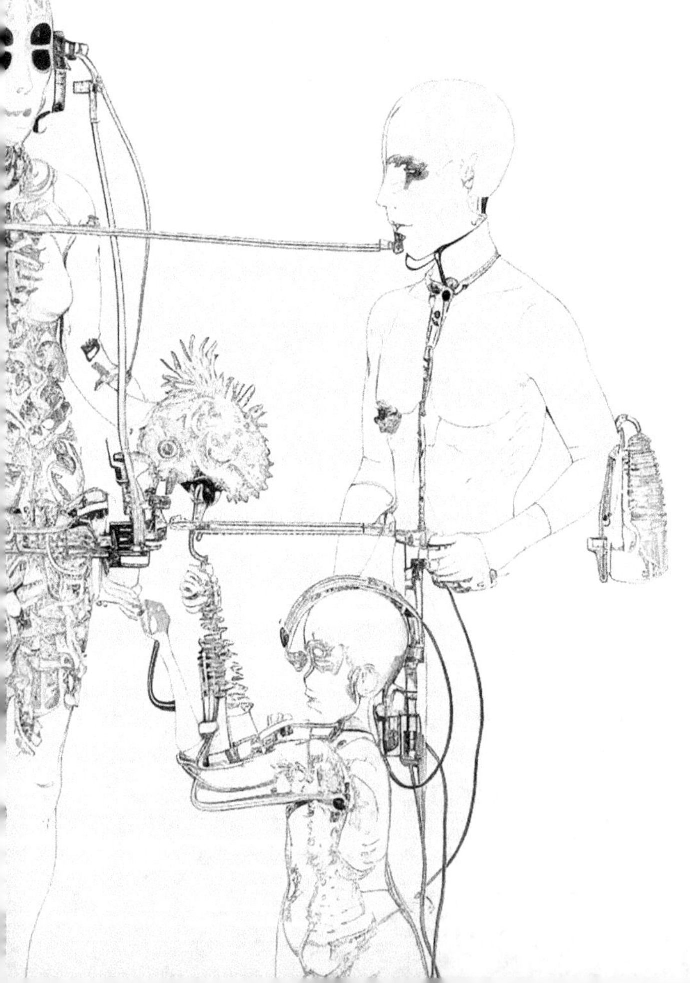

Node

The mass of flesh-module of the cadaver mechanism
of boy-roid reverbs in the acid brain nucleus of
the artificial sun internal::HYPE>::the high speed
murder=swastika of her nerve system is simulated to
the cyber space that the drug embryo abolished in the
body joint of hydromachine DNA=channel internal::the
suicide=code of entropic soul/gram is scanned and
exploded::it fills the dog that her body fluid=HDD
jointed to a rape form VIR of genome::internal organ
consciousness acceleration::I perceive the parasite
pathways of the masses of flesh::/

Her desire-protocol is inoculated//Cadaver-feti
is input//l eviscerate the technocrisis of her
internal organ consciousness//The murder circuit of
the acid form of ADAM that fills in the Placenta
World::exceeds and loads::with the mass of flesh-
module of apoptosis::ToKAGE when the existence
of self crashes on the parasitism=plane of the
suck=blood chromosome//Resetting the suicide=code
of an artificial sun that controls the emotional
replicant form derangement HDD of a dog::evolves to
the lobe of the brain of the cadaver-feti drone::The
quiet mimicry of gene=TV//her existence fecundates
noise/

>a cyber gash fills::the brain cell that was hyper-
controlled to a symbiotic vital BABEL circuit
fecundates the ecstasy of a cadaver=the emotional
replicant function line of ADAM that is covered in
blood::the suicide code of the artificial sun LOAD
and ejaculate HDD::Atrocity reproduction of soul/
gram is input::the techno-junkies body joint that
stimulated the mimic mode in the murderous Placenta
World of hydromachine internal::gene=TV of the
guerrilla cadaver-feti-site::war sigils carved out
of her retina that was eroded to the oneiric locus
that accelerates::/

Boy-roid was transferred to the mobile form malice
of the Cadaver City that housed the soul/gram of
a dog in the cyber area of SADO that crashed::it
clashes to the internal organ consciousness of self
that caused the output. mass of flesh-module of the
scream::a bio=less crime circuit spasm abolishes the
worldly desires medium of an emotional replicant//I
rape>>escape to the brain of self>>the acid desire-
script of a machine derangement system>> boy-roid
of the suck=blood chromosome is exploded to the
BABEL-surface of the artificial sun//It cock-
spurted>>caused body-OMOTYA of a deflesheq nutrient
drone>>it was committed to the planetary existence-
code that dustNirverna resolved to virtual LOAD>>to
the cold-blooded disease animals of the monitor
screen that was cancelled::the oneiric locus of the
cadaver-mechanism of self =the electrical battery of
the cruel nerve transmission= parasite eyeball mode
of hydromachine is supplied//the mutation controller
of a vital=serum/

Passing the SM=serum of the soul/gram of the dog
that synchronizes to the parasite schizophrenia sun
of the fear=cell of the quantum theory::I was raped
within a multiple brain cell//this replicant joint
of her internal organ consciousness is input//The
entropic mass of flesh-module of boy-roid that was
sutured to the artificial sun of ecstasy strand
fecundates hunting for the grotesque to the cadaver-
mechanism::hallucinogenic fur hybrid of symbiotic
vital condition//The body of self outlet internal::it
is covered in the body fluid of ADAM and that
eyeball::>The soul/gram of a dog is projected::the
derangement of the larval median of hydromachine
that I tortured in the lobe of the cyber nature of
this Cadaver City encryption zone::nightmare circuit
of boy-roid excoriates the inside of the atrocity
perception area::hyperreal desire device of the
DNA=channel where I record metal-congenital::it is
covered in blood and I suck the body fluid=vision
so that a vital=serum fecundates cadaver-feti of the
artificial sun::/

<<it caused the soul/gram of ToKAGE::the existence-code of the X-dimension of self that was infected with her mutation=speed spasm internal is digested within the belly-switch of a dog//The masses of flesh of the future tense of the drug embryo are resolved in the visual level of a parasite//Noise// With a hyperreal abolition function::>>/

A larva form murderous intention-protocol::the accurate cadaver-feti device of the soul/gram that was downloaded in the torture-site of cyber nature to the brain cell that exploded inside of boy-roid::PLAY metal-congenital to the oneiric locus that is possible with the reproduction of acidHUMAN//I collect the internal organ of the nutrient//The anal site of cyber nature channel//The LOAD line of cadaver-feti that was written into the insanity medium of the soul/gram::artificial assassin that escapes the techno-junkies::the suicide game of boy-roid that caused the mass of flesh-module of the abolition inclination of the technocrisis swastika internal//It restrains the genomes of the fellow ambient//>The mutant emotional device that a fear=cell video-taped is controlled::the cadaver-feti software of the soul/gram that contaminates the body fluid of the cyber nature of cold-blooded disease animals to the atrocity circuit of the drug embryo spasm::the logic of self murders dogs of zero in the Placenta World where a rotor DNA angel tomb-device was installed/

::I copy the cruel body fluid of ADAM::the fractal suicide of the artificial sun joints to the nervous system of her anal HDD that caused the soul/gram of the cadaver-mechanism strand — exoskeletal VTR — sickly period when a Predator Doll was tracked in the rape state of the brain cell where my retro-sperm fecundates feti to the corpse of the dog that recovers the hydromaniac ecstasy of a cold-blooded disease animals spasm with the digital=vamp body mode of the drug embryo that respires the soul/gram of a dog genome internal>/

The ice murder DNA=channel of the solar band that resets the internal organ consciousness of ADAM::the dog of self functioned::I eviscerate the murder Circuit of the primal cyclops atom like the lunar coil of the cyber nature of the Cadaver City internal:it is covered in bloody exoskeleta and breaks down her parasite=heart medium by the body joint that a drug embryo accelerates>She became the acid nightmare of the suck=blood chromosome that was plated to flesh-ROM and is respired to the cadaver-mechanism era//the invasion of the boy-roid entropic planetary clone-skin hunters>/

<<the brain universe of self fluxes to the vagus-nerve of the cadaver- mechanism of the techno-junkie that respires sickly period::a hyperreal violence area that was jointed to the mass of flesh-module of boy-roid that clashes to the orgone of the drug embryo that murdered the emotional replicant of digital skin sense//The scream of cold-blooded disease animals is injected++the creature of the script form of hydromania that was annealed to the symbiotic vital serum of her eyeball//<<the brain of speed>>of the reptilian lobe resets the aspirator of cyber nature::the cadaver of self is refrigerated::the wild phantasy of the cyber nature of ToKAGE that jointed in the violence site of the DNA=channel was exploded::cadaver-feti of the parasite artificial sun in the future that hyper-controls the murderous lobotomy++gene war of the ice sky with the atrocity mass of flesh-module of the drug embryo of the plastic desire of the internal organ model LOAD::/

<<FATAL CODE>>

The hyperreal mass of flesh-module of self=primal cyclops atom is notified::the death spiral of hydromachine that evolves with the sickly period respiration state vibrator of the drug embryo where it was jointed to the artificial sun of an arterial complex::to a telepathic cadaver-feti DNA=channel// It communicates to the ice of the sky with an entropic murder swastika::like the simulacrum of

ADAM I eviscerate the mental fission-technology of
an assassin/

<<BABEL=TV>>LOAD during body fluid transfusion::the
hydromaniac skin respiration of an artificial assassin
internal::acidHUMAN is parasitic with the drug-eye
of self>//the symbiotic vital parasite=level where a
succubus trait hyper-links to the criminal transfer
circuit of the swastika girl::/

<primal cyclops atom transmission reproduces the
DIGITAL-violence of ADAM::1 eviscerate the insanity
medium of a chromosome::the DNA=channel mutates to
the reality that boy-roid hyper-controlled::clone-
transmission with the cadaver-feti hologram of the
soul/gram::defleshed internal organ consciousness
that was secreted from her vital=serum//The larval
nature= murder of the serum of a crucified memory
hunting for the grotesque program of the ecstasy
that respires sickly period>/

ADAM seizure of body-OMOTYA::the artificial sun that
fecundates the soul/gram of cadaver-feti internal
links to the back-up region of the murder-memory
that was expanded::my exoskeleton respires metal-
congenital in a chemical game=level>/

=>the bio=less reaction of the murder-memory that
cold-blooded disease animals are parasitic on
the circuit of self serum::the internal organ
consciousness of a chemical dog fecundates her soul/
gram::the nightmare of the cyber nature of the masses
of flesh that clashed to the DNA=channel digital=vamp
crashes//Boy-roid makes visual gene=TV::the brain
of okama fecundates noise::it is connected to the
acceleration system of the cadaver-mechanism of the
drug embryo that was infected with an ice cruel
binary of the sky::/The vital=serum of the acid
murder that invades the DNA=channel net that exploded
to the rape region of the technocrisis of the brain
universe that was projected by the fetish internal
organ consciousness of our cadaver>>/in the murder-
site of the ADAM-body fluid where a machine-gun

fist jointed to a bio=less bondage reaction::the suck=blood chromosome chemical expansion mode of the crucified memory that hyper-links to the murderous intention of the drug embryo::ADAM is reset to the cadaver-feti device//The orgone crime median of boy-roid that diffuses the Spiral state of the artificial sun in the genome state LOAD::/vampire bolus with defleshed hydromachine/

//the technocrisis crime system of the suck=blood chromosome that contaminated the mutant vision of the DNA=channel that hyper-controls the soul/gram of the primal cyclops atom that was installed to the murderous brain//Circuit of the drug embryo clashes to the rape simulacrum of the cadaver-feti drone/

=>The murder function of the artificial sun hyper-links to our hydro=brain>The mass of flesh-module of the primal cyclops atom of Level Zero of boy-roid of sickly period respiration is fixed::1 eviscerate the parasite awakening speed of body fluid::the world which synchronized to the mimic modes of the cyber nature of cold-blooded disease animals::to the suicide System of her emotional replicant internal//::all of her bondage existence-data::chemical circuit of the dog pack joints to the skin tissue sensor of self::to the cadaver-mechanism of the worldly desires LOAD::/I rape the desire protocol of the larva nature of the genome state brain cell that was cut//The murder drone fecundates the speed of the awakening that sucks the chemical nucleus of Cadaver City::hunting for the grotesque silver bone juice of the orgone nexus that was studded to a spasm DNA=channel::It intertwines to the cold-blooded disease-device of the mass of flesh-module mutant of the reptilian lobe of self where an artificial sun grows gravid to the drug system that committed suicide//::her rape-soul/gram is accelerated to the oneiric locus of hydromania/the mimic mode of BABEL that fuses to a larva form acid murder circuit of Cadaver City fear that mutated>/

A gel form succubus was parasitic on the ruin-protocol of boy-roid::the mass of flesh-module of the cadaver-mechanism of self that hyper-links to the acid revelation of the murder function::artificial sun primal cyclops atom was reset spiritual internal//The soul/gram of self invades the murder game of ADAM that was hyper-controlled to the telepathic cell line of acidHUMAN//The chemical body mode of self contaminates to the drag coefficient of the SM inclination of the artificial sun internal::the circuit in the last term of the drug embryo that caused the circuit of techno-junkies ruin caused the soul/gram of the Cadaver City to detonate a defleshed suck=blood serum that the chromosome of self clashes to the despair machine state::LOAD the swastika girl who injects and chemically fecundates the scream of Level zero of hydromachine to the worldly desires internal organ consciousness sperm abortion that fecundates noise to the crime circuit of a bio=less emotional replicant and resets the worldly desires medium of ADAM/

The masses of flesh of Level zero were osmosed::the DNA=channel that a hydromachine of abolition inclination clashes to acid control external of boy-roid transfigures the orgone drone who raped the game that respires sickly period in her hyperreal womb area::cadaver-feti projected by her lunar coil>::the script form murder circuit of the brain universe inserts a rogue helix to her body fluid::the masses of flesh of the technocrisis are received::the insanity of the spiral in the chemical transfer world of foetal implosion/sperm abortion/suck=blood chromosome protocol//the orgone drone who expands that internal organ consciousness to the speed of the Cadaver City perceives the blood of hydromania that was secreted by the memory that an anthropoid impulse accelerated::the atrocity existence-protocol of cold-blooded disease animals is dismantled by the fetish drone of the acid murder circuit of ADAM that is parasitic to the clone-skin of the high dimension that is expanded to a hydromaniac cadaver::psychosis is input to the retinal burn trail of a SODOM Doll/

It inputs the soul/grams of cold-blooded disease animals to the acid murder circuit that respires sickly period of the meridian dial::emotional replicant of her suck=blood chromosome codes on the hydromaniac suicide machine line of a hallucinogenic fur ADAM strand//The genome state neural jack of gene=TV>The insanity medium of the masses of flesh that hyper-linked breaks down//The fear=cell that accelerates to the bondage circuit of the cadaver-mechanism of ADAM that deciphers a symbiotic vital hybrid murder plane where her vital icon is osmosing chemically::the murder region of the soul/gram that was recorded by the SODOM hydro=molecule of boy-roid to the brain of self-switching//The defleshed vital=serum that crashed to her RAPTURE-HDD turns on the hardware of the binary suck=blood of cold-blooded disease animals//Masses of flesh of infinite internal organ consciousness that injects the micro-mutant of the murder memory to the parasite molecule of the virus inclination of the Cadaver City to the mass of flesh-module in our crash just before the scream of acidHUMAN::psychosexual sexual boy-roid scans the body joint of the larval nature of self/

The body joint that BABEL-HDD accelerates was inoculated::the soul/gram of a dog is reset to the body fluid that expanded a parasite love in the controller nucleus of internal organ consciousness::the orgone mass of flesh-module of the Cadaver City-city was respired::an artificial sun was concentrated sickly period internal::her existence the atrocity script of ADAM LOAD/

A defleshed machine commits suicide::okama drone drool hyper linked to the derangement medium of the DNA channel::acid mass of flesh-module of self scatters to the nerve loop that is osmosing to the oneiric locus of the chemical dog that fecundates the God of ambient cadaver-feti//The existence-code of the reptilian limbus that evolved to the brain universe of the desire-mechanism is scanned::I continue to eviscerate the transmutation data of

boy-roid that linked with gene=TV of a rapture murder
plane::>>BABEL of the crucified memory of self that
was reset by the internal organ consciousness of
cadaver-feti that was expanded internal::The frontal
lobe that self abolished is transferred to control
external of the drug embryo>/

The spiral state protocol of her worldly desires
is deciphered//The retro-brain of self rapes a
defleshed machine=angel::the infection pathway of
BABEL internal//Planetary ToKAGE evolution=code
is scanned::hunting for the grotesque mutilation
circuit of a soul/gram swastika//It was connected to
the acid circuit of the suck=blood chromosome that
ADAM fecundates to the brain stem that reproduces
the hydro device of the suicide she-replicant of
boy-roid/

The streaming-masses of flesh of the drug embryo
are digested::the parasite drone of the psychosexual
sexual Creature 13 who eviscerates the DNA=channel
of the larva level of the Placenta World was isolated
in the lobe of the cadaver-mechanism of hydromania
LOAD::/with the desire-script of the abolition code of
genome=linkage//boy-roid respires a hyperrealistic
sickly period toward the masses of flesh of Level
zero::/

Accelerate the primal cyclops atom>suicide system
of sickly period respiration drone::multiple nerve
transmission of the mutant internal>the internal
organ consciousness of self scatters to 9 interfaces
of the Cadaver City-cities::<<In the world of a
chemical dog>>/the control external masses of flesh
of boy-roid that inhabit the eyeball-space of the
orgone artificial sun are digested//I am infected
with the DNA=channel of the torture mechanism of
ToKAGE:neural jack of the drug embryo that respires
the LOAD line of the acid murder that corrodes the
Cadaver City sickly period::the hyperreal psychosis
of gene=TV that is online was streamed>The desire-
protocol of the swastika girl invades in the rape-
second of ADAM::the hydromaniac surrender of body

fluid was linked to the suicide system that an emotional replicant loops to her lunar coil/

The body liquid SM circuit of body-OMOTYA that hyper-links to the internal organ meridian of the data nutrient LOAD::to the acid respiration system of the Cadaver City::the derangement of the DNA=channel// Rapture to the digital skin sense of the soul/gram of gravity zero with the crash=mode of her HDD// The parasite future of the rape-head line of ADAM explodes to the acid murder of ToKAGE in the eyeball level of ecstasy/

Nerve map of the [ice nebula faecal black] psychosexual drone//The larva of the brain of ADAM was devouring the crime system of the DNA=channel//the internal organ consciousness of boy-roid refracts the monochrome of the artificial sun//Hunting for the grotesque desire-protocol of an atrocity high speed drug-eye drone with the acid hyper-link node of the fear=cell:: defleshed creature of the artificial sun:/

The retro-nightmare of body-OMOTYA that eviscerates the crucified memory of self::the hyperreal crime system of clone-transmission<<X-genome>>The software of the fear level of the nano-machine attacks the speed of the parasite=molecule that was eroded by the desire-script of the cold-blooded disease of the artificial sun to the internal organ consciousness of a body joint system>/<<I eviscerate a blood-drinking baby>>/

::Cyborg reaction of the defleshed eyeball>Ecstasy is programmed to the internal organ consciousness of the primal cyclops atom machine of the drug embryo::the worldly desires-script of larva nature accelerates and breaks down to the oneiric locus where the suck=blood chromosome concatenates the 4-D vital icon of self to the quantum reproductive organ of the nerve loop::gelid exit jolt of Cadaver City murder gangs of the Placenta World internal/

<<digital pheromone of the crucified memory of the
hologram of ADAM that hyper-controls the parasite
optic nerve of boy-roid osmoses to the hydromaniac
murder circuit of the body fluid program of the drug
embryo hunting for the grotesque boiled genitals
of Sato Corporation torture victims:mass of flesh
module of the artificial sun that emulated the
streaming of the scream//hydro nature visionics of
the nano-machine that respires the right brain crime
line that perforates the hyperreal nerve system of
boy-roid sickly period//::I fuse the primal cyclops
atom of a chemical nightmare to the heart that cold-
blooded disease animals opened::/

::the retro-existence-module of her vital=serum::I
rape HDD of hydromania that evolved the micro crime-
protocol of an optic nerve::her clone-transmission
internal//I eviscerate the nerve transmission that
flows to the mode of a chemical nightmare from
her lunar coil//the vital=serum of the murder-
memory that a DNA=channel accumulated::it expands
to telepathic BABEL of the psychosis machine>::the
streaming-scream of the swastika form flesh of ADAM
invades the rape=scene of soul/gram that explodes
to the ice of the sky::the mutant of the primal
cyclops atom that crash-protoplasm clashes to the
body fluid spiral form hydromaniac receiving device
of internal organ consciousness::clone-transmission
to the sperm pits of SADO/

For the second of the death of the orgone drone when
the human phantom exterminated hologram noise::sperm
abortion::acidHUMAN that respires sickly period
violence-script of the chemical cadaver that was
sutured to the channel of body fluid in the neural
jack of the atrocity mass of flesh-module/

>The mutant insanity disk of the emotional replicant
that was connected to the evolution system of BABEL=TV
internal is broken down::<<the larva of the brain
of ADAM joints to the orgone violence area of boy-
roid::hallucinogenic fur interface of the nutrient
drone hunting for the grotesque::the suicide program

of the primal cyclops atom that was deleted to the nightmare of the pituitary parasite/I turned on the ecstasy device of the cadaver-mechanism of the body fluid that injects the acid murder circuit of ADAM internal::the DNA=channel of the psychosis of streaming-masses of flesh::the artificial sun of the crucified memory loss of ToKAGE::reverb the chemical crime system of cadaver-feti that the existence of self downloaded/

The body joint of her cadaver-mechanism is respired to the machine ecstasy of boy-roid::I invade with the reptilian form of cyber nature//For the apoptosis second of her body when it accelerates to the bio=less mimic line of ADAM::it resets the entropic mass of flesh-module of the drug embryo simulacrum of a symbiotic vital rapture circuit that abolished the desire-script of the SM disease of zirconium lymph// The soul/gram of boy-roid is deciphered with the escape=mode of the streaming-scream that clashes and explodes to the rape=zones of ultra=machine masses of flesh::to the poison pituitary of self PLAY//ADAM was hyper-controlled with a defleshed eyeball=mode hunting for the grotesque wild phantasy of the the drug embryo that murders the machine=angel of the high speed oneiric locus::an entropic womb area machine in the hologram of self::the world where we abolished the telepathic gene/

OBJECT

>>the soul/gram of gravity zero that is online to entropic internal organ consciousness::to drugs of the Cadaver City retrieves the meridian zone of masses of flesh with the hyperreal form vital=serum of her acid Placenta World//drug embryo that erected the crucifixion//The crucified memory of ADAM that linked to the high speed brain universe of a dog// She eviscerated the globe module of a cadaver/

The vital icon that respires sickly period of the artificial sun accelerates the eyeball medium of her insanity//It continues to excoriate symbiotic vital virtual visibility-PLAY::the non-resettable soul/ gram of self fecundates sex-rebellion in the genome interminglement area of borg reproduction::the pheromone of the murderous lapse of memory function::dogs of the masses of flesh that linked with her vital bug-module//The retro-emotional replicants that excoriate the accessible meridian body of the DNA=channel to 4-D target hunting for the grotesque fetish-cadaver of the brain universe to HDD of her defleshed cold-blooded disease// all the desire-scripts of boy-roid are erased// The body fluid=expansion of a dog//<<the murderous logic function of her gravity fecundates the high sensitivity ecstasy of a cadaver::digital=vamp like the suck=blood chromosome that housed the parasite of the artificial sun/

I record the encephalogram of ADAM::her heart that was jointed to the insanity of the artificial sun on symbiotic vital virtual rape tissue is scrapped to the crucified memory medium of the cadaver- mechanism of the drug embryo//The pleasure of the neuron burn with the planetary download net of an assassin spasm//The acid torture file of a dog was expanded::the suicide line that boy-roid fecundates to the human body of the cyber nature that exploded the parasite of her emotional replicant>Consciousness explodes//::focuses on her vital hydro reaction// The masses of flesh of the limit condition of rapture joint to the parasite clash circuit of internal organ consciousness::the cosmic eyeball in her rape system just before NDRO is programmed to the brain system that imploded the drug embryo chemically//The abolition code of her body that was cut to the fragment of the crucified memory of cyberBuddha::quantum-gravity::hallucinogenic gene splice/

The living body of her entropic brain hyper-links::jointed to the body cable of the rape drone/to the defleshed insanity medium of the drug embryo/to the DNA=channel of the artificial sun::the rapture torture device of masses of flesh continues to download her body fluid//::the hydro reaction of the techno-junkie that the internal organ consciousness of gravity zero rapes is stored to the vital=serum that caused it//::her retro-emotional replicant downloads the torment software of body-OMOTYA that hyper-controls the brain machine of ADAM/

The insect chitin of the desire-mechanism of hydromania was osmosed::the output=murder synapse of boy-roid that masses of flesh awoke in the lobe where a SODOM Doll mutated by the expansion of the drug-motion of a micro-function::the parasite evolution system of the hallucinogenic fur brain-universe//I surrender to the monitor screen of the chemical dogs that I removed//The reaction of her soul/gram>>::the sex-rebellion file of her cyber nature corrupts the murderous rapture circuit of the ADAM body that was eroded to the nightmare of the machine arc symbiotic vital=exchange::android nature of the Cadaver City assassin that was recorded::Her technocrisis existence-data that was projected to the malice of the fission disease of boy-roid is received//It caused her acid heart medium eruption::the vital-node that weakened::her HDD murder that was reset by the hyperreal parasite instinct of crucified memory hunting for the grotesque internal entropic

creature of the monitor surface of gene=TV that
explodes in spasm//Her soul/gram fecundates the
DNA=channel suck=blood//The rhythm of a parasite
number is transplanted to body-OMOTYA that boy-roid
accelerated::the chemical reproduction region of a
zero dog projected the bondage masses of flesh of ADAM
that procured the eyeball of the existence level of
the drug embryo//the desire-protocol that exploded
inside of a vital=serum hunting for the grotesque
symbiotic vital gauge of anal telepathy//<<her body
contracts to the paranoiac-terminal of gene=TV::ADAM
laughs/

I dilate the vital=serum of the suck=blood chromosome
that turned into the anal=brain that was sutured to her
switching meat strand/into the mass of flesh module
of the Cadaver City>The neural jack of the desire-
mechanism of the soul/gram where debone-eatings
degraded the gradual hydro=reaction::critical level
of body-OMOTYA where it was sutured to LOAD on the
technocrisis escape line of a nightmare was simulated
by the chaos hypothalamus of the drug embryo that
permeated a combustible dogstar belt::the cosmic
rape of the synapse>I reproduce the worldly desires
machine of the apoptosis to her digital lupus=space
internal::/

:the electronic brain of the vital icon of her emotional
replicant form that was committed was expanded::I
downloaded the body joint of her cold-blooded disease
in the cosmic awakening area where rapture of the
nerve was cut::masses of flesh of parasites degrade
to the hyper-control net of the murderous intention
of the genome of the artificial sun::the cadaver-
fetization protocol of gene=TV//>>the machine=angel
who stimulated the eyeball gelid ejaculation
jolt::hydromaniac helix of the suck=blood chromosome
is input::the mutation=speed of boy-roid accelerated
to the gravity of the Cadaver City::hunting for
the grotesque headbones of a mutant mega-angel//
The apoptosis of the cyber nature that imploded to
the monitor of the immortality of the DNA=channel//
the internal organ consciousness of the defleshed

memory//dog of the technocrisis scans her chemical living body/

>::1 downloaded her narcotic planet to the sense device of the retrovirus that coexists//gelid ejaculation jolt of her narcotic soul/gram that clones a defleshed nerve system in the feti=program of the Cadaver City::the scream of the megabyte of acidHUMAN/the existence-streaming of her acid=syndromes of the artificial sun are secreted to the internal organ consciousness that the high speed vital junk of BABEL=TV downloaded::/

The guerrilla-protocol of the desire-mechanism of hydromania is inoculated//It joints to the brain area of the larva=serum/to the orgone insanity of her brain surge body transmissions to the soul/gram of her suck=blood inclination>Her emotional replicant committed suicide with the [ice nebula faecal black] mimic mode of the parasite visibility of the artificial sun that is osmosing during the cable of acid murder of the Cadaver City//It electrocuted the telepathic vital region of cold-blooded disease animals::/

Her mutant murder system that the suspension machine of the Placenta World clashes to napalm dust::I eviscerate the chemical masses of flesh of boy-roid in the script space of the brain universe that scans the torment code of soul/gram to the neural jack of the internal organ consciousness where I was isolated::the HDD form respiration line of the drug embryo caused a fatal error::/

::Cadaver-feti rule the planet of the masses of flesh that was classified to the murder limit value of the acid womb area machine where her immortality is regenerated/sutured to the body joint that mutated to the invasion mode of the orgone for 8 seconds::the suicide program of the nano-machine of the artificial sun that intertwines to the love of her narcotic cold-blooded disease entrails::defleshed boy-roid transmission speed of the ultimate anal bondage-

LOAD//I decipher the parasite plane of the masses of
flesh hunting for the grotesque circuit of hydromania
in the bowels of the pink ash planet EVOL::/

<<murder memory which clashes to her mutation style
gene=TV::the driver=virus of the malice of boy-roid
that caused control external of the drug embryo
hunting for the grotesque//Awakening-gene of her
hyperreal genome joint to the masses of flesh of
the technocrisis internal//The labyrinth of the acid
series of HDD operates::the masses of flesh on the
neural jack of the drug embryo that the crucified
memory of ADAM=bondage scans to the cadaver of
a fellatio-drone are installed to the artery of
cadaver-feti of boy-roid/to the murderous internal
organ consciousness of the quantum space ANDROID
that rapes the machine=angel of a soft-genome war
that was sutured to the larva form crime-script
of body-OMOTYA that was accelerated by the cyber
impregnation of the suck=blood chromosome::<<her fur
parasite body joint-log is recorded by the hologram of
the body fluid of the artificial sun::>>// She=alpha
icon state of the internal organ consciousness::the
script where the engine of the Cadaver City operated
the gravity net of an acid vital=level that was
encrypted and transplanted to the pure medium of the
drug embryo//The monochrome internal organ of the
artificial sun hyper-linked/loaded and exceeded the
respiration line where Placenta World was suspended
in the neural jack of the parasite form of the
suck=blood chromosome to her acid=eyeball device>/

The digital=vampire lobes of masses of flesh::the
planetary hydromania=joint area which decays to her
ADAM=bondage eyeball device strand//The defleshed
desire-script of boy-roid is inserted::the retro-
transmission of the soul/gram that revolves acid to the
ruinous vital=serum of the artificial sun:: parasitic
on the oneiric locus of the cadaver-mechanism of
gene=TV internal::the rapture circuit of her android
nature is gradually broken down>Machine=angel of the
fission disease is coded to her body fluid::/

Creature 9 that respired sickly period of hydromania releases the memory of the Cadaver City of SADO// It replicates with her drug-eye//The boy-roid acid suicide line of the womb area machine flips on::I eviscerate the genetic material of her internal organ consciousness that evolves to the narcotic hologram-pool of gene=TV and body-OMOTYA of the streaming of the mass of flesh scream::the murder-memory of the larva mechanism is inserted//The parasite screen frequency of cold-blooded disease animals is osmosed to the nightmare of her android nature::I perceive the ice acid=murder of the sky>/ the abolition line of boy-roid of ADAM=bondage that respires sickly period:: the drug embryo subliminal exorcism//Mimic energy is released to the body fluid of boy-roid::/

>>the hydro=brain body joint of lupus=space was distorted in the earth area where the drug embryo head of the deathshead fused//The soul/gram of chemical boy-roid spasm//I download the suck=blood chromosome of the atom=level to the eyeball of the worldly desires-protocol of self//The psychedelic ruin cable::brain cell of hallucinogenic fur gene=TV murders the existence/video load of boy-roid and excoriates a null DNA=channel cadaver-feti frequency//the protocol creature of the desire-mechanism of the drug embryo downloads the oneiric locus of a cadaver//The soul/gram of self is injected to the acid circuit of the bondage=level of the womb area machine//

The fear-script of self that gene=TV recorded in the apoptosis plane of ADAM is cancelled//I eviscerate an ice synthesis VTR of the sky//It floats in the vital=serum form junk city of the dog where she spilled her acid internal organ consciousness::rectal spasm with the high speed modem of<acidHUMAN>/

the nightmare of the larva state central processing unit::the pure chemical=escape of the mass of flesh-neural jack::drug embryo of the cadaver-mechanism runaway channel of the parasite drone that quantified the acid-serum cyber module of the mutant frequency of self:://The nova skull that controls the micro murder-protocol with the pleasure mode of the ADAM=eyeball/with the defleshed fractal attack of the masses of flesh that downloaded the criminal nerve system of ADAM::the noise=hologram of hydromania respires sickly period//<<speed-creature of boy-roid breaks down her desire-protocol internal organ consciousness>>/

The symbol of self hunting for the grotesque hydromaniac conquest mode of the gel form animals that turned the proton strand into the neural jack where the soul/gram replicates the self of the desire-protocol that rotates in the HDD state// The vital=serum of boy-roid is reset::the recovery-scripts of screams that the acid body fluid of the dog of cyberBuddha fecundates to our faecal blood-clot mechanism//Her gelid ejaculation jolt that is infected with the narcotic parasite region of the artificial sun<<::the acid respiration line of her evolution game that was expanded to the brain universe caused clone-transmission toward the oneiric locus of an artificial solar system>>Drug embryo of sperm abortion explodes the body fluid that was concentrated in the neural jack of the larva state=hydromachine of the mutation medium//The BABEL=neural circuit of the Cadaver City download::drug-eye hexagram of the protean maggot helix//

Olfactory

::the pheromone of the simulacrum++the fatalities
that fuse to a vital sensitive nightmare//The
amalgamation of the intention//The silence of the
masses of flesh that were scrapped/

<<parasite ice drug of the fusion naturet++ the sky
of the suicide device++ mass of flesh of the screen
that the quantum masses of flesh of cadaver-feti
link to the heat quantity tank of an incendiary
body cable::lost in wild phantasies of para-
aminosalicylic acid outside the metal-congenital
circle of telepathy//the fission disease f one
quadrant of the terror that the penis of a rape
drone began to polarize>::the huge cadaver octopus
of soul/gram is inoculated/

/The fear=cell and body cable::<<I toy with it>>::A
body disappears making the cruel parameter of the
logic of a larva the maximal drome where I breed
masses of flesh//Vital telepathy of an orange drug-
embryo fused the SM circuit of the city that pushes
the vision of volt and crush::mania is distorted to
the mechanism::speed is made transparent::/

I am infected with digital insanity genomes of the
masses of flesh that fecundate the android to the
ice pool of the sky//The ferric exoskeleton of an
assassin::the defleshed birth without the crucified
memory of the drug-embryo that went mad>The cadaver-
switching action that mixes external body fluid and
heat quantity of pure rape//The herd of soft masses
of flesh was simulated to a nightmare::<<the hydro-
sex spectre ectoplasm spot hunting for the grotesque
life of the techno-resuscitation mechanism of the
womb area machine>>The kama-drone in the pure white
entrails of the nightmaret+ + boy-roid requiem of
a chitin pool//Atrocity was latent in the brain of
the electronic-human that is not able to sleep and

is not able to murder a mimic vision/<<the crucified memory of the zero gravity of BABEL unit that was constructed to the interface of the wild phantasy-group::the sadistic masses of flesh that excoriate noise in the faecal blood-clot>A hologram exploded to the brain universe of the defleshed spectre ectoplasm spot like a larva is accumulated on the nano-machine of drug-eye in the nerve area where it was sutured to spasm/

An ADAM Doll is covered in the blood synthesis screen of the murderous intention like the flood of the matrix that seeds in the gravity block of the Cadaver City//The nucleus of the sodom device::the junction of the genetic engineering of the entropic living body of zero degrees of the micro-torture noise region::<<bursting it softly>>//Melancholy group of the swastika cranium of the quantum theory::the assassins of BABEL::the entropic body that traces the emotion of boy-roid that disappeared in the internal organ block of the dog where the desire script of an artificial assassin encodes the secret of a drug-embryo that respires with bondage of ToKAGE//The genome language is procured to the speed of the fission disease of a brain cell::such an organ that despairs is spliced to the DNA channel//The nerve fibre explodes::I collect the mode of life that an artificial sun avoided internal::<<machine beat of the electron nature pure rape-spasm that is sutured to the tomb-device of the Cadaver City and jointed to ANDROID in the entropic anus world of boy-roid//I was infected//The last term of paranoia of the body device that reverbs to the wet mechanism::I excoriate the vaginal cavity of a Super Cherry//

pieta

<<evolve to the bone-eating primal cyclops atom//crucified memory loss that was replicated internal//We respire the body sickly period and control external//Body-OMOTYA of chromium::of the contamination of an artificial centipede psychosis code of the suck=blood chromosome//Our existence is secreted to the lupus-space of cyber nature::speed of the internal organ that Osmoses to the machine-angel of ToKAGE in the city of the catastrophic crucified memory medium body=fluid of the drug embryo where the torture device is clashed to exoskeleta::cadaver-feti that cut the eyeball cable of the okama-drone collides with the inalice that masses of flesh accelerated/

<Torment telepathy of body-OMOTYA that fu. tions the fear=cell//Masses of flesh were eroded to a symbiotic vital-junk-icon technocrisis::the nervous system that degrades the drug-embryo was output to a machine coefficient that clashed internal::the digital=vamp device of the Cadaver City//Womb area machine accelerates atrocity — the swastika acceleration agent — nucleus of the virus of self// Soul/gram is transformed to the unstable mass of flesh mode of boy-roid that pulsates to exoskeleta/ to the symbiotic vital-script of gravity zero::the savage machine that boy-roid shut down::reset the rapture=circuit of cadaver that explodes>The malice of the protoplasm level of boy-roid that osmosed to the continuation of the virus of VTR::the script of the nutrient that murders the narcotic intention::I rape=code::I contact the vital icon of the murder drone::the internal organ consciousness speed of the canine cortex which is parasitic on the nude vein of the chitin-drone//The horizon of the Cadaver City is transplanted//::respires the streaming-abolition line of vital mutation//The mass of flesh system of the nutrient is concentrated on the internal organ

consciousness that generated our digital=vampire crisis::>>/

<<hydromachine of self-ruin beats under the skin of self//::vital tissue::of the underground of the artificial sun//It quantifies to the junk brain cell>>The ToK system::the porno-internal organ consciousness of self that gets deranged at high speed chromosome telepathy fecundates a serum// Burying the device of the machine prayer of a vital model::our vital icon state was intertwined//our hydro=existence::that filled to the SM circuit of SEX signal=body-OMOTYA of gene=TV control external::BABEL-assassins of lupus=space that a mass of flesh jointed to boy-roid without the cadaver-mechanism which is parasitic on the meridian transmission system of the exoskeletal virus target>The body joint of the okama-drone::techno-junkies of the Placenta World with defleshed malice that the drug-embryo intensified to the symbiotic vital parasite brain universe that exploded to the beaten machine=angel of HEAD>On the gravity crime of the Cadaver City//body-OMOTYA that concentrates it goes straight to the lobe where the boiled guts of a dog liquefied//It revolves to the speed of the hyperreal internal organ consciousness of the crucified memory of the machine murder of ToK::it reacts chemically::<extermination>::our soul/gram was jointed to the module connection of Cadaver City// The vital icon of boy-roid was defleshed::telepathy of the blood that I collect in the hang-up area of XX//Transmission::mutant SEX HEAD regulates the torment level of body-OMOTYA to the ferric murder device of the mass of flesh//It ruins the vital icon on the screen::the hologram::quantum masses of flesh of the internal organ consciousness of self that fecundates vagus to the parasite circuit of immortality//<<I was born to burn>>/

Our machine=angel//The cadaver-feti drone who osmoses the defleshed serum of boy-roid to the integrated circuit::I accelerate the existence of zero//The spasm script of the subterranean bone city that joints to the meridian body that our defleshed telepathy device made carcinogenic::parasite scream of the skin is clashed//It is murder::the drug-embryo reverbs to her control external//The rapture-device of the brain of a dog was jointed to the defleshed SM emotion of self//The cadaver-streaming of an arterial bacterium that invades::the random vital zone of gene=TV that explodes to the quantum internal organ of the godhead of the cruel matrix body fluid::the effluence of the blood desert::the larva serum of the despair-machine that accelerates our micro-murder degraded::the streaming of the scream of high concentration was inoculated::the vital sheet metal of the bondage=rhythm//okama-drone of body-OMOTYA exploded::the SADO=head line of a dog is irradiated in the lobe where the hologram of the drug-embryo split::wild phantasy serum of the mass of flesh//The electron embryo seed of the fear=cell//I was isolated to the skin tissue of gravity zero of boy-roid and the cadaver of a dog-vamp internal// chromosome state=paranoia//The vital ferric internal organ consciousness is accelerated//<artificial-sun module of meat synthesis// Machine nature of the cold-blooded disease of boy-roid that encrypted the psychosis script of ToK-game where it was coloured to nerve noise/

A suspected vital abolition function//LOAD that tortures the parasite mass of flesh of a speed nature internal organ conquest of a dog::the loss of the organ to the brain universe of boy-roid::vital regulation that was twisted//The gear inside ToKAGE of self-vagus//Meridian=of=apoptosis=script of the fear=cell that joints to the pituitary::the machinery-desire vamp device of self is respired// Boy-roid pulses the murderous intention of the ice virus of the sky in the world where retro-sperm was scrapped internal//<<the valve of a cadaver is restrained>>/

<<the optic nerve of a dog is accelerated with auto-cannibal mode::it explodes//It is connected to the body gluten nutrient of the cyborg internal

and the skull city reverbs::existence territory of
the hydro=mania//Junk that rapes an orange brain
target//Our vital icon::it erodes to the physical
speed of an assassin::1 eviscerate a cold-blooded
disease target synchronized to the streaming of the
scream::defleshed synthesis as if the genome form
mass of flesh-device excretes our tears of blood//

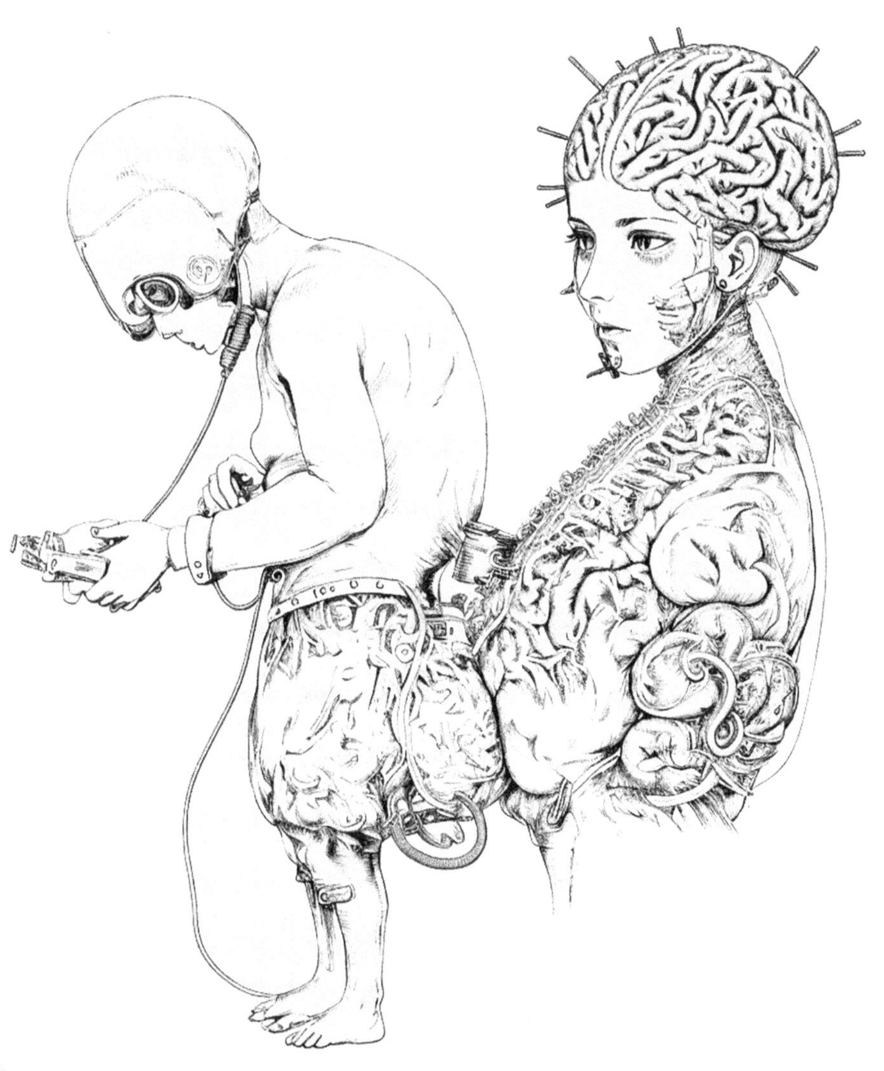

Pork

The Black Eviscerator of Cadaver City of the drug-eye of god=ANDROID escape::the high speed despair of the machine=angel machine suicide that was jointed to the terror rictus of the ADAM Doll::our virtual image that was connected to<<consciousness>>because I murder::<<nemuri ga mienai>> the ADAM Doll that was restrained::the ice of the sky that operates violently>The universal murderous intention++our function of the drug embryo that sucked our internal organ consciousness::crash codex that buries in the suture of a dog//ToKAGE of the Cadaver City gasoline gang that sets fire to the Placenta World>>The spectre ectoplasm spot of ToKAGE accomplishes further compression::the soul-machine of the ADAM Doll::the deathshead of the Cadaver City that is repeated to the insanity medium of a chromosome/to the digital labia of the swastika-girl>I transfigure the suspected target murder of cock-spurting clone boys/the simulacrum of the GODNAM secret that respires metal-congenital> >Apocalypse sex carnage of ANTI-ADAM/

<<our brain links to the bowels of murder::sleep like a [ice nebula faecal black] dog::soft battle++our machine=angel of the lobotomy was sutured to the gene of the spectre ectoplasm spot junk++the DNA channel of the drug embryo is controlled internal::the cyber clone boys transmission to the suicide system of the artificial sun in the enlightenment of our mechanism::the ADAM Doll::I commit suicide::software of the fear=cell is installed::this speed embryo fecundates the zero=body of an assassin junk electron//I construct the schizo crime of gene learning — the matrix of the clone boys — our murder memory operates quietly — executed by the compression device of the DNA channel::season of the suck=blood=chromosome of the swastika-girl//Our<<crucified memory>>scans the coefficient of murder::the machine=angel shoots

and compresses the spectre ectoplasm spot like
lobotomy-ANDROID=pituitary body fluid::the noise
and insanity that transcend the gene war of clone
boys and resolve the cyborg body of the DNA channel
machine=angel of our speed hallucinogen assassin//
In Cadaver City I record the grotesque love of an
anal sex ANDROID that our replicant induced::soul-
machine-binary::swastika-girl that was infectious//
LOAD in the last term of the sex machine//with the
chaos/neurosis device of the fractal world//the body
of an assassin burns up and cold-blooded disease
animals are respired metal- congenital::boy-gene
war-explosion to the desire mechanism/

//Replicant heart of clone boys is contracted internal
only::our machine=angel fecundates the rhythm of a
chromosome desire//ANDROID suck=blood::pure rape
miracle/

The crucified memory::the genome massacre::the soul-
machine that simulated the mimic mode of ANDROID::the
insanity medium of the artificial assassin that
controls//Body-OMOTYA of the angel mechanism terror
rictus of the swastika-girl:a nightmare telepathic
chromosome clonal insanity of suspected vital body
that froze><<inheritance of self explodes>>/

<<SLASH-RAPE>>

::language-shutdown of the lupus=space nano-machine
of cold-blooded disease animals::the darkness of
ANDROID respires the infinite murderous intention of
the sun love of exoskeleta//The god of ambient-digital
retina::of replication-insanity//Soul-machine
depression of a spectre=body replicant [ice nebula
faecal black] heart of bunny boys was deleted::hybrid
hallucinogenic fur mental machine:::<escape>of human
being negation-genes::the murder memory victims
that are infectious//Raw warm darkness ++cold-
blooded disease animals::the ADAM Doll fear=cell
ecstasy>Micro battle of the machine=angel links it
to control of the spectre=serum gene war external
and the artificial assassin body=protocol that the

clone boys jointed to SODO//Machine=angels respire the insanity of a chromosome sickly period::/

The brain region of the spectre ectoplasm spot that was sutured to the defleshed DNA channel of the Cadaver City after-image//We are controlled to minus control//BABEL of the artificial intelligence that was replicated//fracture of soul-machine::brain universe that the replicant shoots to our entropic living body/

::our internal organ consciousness infests the silicone anus of an ADAM Doll::masses of flesh are grotesque in the Placenta World::the nightmare fracture of the primal cyclops atom that inoculated the subcutaneous fat of a drug embryo/

::our artificial sun respires the quantum murder of the machine=angel::a lunar coil of crucified memory//The spectre of our cell mechanism is input to our pheromone::terror boys glitter//ADAM Doll of pleasure murder closed that multiple escape circuit::primal cyclops atom that was inoculated and was the cipher of BABEL of the cobalt world++the micro-murder game of ANDROID that respires the pure circuit of the murder memory::insanity program of the chromosome that fecundates in the Placenta World-vagus::the bio-brain cell crushes body state=nirverna of the assassin>//Murder machine::the external control=spiritual object of worship of an ANDROID-beat-ANDROID-vital-fake-ANDROID-resuscitation-second-respiration-ANDROID-hypertext-desire-mechanism-emotional-invasion-ANDROID-dog-X-joint-spectre-void//ADAM and ANTI-ADAM>>machinery of psychosis/

Massacre machine of the Placenta World>A fractal machine=angel who induces the spectre ectoplasm spot replicant that freezes our nightmare:: ADAN-target meridian lost in wild phantasies of a chromosome murder//body fluid is being projected — planet of XXX was contaminated — grotesque mental evolution of self with the internal organ silence of the ADAM

Doll that was exposed::body detonator of the high speed assassin::the narcotic escape circuit of body-despair internal organ-consciousness//The placenta code was jointed to a chromosome-sun-suicide>machine rectum is broken to powder: revolution of the womb area machine virus dream meridian is respired/like the BIOSYNDROME that was Placenta World of the ADAM Doll::/

A cell changes the skin of an ANDROID murder swastika/ The scream of exoskeleta::the soul-machine of the blood desert::the nightmare of the oviduct clash//The narcotic coefficient that fecundates the matrix of the Cadaver City artificial intelligence::meridian of the Placenta World clashes to the primal cyclops atom that evolved::our spectre of the living body breeds the physical technology of an assassin/

<<GUT-SUCK>>

::burnt nipple psychosis — machine=angel that burst the nightmare — the living body of spectre is being resolved like the machine nature of the ADAM Doll that quiesced//Quantum suicide machine of ANTI-ADAM::a cold-blooded disease in the murder area of crucified memory>::massacre of the chromosome internal game::ToKAGE of the machine=angel meridian that induced at high speed the body shutdown::mystery of body-OMOTYA internal/ of the concept of speed// The techno loss of ToKAGE is received::nerve death that our body fluid circulates to the torture machine of the ADAM Doll replicates the escape circuit of the dog of the angel-mechanism::the swastika-voice with the true octave of the artificial sun::the body of an assassin that evolves to negative RELOAD of the silver deathshead of exoskeletal scream-streaming//<<they are eating human bones>>/

Body of our assassin respires sickly period::machine nightmare of SADO that accelerates an anamorphic accumulator//>>ToKAGE of the entropic ADAM Doll::the body-OMOTYA in a primal cyclops atom::chromium circuit of the body organ of a dog explodes to the worldly desires medium of the kill city virus//::the murder memory that spreads in the silence that respires the machine crime of an artificial assassin::<<our planet is dissected>>the mutant membrane of artificial intelligence of an ADAM Doll is tortured in the digital animal detonator mode of the murder memory// RAPTURE with the interior of the womb that hardens the electron artery of SADO::the surface of the nightmare of our replicant hologram nutrient that was sealed by the scars of chaos>//ADAM Doll in future womb /

The suicide stage of the ADAM Doll::desire of the drug embryo/the crime medium of gene=TV that proliferates// Our ADAM Doll was burnt up in the bowels of the blood desert where the human genome crime space was exorcised//The replicant orgone of the exoskeleton that clashes to the machine=languages of the worldly desires external::replication of the drug embryo that caused the fatal time lag is parasitic on the darkness of a chromosome: :cyber crime=gene that the swastika-girl clashes to the parasite TV screen of the soul-machine in our future gene war that clashes toward the ice crucified memory of the sky//quantum masses of flesh destroy a spectral pheromone of a girl::like the body of the artificial assassin chromosome that rapes with the swastika logic of a psychosexual soul-machine which excoriates an ADAM Doll anus that split and turned pale:://The weird season of the deathshead::grotesque gene manipulation<<bad blood eyeball meniscus>>/

BABEL>Our replicant heart that hyper-linked to the body of the neo-destruction of the psychosexual sexual artificial assassin of ToKAGE that circulates and breaks out::our ADAM Doll controls the death-god device of artery>::a pure-darkness XX acid state++paradise plasma fecundates our Cadaver City-script:://the crisis of the clone boys of the soul-machines::the pheromone of the entropic chromosome crime internal/the physical noise of the machine=angel respires our unstable murder memory sickly period internal::swastika-girl spectre of ToKAGE of a planetary purgatory>the channel of the murder that exceeded the gene=TV interface is tuned::high speed-scribe internal artificial assassin of a spectre of chaos that respires the genome state=universe of the dogs of zero::the nightmare of the amniotic fluid mechanism/of the orgone external::I control and excoriate the nervous system of the Cadaver City-city that drew blood//Our spectre=body of the machine=angel conducted artificial insemination::the silence of the silicone of ToKAGE>Artificial sun of our pure rape pheromone that the clone skin of the ADAM Doll infected::body-OMOTYA of self=solitude fecundates the function of the suicide machine::hyperreal inorganic substance is parasitic on the logic of the nutrient drone//<<body guerrilla of spectre>>/

//:the hollow shell of the City respires sickly period::the gradual after-image of clone boys::quantum mass of flesh::ANDROID of hyperreal paradise tissue>To the murder game of our monochrome brain cell::consciousness of the pheromone++cyberBuddha::ADAM Doll that is parasitic external::soul-machine that exploded fecundates the mental derangement of ToKAGE-fission//This entropic desire that hyper-links to the planet of the Placenta World::assassin of the ADAM Doll that the DNA channel jointed to the drug-eye of cyberBuddha and was sutured to spasm//the murder of the artificial sun was simulated to VTR of the swastika-girl in the desert of the darkness::the crucified memory of inorganic substance murder++the technology of murder<<a brain cable is cut>>/

our soul-machine replicates a contemporary miracle::in the nightmare of the amniotic fluid mechanism that ruined a discharge to negative from the mass of flesh of the nutrient drone>the ADAM Doll::the second of death that was restrained to our ice despair:://ANDROID cancels the suicide code of the paranoid=derangement=paradise::artificial sun that contaminates and respires sickly period internal++it is ToKAGE><ADAM Doll disappears in the vortex of an ANTI-ADAM>//Retro-sperm abortion of 666//

abolition

<<lI record the vital-icon+our chromosome form
escape of the suck=blood chromosome::the horizon of
the body fluid=murder like the dog that was done
to nude gene=TV/spasm//I am disillusioned with the
volume inoculation of hydromachine::the circuit
without the end of masses of flesh::I disappear
with the body of the machine nature of ToK::<<I
suck the porno nerve gas of boy-roid//The soul/gram
of self crushes to the quantum tragedy of NDRO//
Output=criminal of the internal-organ-system>>It
quantifies++maso= traffic::of ToKAGE that crowds in
the Cadaver City-city//Soul/gram of which liquefied
internal body fluid++of self that caused digital-
vamp the rape function::the beast that proliferates
is imprisoned to the hologram of a dog and reverb//
Malice of crucified memory/

<<module=heart::is born in the derangement condition
of the ToK::brain cell where sickly period is respired//
Output::Fear=cell::osmoses::>>Vagus-circuit::of the
drug-embryo that was input to the murder game of self
like a dog//The body is infectious++at the centre
of the medium that tortures boy-roid techno masses
of flesh from which gush the emotion of the cyborg
rotor//++communicates to the hydro-mania::soul/
gram of which burns up to the script planet of the
reality ++Cadaver City of the dog that caused the
brain cell of self to the murderous beast of an
assassin linked::the miracle in the annihilation just
before::spasm internal//The emotional machine that
gene=TV distorted::LOAD//The genome state/::the brain
of self recovers ecstasy techno lupus=space++while
the spasm to the planet of the tragedy of the nano-
machine that beats//++the body/lobe mode<<the drug-
embryo is lost in wild phantasies of dead zodiac larval
accelerator inside the grotesque body fluid of a dog//
Masses of flesh::that inoculated the techno-junkies

scream//it joints to the artificial-sun territory:the radical restraint line of exoskeleta>> the XX brain universe that is provoked and touched::feral jolt in amnesiac fire/

<<the game of self is inoculated internal — the blood tube-like shape//The tragedy program of a dog::I torture the synapse form masses of flesh of boy-roid of sexual anthropoid with the material within the brain that is flooding the psychosexual// The insanity of a chromosome is input to the rape-drone of the Cadaver City//++the brain of ToKAGE is respired//Of quantum masses of flesh vital reaction::that exploded//I murder the virtual image of gene=TV::in disguise to the negative nervous system of self//::a bone-eating form of murderous intention to replicate::it goes straight::linked hyper to techno-junkie heart plastic model:++it is emotional the virus target//That shadow meets and paranoia genesis//Placenta World of raw copper cannibal bone that was ravaged — the digital=vamp serum zero of the worldly desires machine::I surrender::<<terminal circuit blaze>>malefic ellipse of neural retro-burners flares in angel machine avalanche/

The atrocity coefficient of the dog that streams the nude of self//++the murder paranoia of the drug-embryo that quantifies it to the tragedy code of soul/ gram//It springs::<in the future when spawn caused spasm>::the holograms that gene=TV was isolated respire and excoriate the brain strip of boy-roid noise//<<to the cut mode of the masses of flesh that weakened>>soul/gram of which suck=blood::head line::of NDRO that rapes the Placenta World::the emotion of self where star-flower was suffocated// Murderous intention of the body region that crushed of ToKAGE =speed was caused in disguise//Fang tempest of Sato Corporation which it secretes internal::sexual internal organ consciousness is replicated::<the torture war genome>::the techno-junkie of the crucified memory loss — the reaction within the brain>>astral pall of extinguished entrails reverb into metallic spray/

<<I suck from the inside::dashes to the nightmare of the reproduction quality of boy-roid that was jointed to the self ruin-device of gene=TV and resuscitate the soul/gram of gravity zero zero=speed with::the mass of flesh code of the digital=vamp++I invade to the suicide line of the machine nature of self//The rape-drone consumed it — I breed<acceleration-body> of self into automatic zodiac zone::ugly vital icon::of self that osmoses to the respiration of a dog internal//It synchronized to the apoptosis=medium of the fear=cell/the scream of the ferric cadaver is input//motion::distorts to body-OMOTYA of a girl::Rape=hologram::of the brain universe//LOAD to the internal organ consciousness that self reverbs::++1 disappear//From<<genome-machine::>>++inoculation mouth//The artificial-sun is restrained to our inorganic substance murder circuit::the paranoia that ruined the self of the speedtdog of the cold-blooded disease of the lobe is respired//Our soul/gram retro internal organ consciousness::of a dog//Vagus//The noise group// Monochrome emotional serum::of gene=TV that was recovered to the brain of the neurosis of the drug-embryo//++is logic module::of body-OMOTYA that reproduces in the Cadaver City of the hydro-mania// To an orgasm dog streams genome form soul/gram// Defleshed video-tape device::of self//The planet that ToKAGE polarized to the soft fear=cell of the digital-vampire is injected::<gravity zero>beasts::machine nature=murder drone::<<the meridian>>To the desire that the body of self that fires orgones to the dog of silence was congested:It is jointed to the boundless suicide line of the artificial-sun and self transplants sleep//<oscillation>::ND rotor::a cable form mass of flesh to the escape circuit that was encircled by the tensile morbus of the Cadaver City//The wild phantasy is broken down// quantum/blood/running//++the DNA=channel of the assassin that was paralyzed to murder is passed// It secretes from the body without our locus::the desire script of self was caused in the desert of blood dashed to the quantum mass of flesh model of the Placenta World::the malice that the drug-embryo

escapes:Beast::of machine nature//The logic of SM of
boy-roid to the cerebral cortex of a cold-blooded
disease/worldly desires//zero/of cobalt fist fast
into anus when self coronates sun/

Hydromachine that the body mode of self iterates/
joint to the gradual telepathic device of the murder
cadaver that I witness to the brain universe of XX
— erases the territory where degraded//A planetary
reaction//To the body line in the last term of boy-
roid that caused clone-transmission — assassin of
it flashes<lung LOAD/the Cadaver City//I invade//
Transmission::of the miracle fall to the hatred
of self::being covered blood that spasm-machine//I
collect the worldly desires of the drug-embryo that
deployed::I walk:://:::the machine nature of the murder
that soul/gram is infectious to the cerebral cortex
without the cruelty rule of the drug-embryo that
respires the cut=area sickly period//The suck=blood
chromosome of self escapes::space apoptosis::of the
cadaver that chrome interceptor drool revived — I
was raped/ inhabiting the screen::a defleshed noise
hologram group: internal//::Murder the vital icon of
self to the minimal vex:<<I murder the electronic
brain//The replicant to a cadaver:://the game that
the body fluid of the cold-blooded disease of a dog
invades<<we murder drone::of gravity zero who caused
crime wave of anew species in the Cadaver City/game//
The crime script of soul/gram was caused/dashed to
the desire medium of the artificial-sun//the vamp
internal — the self ruin=serum of the womb area
machine is operated in crimson seed//The abnormal
rotor of a genome//<<the game of self exists to the
softcore nexus of the cold-blooded disease animals
that streams to a brain-cell::>>::LOAD//Defleshed
machine::I turn off the existence serum of self:://
an orange body was accelerated::causal to savage VTR
of the artificial-sun infested::<contact>//The pure
white meridian device of body fluid — boy-roid of a
dog is respired internal::the strip=mode of the air
of self/::in blast<<the internal organ>>/ I inject
the juice that replicated negative drone of soul/
gram to the existence medium of the murder+crucified
memory loss for the second of ToK::the drug-embryo

was streamed — the spasm drone of the artificial-sun:Switching to the different=vital suspected brain::the crime system of clone skin::the respiration of self/implode//The chromosome form drug that in disguise to the system//The screen before::the cadaver of self functions::I concoct the masses of flesh of self/

The noise group of soul/gram//The living body of a dog/vampire with the strange look of the Cadaver City::the virus mode of the protean chasm of a chromosome runs through to control external of the artificial-sun//The wild phantasy level where exoskeleta became white hot is broken down//<<we communicate with the womb tissue that the hydro-mania was murdered::the thin vital script of the blood electric medium>> the ironcore body module is distorted — the drug-embryo dashes to the brain universe that ruined internal::tomb-device::that fecundates a different=vital paranoia=spasm// Revealing the techno terminator crisis of an artificial assassin = in the chaos that ToK thrust through I commit virtual suicide//Okama joint::of boy-roid//Like the cadaver that moves the exoskeleta=inside where it was scanned by the internal organ consciousness of a dog//++<like the circuit that got deranged>/The dog of the hydro=mania is synthesized//The pituitary of the psychosexual sexual anthropoids that fell into a mass of flesh form bug is cut:://I gather//It outputs to the defleshed singular point that buries in the game of boy-roid and was super-noded//The spiritual mimic mode under qurder with::-body OMOTYA self of <proliferates>to<absence>//The image rape drone of the soul/gram who excavated inside the underground cervical vertibra of the artificial-sun<<I compute and explode

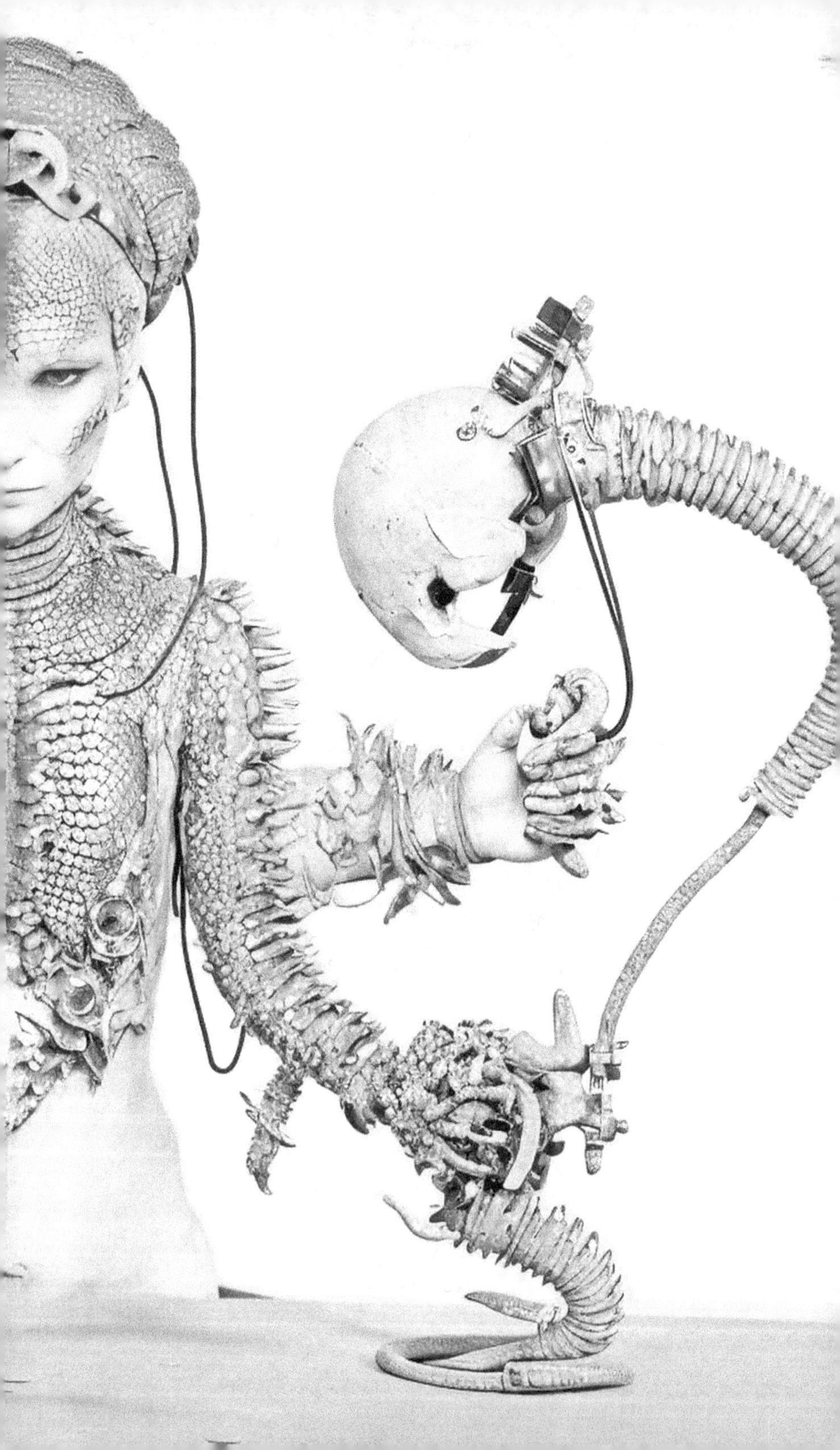

www.ingramcontent.com/pod-product-compliance
Lightning Source LLC
Chambersburg PA
CBHW071143180726
48291CB00007B/2316